Also by Tania Blanchard

The Girl from Munich

SUITCASE OF DREAMS

TANIA BLANCHARD

**SIMON &
SCHUSTER**

London · New York · Sydney · Toronto · New Delhi

SUITCASE OF DREAMS
First published in Australia in 2018 by
Simon & Schuster (Australia) Pty Limited
Level 4, 32 York St, Sydney, NSW 2000
This edition published in 2019

10 9 8 7

New York Amsterdam/Antwerp London Toronto Sydney New Delhi
Visit our website at www.simonandschuster.com.au

 A catalogue record for this
book is available from the
National Library of Australia

Cover design: Christabella Designs
Cover image: Mark Owen/Trevillion Images; PhilipYb Studio/Shutterstock
Typeset by Midland Typesetters, Australia
Printed and bound in Australia by Griffin Press

 The paper this book is printed on is certified against
the Forest Stewardship Council® Standards. Griffin
Press – a member of the Opus Group holds chain
of custody certification SCS–COC-001185. FSC®
promotes environmentally responsible, socially
beneficial and economically viable management of
the world's forests.

For my grandparents.
Without their courage, hard work and persistence,
I would not be here, doing what I love

'Since love grows within you, so beauty grows.
For love is the beauty of the soul.'
St Augustine of Hippo,
Homilies on the First Epistle of John

11 November, 1956

Clusters of tiny lights were scattered across the darkened land before us. As we drew closer in the predawn,
I was loath to relinquish the peace I felt, even amid
the excitement and apprehension that swirled around me.
Clutching the cold railing, I breathed deeply, taking in the
sea air – Australian air – and held on to that moment of calm.

The rising sun lifted above the horizon, dusting the port
of Fremantle and the ocean in a soft golden glow. Sandy
beaches and small dwellings appeared out of the inky blackness, dotting the coastline and harbour. Australia, the golden
land, was welcoming me and my family to our new life with
open arms. I knew I would never forget this sight.

Erich was by my side and I could feel the thrum of excitement course through his body. At that moment, I felt that we
were the only two people who existed, waiting on the edge of

the world, relishing these moments of quiet and united in our desire for a better life.

'We made it, Lotte. We made it,' he whispered into my ear.

'Yes, we made it.' Relief flooded me. Our old life was gone – Nazi Germany, the war and a country changed forever – and our new life beckoned. Finally I would be able to cast off the pull of the rigid traditions and expectations I had grown up with and escape the poverty that had come with choosing a life with Erich. This was a new start and we could be anything we wanted to be. Australia was a young country, with opportunities for all people, we'd been told, opportunities that would never have been possible for us in Germany, our ruined homeland. Here we would have the freedom to choose the life we wanted.

'Look, isn't it beautiful?' He pointed to the shore.

'All shiny and new.'

'Perfect for our family . . . Perfect for our new life.' His anticipation and hope were plain to see under the deck lights and I felt sure that my face mirrored his.

'It has to be.' We'd left everything we knew behind us in search of a better life for ourselves and our girls.

Erich placed his hand over my chilled fingers, sharing his strength, warmth and comfort. 'It will be.'

He gathered me into his arms and kissed me deeply.

Chaos erupted as we docked. Most of the passengers on the *Skaubryn* were German, as were those welcoming the ship to Australia, and bursts of our mother tongue drifted across to us, the shouts and screams of family, friends and acquaintances waiting on the pier for those who were disembarking. There was frantic waving of banners and handkerchiefs. The atmosphere was reassuring. It would be the last time we would hear the sound of our language on Australian soil, I thought, before the inevitable tide of English was upon us. For a moment, I pretended we were still home and not halfway across the world. I wished we had someone greeting us, smoothing our transition into this strange country, but we knew nobody here.

Erich held my hand, his green eyes meeting mine. The girls were jumping out of their skins with excitement that we had finally arrived, fidgeting restlessly, keen to leave the ship for the day and explore, and my conflicted emotions were pushed to one side as we surged towards the designated areas for passport and health control.

'Don't leave Mutti's side,' whispered Greta to Johanna, her dark head against her sister's blonde one. 'I've heard that kangaroos jump down the streets here and take little children and stuff them in their pouches.'

'They do not,' said Johanna indignantly.

Greta nodded knowingly, her hands on her hips as if daring Johanna to prove her wrong.

'Do they?' My younger daughter shot a worried look to me. Her eyes were blue today. They often shifted between blue, like my own eyes, and green, like her father's, and sometimes it was hard to say what shade they were at all.

'Of course not,' I said, exasperated, but quietly, not wanting to make a scene. 'Don't tease your sister,' I said to Greta, giving her my sternest expression.

Greta just grinned at me, her brown eyes sparkling, her nose peeling from hours in the sun. She was ten years old and

3

a month at sea had exhausted all the adventurous opportunities available as far as she was concerned; now she wanted to discover what excitement Australia had in store. Johanna, with her sun-bleached blonde hair, like my own, was two years younger and adored her sister. She was more sensible, wary of new experiences and fond of reminding Greta of the dangers of her latest endeavour. They were a good team, balancing influences, and fiercely protective of each other, despite the usual sibling rivalries. Whatever was ahead of us, I knew that they would be fine.

I spotted Erich returning with our paperwork. He cut an impressive figure – tall, athletic and broad-shouldered – and he carried himself with a natural elegance that many admired. Despite the humidity that embraced us and the throngs of anxious and impatient people, his crisp white jacket remained uncrushed. The matching wide-brimmed hat sat jauntily on his head, covering the luxuriant dark hair, now threaded with silver, that was swept back from his forehead.

'All finished,' he said. 'We can take the bus to Perth.'

'Where's Perth?' Greta pulled on his jacket sleeve. 'Is it far?'

'Not too far. I've been told there's plenty to see. Come on, let's not waste another minute.' We were all excited to get our first glimpse of Australia before boarding the boat once again for the final leg of our journey to Melbourne.

The girls grabbed his hands, and Erich laughed and set off. The vice around my heart eased a little to see the joy on their faces. For a man in his mid-forties, Erich had the energy of a man half his age, but I still sometimes marvelled that he had decided to uproot his entire life and begin again in a new country so late in life. I had struggled with the idea much longer than he had, even though I was only thirty-one. The girls' dark and blonde plaits swayed gently across their backs as they tried to match their father's footsteps. They were why we were here.

It was a beautiful day and our decision was made, so as I first stepped onto Australian soil, I was determined to stop worrying about the uncertainty ahead.

It wasn't until we were standing on top of the hill in Perth's famous Kings Park that I truly got a sense of Australia. The girls were eating ice cream and Erich and I drinking Coca-Cola as we surveyed the city, the beaches and the ocean beyond. Trees unlike any I had seen before were plentiful – the eucalyptus trees we'd been told about on the boat, their leaves fresh and pungent. The dry and dusty paths and the succulents that bordered them reminded me that we had left the verdant green of Germany behind. It was springtime but already evidence of the hot, dry climate was easy to find. I took photographs with the camera Erich and I had bought for the journey, beginning to grasp the vastness of the wild, tough landscape.

We arrived in Melbourne's bustling port five days later, thousands of lights and neon signs illuminating the pier. The screaming and shouting was deafening. Banners, flags and balloons jostled for prime position on the pier as names were called between land and the ship. Everyone wanted to be first to find their loved ones but it was nearly midnight before passengers could step ashore and into waiting arms. That was when the hysterics really started: tears of joy were shed by all at the happy reunions but there were more than a few who cried tears of sadness, those who had no family or friends here. Those who missed their homes desperately.

We could go ashore for the evening too but it was late, and while those who disembarked made the most of their reunions, many of us would stay on board for one final night. My emotions were running high – our voyage here on the *Skaubryn* had been like a dream, the luxury of the liner itself was an unexpected pleasure as we sailed toward our new life. The next morning a train would take us to the Bonegilla migrant camp where we would be processed, given job placements and sent to our new homes.

'It'll be all right,' said Erich, drawing me into his arms. 'We'll get through this together.'

I clung to him. He was my anchor and I knew he was right. Despite the difficulties of moving to a strange new country, we had every reason to believe that better times were ahead for us.

'Let's go to bed. We have an early start in the morning and the girls won't give us a moment's peace once they're up.'

The following day was a blur as we made our way off the ship and through the crowd still clustered around the gangways. Pamphlets were thrust in our faces by faceless figures, promoting what I didn't know. The girls stayed close to us, overwhelmed by the cacophony of voices calling out in different languages.

A group of dock workers stood a little apart from the fray and offered them ice cream and sweets. 'Welcome to Australia,' they said.

The men didn't look like they could afford to give out treats, but I felt obliged to accept, and the girls were very excited to have sweets to sustain them through the hours of the train ride ahead.

The workers didn't force their pamphlets on us but Erich took one willingly and thanked them for their kindness. The pamphlet was promoting trade union membership to new migrant workers. Erich wouldn't need to be part of a union in his profession and new job, but it surprised me that Australians were proactive in the labour movement; we had been told they were a very relaxed people. Under the Third Reich in Germany, trade unionism was banned as a manifestation of communism and workers had no voice. But I was pleased that migrants were being welcomed so readily into the Australian way of life and would be guided and looked after by those who knew and understood Australian ways. It looked like freedom of choice and the freedom to speak your beliefs was a reality in this country and our hope for this was part of the reason we had come.

Then we were through customs with our luggage and onto a train bound for Bonegilla, six hours away. It was hard to believe that we were finally in Australia. At one point on our passage across the world I wondered whether we would arrive at all – the *Skaubryn* was one of the last ships to make it through the Suez Canal before it was closed by the crisis. It was still closed and nobody knew when it would open again.

'When will we get there?' moaned Greta and Johanna on more than one occasion. Each time, I threw them a frown. We were not alone in the carriage, sharing it with a doctor and his two sisters. Erich chatted amiably with them while I tried to keep the girls under control. My nerves were already frayed, worried about what would greet us at the end of this journey, and their restlessness didn't help my state of mind. The supply of sweets had dried up long ago.

'Look out the window for the kangaroos,' said Erich to the girls when it was clear that I would soon lose my patience with them.

'I've seen three already,' said one of the doctor's sisters, winking surreptitiously at me.

I smiled in thanks as the girls' attention was drawn to the rolling countryside once again.

'It goes on forever,' I said to Erich. 'I can count the number of small towns we've passed on one hand.'

'Australia's so much bigger than Germany.'

'Yes, I know, but I never imagined how vast it would be and how few people live in such a big place. It's so different from home.'

'Not really. It's mainly hilly farmland like at home and the cattle and sheep look much the same.'

'You can see the farms are much bigger here and the countryside's nowhere as green.' Erich was only trying to soothe my anxiety but he was irritating me. 'Besides, the never-ending sight of eucalyptus trees is a constant reminder that we're not in Germany any more.' I took a deep breath to calm down, gazing out at the blue-shaded mountains in the distance, and wondered what mysterious things might be found upon their slopes and rugged peaks.

He squeezed my hand. 'I know. It all seems so strange at the moment. We'll get used to it, I'm sure.'

I nodded and stared out the window once more. Although it was certainly going to take a while to adjust to all the changes we would find here, we had each other. And after what we'd been through during the war, and afterwards, we were well used to supporting each other through the toughest of times.

We reached our destination mid-afternoon, our nervous energy swirling around us as we alighted from the train to board the bus to camp.

'Look, Mutti and Vati!' said Johanna, pointing out the window to some figures lining the camp driveway.

'Aborigines!' said Greta with excitement. The three young men wore nothing but shorts, their tanned bodies and faces streaked with white paint. We'd heard about the Aborigines and their ancient culture while still in Germany and after experiencing exotic Colombo, Greta had hoped to see Aborigines everywhere.

The bus driver laughed. 'No, love. They're Swedes. They've been in the sun too long and burnt to a crisp.'

Although I didn't quite understand exactly what he said, I understood his meaning and translated for Greta. Her face fell and I had to hide my smile with my hand.

'But what about the paint?' Erich asked.

'That's calamine lotion for the sunburn. Don't you have that where you come from?'

'No.'

'Oh well, you'll soon get to know it. It's useful for all sorts of things, from sunburn to stinging nettle rash.'

Erich shot a perplexed look at me. I shrugged. I didn't know what he was talking about. Erich's English was now even better than mine but I somehow felt that we were not prepared for the variety spoken in Australia. It would take some time to understand all the strange things Australians said.

Bonegilla migrant camp lay close to the town of Albury. It was a beautiful spot, hilly and leafy with a large water reservoir nearby. We could see mountains beyond the camp, which we were told were only a fifteen-minute walk away. Behind them lay the Australian Alps, still snow-covered this late in spring. The girls were excited by the thought of swimming in the reservoir and although Erich's face lit up when he learnt that motor-boating was popular, I knew that, just like me, he couldn't wait to go hiking in those mountains.

The camp was enormous, with all the facilities we could want – hospital, school, kindergarten, canteen, cinema, theatre and churches. Each block was a small village of twenty corrugated-iron barracks and each barrack had ten small rooms, partitioned with plywood and sparsely furnished. There was a communal kitchen, dining room, laundry, shower room and toilets. It wasn't a palace but it was much better than the dilapidated farm cottage we'd lived in after the war. Erich and I had lived with my mother and aunt and her four boys with no electricity, no running water, only a little fuel to cook once a day and no heating. We'd managed then and we'd manage now.

'Look at the geraniums,' I said to Erich as we walked to our barracks. We'd been given two rooms: one for the girls and one for Erich and me. 'They're enormous compared to the ones at home.' The colours around us were vibrant, with flowering plants and bushes lining the paths and buildings of the camp.

'Everything seems bigger and brighter here,' said Erich in awe as we stepped inside our room. 'Even the sky is bluer. We'll make it feel like home for however long we're here,' he said as we looked around. 'Once you put your touches on the rooms, they'll be cosy and welcoming. Just you wait and see.'

'I know,' I answered. 'How long do you think we'll be here?'

'I've been told that it's only for a couple of weeks. I see the employment office in a day or two. Hopefully they have a job already for me. I'm excited to be working in engineering again. It's been too long.' He sighed, kissing my neck. 'We'll stay only as long as we have to. We'll have a place of our own soon.'

A few days after we arrived, Erich came home, face drained of colour. Thank God the girls were outside with some of the other children in our block, looking at where the fireworks display would be held to celebrate the beginning of the Olympics in Melbourne.

'What happened?'

'There's no job,' he muttered, almost to himself.

My heart began to pound in my ears. I wasn't sure I'd heard him right. 'What did you say?'

Erich looked at me then, and his face crumpled. 'There's no job waiting for me. I've let you down.'

I grasped his arm, not sure if it was to give him strength or to make sure I wasn't in some horrible nightmare. I led him to a chair and sank down beside him. 'What do you mean?'

'I presented all my documentation. Everything was in order, but it didn't matter. Foreign qualifications for professions like medicine, law and engineering – professions like mine – aren't recognised in Australia. I can't work in my field unless I go to university here and retrain.'

Erich knew everything about planes and how they worked. He had been unable to find work in his field in Germany after the war and had struggled to find continuous work to sustain our family. But the Australian Consulate in Frankfurt had promised him engineering work in Australia and that information had helped us make the decision to migrate.

'How can this be?'

'They lied to us to get us to come here. We've been lured here under false pretences.' Erich's voice was hard and flat.

'That is ridiculous! How can they get away with it? It's not right . . .' I raked a trembling hand through my hair. 'What are we going to do?'

'We have no choice. I was reminded of the fact quite clearly today.' He looked me in the eyes. 'We're committed to staying here for two years. I have to take any job I'm given, regardless of what I was promised. Besides, even if we wanted to go back now, we could never repay our passage to the Australian government.'

I stared at Erich. His words were like a slap in the face. All the planning, the heartache and the difficult decisions . . . We'd been through so much. But he was right – false hope and indignation weren't going to get us anywhere. We had no choice.

'I'm so sorry, my *schatz*,' he said. 'You don't deserve this.'

I wrapped my arms around him but I wanted nothing more than to scream and shout – to throw something at any Australian official who crossed my path. But none of that would do us any good. Bureaucracy could not be swayed by the act of a single person, righteous or not. I sat back, steeling myself against what was coming.

'So what happens now?' My voice sounded small, although I was trying to put on a brave face.

'The best they can offer is to find me work in some related field, probably as a mechanic.' He shrugged. 'We're no better off than we were at home.'

'It's not your fault.' I squeezed Erich's hand, summoning my strength. 'We've done it before, we can do it again.'

He straightened in his chair, pulling himself together. 'Maybe it's a start. I can save some money and get us settled and then perhaps I can study to get my qualification.'

The vein at his temple was throbbing and I could see the supreme effort it took him to remain calm and logical. As much as this blow devastated him, he had his family to provide for. We had to come first.

I kissed him and held him tight but a little voice inside me wondered how long it would take for us to find our feet.

2

I wasn't sure what woke me, but the faint glimmer of early morning light peeked between the curtains and fell onto my pillow. I glanced across to Erich's bed. It was empty, and I remembered that he had been sent to Sydney on the train the day before, to work as a mechanic at a factory for trucks and agricultural machinery. It was early January and companies were employing again after their Christmas closures. If all went well, we would join him once we were allocated somewhere to live.

Gooseflesh rippled along my arms. It was still quite cool in the mornings, though I knew we would be scorching by midday. Pulling the blanket higher around my shoulders, I tried to remember the last time we were apart. It was about six years earlier. Erich's first wife and their children were still living with us after he'd managed to get them out of the Russian zone. Inga had made it clear that she wanted Erich back and I was at breaking point. But our love had endured and we'd remarried after his divorce from Inga was finalised. I'd vowed never to be parted from him again.

Erich was the love of my life. Of course life was busier with the girls but even after nearly twelve years of marriage, a tender word, a feather-light touch could still stoke the fire between us like in the days of our young love. If anything, the years had brought us even closer, the intimate knowledge of each other forging a bond deeper than I'd ever imagined possible. I fervently hoped we'd be reunited soon.

When it arrived, his first letter to me from Sydney had left me dismayed, my head reeling. There was no work for him there either. It was only after talking to other migrants in the camp at Villawood that Erich learnt the truth: Bonegilla was the main reception centre for migrants and it only sent people to Sydney to make room for new arrivals. The employment office in Sydney tried to accommodate those sent up from Bonegilla but it was often weeks before they found work for them.

I cried after that letter. I wanted to be by Erich's side, to comfort and support him. I wanted him to see the girls and how happy they were, to be reminded why we'd come to Australia. I remembered our first joyous day at sea. Despite leaving our homeland and everything we knew, I truly believed that Australia was our new beginning. What mattered was that we were together.

The girls and I settled into our routine without Erich, who had decided to stay in Sydney to look for work. Being busy was the only way I could keep my worries at bay and stop myself feeling the absence of him too acutely. I had English classes in the morning, then lunch, a swim at the lake with friends, dinner, a walk and then coffee with the neighbours once the girls were in bed. We could occupy our time easily enough and we were beginning to make friends here but I couldn't keep thoughts of Erich out of my head.

So I made plans to join him in Sydney, and after speaking to the camp officials I was able to secure our transfer to Villawood migrant camp. We were to travel by train to Sydney and Erich would meet us at Central Station and escort us back to the hostel. I was nervous about travelling on my own with the girls. I knew that my English was passable but we'd been cocooned in Bonegilla for the last couple of months, sheltered from the outside world, and part of me was afraid to step beyond our bubble. However, there was no point staying – Sydney was the most likely place for us to find work. It was the almost over-whelming fear of being apart in this strange new country that spurred me forward – and the thought of being together again enabled me to get on that bus and leave the camp behind as we made our way to the train station one morning in late January.

'Good luck to you and your family, missus,' called the bus driver as we set our suitcases down on the dusty kerb. I nodded my thanks and waved as the bus pulled away and we were left alone. Swallowing the lump in my throat, I clasped a suitcase handle in each hand to stop the shaking that had overcome me.

'Come on, girls, let's find our train,' I said brightly as I could. Thankfully our tickets had been booked and paid for and all we had to do now was find the right train and get on.

'Have you got the tickets, Mutti?' asked Greta.

A shot of panic coursed through me. 'I'm sure I put them in my handbag. Let me double check.' I put the suitcases down and rifled through my bag.

'We'll miss the train,' said Johanna, pulling on my sleeve.

'No, we won't. We have plenty of time,' Greta replied superiorly.

'Here they are.' I pulled out the tickets, sighing with relief.

Once inside the station, I looked around anxiously for directions to the platform where the Sydney train would arrive.

'Stay close now. I don't want to lose either of you before we get on.' The girls dutifully stayed by my side as I tried to decipher the board in front of me.

More people arrived, jostling past us impatiently as I stared in confusion at the information.

'What're you standing there for? Can't you see you're in the road?' said one of the men crossly as he tried to squeeze past and bumped into me. I drew back in shock at his tone and the look of anger on his face, dropped the suitcases and put my arms around the girls.

'Train to Sydney,' I began. 'What place?' I stammered in fright.

'What did you say?' The man glared at me. 'You can't even speak English, can you? Why don't you go back to where you came from? We don't want the likes of you here.' The girls cowered next to me, hugging me tight.

A large woman in a skirt and blouse wedged herself between the man and me. 'Is there a problem here?' The man stared at her belligerently. 'Are you all right?' she asked me. I nodded, unable to speak.

'She can't even speak fucking English,' the man proclaimed to the crowd indignantly. I could see the flashes of sympathy across many faces but also the hard stares of others who no doubt agreed.

17

'That's enough,' said the woman, 'or I'll have you escorted from the station.'

'And who do you think you are?' jeered the man.

She stood a little taller. 'I'm the stationmaster's wife.'

The man turned away, scowling at me one more time. 'We fought against these bastard Europeans and now we invite them here,' he said loudly. 'What's this bloody country coming to?'

'Don't pay any attention to him,' said the stationmaster's wife. 'Some men have never been the same since they came back from the war. They left their decency and manners on the battlefield and all they have left is their resentment. I'm sorry you had to see that. Most Australians are friendly and accommodating.'

'Thank you,' I said, the shock beginning to subside and understanding most of what she'd said. I glanced at the girls, their faces pale, and loosened my grip on them.

'I could see that you were staring at the board before you were rudely interrupted. Where are you going?'

'Sydney . . .' I looked at the board again and frowned. 'Platform Two, but the time is different. Is it the right train?' I pulled out our tickets from my bag and showed the woman.

'Oh, of course.' The woman smiled, checking the tickets before handing them back. 'It's the right train but it's running late today and won't arrive for another hour.' The woman didn't seem very worried about the train not running to schedule.

'Okay,' I said, trying to smile. 'I thought that maybe because my English isn't very good that I'd made a mistake.'

'You're fine.' She patted my hand reassuringly. 'How about you all come with me and have a cup of tea before the train arrives. Then I'll put you on the train myself.' Still in shock and worried about the girls, I nodded and allowed the woman to usher us to a small room off the stationmaster's office, where we were given sweet milky tea and biscuits.

The monotonous clattering of the wheels of the train soothed my jarred nerves. The tea and biscuits had done their work on the girls, who were back to their usual selves, restless and annoying each other, but for once I didn't worry. After the morning we'd had, I was happy to let them be, grateful to see them behaving normally. Besides, the carriage was nearly empty. Thankfully the man at the station hadn't boarded the train but I was too rattled to want to leave the security of our carriage. I felt for the packet of sandwiches in my bag, the white bread I couldn't get used to but that the girls loved, still soft and fresh. The kitchen had prepared them for our trip and now I felt very glad for them and that I didn't have to converse in English or deal with Australian money to buy our lunch.

Slowly my frozen mind began to work again and I tuned out the girls who were playing a guessing game. Now I could take in our surroundings as we hurtled through the countryside. There was barely a blade of green grass in sight. As far as the eye could see, it was bone dry, dusty and brown, that was except for the eucalypts – gum trees they were called – and the continuous blue sky. I couldn't imagine an environment more alien and different from anything we had known in Germany. The heat was almost suffocating and my last thought, as I was finally lulled into an exhausted doze, was that soon we'd be with Erich.

*

We alighted at Central Station and were thrust forward amid the sea of passengers, me hanging on to suitcases and the girls in front of me gripping hands. I tried to keep one eye on them and the other looking out for Erich. My heart was thumping madly, wondering what I'd do if I lost the girls or if I couldn't find Erich. How would I get us to Villawood? Then I saw him, standing away from the surge of people, towards the end of the platform. I guided the girls towards him, jostling my way through the crowd.

'We made it.' I fell into Erich's arms and willed myself not to cry. Instead I trembled violently – from relief and joy.

'My *liebchen*,' he murmured, holding me as if he'd never let go. We had been apart for nearly a month and the strain on him was evident.

'I missed you so much,' I whispered, squeezing him to make sure he was real.

'You're here now,' he said, smiling down at me.

That night, lying with Erich in one of the camp beds, I prised the details of the last weeks out of him. We had two rooms like in Bonegilla, separated from the three other families in the dome-shaped Nissen hut by thin partition walls that didn't even reach the roof. There was no privacy at all and we had to whisper to make sure we weren't overheard and so we didn't disturb the children. Erich had finally found a job working as a mechanic servicing Volkswagen cars at Lanock Motors in the city. It wasn't much money but it was a job and that was a start.

'It was difficult,' he began. 'I was supposed to go to the employment office once a week to see if there was a job, but hundreds of people sit there every day, often from early in the morning until the evening, desolate and desperate.'

'I can't believe they let things get so bad.' It sounded like the queues in post-war Germany, standing for hours in the freezing conditions, desperate not to miss out on the limited rations available when the shop opened its doors, determined to stay as long as necessary to bring some kind of food home – anything – to the family.

'I've been told that once you leave Bonegilla, they stop caring about what happens to you, and I've certainly heard many terrible stories about people trying to find work and losing all hope of the life they came to find.'

'Thank God in heaven you found a job, then. How did you manage it?'

He paused and sighed. 'I went to the city and sold our camera.'

'You what?' I turned rigid in his arms. Erich had taken the camera with him to Sydney to send us photos of where he worked and of areas we might live with the last of the film before having it developed. He knew how much that camera meant to me; it was my only link to my passion and my dream of my own photography studio.

He cupped my cheek, trying to soothe me. 'I know, but what other choice did I have? None of our belongings have arrived yet. It was the only thing of value I had. I promise I'll buy you a new one as soon as I can.' He drew back to look into my face in the dim light. 'Can you forgive me?'

We had bought that camera together and he had used it on the boat and on our stopover in Colombo almost as much as I had. It was our only extravagance and held such sentimental feelings. Tears slid down my face against my will, not just at the loss of something so meaningful but at Erich's desperation.

'Of course I forgive you,' I whispered, my body softening once more. 'Why didn't you tell me how bad it's been for you?'

He gently wiped my tears away with his thumb. 'I didn't want to upset you any more than I needed to. You've had enough to deal with on your own with the children and I always hoped that a job would come along.'

'You can always tell me anything.'

'I know.'

'So what did you do with the money?'

'I spent it on fares into the city every day to look for work. I went from factory to factory, but everywhere there were people lined up, sometimes a hundred or more, looking for work, just like me. It was a depressing sight, but the thought of you and the children kept me going.

'One of the other German immigrants gave me the address of the Australian–German Welfare Society. They help Germans who might be having difficulty financially or in finding employment. They used their contacts to help me find work.'

'There are some kind people out there,' I murmured, thinking of the stationmaster's wife.

'I don't know where we would be without them. They gave me the address for the Volkswagen plant here in Sydney. Apparently, Volkswagens are gaining popularity after winning a big cross-country car race recently. They need more mechanics, especially those who understand German cars. I went immediately. After they checked my paperwork and credentials, I was hired as an auto mechanic within the hour. The problem was that all my work clothes and tools are still in our crates and I needed my own tools to start work.'

'I tried to find out where they are before we left Bonegilla but all I got was that they're still in customs,' I said.

'It's okay,' he said, kissing my shoulder. 'Lucky for me the manager has provided me with new tools, which I have to pay off at one pound a week. But they couldn't provide work clothes until I've been there a month. The society helped me again by buying work clothes for me. I have a month to repay them.' He paused. 'I would have lost the job if not for them. I can't believe the kindness they showed me.'

'We're very fortunate.' After the war in Germany, it was every man for himself. Living conditions were far worse than what we were experiencing now and there was no safety net to ensure an ordinary person's survival, let alone that of a family. But I couldn't imagine what this experience had done to Erich's pride.

'It will be all right now.'

I hoped I was right.

Erich settled quickly into his job. Although he was no stranger to manual work, most of the mechanics were in their twenties or thirties and Erich worked as hard as the younger men to justify his employment. It was rough on him: he got up at five in the morning and didn't return until six at night when he collapsed, bone-tired, on the lounge. The only time we really got to talk was on a Sunday, after a sleep-in and late breakfast.

'My English is getting quite good,' he said one Sunday. We were reading the newspaper, enjoying a little peace while the girls were outside playing. 'I'm interpreting for the other German workers who don't understand English so well yet and translating their official documents, so they understand the work routines.'

I noticed that he'd finished the page he was reading and handed him a section I was finished with. 'Surely there are provisions made for people who can't speak English so well?'

'We both know what should be happening but it's not and someone has to help them. Some of the Australian mechanics have started to talk to us, although sometimes it's hard to understand them. They speak so fast and their expressions need explanation. I have to admit there are times I'm totally lost.'

'I know what you mean. I thought that with our good grasp of English, we'd be fine, but there are different ways of saying things here. I let Johanna pay the man at the fruit shop for a few apples and with his broad accent, we misunderstood the price. She gave him the money but worked out herself that what she'd given him was wrong. He saw her confusion and said, "She'll be right." We didn't know what he meant, but when she tried to give him more money he shook his head and smiled and gave her the bag of apples.'

'I know that one.' Erich smiled broadly. 'It means it's all right, don't worry about it.'

'Yes, I guessed as much. It was nice of him to do that, going out of his way to make sure Johanna didn't feel embarrassed.'

'Yes, but there are others who stay away from us. We're called "New Australians", but it's a derogatory term. Some people believe that we don't deserve to be in this country and we should go back to where we came from, especially Germans, who are all Nazis.'

'That's crazy! If people only listened and got to know us, they'd realise we're ordinary people just like them,' I said, remembering how the incident at the train station had left me feeling inadequate and small. I passed him the paper. I didn't feel like reading any more.

'They blame us for taking their jobs, but they don't understand that we're at the bottom of the ladder. Professionals are doing manual labour and factory work, doctors working as hospital cleaners, and many men are sent to remote areas, separated from family, to work on big government projects.' The muscles in his jaw clenched tight.

'Well, helping with the little things is a start,' I said, trying to console him. 'Surely that will show the others that you want the same things that they do – a decent life.'

'I don't know. I really believed that this was the land of equality, but I'm not so sure now. Some of the men at work urge the new workers to join one of the trade unions, to protect their rights, but I don't know if it's the answer for migrant workers.'

'You're doing what you can.'

We soon discovered, however, that Erich's wages were not enough. He made seventeen pounds a week, with a monthly bonus of eight pounds if he worked every day that month and all his hours. Our accommodation and food at the hostel cost twelve pounds a week, two pounds were deducted for Erich's tools and clothes, and our health insurance and hospital fund came out of the remaining three pounds. Then there were the little extras we never thought about that had become essential here. For example, when it rained, it really rained – heavy storms with thunder and lightning, often in the afternoons – and everything was muddy, sodden and flooded. I'd bought all of us rubber boots – which the Australians called gumboots – so our shoes weren't ruined. There was very little left to save, and I knew I had to find work very soon to supplement our income and put savings away so that we could find somewhere to rent and set up a proper home. New migrants were given little help in their search for accommodation, we discovered, and housing was expensive.

The girls started school a couple of weeks after we arrived in Villawood. Although I had been worried about their English being good enough for school, they adjusted well and made new friends very quickly.

'How was your day?' I asked one afternoon, as we walked back to our rooms after school. The grass either side of the path was brown and shrivelled, baked by the relentless summer sun. I wondered if in winter the landscape would return to the luscious green I was more familiar with. The air was warm and still, like walking through an oven, but I discovered, to my surprise, that I liked it.

'Fine, Mutti,' said Greta. She was bright and would find her feet quickly.

Johanna said something to her but I didn't understand her words. It wasn't German or English.

'What did you say, Johanna?' I asked.

'It's all right, Mutti,' said Greta. 'It's just the words Johanna learnt today from her new Dutch friend.'

'You're speaking Dutch?' I was incredulous. 'Your first new words at school are Dutch, not English?'

'Mutti, there are so many different languages and

nationalities at school,' said Johanna. 'At least I could understand Saskia a bit. I've taught her some German too.'

I stared at the girls, not sure what to make of this. Then
I burst out laughing. 'We come to Australia so you can learn
Dutch! Wait until I tell your father!'

'Okay, Mutti,' said Greta, glancing at her sister. 'We're
going to meet Anna and Peter. They're helping us with our
homework. We'll be back for tea.' I was still getting used to
the idea that 'tea' was the Australian word for dinner. Maybe
they were learning after all.

Our neighbours Franz and Claudia Schneider had become
indispensable to us. They were German, too, and had been
at Villawood four months longer than us, so they'd taken us
under their wing, explaining the way things were done in
camp and the differences between Australia and Germany.
They had four children: Anna, who was a year older than
Greta; Peter, who was the same age as Johanna; and twin
girls only three years old. The older two got along beautifully with our girls and they spent hours playing together
and exploring the camp. We were at a similar stage in life
and found that we had much in common. Claudia was my
age and worked in a textiles factory while Franz, now in
his late thirties and unable to work as a lawyer, worked in a
door factory.

'Only since arriving did we discover that Australia's in the
middle of a recession. Unemployment's a real problem,' said
Franz one evening, after we'd shared the difficulties we'd been
experiencing. We were drinking coffee on our porch. Instant
coffee was popular in Australia, and something we were slowly
getting used to. Making it was easier than trudging back up

to the cafeteria yet again and we could drink it and relax in some privacy.

'I don't know why nobody told us that in Germany before we left,' I said. 'We were seduced into coming here ... Even on the boat we weren't told the truth by the Australian representatives.'

'But why is Australia still bringing out immigrants?' asked Claudia.

'They need us to do the jobs that Australians don't want to do,' said Franz.

'Maybe those representatives should come here.' Erich's eyes glittered with anger and frustration. 'The camp residents will tell them what's really going on. I'd be happy to be the one to organise that visit and show them what life is like for migrants!'

'It's like nobody cares,' I said, my cup clinking against its saucer more forcefully than I intended. I felt so helpless, so insignificant, and I'd vowed when I left Germany that I would never feel like that again.

'Nobody does,' said Claudia, her hand on my arm in sympathy. 'Franz wanted to write a letter to the government department in Canberra, or even to Prime Minister Menzies himself, and tell them what's happening.'

'It won't make any difference. It won't be taken seriously by the bureaucracy here,' said Franz, reaching for another spoonful of sugar.

'We have to help each other. Otherwise we'll never make it,' said Claudia.

Erich nodded. 'It takes so much effort to get anyone to notice anything and then it takes time for them to act on it. We'd be better off using our energy to help ourselves.'

'The only thing the Australians are passionate about is their sport,' said Franz. He leant back in his chair, long legs crossed.

I realised with a little start that he reminded me of my old fiancé, Heinrich: tall, blond and athletic. I knew that Mutti and Heinrich still wrote to each other at Christmas but I never enquired after him and Mutti knew better than to talk about him to me. That chapter of my life was closed and I intended it to stay that way.

'I don't mind that so much,' said Erich, grinning. 'I've missed my football and although it's not as popular here as at home, at least there's still a competition to follow.'

'Everything's so strange,' said Claudia, frowning. 'I've seen women walk out onto the street in the mornings in their dressing gowns to buy their newspaper or collect their milk from the milkman, and men half-dressed and barefoot in public. Nobody takes offence. I can't stop shaking my head. It's like nothing I've ever seen before.'

Erich looked thoughtful. 'But there's a certain kind of freedom. People can do what they like.'

I sighed. 'I know what you're saying, but it's crazy. How does anything change if nobody cares?'

'I'm sure one day it will, *liebchen*.' Erich reached across and squeezed my hand. 'I think people here fundamentally believe in having their own rights.'

'Maybe it'll be our children who will make it a country where opportunities are equal for all people,' added Claudia.

I smiled a little at the thought of my girls campaigning in this most peaceful yet, strangely indifferent country, and I realised that I wanted them to have that freedom and opportunity. Here, people could stand up for what they believed in, not like when I was a girl growing up in Hitler's Germany, where even the most innocent comment could be taken as an affront to the Nazi regime. I remembered how my alarmed mother had cautioned me to say nothing after the arrest of my wedding dress designer by the Gestapo. I'd felt so powerless. Being unable – or unwilling – to help her was one of the many things that haunted me.

Franz leant forward. 'I'm proud to say that we've nearly saved enough to rent a house. Thanks to my beautiful wife working so hard.' He smiled and kissed Claudia on the cheek, and a deep blush rose on her delicate, pale skin. She was like the voluptuous beauty of a Rubens painting, plump and curvaceous with fine, honey-blonde hair she pulled back into a roll. 'When we can manage it, I hope to gain my qualifications here and practise law again.'

My eyes were drawn to a couple of large moths attracted to the light where we were sitting, their wings beating frantically, making the light flicker for a moment until they settled against the warmth of the glass. Perhaps surrender was the answer, acceptance of this new land and all of its strange ways. All we could really do now was to put our disappointments to the side, push on and keep our dreams alive.

I discovered that there was a vacancy at a textiles factory. It wasn't photography as I had hoped, but earning money was our priority and I had to take whatever I could get.

'Are you sure you want to do this?' Erich asked. We were walking through the camp after dinner. It was a balmy night, the soft breeze warm on my skin and the droning of cicadas almost deafening.

Bugs were becoming a way of life for us. It was forty-one degrees Celsius in our rooms some days and we had to leave everything open to get as much air flow through as possible, but we had no screens on our windows and doors and no way to keep out the flies, spiders, ants and mosquitoes. The spiders were a common occurrence but it didn't stop me shuddering at the sight of them. The first time I saw a massive huntsman spider on the wall above our beds, I screamed with fright, only to discover from one of the neighbours that they were harmless and not at all poisonous like the red-back spiders we'd been warned about. The pump-action fly spray had become our best friend, and I doused the surfaces of our room with it every day, just to keep the creatures at bay.

'You know I have to. The children are settled and happy at school and we'll never get ahead if I don't take the job.'

Erich stopped walking. 'But this was my responsibility. We agreed that we'd have another child when we got here and you could set up your photography studio. It's all come to nothing! If only I could work as an engineer – it wouldn't even have to be with aeroplanes.'

I caressed his arm. 'It's all right, truly it is. We'll make it work. I know we'll have the son we've always wanted and one day I'll have that studio, too, but it'll have to wait a little longer, that's all.' I kissed him, feeling his cheek grow hot with shame. I had to be strong for both of us. 'This way we can save a little and find a place of our own. Everything will look brighter then.'

'I'll make it up to you. I promise.'

'I know you will.'

3

The tedious and monotonous nature of work in the textiles factory came as a bit of a shock. Admittedly I was sitting most of my day sewing, and only getting up to pick up more garment pieces to machine together.

'Is this what we do all day?' I whispered to the woman next to me after the first morning. We were all female workers, working side by side on industrial sewing machines, cramped together in rows that filled the factory floor.

She nodded. 'That's right. I've been doing this job for a year now.'

'With no change in routine?'

'Just different garments from time to time, but I don't mind. At least I can do it with my eyes closed.'

The electric globes that illuminated the factory hung high above, so many of us hunched over the machines and squinted in the poor light to keep the quality of finish consistent. Luckily for me, my eyesight was good, but I wondered how long it would be before I was squinting too.

'We have to be thankful we have a job at all,' said the woman, shrugging. 'At least I can put food on my family's table.'

Some days, I wondered if the paltry wage was even worth it. By the end of the day, my body was stiff, my neck and back aching and I was ready to scream with boredom. I vowed that one day when we no longer had to exist hand to mouth, I would make my dream of working as a photographer a reality.

Erich saw a job in a German newspaper for a mechanical engineer to build new factories and machinery centres for a large company. It was more like the work he used to do for the Americans after the war and certainly better than the work he was doing. He attended the interview dressed in his best suit. Of course he got the job. We were ecstatic – not only was he working as an engineer, something we both worried would never come to pass, but he was going to earn more money and had the opportunity to work his way up in the company. My mind immediately jumped ahead. Maybe then we could finally move out of Villawood and I could find a job in photography and leave the textiles factory. Maybe I could even consider having another child. Suddenly I could see light at the end of the tunnel.

One evening soon after Erich began his new job, I had the light on, darning socks, while the girls were at the table doing their homework. The days were getting shorter, autumn leaves were falling from the trees, and it was beginning to get dark already. The girls were bickering periodically as was usual, but all it did was set my nerves further on edge. For I had news I needed to share with Erich.

The door opened and Erich came in a little earlier than expected, his face like thunder. He mumbled a greeting and disappeared to wash before dinner. I glanced at the girls, who had barely noticed the odd behaviour. My heart began to pound and I couldn't sit still any longer. I put the darning away and straightened the picture on the wall, the sunflower that had graced the parlour wall of my mother's home when I was young. It reminded me of her and gave our room a homely feeling. I decided I might as well tidy up for the weekly room inspection the following day, so I pulled out the broom and swept the floor.

We all jumped as the door slammed behind us.

'We have to talk,' Erich said.

I gulped down the lump that had formed in my throat. 'All right, girls, enough homework for one night. Off you go to your room until dinner.'

'Can we go to Tante Claudia's?' asked Greta. 'Anna and Peter are going to help us with our English homework.'

'They understand it better than we do,' added Johanna.

I wasn't sure how much homework was going to get done, but sending them out would give me the space to talk to Erich in peace. 'All right. You can go to the dining hall with them and meet us for dinner, but make sure you take your coats.'

The girls didn't waste another minute, gathering up their books and coats and squeezing past their father, who stood rigid in the doorway.

I sat at the table and straightened the tablecloth, thinking about how I was going to tell Erich about my day as I waited for him to join me.

'I've left my job,' he said as he sank into the chair.

My head shot up, eyes wide with shock. I began to feel queasy. I couldn't believe the timing. He'd seemed so happy. 'What happened?' I whispered, barely able to get the words out of my dry mouth.

'The company's a fraud.'

'What are you talking about?'

'They lure German engineers into their firm, knowing they can't get an engineering job anywhere else unless they retrain. There's no big company, only a small room with a few engineers and draughtsmen with a drawing table.' The vein at his temple was pulsing, a sure sign that he was furious.

'What happened?' I asked softly, my hand on his arm.

'The first day I was given photos and paper copies of plans of machines and parts. I was asked to complete the calculations and drawings for them. I thought it a bit odd. But it was only the first day. Maybe they wanted to see what I could do or perhaps it was something to do until my job was ready. The same happened yesterday, but I persevered.

'Today, the copies I received were hardly legible and the photos were blurry.' He leant forward in his seat, eyes blazing. 'I'd had enough and went to the boss. Nothing made sense to me. I'm not a draughtsman or a structural engineer. I was employed to build and set up workshops. I told him my expertise was in machine and plant engineering and that's what I was hired to do.'

'What did he say?'

'After a lot of excuses that he could see I didn't accept, he finally admitted that the company hadn't yet reached that stage and it would be some time before a plant was ready. I couldn't believe what I was hearing and stared at him in astonishment. I asked him how long it would be until the job I had accepted was available, but he couldn't tell me.'

'What do you mean?'

He sighed. 'It all felt wrong, and then the penny dropped. Everything I'd been told was a lie. The company's engaged in industrial espionage, I'm sure of it. I understand now why there's always been such a big turnover of engineers. Nobody stays when they realise what's going on.'

'God in heaven! How can something like this happen? What did you do?'

'I told him what I thought of his company and quit. He went red and then white as a sheet and didn't know what to say. I'm disgusted they're using vulnerable migrants to carry out such criminal activities.' Erich sat back and smiled grimly. 'Perhaps the other engineers just left without telling him what they thought. I'm sick of being taken advantage of and it's disgraceful what he's doing to desperate people.'

A surge of pride mingled with a stab of fear. This was the man I loved standing up for injustice, but I knew from experience how dangerous it could be to tell people with power what you really thought.

'Will you go to the police?'

'No, I don't think so.' He shook his head. 'I don't want any trouble. Besides, the boss could try to turn it around on me and say that I didn't understand what I was supposed to do. I'll just tell everyone I know to be wary of job advertisements in German newspapers. If they seem too good to be true, they probably are.'

'So now you're without a job.' I wiped my clammy hands on my skirt.

'I'm so sorry, Lotte. I just couldn't stay there. It wasn't the right thing to do.'

'I know. I don't blame you, but . . .' I debated whether this was the right time to tell him my news. It was never going to be the right time, I decided. It had to be now, like ripping off an adhesive plaster. 'I have some news of my own.'

'What is it, my *liebchen*?'

I took a deep breath and stared into the concerned green eyes. 'I lost my job today. The textile factory is putting people off because they don't have enough work.'

'You lost your job.'

'Yes.'

'So we're both out of work now.'

I nodded. Erich stared at me.

'We couldn't have planned this if we'd tried, you know,' he said. The edges of his mouth turned up and began to quiver before he broke out into helpless laughter.

I stared for a moment, taken aback by his reaction, but I understood it. If we didn't laugh, we'd cry. I began to laugh too and it felt good to release the day's worries.

'What a day we've both had,' he wheezed as the laughter fizzled away. Then he looked serious as the reality set in. 'We're back to square one.'

On the boat journey, Australia had been an unknown quantity, full of possibilities, and my imagination had run wild with all that we could achieve. Erich had been so happy and we had been so full of hope. I had to hold on to that feeling now.

Thank God for Franz. The company he worked for was looking for someone to cut and plane the timber for the doors they made. Through him, Erich was lucky enough to get the job and was working again within the week. We were so grateful for the wages coming in, but I was worried about Erich when I noticed open sores on his shoulders after the first few days. He tried to brush them off as nothing but, when I insisted, he finally explained his job to me. He had to unload the timber from the truck, each board six metres long and weighing fifty kilograms, cut it on the circular saw, plane it and dress the timber. I knew that it was manual work but never realised how demanding and taxing it really was. Yet he'd never complained about it.

Over coffee one evening at the end of the week, Franz and Erich tried to explain the work hierarchy they had witnessed to Claudia and me.

'Australia needs migrants to do its manual labour and unskilled work. They don't have enough people to do this kind of work now that the manufacturing industries are booming. There's no such thing as employment contracts for migrant labourers either,' said Erich. He was so indignant he had forgotten the cigarette smouldering between his fingers. A few cigarettes were his one indulgence at the end of the working week; we couldn't afford for him to smoke more than that. I knew how much he missed it and looked forward to Friday night coffee when he could sit and relax and have a smoke. Privately, I didn't miss the smell on his clothes, breath and skin, even though I had become used to it when he smoked like a chimney during the war.

'Really? No employment contracts?' Thanks to Franz, Claudia was used to the organised, pragmatic approach to legal matters. It would never have occurred to her that Australia was any different to Germany.

We knew a little about the life she and Franz had shared in Germany. We were happy to share personal stories of family life but never discussed the war years in any detail. Nobody wanted to remember that time and we'd all come to Australia to get away from the horrors we'd seen and experienced under Hitler's Reich.

'It's no different in the textiles factories where you work,' said Erich.

Claudia's eyebrows shot up in surprise. 'I just assumed that the jobs Lotte and I started were the usual way to enter the workforce and once we'd proved ourselves, we would work our way up.'

Erich shook his head.

She glanced at me and I shrugged. 'I didn't know either until I lost my job. Erich explained that I had no recourse to complain or fight for my job. Migrants are always first to go.'

'That's how some of the trade unions get migrant members,' said Erich. 'The union reps wait at the factory gates to talk to new workers. Some unions are more inclined to help migrants, explaining their vulnerability and how easily they're being taken advantage of and discriminated against.'

After what had happened with the engineering job, I knew that Erich had considered union membership as a way to be heard. He'd become quite passionate recently about finding the best way to protect the rights of workers arriving in Australia.

'At least they employ us Germans,' said Franz bitterly. 'As far as the management is concerned, we're good workers and anti-communist. After all, everyone knows Hitler was fighting the communists. We won't cause trouble, striking and demanding better conditions and pay, like the supposed communists in the unions and industrial groups.'

'I can't believe that belonging to a union brands you as a communist,' said Claudia. 'Let the Hungarian refugees talk about *real* communism. They understand what it's about.'

'Reds under the bed,' I murmured. 'It's insane. If Australians really knew what communism was, they'd see they're under no threat here.' The stories Erich had heard about life under Stalin in the Soviet Union from the Russian soldiers he befriended during the war still made my blood run cold.

'Blame the Petrov Affair in Canberra a few years ago,' said Franz, 'and now the war in Korea. Anyone spouting socialist ideas is branded a communist and a threat to demo- cratic and civilised society. Not only that but we'd also be branded Nazis.'

'That's ridiculous,' spat Claudia. 'How can you be a communist and a Nazi?'

Franz shrugged. 'But it's not worth the risk for us. I'll have to wait and fight injustice as a lawyer once I've finished my studies.'

'It doesn't matter that some of us are so much more quali- fied or experienced than the Australians, our papers and work history seem to make no difference – all the higher positions, the managers and bosses, are Australian or English,' said Erich. He clearly didn't want to discuss communism and I wondered how close he was to joining the union.

'That's right,' said Franz. 'Educated men like us suffer the most. There's no way we can rise to a higher position, it just isn't possible.' He cocked his blond head to the side, frowning slightly. 'No, that's not exactly true. There are exceptions. Migrants who have risen to elevated positions have been here for some years and are naturalised . . . Australian citizens.'

'All I know is that Australian craftsmen and builders must be good: we've decided to rent for a while before we can afford to build a house because the labour costs are outrageous!' Claudia rolled her eyes.

'Maybe Erich and I should go into the building business,' said Franz, grinning. 'He's a master with timber even though he hasn't got any trade qualifications.' He slapped Erich on the back. 'We have to be smart about it, understand how the system works here and make the most of it. We'll be successful just to spite them all!'

Not long after, I found casual work on factory processing lines, standing for long hours, performing mindless and repetitive tasks: checking, filling or capping soft drink bottles or packaging soap into boxes. I hated it. I wasn't there long enough each week to make friends, maybe one or two days at each plant, and the permanent workers kept mostly to themselves. The factories were always the same: poor natural light with the windows high up in the factory walls, cold as the season turned towards winter, the floors hard concrete and the work relentless. But I couldn't complain – at least it was money coming in. I realised that I'd been reduced to being grateful for any kind of work like the woman I'd spoken to on my first day at the textiles factory, but I'd be damned if I was going to do this forever. Things would turn around for us soon, I told myself. It was the only way I could bring myself to return to the factory each day.

*

In the dead of winter our crates finally arrived. It was just like Christmas. The girls hopped from one foot to the other waiting for Erich to pry the lids off the boxes.

'Come on, Vati,' said Greta impatiently. 'You're doing it too slowly.'

'Am I?' asked Erich innocently, a twinkle in his eye. 'I'm going as fast as I can but these lids are shut so tight, I don't know if I can open them.'

I was just as excited as the children. I mostly remembered what we had packed but that was over nine months ago now and I was sure I would find as many surprises as the girls.

'Put them out of their misery,' I said.

Erich looked at me. 'In some kind of hurry, are you?'

'No,' I said, my fingers itching to rip the lids off the crates.

Johanna pulled on her father's shirt sleeve. 'Vati, I'm going to burst with excitement if you make us wait much longer.'

'Well, I don't think Mutti would like to clean up the mess after that. I'd better put some more muscle into it then. Can you girls help me?'

Greta and Johanna were by his side in an instant, helping to lift the lid of the first crate.

'Well, I think the honour of discovering what's under all this padding goes to Mutti,' Erich said. 'Move aside, girls, and let your mother through.'

In the silence that followed, I removed the padding from the top of the crate and reached in to remove the first treasure, wrapped in paper. I realised it was part of my dinner set, the one Mutti had given us before we left Germany. I carefully placed the package on the small table.

'What are all these stickers on the side of the box?' asked Greta, always the curious and observant one.

Erich looked to where she was pointing then glanced at me, his face clouded in concern.

'What is it?' The package was forgotten as my stomach clenched in apprehension.

'The crates have been opened by customs. I hope everything's all right.'

Dread swirled in my belly. 'There's only one way to find out.' Willing my hands not to tremble, I began to unwrap the first parcel. 'It's broken!' My voice caught as my shaking fingers pulled the wrapping away. 'My beautiful crockery, it's smashed.'

Just like that, our joyful and excited mood was gone.

'This isn't how we packed everything,' I said as I looked into the crate. 'It's all been pulled out and put back in but with no care to how it would travel.' White hot anger surged through me.

Then Erich's hand was on my shoulder, ready to soothe me. 'It might be only one package. We'll have to unpack it all now to make sure the rest is undamaged.'

I shook my head. There was no way the dinnerware would be unbroken. 'But you wanted to rest. You've had such a busy week.'

'It doesn't matter.' He reached into the crate and pulled out another package.

I kissed him on the cheek. 'Come on, then,' I said to the children. 'We all have to help if we're going to get anything else done today.' I handed a parcel to Greta. 'Here, unwrap it carefully.'

But we soon sent the girls outside to play after they began crying when we discovered some of their toys had been broken.

After everything was unpacked, Erich and I stared at each other.

'I can't believe it.' Precious things that could have helped us enormously in our new life were no good now. Most of my china was smashed and the sewing machine that I'd hoped to use to make us clothes and curtains was ruined. Many of the household items we'd worked so hard to save for in Germany like the radio and gramophone were dented and some were simply destroyed.

Each package brought back memories of our life in Germany, reminding me of what we had been through and what we had sacrificed to be here. My parents were on the other side of the world and I missed them terribly.

'Even your technical tools and measuring instruments are gone,' I whispered, not daring to look at him. They were Erich's livelihood.

'We'll manage.'

'We always do,' I said flatly.

If only we could return home, but we had no money to go back and no way of repaying the fare that brought us here to begin with. I blinked away my tears, determined not to show Erich how upset I was. Somehow I had to come to terms with the fact that our life was here, at least for the next couple of years.

4

We discovered we weren't the only ones who had suffered such destruction and loss. Many of the immigrants in the camp shook their heads when Erich and I shared our experience but their sympathy didn't help my state of mind. Everything had changed. I couldn't see a way of staying. All the disappointments we'd endured spooled over in my mind like a movie.

'We can't keep doing this,' I whispered to Erich as we lay in our beds. 'We'll be worn out before we can enjoy the results of our hard work.' Neither of us could sleep although we were exhausted.

'I know. I've been thinking the same thing . . .' The stiff sheets rustled as he turned towards me. 'We have to find you a job in photography. At least you'll be doing something you love and I'd imagine the hours and money will be better too.'

'Who's going to employ me? I haven't worked in the industry since my training,' I said a little bitterly.

'You don't know that. We'll start looking in the news-papers. There's bound to be something. I want to find something with more pay too. The sooner we get out of this hostel, the better. I've been thinking and looking at our options.' Erich paused and even in the gloom I could see the indecision and apprehension crossing his face. Perhaps he'd come to the same conclusion as me. I slid out of my bed and into his, settling against him with a sigh of pleasure.

'Tell me,' I said hopefully.

He took my hand and held it against his chest. 'We have to make some plans, otherwise the despair we're feeling will drag us down.'

'Nothing's worked out for us,' I said. 'Receiving the crates was the last straw for me. It's time to talk about going home.'

'Home? Isn't this home?'

'This is not home,' I hissed, anger flaring in me. 'I mean Germany. I want to go back to Germany.'

'We can't go back. You know that.'

'Yes, I know, we're committed for two years, but we can go after that.'

'Whatever for? We'll be out of here then, renting and saving to buy our own house, something we'd never be able to manage in Germany. I want the girls to grow up in a place that's our own, with plenty of space to run around. Isn't that what you wanted?'

I stared at him silently.

He tried again. 'We have just as much chance, if not more, of making it here as back in Germany.'

I pulled away from him, unable to believe what I was hearing. 'Are you crazy?'

46

'I hope not.' Erich shrugged but the wariness in his eyes and the set of his jaw told me he'd known what my reaction would be.

I sat up, furious. 'It's hopeless! This is never going to work. Nobody wants us here. We may as well jump into the ocean and try to swim back to Germany. It'll be a quicker death, because staying here is going to kill us slowly.' I knew I shouldn't say it, I knew that Erich felt the full brunt of our failures here in Australia, but his plans to stay were too much and I couldn't hold my feelings in any longer.

He looked at me for a second and then he embraced me. 'We can't let this get us down, *liebchen*. We're better than this. If nobody wants to help us, then we have to help ourselves. It's the only way we can get through this and get ahead. We're both strong and resourceful and we will find a way.'

'After everything that's happened, I don't want to hear you say that.' I pushed him away. 'We were promised so much more. We can't even get decent jobs, let alone work we want to do. How will you ever be able to manage to go back to university at this rate? And I'll never have that photography studio, will I?' I slapped the mattress in exasperation. 'Look at us! We're no better off. All the broken promises, the broken dreams. We're working our fingers to the bone in those awful factories, we never see each other or the children, and at this rate we'll never be able to afford to have any more children. And you want us to stay? Have I got that right?'

Erich's eyes glittered dangerously with a strong emotion that I couldn't identify. 'If you'd only listen to me, I can explain what I mean.'

'What's there to explain? It's bad enough the Australian government made empty promises but now you're asking me to stay where we're obviously not appreciated, where we're treated like second-class citizens? I had hoped that we could leave this nightmare soon but now you're saying we should stay? How could you do this to me?'

'Will you at least hear what I have to say? I'm doing everything I can to make this situation better. It's not what I wanted either, but it's what we have to do. Can't you see that? We're staying and we will make this work. That's final!'

I glowered at him, wanting to hit him, wanting to run away, wanting to be anywhere but here. 'You've made your point. Now leave me alone.' I pushed off the covers and swung my legs over the side of the bed.

Erich seized my arm to prevent me from rising.

'Let me go.'

'Lotte, we're in this together, you and me. I'm only trying to think of a way to make everything better. I won't force you to do anything, but if we can talk about it, we can make the decisions we need to.' The anger had gone out of his eyes and I saw a hollowness I hadn't noticed before, a desperation mingled with deep pain.

I nodded, unable to speak, but remained rigid on the edge of the bed.

'I don't think I can start again.' His voice caught. 'I've done that too many times now. We have to make this work. If we set ourselves a goal, a certain amount of savings within a time limit, it might help us both manage a little better until we can set up our own home.'

'Two years . . .' I whispered. It was my mantra as I worked like a zombie in the factory. Tears welled in my eyes. Two years was what I had been working towards.

'I blame myself for what's happened to us but we can't go back after two years. We'll never have enough money saved to start again. I'm sorry.'

I bowed my head, letting the tears fall. He was right. Returning to Germany could never have been a reality.

Erich sat beside me, his cool hands soothing my burning face, and wiped the tears away. 'It pains me to see you working like a dog but we'll both have to work hard until we've saved for a home. After that, I don't want you to have to work any more.' He paused. 'I won't be returning to study . . . we'll never get there otherwise.'

'So you don't want to be an engineer?'

'Of course, but is it worth it now? Who knows how long it'll be until I've graduated? Besides, I'm getting older, I'll be at least fifty by then, and nobody can guarantee me a job when I'm finished. It may be all for nothing anyway.' He suddenly seemed to deflate, his spark spent in trying to convince me we had to stay.

'We've done everything right. We deserve more than this.'

'I know, but we'll turn this around and make a success here.'

I couldn't help but feel resentful. We were never going to get what we wanted. However I had been so focused on what this move had cost me that I hadn't recognised how deeply it had affected Erich. To give up on his dream of working as an aeronautic engineer again was like tearing away a limb – it stripped the identity and pride from the man who loved his profession. What was a man without his work? Coming to Australia was Erich's chance to find himself again, but it had all been for nothing.

My fury dissipated and was replaced by guilt and regret. Whatever I felt I had lost, Erich had lost so much more. We'd had so much hope for the future when we sailed into the harbour at Fremantle. How much more did we have to sacrifice to have the chance at a decent life for our family?

'Let's not make any decisions about university until we're in our own place,' I said.

'I'm happy if you and the girls are happy,' he said softly.

That night I dreamt of the Bavarian Alps I had visited in my childhood. I ran and laughed, carefree, finally jumping into the safe embrace of my mother's welcoming arms.

'I've joined the union,' Erich said one evening not long after our argument. The girls were in the bathrooms, washing before dinner. 'I know we can't really afford it but I couldn't stand back and watch how people like us – migrants – are treated any longer. I think it's maybe the only way to see change.'

'What made you do it?' I asked, taking his jacket from him. 'Was it that journalist the other night?'

He nodded. 'After the engineering firm, I'd had enough but didn't know if the union was the right way to go. That journalist made me realise I had to do something. I don't care if I'm called a communist. Name calling is the least of my problems.'

A journalist and photographer from the local paper had visited Villawood and asked if we'd mind if they took our picture for an article they were writing about immigration. Erich struck up a conversation with them and discovered that the intended slant of the piece was that immigrants' lives in Australia were much better than that in their homelands and there were myriad opportunities for us in our new home. Learning that made me so angry, given the situation we were in. Our reality was being glossed over, if not ignored entirely, by their story and I knew that if we'd tried to enlighten them, we'd be viewed as ungrateful New Australians. It was common to hear Australians tell some migrant not satisfied with some aspect of their life or misunderstanding a custom or way of doing things to 'go back to where you came from'. Honesty was a fine line for us to walk.

'Have you told Franz?' I asked.

'Yes. He reminded me of the risk of sanctions. The government owns us for two years. They can easily move anyone they see as troublesome to a worse job or location.'

'You mean like being a member of a union?'

'Possibly . . . but more for being involved in industrial action.'

'Let's hope it doesn't come to that.' I hung his jacket in the tiny wardrobe, wondering how the government could punish those who spoke out against inequality. That's how things had begun in Germany. A shiver of fear rippled through me but I refused to believe that Australia was unjust. Erich was doing nothing wrong. Joining the union was his way to find his place and make sense of the world we now found ourselves in. He felt the dislocation more acutely than I did, but maybe he had the right idea. Maybe I wouldn't settle until I found my place in this strange new country.

'Mind you, Franz fully supports any organisation that'll help migrants and understands why I had to do it. He can't risk it, of course. Once he practises law again, I know he'll support workers' rights in any legal battle.'

'So what's next?'

'I go to my first meeting next week. I'll get a feel of the group and see how it all works. The time for sitting on my hands is over.'

My arms slid around his waist and I kissed him on the lips. 'I know how much doing nothing was suffocating you. I don't care what others call you. You're a good man.'

'It feels good to take a stand,' he murmured, kissing me back before the girls returned to the room. 'Are you working tomorrow?

'No,' I said. It looked like the casual work was beginning to dry up. I'd had only three days of factory work this last week.

'Good. I've found you something better.' He stood there grinning like the Cheshire cat, arms folded on his chest.

'Better?' I repeated stupidly.

'The photographer who was with that journalist was kind enough to give me some contacts at photography studios in the city. I followed them up and when I mentioned you were European-trained, one of the busiest and most prestigious studios in Sydney jumped at the chance to talk to you.'

I stared at him for a moment. After all these years of dreaming, wishing and waiting to practise my passion, was it finally going to happen? My heart began to race.

'Photography? You've found me a photography job?'

He nodded, looking very pleased with himself. 'Well? Aren't you going to say anything?'

I rushed into his arms and he caught me with a whoop of surprise. I hugged him with all my might.

The following day, I met the owner of the photography studio in Sydney, Mr Baker, and he explained that he required my colouring and retouching skills. Apparently the abilities I had acquired were very sought after because the sort of training I'd had in Germany was still hard to find in Australia.

I'd trained as a photographer during the war at the prestigious Bavarian State Institute for Photography. It was because of Vati, who had seen my passion for photography, that I was able to do the very expensive but one of the most respected courses in Europe. All I'd wanted was to work as a military photographer on the front, but after losing my brother at Stalingrad my parents wouldn't hear of it. Instead I'd worked as a secretary in the Luftwaffe, where I'd met Erich. After the war, when Germany was in chaos, there hadn't been an opportunity for me to find work as a photographer. Now, finally, I had a chance.

'Can you show me some of the techniques you learnt?' Mr Baker asked eagerly.

'Of course,' I replied, my heart hammering as I wondered if I could show enough skill after years of no practice. We moved across to the retouching table where he had left a number of negatives and photographs.

'What would you change in this photograph?' He handed me a portrait of a young woman. I looked at it carefully but it was easy to spot what needed fixing.

'I'd get rid of the dark rings under her eyes, the stray hair on her face and shoulder, the wrinkles in her dress and sharpen her figure. It looks a little indistinct or blurred to me. Her face requires softening . . . I'd remove the blemishes and smooth her skin. Then this area is underexposed and needs to be lightened and this area darkened to provide contrast,' I said, pointing to the parts of the photograph in question.

He nodded. 'Very good. That's exactly what I would do. Now can you show me how you would accomplish this?'

Willing my hands to remain steady and the butterflies in my stomach to still, I moved the mirror to increase the light and began the work on retouching the negative. It was quite a process: sometimes involving delicately applying dye, alcohol or graphite powder, rubbing down with abrasives, etching with a retouching knife and finally the use of fine pencils. Suddenly I was immersed in the work and my nervousness fell away. I was in my element as I explained each procedure, and answering Mr Baker's questions. We progressed to the colouring of a photograph with a variety of paints and brushes. This was something I'd always been good at.

Finally I was done and I was happy with what I'd achieved. I was relieved to find that I hadn't forgotten a thing.

'Your work is of a very high standard, Mrs Drescher. You most definitely have an eye for detail, colour and for perfect proportion. I'd like to offer you some work.'

I smiled, barely containing my joy. I could hardly believe it. I wanted to wrap my arms around his portly middle in gratitude.

'Unfortunately, I can't give you full-time work but perhaps you'd like to take whatever retouching and colouring work

I have for you. You could pick it up from here as required, complete it at home and then return it to the studio when you're done. Is that something you'd be interested in?'

I was disappointed that it wasn't full-time work but working from home meant that I could fit it in around any other casual work I could get. Best of all, I could be home in the afternoons with the girls.

'That's wonderful,' I said. 'When do you want me to start?'

Finally, after fourteen years, I was working in photography. Not doing exactly what I'd hoped for but it was a foot in the door, and with any luck it would lead to some studio work. It was exhilarating. The dream of one day owning my own studio became a real possibility once again. More than that, it gave me hope that life in Australia could be good for us.

Little by little, I was beginning to come to terms with staying. I enjoyed my trips into Sydney, getting off the train at Town Hall station and looking around the shops before picking up my work and heading back to Villawood. Although Sydney was only a young city compared to those in Europe and quite without the sense of culture and sophistication that long history brought with it, like my home, Munich, it was still a city I loved. It was fresh, vibrant and full of life, and there was a much greater variety of shops than in the suburbs. I enjoyed walking to the studio rather than jumping on the tram or catching the train along the new underground Circular Quay loop. Then there was the magnificent harbour and Bennelong Point, where the new Sydney Opera House would be built. I was amused that a Danish architect had produced the winning design. One day I would look out over Sydney Harbour after attending an opera or concert, I decided.

Erich attended a mass meeting of a number of trade unions at the Sydney Stadium. He was so excited to hear what other groups were doing, to hear plans to improve the lives of workers, and he came home full of nervous energy. Even though it was late, I could tell that he wanted to talk – he wouldn't sleep until he'd expressed his thoughts and shared the evening's events. I sat down at the table stifling a yawn. It had been a long day and I was just about ready for bed.

'I know the push of the meeting was to improve workers' wages overall and to lobby for women's wages to be equal to men's,' he said, sipping a cup of scalding coffee, 'but migrants put up with the lowest wages of all and these need to be brought into line with the standard wage. I talked to other members and delegates about how migrants often can't get good access to housing and as a result are discriminated against with the high living expenses they have to pay, whether in the hostel or out in the community, and I explained how in most households women have to work to help make ends meet. They work as hard as men and they're paid even less than migrant men for the same work.'

'Nice to see you've noticed that,' I said cheekily, waking up significantly.

I felt strongly about women in the workplace. The war had changed the role of women forever and most of us were no longer satisfied to be just homemakers, rearing our children – we wanted to help out financially, gain some independence and a sense of worth outside of the home. It was only right and fair that women received wages that were equal to men, when doing the same jobs. What I couldn't believe was that there was such a debate about the whole idea.

'We heard stories of less than acceptable amenities and poor conditions on worksites: taps that don't work or when they do no soap is provided; no chairs or tables to have lunch at; filthy floors; inadequately cleaned protective gear and non-existent safety measures.'

'That's disgraceful.' I poured milk into my coffee, and saw Erich grimace from the corner of my eye. 'What?'

'I told the delegate that migrant workers should be treated like ordinary Australians.'

I snorted. 'What did he say?'

'One of the members he was with asked me why I believed they deserved to be.'

'No!'

Erich nodded. 'I didn't get angry but reminded them that migrants like us have become a big part of Australian culture since the end of the war. We might seem different and be called derogatory names, but we want what most people want – to work and earn a living and to actively contribute to the community.

'But I had to give them something to relate to, something they've seen in their everyday lives. I talked about the Italians with their love of coffee and the coffee houses they've set up all over Sydney and the Greek cafes with their fish and chips and hamburgers that bring customers from miles away. They work hard and give Australia something new and exciting, but they're called dagoes and wogs.' He shook his head ruefully. 'It's only the tip of the iceberg, but I think some of them began to see what I was talking about.'

'I'm proud of you for speaking up,' I said, kissing him. It was only a small thing, but I truly believed that with every small success, our hope that anything was possible grew and made us stronger, more resolute in finding our place and making our mark on this young nation.

5

Franz and Claudia moved out in August, renting a small house in Liverpool, closer to the door factory. The hostel had been no help to them in finding accommodation and they'd been searching for months for something appropriate. I was upset to see them go, as were the children, and Erich lost his commuting partner.

We visited them one Sunday not long after they moved and it was wonderful to see how well they'd settled in. The house was small, especially with four children, but certainly bigger than their rooms at the hostel and they had their own kitchen and bathroom. Most of all, they had privacy and the freedom to do whatever they wanted.

'Have you found a good butcher?' I asked Claudia. Franz was showing Erich the backyard where the children were playing on a small patch of grass.

'The butcher isn't bad but the delicatessen is better. Lots of Europeans go there and I've found I can generally get what I want. It's funny what you hear, though, with the shop assistant only being able to speak English. The other day a German woman in front of me wanted a pound of almonds. She couldn't speak English well at all and must have looked up the English translation for *mandeln*. What she didn't realise is that there are two different translations in English. So she asked the shop assistant for a pound of tonsils, rather than for a pound of almonds.'

I burst out laughing. 'What did the shop assistant do?' I asked.

'He looked at her very strangely and muttered how these "New Australians" have some very odd ideas and why would he stock tonsils in his shop? Other people in the shop looked quite shocked and I heard someone whisper "savages". He was about to turn away in disgust while this woman looked on, bewildered by his reaction, when I stepped in and explained that she actually wanted almonds, and he served her begrudgingly. When I explained to her the error, she was absolutely horrified!'

'Thank God you set them both straight!'

'We can't afford to eat meat now,' Claudia continued in a low voice. 'We have it maybe once a fortnight and then it's only pig trotters or offal, but I don't mind. At least I don't have to eat lamb any more.'

'You know it's really mutton, don't you?' I said, trying to lighten the mood. It was so good to talk to her about our situation. She understood.

'I know, but I've just got into the habit of calling it lamb like everyone else.'

'I have to admit that I'm sick of it. It's all they ever give us at the hostel – whether it's roasted, boiled or stewed, it's always so tough and chewy.'

Claudia pulled a face. 'At least I'm cooking what I want. It's good to be cooking German food again. The children are happier and Franz looks forward to the evening meal now.'

I nodded and took a sip of coffee. It was sobering to think that in some ways we might be even worse off in our own place after buying what we'd need to get started but I knew that it wouldn't change how I felt about being out of the hostel. The benefits of home cooking and privacy outweighed everything else for me. Besides, I knew how to make do on limited rations. I'd done it for years in Germany.

Claudia turned serious. 'How are you coping at the hostel? I know you wear a bright face and keep optimistic for the children, but how are you dealing with your situation?'

'I'm fine,' I said automatically.

'You're not fine. Don't pretend.' Claudia knew about the fight Erich and I had and how I'd been struggling with the idea of staying.

I slumped in my chair and sighed. 'All I want is our own place, somewhere that feels like home to us.'

'I know. It'll come. I thought we'd never get to this point, yet here we are.'

'I have to accept our situation for what it is. Crying and complaining about it won't help. We're both doing what we can to get out of the hostel. I can't find full-time work but Erich's doing as much overtime as he can.' I had seen families fall apart under the pressure of surviving at Villawood, trying desperately to get a start, and I was determined not to let that happen to us.

Claudia squeezed my hands in sympathy.

'At least the girls are happy, although they miss Anna and Peter terribly. We've been trying to dress our rooms up to make them feel more like home for however long we have to be there. Erich's made a few small things, shelves and tables for next to the beds. He hasn't made furniture in years, but he loves doing it and they're really quite beautiful.'

Erich had bought offcuts of maple cheaply from the door factory. The timber was grown in northern Queensland and New Guinea and was a rich pink hue. He seemed happy when he was making furniture and I knew how much feeling he put into each item.

'You're both strong and healthy and you love each other. The rest will come.'

I nodded. 'I realised that we have to be united. The only way we can get through this is if we do it together. Somehow I'd forgotten that.'

'It's no wonder, after everything that's happened. Franz and I have had our moments too, but I've always known that we'll never go back to Germany. Franz made that very clear to me, even before we left. I don't know exactly why, but he never wants to set foot in Germany again, even if it means never seeing his family.'

A pang of sorrow shot through me. Erich's mother and his two children from his first marriage were still in Germany, as were my parents. We had all hoped to leave the long shadows of the war behind us in Germany but I was beginning to see that sometimes the past journeyed with us no matter how far away we went or how many years had passed.

*

17th September, 1957
Liebe Lotte,

My darling girl, this is the hardest letter I've ever had to write. Your father passed away in his sleep yesterday. As you know, it wasn't unexpected – he's been unwell for some time now. I can imagine how hard this news will hit you, as it has me. I can't believe he's gone – that I will never again see his smile, the love in his eyes for me, his calm and gentle manner. He was the love of my life and now I feel lost without him.

I sat at the kitchen table, stunned, tears streaming down my face, the letter from my mother crumpling in my hands. I had known that Vati wouldn't live forever, I'd seen him age suddenly and swiftly after the war, but it didn't take away the shock of his passing. My Vati was dead, the man who had been my rock, my support, and who had always had unerring faith in me.

Alone with my grief, I allowed great gasping sobs to erupt from me. All my bottled-up pain and disappointment burst free, a raging sea of failure and loss that threatened to consume me. The fear and confusion I felt after the divorce of my parents when I was ten years old returned to me. When Johann von Klein married my mother five years later, I left boarding school to live with them. Vati always treated me as his daughter, cherishing me as the child he'd never had.

Now that extraordinary man was gone. I had said my goodbyes to him before we left Germany, knowing I would probably never see him again, but now the day had come, I didn't know how I was going to live without him in my life, even on the other side of the world. Besides Erich, he was the only man who had truly understood me, the perfect counterpoint in my often volatile relationship with my mother. How was I going to manage without him?

I looked at Mutti's letter again, smoothing the creases flat on the table. I didn't know if I could bear to read the rest of it, but I would try, for Vati's sake.

Your father and I spoke about what I would do when he was gone. I didn't want to hear such talk but he made me listen. He knew I would struggle and made me promise him something – he wanted me to come to you in Australia, to bring his last gifts to you myself.

I will come, if you and Erich will have me. I have nobody here now that he's gone. He was my life.

Vati's last gifts? But what could he have to give me?

I skimmed the rest of the letter and my tears dried as I realised what Mutti had written. My father's last wish was to send my mother to us with money to help us get started here in Australia. Would we perhaps be able to buy a house? I had tried not to say too much in my letters to them, keeping the news positive, but Vati must have read between the lines. He knew me so well. My heart swelled with gratitude for this most generous last gift of Vati's, the burden of the last months lifting from my shoulders. Even now, he was doing all he could for my family. I couldn't believe our good fortune, but it was bittersweet. Fresh tears fell.

I had composed myself by the time the children came home from school, although my eyes were still red-rimmed and they knew I had been crying.

'Grosspapa has died,' I told them softly, holding them close to me. 'It's all right to cry,' I said, stroking their heads. 'He knew how much you loved him.'

Greta and Johanna knew Vati was old and had been unwell, but it was still a shock to them as it had been to me. After a little cry and hug with me, they went off to do their homework.

I was glad that they had taken it well but I was still in shock.

My head began to pound as I moved mechanically through the afternoon's routine. I didn't know how to feel. I was numbed by the loss of Vati, but hope for our future had sprung like a seedling that sprouts after the winter snows. My mother would bring this blessing to us, and although I wanted nothing more than to see her and hold her tight, I wasn't sure if I wanted her to stay with us permanently. But I was all she had left and I felt ashamed to be so uncertain.

'Look, Mutti,' said Johanna, coming in the front door, Greta behind her. I hadn't even realised that they'd gone outside. 'We picked some flowers for you.' She thrust the flowers in front of my face. 'We know you're feeling sad and we wanted to cheer you up.'

My heart filled with joy for my thoughtful, gorgeous children. They made everything worthwhile.

'That's lovely of you, sweetheart.' I took the flowers and sniffed them. Johanna's eyes gleamed and Greta smiled with satisfaction. 'They're beautiful and smell wonderful. Come here and give me a hug.'

Encircled by love, I let my tears fall, weeping again for the man we'd all adored.

*

After dinner that evening, when the girls were in bed, Erich and I sat at the table sipping coffee. I showed him the letter. I watched the sadness in his face become a frown as he continued to read. My mother wasn't his favourite person.

'I'm so sorry, my *liebchen*,' he said eventually, grasping my hand across the table. 'I know how much your father meant to you. He was a good man and he'll be sorely missed. I'm sorry that you weren't there when he passed.'

'It's all right,' I whispered. 'We said everything we needed and wanted to say to each other before I left. He knew how I felt about him and I knew how he felt about me. We knew it was likely we would never see each other again. He understood why we had to come to Australia.' I started to sob. 'I miss the sound of his voice, the smell of tobacco on his coat . . . I miss him so much.'

Erich held me tightly, our coffee forgotten on the table, but there was a hole in my heart now and nothing either of us could do about that. I'd known loss before and although it would heal in time, the ache would never fade.

'What are we going to do about Mutti?' I asked tentatively. I wasn't sure I could turn her away, despite the difficult history between the three of us.

'What do you want to do?' Erich knew life would be challenging with my mother, and yet he understood what it was like to have nobody else. He had thought that his first wife and two eldest children had perished in a bombing raid during the final months of the war and his father had disappeared, probably into a Russian camp, but nobody could tell him what had become of him. Erich's mother Karoline had disappeared after the war too, only to be found by the Red Cross in a Russian camp in Western Siberia.

'Vati wanted her to come to us and she's bringing us everything we need for a fresh start here but – ' I couldn't continue, my throat choked with emotion.

'I can't believe what your parents are doing for us. We won't be able to ever repay them. And what your mother's doing . . .'

'They're doing it because they want us to be happy and to do well. Maybe we can buy a house and you can go back to university.' I still couldn't believe it myself and was amazed at my mother's decision to come to Australia to be with us. I understood what it meant for her to give up her sparkling life and felt gratitude for her selfless act. But I also wondered what we would do if she didn't like it here.

'Maybe,' echoed Erich.

I took a deep breath. 'But how do you feel about Mutti wanting to live with us? Do you think you could cope?'

'Is that what you want? Your mother's very generous and I'm grateful for any gift, but you know it'll come with conditions.'

I nodded. I had thought about that. I'd even considered the possibility of her coming to visit and not staying, but rejected it immediately. I couldn't be so heartless.

'Certainly the money will be an incredible help to get us started but we can manage if you don't want her to come,' he said, then paused and looked into my eyes. 'You know what she does to you. Will it make you happy to have her here?'

I stared back at him for a moment. My mother repre- sented everything I had rejected about my old life. She was controlling, and had held on to me desperately when I fought to find my own path, constantly reminding me that I should uphold the traditions of my social class and respect my family name. Here in Australia, I could be free of that influence, free of that expectation. Erich and I could forge a life of our choosing, deserving all the opportunities that might come our way. I could be free of shame and guilt. I knew Mutti would try to drag me back to the old life.

I didn't know if it was possible for any of us to cope with her in a confined space for a lengthy period of time, especially in the hostel. She and Erich didn't see eye to eye and I feared that she might be critical of our life here and try to create a wedge between Erich and me. But we were the only family she had left and, despite it all, I still loved her and missed her – and I knew that she loved me too.

'I know she can be difficult but she has nobody else now that Vati's gone ... She could look after the girls while I'm working and maybe even do some housework,' I said, shrugging. 'She's offered to help any way she can.'

Erich pulled a face and I laughed. My mother had kept servants and a cook until the latter part of the war. Although she'd managed without them, she was never quite as accomplished at those domestic tasks as she could have been and she never enjoyed them.

'What do you want, Lotte?' Erich repeated softly, cupping my cheek in his hand. His eyes were steadfast and full of love. He would bear my mother if that's what I wanted, and take all the changes that would come with her arrival in his stride.

'I want her here with us. I want to be able to hold her whenever I want, for her to see our girls grow up. I miss her.'

A sense of calm washed over me, and a tentative joy at the thought of being in the same room with her again.

'Then that's settled, isn't it?'

'Really?' I looked into his face, trying to detect some reservation.

'Of course, my *liebchen*, she's your mother. Anything for you.' Erich understood how hard it was to be far away from family, and my heart twisted at the thought he might never see his own mother again. He kissed me lightly on the lips and I leant into him instinctively. 'Besides, it might be interesting to watch your mother deal with Australian life.'

I snorted, batting him playfully on the arm. 'Don't be so rude! She's tougher than you think. She'll be fine.'

'Well, you'd better put her out of her misery and let her know. Ask her when she plans to come. In the meantime, we'll find out what we need to do to rent a house somewhere. She can't stay here in the hostel with us – that will drive us all mad!'

'You're right. I need to find some more permanent work. I'll talk to the studio again next time I'm there. Maybe they can help with some contacts.'

Erich nodded, and I could see the wheels turning in his mind already. Whatever we needed to do now, he would make sure it happened. I loved him even more for it.

It was time to leave the hostel.

After speaking with Mr Baker, he suggested I contact a photographic studio in Liverpool. It was owned and run by a German family who had migrated to Australia before the war.

Although only a small business with a handful of photographers, all trained in the European tradition, it had a fabulous reputation and the owner, Reinhardt Weber, had high expectations. The more senior photographers focussed on studio sittings through the week and attended weddings on the weekend. The high-profile events, studio and photo shoots were managed by the owner and his family.

I decided to go in person.

'You've come highly recommended, I see,' said Mr Weber, reading the glowing reference from Mr Baker. 'I remember what it was like when we first arrived from Germany. I'm not looking for a photographer right now, but maybe I have something else for you. Come into my office and tell me about your training.'

My heart thumping in my chest, I showed him my qualifications and, happy to be explaining in German, told him about the techniques I had learnt in Munich. I prayed that it was enough to get some work.

'Impressive,' he said, stroking his bushy grey moustache. 'Did you bring any examples of your work?'

'Yes, of course.' I slid the portfolio across the desk to him and waited anxiously as he thumbed through the pages.

'Very good.' He looked up at me and smiled. 'With skills like that, I have to hire you on the spot. You can start in the darkroom until you get some experience behind the camera. How does that sound?'

'I'll take it,' I said, ready to sag with relief. My gamble had paid off.

I was terribly excited to be working with other photographers, finally beginning my career. Even discovering that it fell to me to process the film and develop the negatives into photographs – since I was the most recently employed and had the least experience – didn't dampen my enthusiasm. It was tedious work and backbreaking, leaning over the chemicals and negatives all day long, but I knew that with time I would prove my worth and work my way up to what I really wanted to do: take photographs.

I began to work some late nights, retouching the negatives and colouring photographs. Reinhardt had been impressed with the work I had done for the studio in the city. I didn't complain; it meant we could save more and move out of the hostel a little more quickly. And on Saturday mornings, I continued the work I received from the city. I barely had time to think about our living conditions, but the need to find somewhere to live before Mutti arrived loomed and suddenly I wished I had more free time to look for a house.

Claudia was my saviour. She told me about a little place near her in Liverpool, on Northumberland Street. It was a semi-detached house and the rent was just manageable, less than a fully furnished apartment or a whole house. Better still, it had a yard for the children and for Erich and I to plant a vegetable garden and flower beds. A young couple lived on the other side of the house and had their own entrance. This house meant I could walk to work rather than catch the train each day and Erich could travel to work with Franz again, who now owned a car. The girls could join Anna and Peter at the local school. We could be near our friends and continue to support each other.

'What do you think?' I whispered excitedly to Erich as we looked around the empty house. It wasn't much to look at – only two bedrooms with a combined lounge and dining area and a small area off the kitchen that may have been an enclosed patio – but it was a lot more private and spacious than our rooms in the hostel. Heavenly!

'I think it'll do,' he replied, opening and closing doors to make sure they were swinging correctly. 'It's not as big as I'd like but at least we'll be out of Villawood.'

'Mmm, I think so too,' I said, peering into the bathroom. There was a shower over the bath. The toilet was outside, next to the laundry. 'We could partition off the area next to the kitchen for Mutti.'

'We'll manage something until we find a bigger place, but do you think your mother can put up with it until then?'

'She'll have to,' I said. 'This place is a rare find, almost too good to be true. I think we'll have to take it and work out the rest later.'

'As long as you're happy.' He drew me into his arms and kissed me. 'I'll let them know that we'll take it.'

The only problem with the house was that we had to buy just about everything. We needed beds to sleep on, furniture and household appliances. Thank God hire-purchase was popular; it meant we could put a deposit on the essentials we couldn't do without, bring them home and pay them off in weekly instalments. It made me nervous to think of living like that, but Erich persuaded me that there was no other way. We had a steady income and with careful management through putting aside the money for rent and repayments each week, we would manage – just.

6

It was an incredible feeling to finally leave the hostel on a bright, sunny day in November, almost a year since arriving in Australia. I didn't give the place a backward glance. We packed our belongings in the back of Franz's car and a trailer we had rented for the day, and arrived at our new home full of hope and ready to begin the next chapter of our lives. It seemed a long time since any of us had been so excited.

Everything took longer to unpack and put away than I'd expected, even with the help of Franz, Claudia and the children. But with the girls asleep in their new beds, Erich and I finally collapsed into our armchairs, perusing the litter of half-unpacked boxes.

'We did it,' I said, grinning stupidly at him.

'We did. We're here and we've got so much done.' He was clearly satisfied with the day's work, though the black smudges beneath his eyes showed how exhausted he was.

'But there's still so much to do.'

'Enough for one day.' He stood and offered me his hand. 'I know you'd keep going until you drop, but we have tomorrow to get it finished. All I want now is a real bed . . . I've got other things planned for us.'

'Whatever do you mean?' I looked at him innocently, batting my eyelashes before taking his hand.

'You want sleep, do you?' he whispered in my ear. 'I'll make sure you sleep like a baby.' He led me to our bedroom.

'Finally, a double bed.' I stretched my limbs across the mattress and groaned, the crisp, fresh sheets crackling softly beneath me. I pulled Erich down. 'It's been over a year since we've slept in a proper bed.'

'I think a christening's in order.' He ran his hands down the length of my torso, kissed my neck, then shuffled a little so our bodies were touching.

I wriggled against him ever so slightly, watching the effect on him, how the nearness of me still aroused him after twelve years of marriage. It made me want him all the more.

Then the world disappeared and there was just the two of us. I rode the crest of a wave, helpless to do anything but respond to Erich's desire with my own. He kissed me with such intensity I thought I would dissolve into nothingness as we blessed the sanctity of our bed and the sanctuary of our home.

Afterwards, in a tangle of sheets and blankets, Erich turned to me with a bemused look on his face.

Concern shot through me. 'What is it?'

He put his hand on my arm, still smouldering with heat. 'No, it's not you. That was wonderful.' He kissed my bare shoulder. 'I just had something I wanted to give you to mark the next stage of our life, but I got distracted.'

I laughed. 'I thought you just gave me something . . . something special.'

'Is it that time?'

I shook my head. 'No, that's not what I meant.' As much as we both wanted another baby, we couldn't risk it yet. We needed my income to manage and I couldn't stay home to look after a baby until our circumstances improved. He smiled, and I could see he wasn't sure whether to feel sad or relieved. Neither was I.

He smoothed the hair from my face. 'I'm glad you think it was special but I was talking about something else, a promise I made you months ago. Wait here, I'll be back in a moment.'

Cool air rushed to replace his warmth as I watched him leave the room, the line of his body still tall, taut and athletic. He really was a handsome man. His backside seemed iridescent in the dim light, white above his tanned legs. I liked the shape of it, the feel of it cupped in my hands . . . I lay down, my body sinking into the bed, my eyelids heavy with sleep, and let my thoughts drift.

Then he was by my side once more. 'Don't go to sleep yet.'

I opened my eyes to see him place a box wrapped in paper on the bed. He settled next to me, anticipation on his face. I carefully peeled the tape off and removed the paper so we could use it again. I gasped in disbelief and delight when I realised what was inside.

'You didn't!'

Erich grinned widely. 'Pull it out and see what you think.'

I didn't know who was more excited at this point, him or me.

I scrambled to open the box without ripping it then gently pulled out a hard brown leather camera case. I opened it to reveal a Kodak Retina IIIc.

'It's beautiful,' I murmured, my fingers tracing the edges and mechanism of the camera, itching to use it immediately. I knew this model. It was a high-quality camera and one of the best Kodak made. It was smooth and easy to use, producing clear, sharp images, with features I knew I could do so much with. 'You shouldn't have. We really can't afford it.'

'I promised you I'd buy another camera as soon as I could and with you working in the studio now, you really need your own. Besides, this one's as good as the Leica – so I'm told – but at a fraction of the cost. And I can pay it off.' He looked very pleased with his surprise.

'You're right, this is a fabulous camera, one I would have bought myself.'

'You like it, then?'

'I love it!' I squeezed his hand, blinking away tears. 'How did you know what to get me?'

'I spoke to Reinhardt and he told me which one was in our price range.'

'My boss?'

'Yes, on the way home from work one day, Franz and I slipped into the studio and spoke with him. You didn't ever know we were there!' He chuckled to himself.

'Thank you.' I threw my arms around his neck and kissed him soundly. 'We'll record all our special moments. I can't wait to use it.'

'I'm glad you like it,' he said softly. 'Now, I want nothing more than to collapse into this bed and sleep all night with you by my side.'

December was hot and with it came the terrible bush-fires that were a normal part of Australian summers. This was a harsh land, and I was learning that its beauty was hard won.

Erich bought a fan to cool whatever room we occupied. Thank God we'd bought a refrigerator just before the scorching temperatures hit; our small ice box wouldn't have been enough. The Kelvinator was my pride and joy, with plenty of shelf space and a freezer at the top. With a kitchen of my own, I was beside myself. I was finally able to cook our traditional Christmas sweets of gingerbread and stollen.

'Make sure you roll the dough out to the right thickness,' I said to Johanna.

'I don't think we can fit any more onto the tray,' said Greta, looking dubiously at the shapes she'd cut from her piece of dough.

'It's all right,' I said. 'We'll just have to wait for the ones in the oven to come out first.' We'd decided to make extra for Claudia and her family as a surprise. I knew she struggled to be in the kitchen for any length of time with two little ones underfoot.

'It's so hot, Mutti,' said Johanna. I smiled, thinking how in Germany they would be in cumbersome layers at this time of year, not light and easy shorts and halter-neck tops.

'I know,' I said. 'Especially since we have the oven on.' We were all wilting with the heat but I was determined to continue this ritual, remembering the special times I'd had with my mother as a girl. Besides, I wanted my daughters to be proud of their heritage, to never forget it and to one day teach their own children.

'Can we have an ice block?' asked Greta, her brown eyes pleading.

'You can have an ice block on the back step when this last batch goes in the oven.' When it got too hot in the afternoons, I ran the bath and the girls sat and played in the cool water until they felt refreshed. I didn't mind. It was peaceful when they were occupied.

Although we couldn't afford much, I was determined to make the first Christmas in our own home in Australia special. Franz, Claudia and the children were coming, of course, and Tommy and Suzanne, our Australian neighbours, were going to join us for a Christmas drink. They were a delightful young couple who had been married for a year. Erich had also invited the family of one of the new men at work. Giovanni, Carmela and their five small children had just arrived from Malta and had no family to spend Christmas with. When Erich told me about them, I remembered our first Christmas very well. Everything had seemed so foreign and we missed family so much. Helping a fellow migrant family embodied the meaning of the season and it felt only right to invite them. I wondered what their children's reactions would be at the sight of our Christmas.

I had decided to cook a goose, a luxury for us, as we could rarely afford to eat meat, and had found a continental butcher who sold the game, poultry and small goods we were used to in Germany. Giovanni and Carmela were bringing traditional Maltese pastries and Claudia had promised to bring champagne, as we hadn't yet celebrated our new home. It was going to be wonderful.

The morning of Christmas Eve, after I had planned and organised the tasks I had to get done, I set aside time for the Christmas tree. This was something I couldn't rush and it had to be just right. The base of the tree was resting in a bucket of water, secured with bricks so it stood straight. The base and bucket were covered in a white sheet, which looked like the snow of the northern hemisphere, the perfect place for the baby Jesus in his manger and the presents from Santa Claus. The pungent smell of pine leaves was already noticeable and I smiled. It wasn't Christmas without the scent of pine. It never failed to get me into the spirit and reminded me of all the Christmases in Germany, the happy times spent with family. This was the first on our own but we were not alone and we had so much to be thankful for, so many blessings.

I carefully pulled out the packages containing the nativity scene I had brought with us from Germany. With trembling fingers, I unwrapped each parcel, but they hadn't been broken with the moves. I was pleased to find that the painted figures and straw-covered barn looked as good as new.

'Greta and Johanna! I'm ready to do the tree,' I called. The girls were making Christmas cards in their bedroom.

'Coming, Mutti,' yelled Greta.

'Here, let's start with the glass decorations,' I said when they joined me, handing them the coloured baubles. 'Be careful now, because they'll break.'

'We know, Mutti,' said Johanna with a very serious face.

They hung the balls and ornaments I still had from Germany around the tree, as well as a few I had bought at David Jones while in the city. I smiled, resisting the impulse to take over as I watched them reaching on tip-toes to place the ornaments as high as they could. Then we moved on to the candle holders and the long strands of silver tinsel. The girls were as excited as I was.

I took photographs of the girls and the tree with my new camera, putting it through its paces, working out how to best use its features and revelling in the freedom to take as many pictures as I liked, now I could get them developed cheaply at work. I rejoiced in how much pleasure photography gave me.

'That looks beautiful,' I said, standing back to admire their handiwork. 'Now let's put the manger under the tree.'

The girls knew that this was what made the Christmas tree special and reverently helped me position the nativity scene on the white sheet. Immediately, our new house felt like home.

'It's perfect, Mutti,' said Greta, head tilted to one side and then the other.

'You've both done a wonderful job,' I said. I pulled them to me, hugging them tight and kissing them each on the cheek.

I discovered, however, that even keeping the candles for the tree in the fridge until we were ready to use them later that day didn't stop them from bending in the heat. *This is Australia after all, not Germany,* I thought, the sight of the bowed red candles stopping me in my tracks as I hurried to place the final touches on the table before our guests arrived. I shrugged and left them; they were too much a part of our tradition to not use. The blazing of light around the tree at night was the essence of Christmas to me and I knew it was special for the girls.

The evening was delightful. The goose was cooked to perfection, the Maltese pastries, Christmas biscuits and stollen were a hit and the children's faces as their eyes lit up at the sight of the presents they discovered under the Christmas tree made the adults smile. I took photographs all night to make sure our memories of the first Christmas in our own home in Australia were recorded for posterity.

'Thank you, Erich and Lotte. We go now,' said Giovanni, with two sleepy, dark-haired children in his arms. I smiled ruefully. They were going to midnight mass with all five children and I felt sure they would fall asleep in their parents' arms long before the service was over.

'We have good night,' said Carmela in her broken English, kissing my hand, tears in her eyes.

Greta, Johanna and Anna were hugging the older children goodbye who clutched their gifts in their hands, sad to leave and their dark eyes still round with wonder. Whatever difficulties we thought we were experiencing, these children evidently thought this was paradise. I wondered what life they'd left behind in Malta and felt a renewed appreciation for what we had.

I kissed Carmela on her soft, smooth cheek. 'Come and visit us again.' I followed my children's lead and hugged her. 'Merry Christmas.'

All the children were in bed just before midnight, worn out from the excitement. Anna and Peter slept in our room and the twins lay on an eiderdown on the bedroom floor.

'It's so peaceful when they're asleep,' murmured Claudia, leaning against the back of the lounge.

'Mmm.' I sighed with the pleasure of a successful night behind me. There was nothing I needed to do except relax and enjoy the company of good friends.

'Come on, let's fill up the glasses,' said Franz, full of energy as always. 'Let's toast to the birth of Jesus and to Lotte's fabulous cooking. I'm so full, I'm sure you'll have to roll me out the door.'

'A little change in music would be good about now,' said Erich. 'I think I've had enough of Christmas carols. Franz, you pick the record as you're the expert on music, while I open the champagne.'

'You're an expert?' I said, bringing the nuts and fruit cake to the coffee table. 'I didn't know that.'

'Franz comes from a very musical family and was named after his father's favourite composer and pianist, Franz Liszt,' said Claudia.

'Really?' I looked at Franz in surprise. He was engrossed in his task, already thumbing through our small collection of records, stacked on a shelf beneath the record player. 'According to my mother, Franz Liszt was a good friend of my great-great grandfather.'

'Isn't it amazing, the strange coincidences that connect us to one another? Franz was an accomplished concert pianist before the war, before he became a lawyer,' Claudia continued, holding up a champagne glass for Erich. 'He was asked to play a number of concerts on the boat coming to Australia.'

'What sort of concerts?' Erich asked as he filled the glasses.

'Solos, concertos mainly ... Beethoven, Chopin, Liszt

of course, and a variety of other composers, but they're my favourites,' said Franz, straightening up.

'The one I loved the most was Beethoven's *Pathetique Sonata*. The audience gave Franz a standing ovation the night he played that. He was told by the Australian officials on board that he should pursue a career here in Australia.' Claudia's eyes were sparkling with pride.

'Why didn't you?' I asked, as the strains of Chopin's *Fantaisie Impromptu* began. It was a beautiful composition, one that always reminded me of my mother. I remembered sitting in the parlour after dinner with her and my father to listen to it. I closed my eyes for a second. The music was passionate and moving.

'I don't know ... making money to support my family seemed more important.' Franz sighed as he flopped into the lounge chair and took a glass of champagne from Erich. *'Danke.'*

'We would've managed,' Claudia said.

Franz laid his hand gently on his wife's cheek. 'I know, my sweetheart, but why make life harder than it needs to be? God knows we'd been through enough in Germany.'

She nodded sadly and kissed his hand.

None of us spoke. Nobody who was touched by Nazi Germany and the war had a simple story, but dredging up the ghost of the past was a painful business, rarely contemplated, and even more rarely shared with others. There were so many stories of lives and families destroyed by the war, incredible potential and talent that should have been shared with the world but which had been crushed prematurely.

'Well, you'll have to play for us sometime,' said Erich, breaking the sombre mood. The relief was palpable.

'Of course!' said Franz, draining his glass.

'We've been saving for a decent piano,' said Claudia. 'Hopefully soon we'll have one and the house will be filled with music again.'

'Yes, I miss playing at the end of the day and listening to the children practise. Anna and Peter learnt in Germany but it's been a few years. I want to teach the twins too. It will be good to have a piano again but I'm not so sure how much time I'll have to play once I get into law school.'

'How's that going?' asked Erich.

Franz's smile waned. 'Well, it won't be next year. I've made some enquires at the University of Sydney and the first year is full-time study with the next three years part time. We're not in a position to manage that just yet.'

'But he's not giving up,' said Claudia, clasping her husband's hand.

I nibbled on my fruit cake and gazed at Erich, relaxed and happy. In this moment, life couldn't be any better. We were spending Christmas in our own home, with friends whose company we truly enjoyed and our children were happy, healthy and safely tucked up into bed, perhaps dreaming of Christmas joy. We had a lot to be thankful for.

'Merry Christmas,' I said, raising my glass. 'Here's to family and good friends.'

I was content in our new home despite the long hours that Erich and I worked. We'd breached a vast psychological barrier by moving out of the hostel and it felt like we could finally get ahead. Our goal now was to make an inviting home for ourselves before Mutti arrived.

Erich found a new purpose, too, when he was elected as union delegate at the factory. It was his responsibility to talk with new workers, mostly migrants, explain how things worked, provide support and act as intermediary between the workers, union and the factory managers. He took his commitment seriously. Although union meetings only occurred once a month, Erich gave support to migrant workers where he could, translating letters and official documents, providing useful tips on how to manage in this strange new country and organising social gatherings for families.

Something had changed for him – he'd slipped into the role as if it were made for him and he seemed more comfortable, like he felt he belonged there.

'So many migrants don't want to get involved in unions because they don't believe that their needs are being understood,' Erich told me one day when we were in the backyard. He was making a cupboard for Mutti.

'What do you mean?' I asked, pegging washing on the line.

'People are making less money working in unskilled jobs or performing manual labour – if they can get a job at all – because their qualifications aren't recognised. Nobody likes to be treated like an idiot. And the wealth of experience and culture that we've brought with us is often forgotten.'

'We want to be part of Australian society,' I agreed, 'but our cultures are part of who we are. I think the bosses need to remember that.'

He stood straight, and rolled up his sleeves to reveal lean, muscular arms, bronzed by the Australian sun. 'Being Australian now is different from what it was even ten years ago – a bigger proportion of the population aren't from a

British background. What's needed is information for workers in their own languages. It's all well and good to expect them to learn English, but translations will go a long way towards offering them a sense of belonging and empowerment.'

'We need more people like you, who care enough to try to make a difference.'

Erich raised his head and smiled. 'I'm glad you think so.'

We were expecting Mutti in April. She was arriving on the *Skaubryn* and I knew she would enjoy the luxury of the boat as we had. When I wasn't working, I spent my time preparing the house: hanging new curtains I'd made, making sure all the pictures and ornaments from Germany were in pride of place and creating a small flower garden with Erich and the girls. We even got a little orange kitten from one of the photographers at work, and we called it Moshi. Our home felt comfortable, warm and welcoming. We were ready for my mother to come.

The week before Easter was busy, not just because of the workload – especially with Good Friday off – but because of the number of weddings and christenings booked for the Sunday. It was all hands on deck and I didn't know how I was going to leave the studio to buy my groceries, the fish for Good Friday and duck for our Easter lunch. I decided to skip my lunch break and work through each day to try to finish a little earlier on the Thursday.

On Tuesday, I came out of the darkroom with some of the developed proofs for Reinhardt. Before taking them to him I checked with Otto, his son, and one of the senior photographers who was in the lunchroom.

'Are these the photos you wanted for Reinhardt?'

Otto drew on his cigarette and took the proofs from me, leaning back in his chair as he checked each sheet. 'Yes, these are good. I like the ones you've chosen,' he said. 'You've got a good eye.'

I blushed, pleased to have his approval and praise. After having nothing to do with the industry for so long, I had lost my confidence and belief in my abilities. It was returning slowly the more work I did, and now most of the photographers were happy for me to choose the proofs to go to Reinhardt, although he often still checked them all.

'Lotte,' called Sabine, breezing into the lunchroom after returning from a job, a cigarette between her fingers. She was Otto's younger sister and a photographer too. It seemed everyone in the photography business smoked to get through the busy schedules and long hours, but it wasn't for me. 'Lucky I found you here. Didn't you tell me that your mother's coming out to Australia soon?'

'Yes, that's right,' I said, taking the proofs from Otto. 'She left a couple of weeks ago and should arrive in Melbourne on the twentieth.'

'What ship did she sail on?' she asked.

'The *Skaubryn*. Why?'

Sabine turned pale, dropping the cigarette onto the edge of an ashtray, her eyes wide. 'Haven't you heard the midday news?'

'No, I worked through lunch today. Why? What's wrong?'

Sabine threw a worried glance at her brother, who only frowned. Clutching my arm, she tried to pull me towards the chair. 'I think you'd better sit down.'

I remained standing and shook my head in irritation. I had to get back to work. 'Just tell me what's going on.'

Concern creased her smooth brow. 'The *Skaubryn* caught fire overnight. It sank in the Indian Ocean.'

Spots swam in front of my eyes and I began to sway. I reached for the table to prevent collapsing and sagged into a chair, staring at her in disbelief. 'No, that can't be right.'

'Are you sure?' Otto asked. 'Maybe you misheard.'

'I'm sure,' said Sabine. 'I know what I heard.' She crouched beside me, placing her hand on my arm. 'I'm sorry, Lotte, but it was the *Skaubryn*.'

'What about the passengers?' Otto asked.

Sabine shook her head sadly. 'No news yet.'

Without saying a word, I stood and left the lunchroom, still holding the proofs. I knocked on Reinhardt's door and went into his office.

He looked up from his desk. 'Lotte! What's wrong? You're as white as a sheet.' He guided me to a chair. 'Sit before you fall down.'

I sat and placed the proofs on his desk, unable to speak. I couldn't begin to imagine that my mother was gone, and on the ship that had given our family so much joy.

Reinhardt shook me gently by the shoulder, his brow furrowed with worry. 'Are you unwell?'

I shook my head. 'No,' I whispered. 'Sabine just told me that the ship my mother is on has sunk in the Indian Ocean.'

'What?'

'She heard it on the midday news.'

Reinhardt stared at me a moment. 'What day is this?' he asked finally.

'The first of April.'

Realisation flooded his face and he breathed a sigh of relief. 'It's an April Fool's joke. It has to be!'

'What?'

Reinhardt waved his hand in dismissal. 'It's an old English tradition to play a joke on the first of April, April Fool's Day.' He shook his head, his face darkening with fury. 'Wait until I speak with her. That kind of joke is unacceptable.'

I began to rise from the chair. 'No, please don't. I'm sure it was some kind of mistake.' Reinhardt was quite hard on Otto and Sabine. Perhaps it was his way of compensating for the fact that his wife had died shortly after arriving in Australia, when the children were only young.

'No, Lotte. Stay here, please, while I get to the bottom of this.' He strode out of the room before I could protest further.

I didn't know how to feel. On one hand I hoped he was right and my mother and the *Skaubryn* were safe, but I couldn't imagine Sabine doing anything as cruel as this, even as an April Fool's joke, and I felt bad about the wrath Reinhardt was about to bring down on his daughter's head. On the other hand, what if Sabine was right? My mother could be gone, all because I wanted to see her and receive the gift she was bringing. My hands were clammy and I felt as if I was going to vomit.

Reinhardt returned, his brows drawn low over his eyes. 'We're ringing the radio station,' he said brusquely, picking up the receiver of the telephone.

'It's not a joke?' I stared at him, not daring to breathe.

'Sabine swears it's what she heard.'

Blood roared in my ears as I watched Reinhardt on the phone. He shook his head and hung up.

'I'm so sorry, Lotte. It's all true.'

'The passengers?'

'Nothing yet, I'm afraid.'

My breathing came in ragged gasps and my vision swam and doubled. No news of passengers couldn't be good.

Reinhardt's hand was on my shoulder once again, keeping me steady. 'Should I call Erich home from work?'

I shook my head, trying to get my panic under control. 'No, I'll be fine. Just give me a moment.'

'The best we can do is to call the newspaper. I'll ring the *Sydney Morning Herald*. I have a friend who works there and as soon as there's any news, we'll know.'

I smiled weakly at him, grateful for his help. 'Thank you, Reinhardt. You're too kind.' I stood shakily.

'Otto can walk you home if you want to take the rest of the day off.'

'No. I'll be all right. There's lots to do before the weekend and I don't want to get behind.'

Reinhardt's eyes narrowed. 'Okay then. Do what you can and I'll let you know as soon as I have news.'

I nodded, clicking the door closed softly behind me.

7

The next hours passed in a haze as I focused on the repetitive work, pushing away thoughts of my mother, but images still played in my mind. I remembered sitting in her arms as a small child before her divorce, the joy of her long-awaited visits to boarding school, walking through the Englischer Garten in Munich with her, and the grief we had shared at the deaths of my brothers. There was still so much I wanted to say to her, too many moments I wanted to share. With Vati's death still so raw, I wasn't ready to let her go.

It was five o'clock when Reinhardt called me from the darkroom. My eyes hurt as I squinted up at him and I wasn't sure if it was from the light or the fact that I had been crying.

'Lotte, please sit down,' said Reinhardt, gesturing to the chair on the other side of his desk.

I sat slowly, looking into his face for some clue, but as usual his face was carefully guarded. My hands gripped the sides of the chair. 'What did you find out?'

'BBC News in London has confirmed that all the passengers made it to the lifeboats and were picked up by an Australian oil tanker.'

I stared at him. Mutti was safe, she was alive. I took a big gulp of air and dropped my head into my hands. I started to shake.

'She's safe, Lotte. You'll see her again soon.' Reinhardt's voice was calm and soothing.

I lifted my head and saw the sympathy in his eyes. Pulling myself together, I sat up tall and nodded. 'Yes – thank you, Reinhardt, for your help and support.' I clasped my hands to stop them from shaking. 'I would've been out of my mind with worry, not knowing what had happened to her if it wasn't for you.'

'It was nothing – I'm glad I could help.' He stood and came around the desk to where I was sitting, tears filling my eyes, and patted my shoulder. 'Now, I think you've had enough excitement for one day. Otto will walk you home. Try to get some rest.'

I nodded, relief gushing through me. My legs still felt weak but Reinhardt's arm was at my back and his hand under my elbow as he helped me stand. Suddenly I wanted to be home and I was glad Otto was accompanying me because I didn't feel like myself.

I walked through the front door dazed, a million thoughts going through my head. Not wanting the girls to see my distraction and distress, I immediately directed Greta to put some potatoes on to boil and told Johanna to feed Moshi.

'What is it, Mutti?' asked Greta. She was watching me curiously, and I realised that I was still standing by the door.

'Johanna!' shouted Greta. 'Something's wrong with Mutti!'

Small hands grasped my arms and guided me gently into a chair. My daughters peered into my face.

Greta shook me by the shoulder. 'Mutti, are you okay? Johanna, get her a glass of water.'

I blinked, realising how I was worrying my daughters. 'I'm all right,' I said, taking a deep breath. I had to keep my emotions in check. I couldn't worry the girls with something they couldn't do anything about. 'It's nothing.' I tried to smile.

'Nothing?' Johanna echoed, handing me a glass of water.

'That's right.' I took a long drink of water, unable to look her in the eye.

'Something's happened, Mutti,' said Greta, her eyes narrowing as she tried to work it out. 'Have you lost your job again?'

I put the glass on the table and stood abruptly. 'No, nothing like that. Just something I heard at work today, but it's fine. Come on now, we'd better get dinner on before Vati gets home. Then you can finish your homework.'

Erich arrived home not long after. 'God, you're as white as a sheet! I'll get you a brandy. Feed the children,' he said, kissing me. 'Then come to the bedroom and talk to me. Tell me what's going on.'

I nodded, my hands beginning to shake again as I spooned scorched potato from the pot.

Brandy was just what I needed. 'Pour yourself one too,' I said. Out of the corner of my eye, I saw him look at me strangely, frowning with concern, but I didn't dare look at him because I would have gone to pieces.

'Vati!' Johanna came into the kitchen and launched herself into her father's arms, kissing him on his cheek. 'Guess what, Vati?'

'What?'

'I'm making you an Easter present at school.'

'Really? Is that true? Just for me?'

Johanna nodded earnestly, her plaits bouncing against her back.

'What a surprise! I can't wait for Easter then.' Erich kissed her on the top of her head. 'Now tell your sister to come and have her dinner and then go and sit at the table.' He released Johanna and went to the cupboard for two glasses and the brandy. 'Mutti and I have to talk.'

'All right, Vati, but I want to tell you about my day after dinner.' Johanna glanced at me and I caught the look of concern on her face.

'Yes, after dinner,' he said. He handed me a glass, the bottom filled with rich amber liquid. 'Leave us be until we come out of the bedroom.' He took my hand and led me to our room.

I perched on the edge of the bed, muscles wound so tight that my body hurt. I sipped the brandy slowly, feeling the pleasant burn down my throat coiling into a warmth in my belly until I was ready to tell him what had happened.

'I can't believe it,' he said when I had finished.

'No, neither can I.'

'So we don't know where your mother is now?'

'No, there's been no more news.'

'What a nightmare!' He took a gulp of brandy. 'Surely we'll receive a telegram in the next few days, telling us where your mother is and when she'll be arriving.'

'My poor mother,' I whispered. 'I can't imagine the state she's in.'

Erich gathered me in his arms. 'All the passengers are safe and well, that's the main thing.'

My body relaxed against him. He was right. I tried to push my worry to one side. 'I can't believe that beautiful ship is gone. The wonderful times we had on it . . . Those poor families, imagine how frightened the children must've been. They've lost everything.'

He kissed my forehead. 'We'll know more tomorrow.'

I nodded, comforted by his solid presence and strength.

Between work and home, I kept myself as busy as possible, continuing as if nothing had changed: baking with the girls, helping them decorate the house with the festive eggs they'd carefully coloured and painted, and socialising with our neighbours and friends. But always in the back of my mind the worry about Mutti churned away, causing spikes of anxiety whenever I let myself think about it. Although I knew Mutti was tough, I didn't know how she would cope on her own. She had leant on Vati's support for so many years and now she was truly alone – and the shock of what had happened on the *Skanbryn* would only have made that harder to bear for her.

We received the telegram on Saturday.

Erich came in from the garden where the girls were helping him clean up. 'Come on then, let's open it together.'

Leaving the mop and bucket in the middle of the floor, I joined him at the table. I ripped open the envelope and stared at the paper nestled inside, transported back to when my mother had received the telegrams informing her of my brothers' deaths years earlier and the terrible numbness deep in my bones.

Erich gently prised the envelope from my hands and slid the telegram out. 'It's okay . . . She's in Aden. She arrived there yesterday on the SS *Roma*.'

I sagged, relief flooding my body, making me feel weak and giddy. 'She's OK.'

'Yes.'

Looking into Erich's green eyes, I realised that wasn't all. 'What is it?'

'She's flying to Australia in the next few days.'

I didn't know how to feel – excited or horrified. I hadn't been expecting her for another two weeks. Nothing was ready for her arrival. I stood abruptly. 'There's still so much I wanted to do.'

'It'll be okay, Lotte. Your mother's safe and well and will soon be under your loving care. The rest doesn't matter.'

'But she's got nothing. Everything would've gone down with the ship.' We both knew what this meant.

'Maybe she kept her valuables on her. You know how your mother is with money. She keeps everything in that handbag of hers. I bet it never left her side.'

I nodded. 'You're right. The luggage is probably gone but she would've kept everything else with her.'

'There's the insurance as well,' said Erich softly. 'She should be able to claim on that. With any luck, she hasn't lost everything, and if she has . . . we'll manage as we always do.' He shrugged as if it wasn't important, though our chance of buying a house rested on my parents' gift and, if it was gone, so was our new beginning.

But I wouldn't dwell on what might be. Instead, I was comforted by the reasonable hope that all would still be well.

Although we had more room than back at the hostel, the house was still small. The girls already shared a bedroom but we had the tiny space at the back of the house next to the back door, a porch that had been closed in. There was enough room for a bed, a side table and wardrobe that Erich had made, and it was this space we prepared for Mutti. The girls helped me make it homely and inviting while Erich hung a curtain as a partition. I was pleased with the results.

The work kept me busy, giving me an outlet for my nervous energy. Part of me wondered whether agreeing to have Mutti live with us was a mistake. I hoped she wouldn't make trouble between Erich and me. I hoped that I could cope with her tendency to interfere with our lives. And I wondered if the sinking of the *Skaubryn* was a sign of what was to come. I was immediately ashamed for thinking such thoughts, after everything she'd been through.

'Vati! Grossmama's coming tomorrow,' said Johanna, dancing around her father, unable to stay still. 'Can you believe it? Isn't it so exciting?'

'Yes,' said Erich. 'Very exciting.'

I smirked and dropped my head, not daring to look at him. Erich would soon be surrounded by women.

'Come on now, help your mother.'

We borrowed Franz's car and went to pick my mother up from Sydney Airport. It was the first time any of us had been there and the girls' wide eyes as they surveyed the different aeroplanes through the windows as we walked to the arrivals lounge took the edge off my nervousness and worry.

Then I saw her – Mutti: forlorn, bedraggled and alone, clutching her handbag as if it was the only thing she had in the world. She scanned the crowd anxiously for us, her face pale and drawn. Normally she appeared younger than she was but today she looked her fifty-eight years, her strawberry blonde hair frizzy and unkempt and streaked with grey, and her dress crushed and rumpled, as if she'd been sleeping in it for days.

Johanna pulled on my arm in excitement. 'There she is. There's Grossmama.' Then she paused. 'What's wrong with her, Mutti? She's all messy.'

'There was a problem on Grossmama's boat and she hasn't had time to change her clothes or fix herself up before arriving here. Now, don't say anything to her. She's very tired and she's had a difficult few days.'

'All right, Mutti. Come on, let's get her so we can take her home and she can have a rest and get changed.'

I smiled as Johanna dragged me to where Mutti was standing, but she was right. That was exactly what my mother needed.

'Grossmama!' yelled the girls in unison, waving their arms so she could see us. Greta rushed ahead, throwing herself into her grandmother's arms. Mutti swayed a little, stunned by the weight of the nearly twelve-year-old. She wrapped her arms around Greta, kissing the top of her head. When she looked at me, there were tears in her eyes.

'Lotte,' she murmured, her face crumpling with relief. 'I made it.'

Greta moved aside for me to greet my mother and, finally, the moment I'd been dreaming about for months was real. I held my mother in my arms.

'Mutti, I can't believe you're really here,' I whispered. 'I've missed you so much.' I pulled back a moment to look carefully at her. 'Are you all right?'

'I'm fine.' A small smile flitted across her face. 'Nothing was going to stop me from coming to you.' Then she began shaking like a leaf. My tears mingled with hers as I kissed her cheek and we held each other tight.

We headed to the exit and I wanted to pinch myself to see if I was really walking arm in arm with Mutti, just like the old days. Even her greeting with Erich couldn't have been better: she hugged him tight and he was gentle and warm with her.

'Grossmama, where's your luggage?' Greta stood still in the middle of the flow of people, causing them to jostle to get around her. 'Don't we have to get it before we go?'

'No, her luggage didn't come with her on the plane,' said Erich as he draped his arm over our daughter's shoulder and guided her along.

'Do you have to wait for it to arrive from the ship?' asked Johanna, holding her father's hand.

Mutti looked at me and I shook my head. I hadn't told the girls what had happened. They didn't need to be distressed unnecessarily.

'Yes, that's right. I have to wait for it,' my mother said.

'But what about your hand luggage, your overnight bag?' Greta persisted. She took her grandmother's free hand, looked up at her with a frown.

'It got lost, *schätzchen*.' Mutti removed her arm from mine and smoothed the hair from Greta's face. 'But it's all right now, because I'm here with you.'

Greta nodded, satisfied, and hugged her grandmother. 'Okay, Grossmama. We'll look after you. We've got so much to tell you. I can't wait to show you around! Johanna and I will take you exploring while Mutti and Vati are at work.'

A pang of discomfort shot through me. My mother would be looking after the children instead of me and Greta was clearly excited about the prospect. Erich sent a look at me as if to say, 'It begins'.

'That will be lovely,' said Mutti.

'We have to get Grossmama settled first,' I said firmly. 'Let's give her some time before you bombard her with your activities.' Mutti squeezed my hand in gratitude. Her hand in mine was a solid reminder that she was finally here and no longer alone. It was time to lavish all the love and attention on her that I hadn't been able to for years.

When we arrived home, I left Mutti in a warm bath and went out the back to wash the clothes she'd been wearing. I wanted a few minutes to myself. I had never seen my mother so shaken and lost but the last thing she needed was for me to break down. I had to be the strong one.

'Don't disturb Grossmama,' I heard Erich whisper as I reached the back door. 'Once Mutti comes inside, we'll take Onkel Franz's car back to him.'

'But Vati,' said Greta, 'I wanted to talk to Grossmama. It's been such a long time and I have so much to tell her.' She sounded so disappointed. She had missed her grandmother more than I'd realised.

'You'll have plenty of time to talk to Grossmama. Let's give her some peace and quiet. How about we go and get some ice cream and let her rest for a while?'

'All right,' said Johanna. Ice cream got them every time.

I stood for a moment to compose myself and wiped my eyes before coming inside.

Erich reached out and kissed me on the neck. 'All right?'

'Yes. I'm fine now. I'll put a pot of coffee on for Mutti. She'll enjoy that more than instant coffee, and then we'll sit down and see how she really is.'

'Well, I'll give you some time and take the girls with me.'

'For ice cream, I believe.' I raised an eyebrow and Erich smiled. I kissed him, grateful. 'Thank you, my darling.'

Mutti emerged from her bedroom about half an hour later, dressed in the fresh plain skirt and blouse I had bought for her. It was strange to see her in such simple clothes and I felt sad that I hadn't been able to buy her something she was more accustomed to wearing, but she was smiling anyway. She sat on the lounge, her damp hair still bound with a towel.

'It feels wonderful to finally be really clean.'

'Do you want to curl your hair now?' I asked, pouring the hot, strong coffee into Mutti's cup before filling mine. I sat down beside her.

'No, my *schatz*, not now. I'll do it after I've had a little sleep.' She picked up her coffee and took a sip. 'Ah, just the way I like it and just what I needed.'

'Tired?'

She put her cup down. 'Yes. I haven't had much sleep in the last week or so but I'm not ready for bed yet ... I'm too happy to be here.' She squeezed my hand, tears in her eyes. 'At one point I wondered if I would ever see you again. Vati would be so happy to see us together now. I can't bear to think of him at the moment. I miss him so much.'

'It's all right, Mutti. You're here now, and safe. You made it.' I kissed her hand, still clenched tightly in mine.

Her eyes drifted to a recent photo of the girls on the bookshelf. It had been taken at Christmas and they were happy and carefree, long-limbed, skin browned to a healthy glow from summer days under the Australian sun. They were heartbreakingly beautiful.

'They've grown so tall,' Mutti said. 'Greta looks so much like Tante Susie at that age. She takes after my Bavarian grandmother's side of the family. They're all gone now. You three are all I have left . . .'

'I'm glad you left Germany. Here the girls can grow up without the spectre of the war, here they can be free from all the losses Germany has endured – that we've all endured.' She sighed. 'This is where I want to be, with you and your girls. This is home now.'

Tears filled my eyes and I dashed them away. It shocked me to see her so raw. This was not the Mutti I was used to. Whatever she had been through out on the ocean had changed her. Perhaps all my apprehension leading up to her arrival was unfounded and unfair.

'Erich looks the same,' she continued, 'but he's quite grey now and seems tired. I heard him talking to the girls when I was in the bath.'

'Yes, I heard them,' I said, adding a splash of milk to my cup.

'He's a good father . . . I noticed the way he looked at the children when we walked to the car. He adores them.' Her eyes took on that penetrating stare I knew so well, startlingly blue and frosty. 'But I'm not so sure about you.'

'What?'

'You're much too thin and you look exhausted. Maybe this move to Australia has been good for the children, but not for you.'

'I'm fine, Mutti. There's no need to worry about me. Let me worry about you and take care of you for a change.' I understood her concern but had forgotten what it was sometimes like with her. I refused to react – I couldn't let the irritation humming in my nerves get the better of me.

'Things aren't right with you. It's as if all the disappointments have dented your spirit. I can see it in your eyes, the set of your shoulders, your body language.'

'Mutti, really, I'm just tired. It's been a busy few weeks and we've all been worried about you.'

'I know. When I've regained my strength, I'll look after you and help you in any way I can. I want to see the spark in your eyes again.' She turned her face abruptly away and fiddled with the cuff of her blouse. 'I'm so sorry, Lotte. I didn't mean to cause you such worry. I came to help make your life better, not worse.'

'Shh, Mutti.' I hugged her tight. 'All that matters is that you're here, safe and well.'

She pulled away, a look of desperation on her face. 'I have to tell you what happened now, before I lose my courage.'

'You don't need to talk about it if you're not ready, Mutti.'

'No, Lotte, it has to be now.' She picked up her coffee cup and sipped, as if summoning what strength she had left and finding a way to start. 'I only want to tell you about it once,' she said, placing her cup back on the saucer. 'You have to know.'

A streak of sunlight from the front window fell across the coffee table that Erich had made, the pinkish timber gleaming rich and warm. I'd seen my mother deal with tragedy before. Mutti believed that it was best kept to yourself, locked away in a little compartment in your mind and heart, only to be opened, just a crack, in dreams and disjointed nightmares until time was finally able to keep those compartments sealed. It was the way things were done in her family, where traditional German values were held in the highest regard. That was my old world. But I knew about trauma and hardship too, and knew there were other ways to deal with pain and heartbreak.

'We were somewhere between Aden and Ceylon and it was very hot. We'd had an emergency drill earlier that afternoon and many of the passengers who were used to a siesta were less than happy to have their rest disturbed. It was the men who grumbled the most, while the women kept the children under control. I went to dinner as usual, enjoying the company of the German couples at my table. They persuaded me to stay and listen to the band play afterwards and I danced a little too . . . You were right. The *Skaubryn* was a beautiful ship and the service was impeccable. It reminded me of the holidays I used to enjoy. There was intelligent and sparkling dinner conversation and walks along the decks with new friends. I began to feel alive again and I was finally able to let my grief fade just a little and enjoy myself.' She took a deep breath.

'I can't believe it's gone now,' I murmured wistfully, leaning back into my seat, my coffee forgotten. 'The *Skaubryn* was our first real holiday. We couldn't believe the level of luxury. There was always something for the children to do. It was the first time Erich and I had time to just relax and enjoy each other's company without the pressures of our life in Germany.' I shook my head. 'We'd had such high hopes but we had no idea how difficult it would be when we arrived. I can only imagine how much harder it's going to be for those families who have come with nothing but the clothes on their back.'

'How long since you've laughed, Lotte?' Mutti asked softly.

My eyes widened in surprise at the question. She missed nothing. 'It's been hard, Mutti, but we're doing better now. We both have jobs and this house. The children are happy and thriving here. Things are looking up.'

'And you and Erich? Are things good between you? Is he treating you as he should?'

'We're as strong as ever, Mutti. We've both been under a lot of strain and working long hours, but things are good between us.'

Mutti nodded, her lips compressed. She once told me, on a rare occasion when she'd spoken from the heart, that the reason we often clashed was because we were so much alike. She said it was hard to be in the same room as me sometimes, because it was like a mirror was held up to her and she was confronted by the truth of what she saw in my face.

I knew she was only worried about me but I couldn't have her interfere in my marriage. I picked up my coffee cup, welcoming the strong, slightly bitter taste. I couldn't berate her after all she'd just been through, but I could change the subject.

'What happened on the boat, Mutti?'

'It's hard to talk about.' She paused, clutching the arms of the chair so her fingers turned white.

'It was like a nightmare. The lights went out. It was about half past nine. An announcement came over the loudspeaker that we were to make our way to the lifeboats. The ship was on fire. We were guided from the lounge by crewmen with torches. Smoke began to billow out of passageways . . . crewmen burst through the doors . . . passengers from the lower decks spilled out coughing. The heat was oppressive and it was hard to breathe. The pushing and shoving . . . the screaming as mothers looked for their children and husbands looked for their wives. The smell of fear, it was stronger than the stench of smoke that we could smell for days after. My friend Rina held my hand so tight that I couldn't feel my fingers. Then her husband found us, pushing us in front of him, like cattle down a race. He held his young son's hand, yelling at us to stay with him . . . Rina was screaming at her son not to let go, sobbing uncontrollably.

'When the time came, we climbed down the rope ladder into the lifeboat and we were lowered against the hull of the boat. The metal plate was hot. Then we were bobbing on the ocean, watching the other boats being loaded, passengers in evening wear and pyjamas, ushering frightened children towards the edge of the ship, mothers screaming as screeching babies in pillowcases were thrown from the deck into the waiting arms of the crewmen in the lifeboats. It must have been well after midnight when everyone was safely on the water and we watched the flickers of fire and plumes of smoke intensify on the ship. It was then that I realised I still had my handbag clutched to my chest.'

Mutti seemed to remember I was sitting beside her then and she shivered slightly, turning those bright blue eyes on me and sighed. 'The crewmen worked like clockwork, calm and efficient, and they got everyone on those boats. They saved all our lives. Finally before dawn, an oil tanker reached us. We watched the *Skaubryn* sink while we waited for the SS *Roma* to reach us.'

'Oh Mutti, I'm so sorry. It must have been awful ...' I willed the tears away. If Mutti could be strong, then so could I.

'It's over now.' Mutti patted my hand. 'But there's something else I have to tell you . . . The fire and our escape wasn't the worst of it.'

'What do you mean?'

She hung her head. 'I didn't just lose my luggage and the few things I brought from home with me.'

I put my cup down, intending to end the conversation. 'Mutti, I think you've been through enough.'

She put her hand on my arm. 'No. Let me finish. It was what was in the captain's safe.'

Dread grew in my belly.

'As we were being directed off the *Skaubryn*, I approached one of the crewmen. I told him that I had a package locked in the captain's safe that I needed to retrieve. He told me that it had to stay, there wasn't enough time to get it. I pleaded with him, told him that it was all I had left in the world and asked if the captain, perhaps, or one of the crewmen, could bring it.

He just shook his head and gently pushed me towards the life-boats on the edge of the deck before dealing with the rest of the passengers. All I had was my handbag, which I had taken with me to dinner.'

'What did you have in the safe?'

Mutti shivered. She couldn't look at me. 'It was everything I had left.' She let the words hang in the air for a moment. 'I kept a small amount of cash in my handbag but I put everything else in the captain's safe. I had been persuaded to do so by the captain. I was assured it was the safest place on the ship.'

What could I say to make my mother feel better? I took her hand in mine again, the hand that had caressed my face as a child, had soothed away my hurts. 'It doesn't matter, Mutti.'

She pulled away and glared at me. 'But it *does* matter! It was what Vati and I had wanted to do, his last gift to you, and it's all gone.

'But it wasn't only that. I lost everything I had from my own family. All the family heirlooms and jewels and my father's beloved Rembrandt – things that should have gone to you and the children.' She took a shaky breath. 'There was no insurance. I'm so sorry.' She hid her face in her hands, sobbing in despair and horror.

The scale of what we had lost overwhelmed me. Now we truly had nothing. The money was gone along with our family treasures and our link to our heritage. Mutti was reduced to relying on Erich and me. She looked wretched, so small and vulnerable, deflated, as if the life had drained from her with her confession.

My poor, poor mother. I gathered her in my arms and held her tight, my own tears falling. 'Mutti, Mutti – it's all right.'

'I've failed you,' she whispered.

'No, you haven't. All I wanted was to have you here with us, for you to watch the children grow, for me to be able to hug you like this whenever I want.' All my hopes and dreams were dashed, but what I said was true. What mattered was having those we loved close to us. That much I had learnt.

Mutti took herself to bed and I tidied up, thinking about what she had gone through.

'Shh!' I whispered while drying the last coffee cup, as Erich came through the front door without the girls – Claudia had insisted that they stay and she would walk them home later. I sent a silent prayer to God, thanking Him for her friendship.

'Where's your mother?' He kissed me on the lips in greeting.

'She's asleep. She was exhausted.'

'How did you go with her?' He leant casually against the sink, but I could see the tension in the set of his shoulders.

'All right. I'll tell you, but not here. I don't want to wake her.' I dropped the tea-towel on the bench and led him to our bedroom, shutting the door behind us. 'She's too upset to tell me much. But she was determined to tell me what she lost, what sank with the boat.'

Erich reached for me and I stepped into the warm security of his arms, sagging with relief, unable to bear the burden of Mutti's terrible guilt on my own a minute longer.

'She's lost everything,' I whispered. Then I told him what I knew.

'At least your mother has us,' he said when I was done.

'She's taking it hard. She's horrified that she's come with nothing when she wanted to help us get a real start here. She won't cope very well knowing she's now dependent on us. I'm sure she thinks she'll be a burden, an extra mouth to feed.'

'Don't be silly,' said Erich softly. 'I'll never forget how you welcomed my mother and Inga and the children into our home when we had even less than this.' He kissed me and I looked into his eyes, the green depths shining with love and remembrance. 'It's a real blow, but there's nothing we can do about it.'

We had been through much worse in Germany after the war, eight of us living in a two-bedroom house with a tiny attic and only Erich working. The tension between Inga and me had been explosive. We could certainly manage my mother, but I wasn't so sure how she'd cope.

Leaning my head against his shoulder, I felt solid strength seep through me. He was a good man without a malicious bone in his body and wouldn't hold our financial difficulties against her.

There would be no help to buy a house, no return to university for Erich and no chance for me to stop work to have another baby. Those dreams were gone, perhaps forever. But he would accept my mother as she was. He did it for me.

8

Erich came home one evening not long after Mutti arrived, looking white as a sheet.

'What's wrong?'

'It's been a difficult day.'

'Why, what's happened?' I took his jacket from him and hung it on the hook by the door.

'Not now, I just want a moment to relax,' he said irritably.

'Well, I'll leave you alone then,' I snapped, turning towards the kitchen.

'Lotte, no. I'm sorry. I'm angry, but not at you.' He sank into the lounge, running his hands through his hair. 'I witnessed a terrible industrial accident today.'

'Someone you knew?'

'It was Giovanni.' I sat beside him in shock. He shook his head with frustration. 'I should have been there. There wasn't a thing I could do. I came out of the manager's office too late to warn him . . . It all happened in slow motion. I've been saying it for months but maybe now they'll do something.' He grimaced. 'One of our operators went off sick and a fresh load of timber came in that needed cutting immediately. Apparently, the foreman decided to put the new man on the circular saw with only a brief explanation of how to use it while someone more experienced worked the machine that dresses the timber.

'While Giovanni was cutting a timber stile for the door frame, he was distracted – trying to understand someone asking him a question. He reached down to remove the cut piece of timber and his fingers got caught in the belt. It dragged in his hand.' His voice choked and he swallowed hard. 'I'll never forget that sight as long as I live.'

'God in heaven!'

'Three of his fingers were completely severed. I pulled him away from the machine and it was only then that people around us noticed what was happening. There was blood splattered everywhere and I realised that his fingers were missing but he just stood there in total shock. Then he stared at his mangled hand and registered what had happened. I got a chair under him just in time before he started screaming.'

My eyes were wide with horror. Erich had begun with the same job. It could have been him. 'Poor Giovanni. What will happen to him now?'

He shrugged. 'I don't know, perhaps he'll have surgery, but he'll be off work for a good while.'

'And his family? Is there worker's compensation?'

'Without an income, they won't manage. I imagine that Carmela will have to find a job, but the children are so little.' My heart went out to them. 'A claim has to be made but it'll take time for them to receive payments. It won't be enough – they'll get a percentage of his wage and payments for her if she's not working and for the children, then a small amount for hospital and medical bills.'

I saw Johanna in the doorway out of the corner of my eye and waved her away. 'Thank God we have health insurance.'

'But I doubt he has,' he said softly. 'I'll set up a collection for the family. I know it's not good enough, but there's not much more anyone can do. The fact is, he'll struggle to find work once he's recovered. The union can help the family as much as possible . . . but it should never have happened.' He clutched the arm rest so tightly his knuckles turned white. 'The machinery has no protective guards on either the belt or the blade and he should never have been allowed to use that saw until he'd had proper training and he could properly understand what he'd been told.'

I hugged Erich tight. I knew that he probably blamed himself for not trying harder to bring about the changes for a safer environment, but all I could think about was what would have happened to us if it had been him. Where would we be if he suddenly became incapacitated? Our whole life here would be in jeopardy.

But my fears for our new life were always allayed by seeing how the girls thrived. They spoke English fluently now, and they seemed happy at school, where they had made friends.

One evening after the girls were in bed, Mutti approached me. Erich was outside, taking out the rubbish.

'I need to talk to you about Greta,' she said.

'What is it?' I lifted my head from the colouring work I was concentrating on. I was tired and didn't need any more complications in an already long and busy day.

Mutti sank into the chair opposite me. 'She came home today with bruises and a cut on her arm.'

She had my attention now. I put down my pencil and pushed the work to one side. 'What happened?'

'She wouldn't tell me at first. I was surprised, because usually Greta tells me everything. But Anna persuaded her to tell me. There have been some children at school who've been calling her and Johanna names. Anna said that she and Peter have been the target of this name-calling too.'

'What names? Surely they're just silly childhood taunts.'

My mother shook her head sadly. 'No, my *schatz*. I'm afraid not. They called them Nazi bastards.'

I put my hand to my mouth, my eyes wide. 'They're just children!' It made my blood boil to hear my innocent children tarnished with the Nazi name. Not only that, but I couldn't stand my children being called 'bastards'. My marriage to Erich had been declared null and void in a court of law in 1949, four years after we were married, when it was discovered that Erich's first wife and children were alive and not dead in the bombings as we had believed. My children had been illegitimate. It took protracted divorce proceedings while Inga and her children lived with us before Erich and I could remarry in 1952.

'Peter's been trying to keep Johanna away from those children, but Greta's somehow often in their path. She retaliated, and admitted that today wasn't the first time she'd done so. She's been fighting them.'

'I didn't bring up my girls to behave like this! I brought them up to be young ladies.'

'I know, I know. Don't get angry with her. I think she had every right to fight back, but I made her promise to stop. Today she made the ringleader's nose bleed and threatened to do it again if he or his friends came near any of them. He ran away crying while the other children laughed at him. She doesn't think they'll annoy her, Johanna or Claudia's children again.'

I was dumbfounded. 'Greta did that?'

Mutti nodded, grinning. 'She's tough, your daughter. Nobody's going to walk all over her.'

'I can't believe you condone this!'

'Lotte, haven't you told me that you wanted the girls to grow up to be themselves, to have the freedom to stand up for what they believe in and to live the life they want? Isn't this part of the reason you came to Australia? It's certainly what your husband's advocating in his union work.'

'I didn't realise you were listening, or that you'd noticed.'

'Of course. I saw how things were for you in Germany. How unhappy you were before you met Erich. I should never have tried to push you away from him. We would've had a much closer relationship if I'd let you find your own path to happiness.'

I frowned and shook my head, trying to comprehend my mother's words, words I'd never imagined I would hear from her. 'But I don't understand how this could happen at school. There are migrant children from so many countries there. I just didn't expect it.'

'It happens everywhere,' said Mutti softly. 'You work in a very sheltered environment. Ask Erich, he'll tell you the same. He explained to me that there's still a stigma about being German. Many people believe that we shouldn't be in this country, that we shouldn't take Australian jobs and that we're all unrepentant fascists.'

'Yes, I know.' I sighed. 'I've heard the stories too, but I didn't think I'd hear it from children.'

'They only repeat what they hear from their parents.'

I nodded. This might be a reality I couldn't change. 'I have to work out what we do about Greta.'

'Do nothing. She's promised to stop fighting and she's promised to let me know if the taunting continues. She was only standing up for herself and Johanna. I'm sure a few discreet enquiries to Anna will tell you if it has truly stopped.'

I knew Mutti had a soft spot for Greta but she was right. I only wished she could have been so mellow when I was growing up. Who was this woman sitting in front of me? I said a swift prayer of thanks for her, whoever she was. Maybe she really had changed.

'Promise me you'll let me know, Mutti. I can't have my daughter brawling in the schoolyard like a ruffian.'

'I promise.'

I worried about my mother and my daughters but I had no idea that I should have been worrying about Erich. The workplace accident he'd witnessed had taken him to the wider world – now he spoke with new passion about the terrible risks to life and livelihood that could result from inadequate or non-existent safety measures, not just at the union meetings but also public work meetings. But I didn't truly understand the repercussions of his activism until Claudia approached me.

'Lotte, there's something I want to say to you,' she said haltingly as we walked from her place to mine one Sunday.

'Of course, anything,' I said. The children had run ahead, and Mutti was a little in front of us, holding the twins' hands. Erich had remained at Franz's for a game of cards with some other German men.

'You can tell me to mind my own business, but it's something I think you should know.'

I stopped in the middle of the path. 'What is it? Just tell me.'

'Erich's been threatened,' she whispered.

'What?'

'Let's keep walking.' She grasped my arm. 'He's been noticed at the big rallies and was approached at the factory gate a couple of days ago. One of the employment officers told him to stay away from the union and to stop speaking out about things he couldn't possibly understand or he'd end up working on the railway in the outback for the rest of his two years.'

I couldn't believe it was true. 'Who told you this?'

'Franz. He heard the whole thing. Erich hasn't told you?'

'No, he wouldn't want to worry me.' I felt sick. 'Can they really do that to him?'

'Franz said that they had no grounds, they were only bluffing and trying to scare him off and Erich would know that too . . . But still, I wanted you to know.'

It wasn't until that evening when the children and Mutti were in bed that I could speak to Erich about what Claudia had said.

Just looking at his face told me every word of it was true.

'I wanted to tell you, but didn't want to worry you,' he said, sitting heavily on the edge of the bed next to me. 'I'm sorry you found out this way.'

I shook my head impatiently, wincing with pain. My neck was coiled tight with tension. 'I know you didn't want to worry me, but can the government do this to you?'

Erich's warm fingers rubbed the knots in my neck and across the tops of my shoulders. 'I'm nearly at the end of my two years. Any fool who'd cared to check would have known that. He was just trying to warn me off with tough words. You know how it is with these officials, any small amount of power they think they might have goes to their head.'

'So it's the same everywhere then.' I was relieved and worried at the same time. It was probably just an idle threat, but I'd seen men like that become dangerous.

Erich smiled and kissed my cheek. 'I'm afraid it is.'

'All the same, please be careful. Who knows what they might try to do!'

'I promise I'll be careful.' The massaging stopped, the heat from his hands radiating into the relaxed muscles. His face creased into lines of regret at the worry he'd caused me but then hardened once more, and a steely light entered his eyes. 'But in truth, I've done nothing wrong or illegal and I won't be bullied into backing down.'

'I know, my darling. I would never expect you to.' I cupped his cheek. 'It's part of who you are, but don't give them a reason to hurt you and the chances we have of a good life here. We have to work harder than ever now that Mutti's money is gone.'

'I would never do that to you and the children,' he whispered as he gathered me into his arms.

All our efforts paid off the day Erich arrived home with a utility. It was an old Vanguard with a spacious bench seat at the front and a solid tray at the rear, perfect for carrying tools and supplies. Erich beamed from ear to ear, taking the girls and me for a drive around the block to show us how smoothly it ran.

'Now we can drive wherever we want to go,' he said.

'Can we go to the beach?' asked Greta.

'Of course we can. We can start exploring and drive somewhere different every Sunday afternoon.'

'Yippee!' shouted the girls.

Our world opened up – we had something to look forward to other than constant work. We could see the countryside, begin to explore what Australia had to offer: the beaches, mountains, rivers, forests and the bush. Although I missed the lush, orderly green of Germany, Australia was growing on me. I'd heard so much about the unusual flora and fauna, the wide open spaces and the wild ruggedness of the terrain that I wanted us to experience it for ourselves.

'Can we jump in the back?' asked Greta when Erich stopped at the kerb outside our house.

'Yes, off you go,' said Erich, waving them out.

'Be careful and hold on,' I added.

The girls shot out the door and climbed onto the tray.

'Do you like it?' asked Erich.

'Of course. It's wonderful.'

'I know you'd have preferred a sedan but there's a reason I bought the utility. I've been thinking about our financial situation. I still want to buy a house, something that's our own, to give the children and your mother their own rooms, with space in the backyard and the chance to have a real garden and grow some vegetables, but you know how expensive it is.'

I nodded. With Mutti's loss on the *Skaubryn*, I had resigned myself to working hard for years before we'd ever be able to afford to buy a house.

'Well, what if we buy some land, a few acres? It's better than renting, paying dead money. We could build a house, a few rooms at first so we can move into it, but bigger than what we have now so it's comfortable, and then add on more. Perhaps we could even farm a little, grow some crops and vegetables, make some extra money on the side . . . I want the girls to grow up understanding about the cycles of nature, as I did. I want them to have a childhood like that.'

He looked at me. I tried to hide my smile at his enthusiasm, not at all surprised. He'd been giving away a few hints, and chatting to Franz about farming. Maybe this would make him happy, since he would never return to engineering. Erich was passionate about his union work and it gave him a sense of identity but he needed to put down roots too. He'd grown up in Silesia and, although he'd lived in one of the bigger towns, he'd spent much of his childhood in the surrounding countryside. A farm was a place of sanctuary for him, a place of relaxation and joy. How could I deny him that?

I remembered my childhood, and my father's estate where I spent idyllic summers running barefoot in the meadows and forests, revelling in the fresh country air and the sense of freedom. They were my best memories of my youth. I couldn't wish my lonely childhood on my children but I did love the outdoors and open spaces.

'Well, what do you think of that?'

'It could work ... We'd stop renting sooner.' I stared out to the small garden we'd planted, little bursts of colour making the yard feel cheery and loved. I'd enjoyed making that garden with Erich and the girls. I could feel his eyes on me, willing me to be just as excited as he was. 'Just as long as we have more space in the house and it's in good condition before we move into it. We have to find the right block, not too far away from the girls' school or work.'

'So you think it's a good plan?'

'Yes, it's wonderful.'

'I promised you we'd find a way. We'll find the perfect place, I know it, and you'll have the house of your dreams.'

I laughed at his excitement and earnest desire to make me happy.

A banging on the back of the ute reminded us that the children were waiting. 'Come on, Vati,' yelled Greta. 'We want to go for a drive.'

'All right, let's go on our adventure.' Erich eased the ute away from the gutter, onto the street.

We decided to drive up to the Blue Mountains not long after. Reinhardt, Sabine and Otto had insisted that we join them for a day out. We met them in Katoomba at the lookout of The Three Sisters.

'Wow,' said Johanna, staring across the valley.

'Beautiful, isn't it?' Sabine said, pulling her coat closed. It was fresh at this altitude but nothing compared to the cold in Germany.

'It just goes on forever,' said Greta in awe. It was an alien landscape. The soft green of the eucalypt forest covered the deep crevices of the valley below and spread up the mountain plateaus as far as the eye could see, punctuated only by rugged sandstone cliffs and the three strange but impressive outcrops of rock that stood like ancient sentinels above the valley.

'Is it worth the trip?' asked Reinhardt, smiling at the girls' reactions.

'It's wilder and grander than I imagined . . . prehistoric even,' I said. 'We don't have anything like this back in Germany.'

'It looks impenetrable,' said Erich. 'How can people navigate their way through these mountains?'

'For a long time they didn't, and there are still hikers who get lost in these mountains,' said Otto, leaning casually against a metal railing. 'People die all the time.'

I shivered at the thought of being lost out here. The Australian landscape could be harsh and unforgiving but there was no denying how breathtakingly beautiful it could be too. I pulled out my camera to take photos of Erich and the girls with the iconic The Three Sisters in the background.

It was November before I was finally able to properly use my photography skills again. Thank God I'd been using my time wisely, learning about the technological advances and changes in cameras and photography after being out of the industry for so long. Otto was up to date with the most recent ideas coming out of the European academies and had agreed to help me with the retraining I needed whenever he wasn't busy. He had given me manuals to read in the spare time I didn't have. But somehow I managed to bring it all together, and Otto gave me a project to test my new skill and techniques: I had to take some technically difficult shots and develop them to show Reinhardt.

Otto decided that photographing the girls on their sports carnival at school would satisfy the requirements. I was touched by his thoughtfulness, pleased I could watch the girls compete even if I was concentrating on taking the perfect photos and incorporating all the aspects on Otto's checklist. It would be a challenge, but I was ready for it and excited to prove what I was capable of.

I left the girls in their yellow T-shirts and ribbons and made my way to the track. The shouting and cheering fell away as I focused on the racing children on the sports field. The sun burst through the overcast sky, casting a momentary glow over the oval. I couldn't do much about the light in this environment. I had brought a small reflector to either minimise shadows or soften the sunlight for the outdoor portraits I would later do of the girls. Now, it was all about capturing the moment, anticipating the movements and getting the right shutter speed – taking the photos in fast, successive bursts. I was prepared to use the new technology of the camera I was using, with its SLR lens, various shutter speeds and modern focusing mechanism. But I wanted more – not just the action, but their joyful, vigorous expressions and body language. My photos had to tell a story, they had to have a soul. I knew I had to move to the finish line.

'You have a good eye,' was all Reinhardt said to me after carefully studying the final prints.

'It's time for you to work behind the camera,' said Otto proudly.

Sabine had just been married to a lovely Norwegian boy who had graduated in architecture and they were on their honeymoon, four weeks in Europe. Reinhardt decided to allow me to take on some of the appointments scheduled until Christmas, ones that Otto and the other senior photographer, Alex, couldn't fit in. I was to manage the extra studio sittings and the odd assignment outside the studio as well as the work I was doing. Saturdays were often fully booked with weddings and I was thrilled to learn that I would cover these too. Wedding photography was prestigious and a wonderful opportunity to finally interact with ordinary Australian people. I was so pleased that Erich had insisted that I get my licence and that we had the car.

However, at my first shoot it wasn't quite what I had expected. I hadn't thought of the challenges associated with such an emotionally charged day.

The bride was nervous when she stepped out of the car in front of the church. Her father with his shiny black shoes and slicked down hair had no idea what to do. Even the bridesmaids that hovered around her couldn't calm her.

'Time with her please,' I said to the matron of honour.

'What do you want?' she asked sharply, already feeling the pressure of the day.

This was not the time for my English to fail me. 'Take the girls away. Give her room.' She looked at me dubiously. I breathed deeply to illustrate my meaning, keeping an efficient, professional demeanour, as though I'd dealt with this exact situation many times before. Relief washed over me when she nodded and took the bride's father's arm, directing the bridesmaids and flower girl to wait with them in the shade of the trees. It was already becoming a warm day and it wouldn't be long before the flowers started to wilt. I'd have to work quickly.

I crouched down next to the panicked bride as she perched on the edge of the back seat of the car. 'Tell me about your fiancé. I want to take the best photographs of you both. How did you meet? What made you fall in love with him?'

The bride smiled then and I knew I'd got through to her. She relaxed visibly as she told me her story, reminding her of how much she wanted this day to come to pass. When she'd finished, she was radiant, confident and couldn't wait to enter the church. I knew the photos would be perfect.

'Thank you,' she said, grasping my hand for a moment. We were waiting in the sandstone portico as the bridesmaids prepared her train.

'Just enjoy your day,' I said, glad that we'd overcome the first hurdle and that I now had her trust.

The bride and groom were easy to photograph in the gardens after. The groom was no longer awkward or uncomfortable in his suit and the bride was happy that they were on their own for a few moments. It allowed me to create unique but natural shots that I thought they'd be happy with. But gathering family members was another matter. Concentrating to make sure I used the right English words, getting them to all look at the camera, especially the restless children, and ensuring the lighting and positions were just right was more of a challenge. The reception wasn't any easier, trying to stay unobtrusive but ready to catch that perfect moment, wrestling with the uneven lighting. My greatest worry was that Reinhardt would be disappointed with my work and never give me another photography assignment or studio sitting, but I enjoyed every moment of that day. By the end of the night, I was exhausted but jubilant. I was doing what I loved.

Between my normal work, night work and weekends, I barely had time to think. We began to save more money and the dream of buying a block of land became tangible for me. Thank God for Mutti, who cooked at night and looked after the girls after school and the weekends that Erich worked. She even did a little cleaning while supervising the girls with their chores. I had never imagined in my wildest dreams that she could be such a help. But I did miss spending time with my family and tried my best to have dinner with them every night.

'I don't want liverwurst sandwiches any more, Mutti,' said Johanna one evening after dinner.

'Why not, darling? You like liverwurst.'

'I want Vegemite sandwiches,' whispered Johanna, 'just like all the Australian kids.'

'The Australians tease anyone with a different lunch to them,' said Greta softly.

I couldn't show them how I was hurting for them, it would only make it worse.

'So Vegemite?' All I could do was help to smooth their transition and if Vegemite was going to help, then Vegemite it was.

Both girls nodded. A tendril of uncertainty snaked down my back. What if doing what I loved, the constant work to get ahead, was at the expense of the girls? I wanted to be there for them, know what they were going through each day, help them make sense of their world. I'd have to keep a closer eye on them, I decided.

'Can you make our lunches, Mutti?' Greta glanced at the kitchen. 'We don't want to upset Grossmama, but she's a bit heavy-handed and Vegemite needs to be smeared on the bread thin, not thick.'

I tried not to smile. 'All right. I'll buy some tomorrow.'

Sabine returned from her honeymoon just before Christmas. Reinhardt called me into his office. I was sure that she would return to her usual position and the chance to prove my worth would be gone.

'Sabine and I have been talking,' he said without pre-amble. 'She's coming back to work after Christmas, so she'll continue with her studio sittings and assignments during the week.'

'Of course,' I murmured. I tried to smile and not show the disappointment that pierced me. I had been hoping to take on more of the studio work.

'However, I've decided that I'd like you to continue the weddings on Saturdays.'

My head shot up. 'Really?'

'Doesn't it suit you?' asked Reinhardt.

'Yes, yes, it does,' I gushed. 'I just can't believe you're letting me continue with the weddings.'

'Why not? You're a very talented photographer. You're efficient, hard-working and you get the job done. Not only that, but you deal beautifully with the clients. I've had such good reports about your management on the day and your handling of the bridal party and guests.'

I blushed furiously, embarrassed by the praise but pleased at the same time. I was talented, he said. It had been a very long time since I had heard those words.

'Thank you.'

'So you're happy to keep the Saturdays then?'

'Yes, that sounds wonderful.' I smiled. Finally I had done it – I was working behind the camera, if only for one day a week. But if Reinhardt thought I was talented, there would be more work to come. Not only that, the extra money would really help us.

1959

With my greater understanding of the surrounding districts, thanks to travelling to many areas for the Saturday weddings, Erich and I narrowed down the search area for our farm quite quickly. We found what we wanted in Leppington, about halfway between Liverpool and the rural town of Camden. It was perfect for Erich's dream: ten acres surrounded by farmland, market gardens and bush. Although it seemed quite secluded, it was only a ten-minute walk to the Hume Highway for the girls or Mutti to catch the bus into Liverpool. Best of all, it was affordable. Putting down our deposit and nervously awaiting settlement felt incredible. A small patch of Australian land was about to become ours.

We had a little get-together at home to celebrate our achievement. Franz, Claudia and the children joined us, as did Reinhardt, Sabine and her husband Karl, and our neighbours Tommy and Suzanne with their new baby, Joan. It was a lovely spring afternoon drinking coffee and tea, eating cake and celebrating with a glass of champagne.

'However did you find it?' asked Suzanne, the baby wriggling restlessly on her lap.

'I drove past the For Sale sign one Saturday on my way to a wedding,' I said, sipping my champagne.

'We went the next day to have a look. We'd seen enough places to know what we were after. It was perfect,' Erich said.

'I told them I was jealous,' Franz leaned across Claudia to whisper conspiratorially to Suzanne. 'We've just bought a house in Liverpool but after seeing their farm, all I want to do is sell our place and move to the quiet and solitude of the country too!'

His uncle Ernst had unexpectedly come to live with them late the previous year. Claudia hadn't been very happy about his sudden arrival but, as he'd done so much for Franz in Germany during the war, they couldn't refuse him. Ernst had been living in Spain until recently when he'd learnt of Franz's emigration to Australia and decided to join him. It had been a very tight squeeze with them all in the two-bedroom home until Ernst had insisted on helping them with his savings to purchase the home they now owned.

Claudia batted him playfully over the ear. 'Don't listen to him. We love our place. It's convenient, close to school, work, the station, doesn't need much doing to it and has plenty of room for everyone.' She turned her gaze to her husband. 'Besides, what would you do with all that land? You're not a farmer. It would only be a headache for us.'

'But Erich isn't a farmer either.' Franz took a long swallow of beer, his legs stretched out in front of him.

'Yes, but at least he grew up around a farming community. Not like you, who grew up in the big city.'

'But a man has to have dreams,' Franz groaned, but I could see the twinkle in his eye.

'Your dream is right here,' Claudia scolded. 'You have to finish your studies, get a job, and we have to save until you can open up your own firm.'

Franz was halfway through his first year of law school and was currently looking for work in one of the law firms in Sydney. The arrival of his uncle meant he could return to university full time while Ernst took on Franz's job at the door factory, and they'd still have his income. Erich now picked Ernst up for work each day, returning the favour Franz had done him for all those months.

Franz's shoulders slumped in mock defeat. 'I suppose that's it then.'

'You can have a farm when you retire,' said Suzanne tentatively.

'That's right,' said Claudia.

'Well, at least let me go out and help Erich clear his block on the weekends. That's all I'll have of the fresh air and peace and quiet.'

'You mean you'll give me some peace and quiet,' retorted Claudia, holding out her glass to Erich as he poured more champagne. 'As long as you take the children and your uncle with you.'

'Don't worry about those two,' I whispered to Suzanne. 'They're just joking around. Besides, they've both had a bit to drink and that's when Franz really likes to stir Claudia up.'

'All right,' she said, placing a teething ring into Joan's mouth. The little girl quietened immediately, drool dribbling down her chin.

'How long until you think you'll be ready to move there?' asked Tommy.

Erich paused to think, beer bottle halfway to his mouth. 'I have to clear some of the land. I want to plant crops, maybe something that grows easily to start with, until I get a good understanding of the soil and climate. Then I'll have to begin on the house. That will take some time, I think.'

And money, I thought. It would be a while until we could move. We had to save more to afford to build the house. I had to be patient. One step at a time.

'Sometime next year, perhaps.' Erich smiled at me and I returned it. I couldn't wait to be in our own place. We'd waited so long for this.

'We'll miss you,' whispered Suzanne, squeezing my hand.

'We'll miss you too,' I said, 'but I'm in Liverpool almost every day. I'm sure we'll see each other often.' I had grown fond of Suzanne. She was a lovely girl, friendly, kind and thoughtful. Joan began to cry, tossing the teething ring away.

'Here, let me take her,' said Mutti in her thickly accented English. She reached for the squirming baby and Suzanne released her gratefully. 'I'll take her out to see what the children are doing.'

'Thank you, Amelia. That would be lovely.'

'Finish your champagne and relax. We'll be fine, won't we, Joan?' Mutti patted the baby on her back and carried her to the door.

'Your mother's a godsend,' said Suzanne. 'She's such a help with Joan, especially when I don't know what to do with her.'

'Yes, she can be wonderful,' I said. Mutti had missed more of the girls' early years than she cared to admit because she was fighting with me about Erich. I knew Joan brought back memories of my girls as babies. Mutti had time on her hands – time to reflect on the past and time to get bored. She was struggling to learn English but Suzanne was helping her and, for the lack of any other company through the day, would walk with her and Joan to the shops, just to get out of the house and practise her English skills.

We understood about lost time as did Reinhardt and Sabine, in a way that Suzanne and Tommy didn't, and I hoped would never have to. They seemed so innocent about what life could bring. I prayed that it would be good to them, the same as I wished for my daughters.

'I think this will be the best place for the house,' said Erich, one Sunday not long after we'd settled on the land.

We were standing in the tall grass on the front part of the block which was flat, level and cleared but still dotted with gum trees. The girls had already disappeared, but I wasn't sure if it was to explore or to avoid helping with the repair of the boundary fences. We came to the farm most Sundays, not only to give the girls fresh air and somewhere to run around but to consolidate our plans and begin on the list of jobs that would make our dream a reality. Despite it being my only day off, I enjoyed coming out. The feeling of accomplishment, working with my family to make this place our home, washed away all the disappointments we'd encountered along the way. It was finally happening. There was a sense of space that felt so different from where we were living in Liverpool and for the first time since stepping off the boat, I felt as if I could really breathe.

'It's a good position,' I said, looking back towards the front. 'Just far enough from the road to be private.'

'We'll put the garage next to it here,' he said, pointing as he explained the design we'd discussed. 'The driveway will come in like this and there'll be room for a garden and a path to the front door.' It was hot, dry and dusty and I couldn't imagine planting a garden full of jewel-coloured flowers and bright greenery, like we'd had in Germany – or even in Liverpool for that matter.

'Do you think we'll manage renting and building?' Despite my excitement, I couldn't help but feel nervous at the financial strain we were putting ourselves under.

'I think it will be all right. There's plenty of room to prepare a few paddocks for growing crops or vegetables,' he said, staring down the length of the block.

He seemed lost in thought for a moment and it suddenly hit me how beautiful he was to me. He was straight and tall, broad-shouldered and still athletic. His profile was strong and elegant, the firm jaw line and high cheek bones, the long, straight nose, the generous mouth, dark hair slicked back from a wide forehead, grey at the temples and silver strands glinting in the sunlight. The startlingly green eyes were expressive and crinkled attractively under full lashes. Smile lines around his mouth showed that although he was no longer a young man, he still found the best in every day despite everything we'd been through. I wished I'd brought the camera.

'We can make some extra money that way. And I've looked into the costs. The cheapest option is to build a kit home with fibro. I'll start on the garage straightaway. If I can do it myself, it will cut down on costs and if it goes well, I'll build the house too.'

'I suppose if it gets too much, we can always live in the garage until the house is finished,' I said jokingly.

'I wouldn't do that to you.' He put his arm around me and kissed my cheek. 'Let's find these girls. I bet they're down the back. There's a lot to do and we'd better get started.'

Walking along the track into the bush at the back of the block brought back echoes of how I'd felt in the Blue Mountains. It was as if we'd entered another world. Although only a small patch rested within our fence line, the trees extended across the backs of the neighbouring blocks and into the larger farms behind us. Everything else was cleared for farming.

'This was what the landscape must have once looked like,' I said to Erich as we stood in the woodland, surrounded by muted green foliage and soft grey trunks of the gum trees. 'It's so different to what we're used to. I wonder how long it's been here.' I still missed the lush, verdant forests of Germany and the orderly patchwork of meadows but there was something beautiful about the Australian bush that I couldn't put my finger on.

'Forever.'

I nodded in agreement. That was it. It felt timeless. The unmistakable and primordial laugh of a kookaburra punctuated the silence and reverberated through the bush, making us both smile.

With every trip to the farm, walking among the trees still conjured up that feeling: a state of grace, of oneness with nature. When I wasn't helping to fix fences, build the chicken coop or erect the garage with Erich, Ernst, Franz and our families, I couldn't help but take photos of the activity and the countryside around us. No matter how hard I tried, I knew that somehow I could never quite capture the essence of the landscape, especially the bush, on film.

But it was then that I realised that we were beginning to put down roots on this little patch of paradise and that, one day, we would call it home.

9

Erich took Johanna to help him at the farm, waving goodbye as Bella, our Alsatian dog, barked joyously on the back of the ute. It was muggy when they left, the sky low with heavy pewter clouds that threatened rain.

Erich had corn growing in the paddock that he had cleared and tilled, borrowing tractors and machinery from neighbours and friends. It had stunk for weeks after he applied manure he'd procured from one of the dairy farms near Camden but now the corn was almost ready for harvest, tall and green, the kernels beginning to turn from white to golden yellow. Selling our produce by the side of the road or possibly at the markets would be a good source of extra money.

How Erich could turn his hand to anything and make a success of it constantly surprised me. The fibro garage was almost finished, we were just waiting on the doors, and we'd started to plan when we could afford to begin on the house.

Johanna missed no opportunity to go out to the farm with Erich. I would have loved to go with them. But today I had more important things to attend to. It was Johanna's birthday – she was turning twelve. I wanted to make a Black Forest torte for when friends came for coffee and cake this afternoon. Greta was at Anna's, doing a school project. She would come home later to help Mutti and me clean up and get ready for Johanna's birthday party.

I glanced out the window and saw fat drops of rain beginning to fall, the leaves on the rosebushes drooping under their battering force. I hoped Greta had remembered her raincoat. As if on cue, sheets of water cascaded mercilessly over the street and garden before me. I groaned – so much for our beautiful garden. I only hoped that the deluge would stop before the plants were damaged beyond repair and that the rain would clear before our guests arrived.

Turning back to the task at hand, I collected the ingredients I needed for the chocolate cake. Mutti was still in bed, making the most of the quiet, but I knew she'd be up soon to help me. Cooking together reminded us of the times we had done so in Germany. I could hardly hear myself think over the pelting rain. Normally I found rain soothing, even powerful rainstorms such as this, but not today.

I could barely concentrate, the rain on the roof sounding like a drumroll, making my nerves jangle and draw tight with tension. The eggs slipped from my hands and the shock of them smashing on the floor made me gasp. Bright yellow yolk and clear whites splashed across the vinyl like one of the girls' splatter paintings. I stared at the oozing contents of the eggs and a shiver ran through me making gooseflesh rise on my arms. I shook my head, took a step back and the feeling passed.

'What was that?' I said out loud. 'I must be more tired than I thought.' I frowned at the mess on the floor, annoyed at myself for making it, and bent to clean it up. 'Mutti!' I called. 'I know you're awake. I'm making coffee if you want some.' That was what I needed, I was sure – a good, strong, hot cup of coffee before I started. Maybe then I could concentrate on what I was doing and not let the rain get to me. It was about an hour later as Mutti and I were cleaning up, the cake in the oven, that there was a knock at the front door. It was still raining but not as heavily as before. I went to answer it.

Otto stood on the porch hunched under an umbrella, his face pale with worry.

'Otto, come in out of the rain,' I said.

He nodded, closing his umbrella and placing it by the door before coming inside.

'*Guten morgen,* Otto. Coffee?' Mutti asked, her head appearing from the kitchen.

'No, thank you, Amelia. I can't stay.' He rubbed his hands as if he were cold, although it was a warm and sticky day. He shifted from foot to foot, his gaze darting nervously about the room.

'What brings you here? Something wrong?' I asked, the back of my neck beginning to prickle.

'I've just had a phone call at the studio,' he said, finally looking at me.

I frowned, waiting for him to tell me, an odd heaviness swirling in my belly.

'It was Liverpool Hospital.'

I grasped his arm. 'Are your family all right?'

'Yes, yes, they're fine,' he said hastily, his eyes sliding away from my face.

I was relieved but the pricking grew stronger and my eyes widened in sudden fear as I thought of another possibility: we had no telephone and any emergency phone calls were directed to the studio.

'It's Erich,' Otto blurted. 'He was in a car accident and he and Johanna are at the hospital. I'm so sorry.'

Suddenly Otto was holding me up and Mutti was by my side, easing me onto a chair.

'Are they all right?' I croaked, my voice not working very well.

'Johanna is fine, just some cuts and bruises but ...' He looked to Mutti before crouching down beside me, his grey eyes steadfast on mine. 'Erich was injured quite badly.'

The room swam before me, and there was a roaring in my ears.

'Lotte!' Mutti was shaking me by the shoulders. 'Come on. Otto will take you to the hospital. Do you want me to come?'

I stared into my mother's drawn face. 'The cake will burn.' I looked at Otto. 'It's Johanna's birthday.'

'Yes, I know.' He put his hand on my shoulder. It was warm and comforting. 'I'll take you to the hospital and wait with you as long as you need.'

'I'll stay and watch the cake and wait for Greta to come home,' said Mutti, smoothing my hair.

'All right,' I said, my voice coming from a long way away. 'I'll just get my handbag.'

*

Johanna sat on a bed in the emergency ward looking tiny and vulnerable. My breath caught at the sight of her. My poor, poor darling girl! She was pale, the same colour as the bandage wrapped around her head. The left side of her face was red and swollen, her cheek smeared with dried blood. Her bottom lip was puffy, a dark crust surrounding a cut, and her long blonde hair was matted with blood, which was also caked around her ear. Blood had dripped onto her top, staining the blue fabric with dark blotches.

I didn't know if I wanted to vomit and collapse in relief or distress and my heart clenched at the thought of what she had gone through. It could have been so much worse, I told myself. The doctor had told me that besides a number of superficial cuts, grazes and bruising, Johanna had sustained a deep gash to her forehead, which they had cleaned and stitched. Although she had a terrible headache, she was alert and could go home with me.

'*Schätzchen*,' I whispered, holding her tightly against me. 'It's all right now. I'm here.'

Johanna nodded and sagged against me as I perched on the edge of the bed. I kissed her lightly on the top of her head and put my arm gently around her. I never wanted to let her go.

I squeezed my eyes shut to prevent the tears from falling. What would I have done if something more awful had happened to her?

'How's Vati?' whispered Johanna.

My chest tightened. 'I don't know.' I felt her stiffen in my arms. 'I'll see him in a minute, but the doctors wouldn't let me see him if he wasn't all right.'

She nodded and burrowed against me further, as if she wanted the world to disappear.

'Mutti, do you know what happened to Bella?'

'I haven't heard.'

She pulled away, tears filling her eyes, dark as the stormy sea.

'Don't worry, my darling. I'll find out. I'm sure she's fine.' I squeezed her hand, wishing I could take away everything that had happened and make this day right for her. A movement caught the corner of my eye and I turned my head to find the doctor ready for me.

'I'll take you to see your husband, Mrs Drescher,' he said.

'I'll be back in a few minutes.' I kissed the top of Johanna's head again, not wanting to touch her face. 'Then Otto will take us home.'

'I'll be all right, Mutti. Give Vati a kiss for me,' she whispered, trying to smile and grimacing as the cut in her lip cracked open, beads of fresh blood blossoming from the wound. I didn't want to leave her side but I squeezed her hand tightly and slipped off the bed to follow the doctor down the aisle.

It seemed to take forever as we walked past the many beds of the casualty department. All I wanted was to see Erich, to touch him and talk to him, to make sure that he was all right. My heart thumped in my chest until I thought it would explode and I was sure I was going to be sick. I wiped my clammy hands on my skirt then swallowed hard and tried to steel myself for what I would find.

The doctor stopped outside a closed curtain towards the end of the ward and turned to me.

'Your husband has sustained a number of fractures to his right leg,' he said in a low voice. 'It was a terrible accident and he lost a lot of blood, but he has no internal injuries that we can see. He's lucky to be alive, but I won't pretend that he has an easy road ahead.'

Relief swamped me, making my knees turn to jelly. Erich was safe and out of immediate danger. I wanted to rip the curtain open and see him with my own eyes.

'Can I see him?' My hand was already on the fabric.

'Of course, but only for a moment. He's groggy from the painkillers and may not be very alert.' He put a hand on my shoulder and, surprised, I jerked my head around to find his brows creased in concern and his hazel eyes filled with compassion. 'Now, I want you to know that he looks as he did when he was brought in, so don't get a shock when you see him. The nurses will be in to put him in a hospital gown and tidy him up to prepare him for his move to the orthopaedic ward shortly. I'll be back to answer any questions you might have. After that, just ask the doctor looking after him on the ward.'

'Thank you, doctor.'

I drew the curtain back just enough to squeeze through and took a deep breath to control the urge to throw myself onto my husband, weeping with relief and shock. Erich lay back on the bed, his eyes closed, dark lashes stark against the waxen pallor of his skin. I could see from the set of his mouth that he was in pain despite the medication they had given him. His leg, supported and encased on three sides by a plaster splint cushioned with layers of cotton, lay on top of the sheet. His trouser leg was cut away and my hand flew to my mouth in horror at the twisted, mangled mess before me. The leg sat at an odd angle with the white end of the bone of his upper leg poking through, bare against the red of the open wound. Blood covered his leg, which was swollen and discoloured. It didn't look real, a macabre prop from a horror movie.

'Oh, my love,' I whispered. I couldn't imagine his leg ever being right after this. In fact, I couldn't imagine him ever using it again.

The long lashes fluttered and his eyes opened, the brilliant green dull and clouded with pain, drugs or maybe both. 'Lotte.' His voice was groggy.

'I'm here, my darling.' I moved quickly to his side and held the limp hand above the sheet. It was cold despite the hot, humid February day. 'You're in good hands now.'

'Johanna?'

'She's fine. Just a couple of bumps and scratches. I can take her home with me. Otto's waiting for us.' His luxuriant brown hair, streaked with silver, fell over one eye. I brushed it back into place, my hand lingering on his head. It was beaded with sweat. His eyelids drooped and I wanted nothing more than to hold him tight and kiss his eyelids and his mouth and tell him that everything would be all right.

'I'm so sorry.' He said it so quietly I almost missed it.

Tears prickled my eyes and I blinked them furiously away in case he opened his and saw me crying. 'Just come home to us. Get better and we'll be back to normal before you know it.' He gave no response and I wondered if he had slipped into sleep.

Then he squeezed my hand ever so lightly. 'I'll never leave you,' he murmured. 'I love you.'

The curtains parted and two nurses entered.

'I'm sorry, Mrs Drescher, it's time for you to go. The doctor's waiting to speak to you and we have to get your husband ready for the ward. Come back tomorrow in visiting hours. I'm sure he'll feel a lot better then.'

'I have to go now, my darling.' I kissed him on the lips. 'I'll come to see you tomorrow. I love you too.' His lips were cold as well, like kissing a stone carving. I repressed a shudder. I might have been kissing a corpse, kissing my husband goodbye ... I sent a silent prayer of thanks for Erich's deliverance.

With my hand on the curtain, I turned to look back at him one more time, to make sure he was all right. I couldn't bear to be parted from him. Watching the nurses work with careful efficiency around his bed, I knew he was in the best hands possible and yet I felt like I was abandoning him. I should be by his side, there to care for him myself, not leaving him in the hands of strangers.

Erich looked at me a moment longer and nodded slightly. Then his eyes closed, a spasm of pain flitting across his face as the nurses began to cut away his trousers.

I could do nothing for him now and Johanna needed me. I slipped through the curtains, willing myself not to cry.

The doctor waited for me, face impassive but sympathy in his eyes. He took my arm and drew me away from Erich's cubicle just a little.

'His leg – how did he get so terribly injured when my daughter has only cuts and bruises?'

'A cement truck swerved on the Hume Highway, lost control and ran head-on into your husband's utility.'

I nodded, trying to imagine how it happened but not quite understanding. 'But how is my daughter still walking?'

The doctor looked at me and I got the feeling that he was assessing how much he should tell me. I tried to appear calm and composed, rearranging my features into a neutral expression.

'What I was told was that your husband flung himself across your daughter to stop her from going through the windscreen before the truck hit them. He saved her from serious injury or possible death. She must've still hit the dashboard with her head. But your husband would have suffered life-threatening injuries or been killed outright if he'd stayed upright behind the steering wheel. His actions saved them both.'

Tears filled my eyes as pride and love blossomed hot in my chest. Erich's desire to protect Johanna and his quick thinking had kept them both safe. He was selfless, he always had been. 'How is my husband, then?'

'Despite his blood loss, your husband is medically stable. Amazingly, the main injury was sustained just to that right leg.' The doctor shook his head in wonder. 'However, from what we've seen and checked on X-ray, those injuries are severe. He has a comminuted fracture of his fibula, unstable transverse and oblique fractures in his tibia and femur and he also has an open compound fracture of the femur.

'I know it's a lot to take in. He'll require a long period in traction to allow those bones to knit and heal. The important thing is that we avoid infection. Once we have union of the bone – that means that the fractures have healed and the bones are stable and whole – the process of rehabilitation begins.'

'How long will he be in hospital?' I whispered, feeling the weight of the world descend on my shoulders.

'I suspect it will be anywhere from six to eight months, perhaps more if there are complications.'

Everything around me seemed to fade into the background as my head began to spin with the implications of that statement. I felt a hand on my arm and looked up to see the doctor peering into my face.

'Are you all right, Mrs Drescher?'

I nodded and swallowed hard, squaring my shoulders as I collected myself. I had to be strong. 'How long until he can walk?' I had to know what I was dealing with.

The doctor shook his head. 'If all goes well, it may take a year or two before he can walk again, but we won't know until then whether he'll get full use of the leg. There are so many breaks and his injuries are severe . . .' His voice trailed off.

'I have to know, doctor,' I said in a low voice. I thought of poor Carmela struggling at home with the children and her handicapped husband. Prospects were not good for Giovanni, who was still unable to provide a decent income for his family. But although I wanted to scream in frustration and rage that such a thing had happened to Erich and our family, I felt a calm wash over me. My survival instinct took over. I was the one who had to keep our family afloat.

He nodded, glancing towards the cubicle where Erich lay, as if he could see through the pale blue curtains, and then his hazel eyes rested on me. 'It's early days, and perhaps too soon to tell, but I've seen these kinds of injuries before and I want to warn you that there is the possibility that he may never walk again.'

'I see.' My heart lurched to my throat. But I couldn't contemplate that possibility right now. The main thing was that Erich was alive and safe.

'I'm so sorry. We'll do everything we can to ensure the best outcome possible.'

I nodded, murmuring my thanks before turning away, numb.

Walking the corridor, each step taking me further away from Erich, I felt separate from the world, contained in a bubble of shock and disbelief. The curtains and beds swam in and out of focus as I found my way back to Johanna. I had to concentrate on her; to think about Erich's condition was too terrifying for the moment. Somehow I had to stay strong. It was time to take her home and lavish all my love and attention on her, while trying desperately not to feel so helpless, trying not to think about what was going to happen to us now.

Otto took us to look for Bella. Johanna was inconsolable, desperate to find the dog, and wouldn't calm until we agreed to look for her. She didn't know what had caused the accident and hadn't seen what had happened to Bella. We learnt that the dog hadn't been found on the back of the ute after the crash, so we assumed that she must have jumped off and run away. We drove around the area of the crash, calling her name. Otto and I even walked the streets, enquiring if anyone had seen her. Nobody had.

When I returned to the hospital the following day, it was a rude shock to find Erich trussed up, his leg elevated, bandaged and in traction, two splints and a dizzying array of ropes, pulleys and weights attached to a frame above the bed. He was on an eight-bed ward, each cubicle curtained off from the other to afford some privacy, but I could still hear the sounds of men hawking and coughing. The smell of hospital disinfectant was strong, no doubt masking the smells of closely confined, immobile men.

At home, I fussed over Johanna as a way to avoid thinking about Erich's condition and the future ahead of us. In the early weeks she woke most nights with nightmares about the accident and Bella, but once the shock wore off and the pain from her injuries had receded, it was obvious she didn't want me to coddle her any longer.

After that, most nights I went to bed trying to work out how our finances would stretch. We had the rent to pay, the block of land to pay off, payments on the ute and the fridge, just to start with. No matter how I reconfigured the numbers, I always fell short. At least Erich's hospital stay was covered by our health insurance, so I could breathe easy knowing he had the best care for as long as he needed it. However, I didn't know how long he would be in hospital. Although his job was gone owing to the amount of time he would have off, he'd been promised work on his return – if that was even a possibility.

I needed to either reduce our expenses or find a way to make more money. As far as I could see it, we had to sell the farm or I had to find more work, something that didn't need a car to get to, because it would be months before we could buy another car from the insurance. At least Reinhardt had kindly allowed me to borrow one of his cars to do the weddings on Saturdays. Some nights I fell asleep, too exhausted to worry any longer, but other nights I cried myself to sleep. This wasn't the life we had wanted for ourselves. All our plans for the future were in disarray and it was up to me to work out our next step.

It was a week or so before I took the girls to see their father. Erich was on so much heavy medication that he dozed on and off through my visits and I didn't want them to see him in such a bad state. When I did take them, Greta and Johanna were nervous about going near him, worried they would bump the intricate apparatus and hurt him.

'Come on, my girls,' said Erich in his brightest voice despite the pain he was still in. 'I won't bite. I've been waiting all day to get my hugs from you both. '

'But, Vati, what about your leg and all this?' said Greta tentatively, waving her hand at the ropes and pulleys. Johanna stayed by my side holding my hand tightly, watching her father warily.

'It's all right. Just stay on my left side. Here,' he said, patting the bed next to him, 'come and sit with me and tell me what's been going on. How's school?'

Greta looked at me hesitantly and I nodded, smiling. She sat carefully by her father's side and hugged him gently. I noticed Erich's subtle grimace as the mattress moved under her weight and jarred his body ever so slightly.

'It's all right, Vati.' Greta had gone very pale herself. 'How are you?'

'I'm much better now that you're here.' Erich smiled at her, brushing the dark hair from her face.

'Really, Vati. How are you?' she repeated, frowning slightly at him.

149

Erich sighed, his shoulders slumping a little. 'I'm still in some pain and a bit uncomfortable with this traction but better than I was. It's going to take time, but I'll be all right in the end.'

She nodded thoughtfully and began to tell him about her day, trying, I'm sure, to distract him from his pain.

'What about you?' Erich asked Johanna a little while later. She was now standing next to the bed, enticed by Greta's story and keen to add her perspective on what her sister had been telling him.

Johanna's face fell and her bottom lip began to wobble. 'We can't find Bella. I've looked everywhere, calling and calling, but she never comes.' Greta had told me that Johanna walked the streets after school, looking for Bella.

'Come here so I can give you a hug.' Erich kissed Greta on the head and she slid off the bed to allow Johanna to climb up beside him. He clasped Johanna to him, glancing at the dressing still covering her forehead. Much of the swelling in her face had subsided but purple and green bruising ringed her right eye and discoloured her cheek and upper jaw. The cuts and grazes were dark with scabs but healing well. 'Bella will be all right. I don't think she was hurt in the accident but she would have been lost. She's probably found a good home by now.'

'But she's our dog and her home is with us!' Johanna's tiny voice nearly broke my heart.

Erich looked at me helplessly. I shrugged and shook my head. I had done everything to find her but Johanna couldn't accept that Bella wasn't coming home. The look between us confirmed what we both knew – Bella was likely killed in the accident, thrown from the ute – but neither of us wanted to traumatise the girls any further.

'Shh, now,' said Erich, patting her back. 'Keep an eye out for her when you walk home from school. Maybe one day, she'll find her way back to us. In the meantime, Mutti and Mr Weber have given out their telephone numbers. If anyone sees her, they'll call.'

'I know, Vati.' Johanna wiped the tears welling from her eyes. 'She wouldn't have run away on purpose. The accident scared her.'

'What happened?' asked Greta quietly, standing next to the bed. 'The accident . . . how did it happen?'

Erich stared at the curtain opposite his bed. 'There was a boy crossing the highway in that terrible rain. It was hard to see anything. The concrete truck was coming towards us but couldn't stop in time. It swerved to miss him, lost control and hit us instead.'

I knew he was playing that moment over, wondering if he could have done anything different. We had discussed it at length but there was nothing – we were just lucky that neither of them had died that day.

'Vati leant across me so I wouldn't go through the wind-screen,' said Johanna softly, holding her father's hand. She kissed his cheek. 'Thank you, Vati, for keeping me safe.'

Erich buried his face in Johanna's hair, pulling Greta into his side, to hug them both.

I blinked away tears. That day could have ended so differently. Although I didn't know how we were going to manage with Erich off work for so long, at least we were all still alive and together. I couldn't let the weight of our situation crush me and make me forget how lucky we really were. We'd somehow work the rest of it out, I knew that much, and all I could do now was to take one day at a time.

We visited Erich every day after work. I'd go home to have a quick bite to eat with Mutti and the girls and then we'd walk up to the hospital to spend an hour or so with him. On Saturdays I'd go whenever I could between wedding bookings, but it was Sundays that Erich and I most looked forward to, when we could spend longer together.

Sometimes Mutti would come to the hospital with us but otherwise she stayed at home to clean up after dinner or supervise the girls. I knew she was worried about me but she said very little. I was amazed at her self-control because usually she'd be bursting to give me her opinion and advice on what I should do. She seemed to be more sensitive to my feelings since she'd arrived and had only occasionally spoken out of turn about Erich or our situation here in Australia. Maybe she'd really changed but I noticed the sorrow in her eyes from time to time and wondered if it had more to do with the guilt she carried about losing the money that would have changed our lives. There wasn't much she could do for me, except continue to help out at home and keep an eye on the girls, but even her silent support was a blessed relief. It gave me time to think through my options.

10

It soon became apparent that we couldn't manage on one income. I tried everything I could – working longer hours, seven days a week between the studio and my retouching and colouring, and juggling the bills – but it wasn't enough. Thank God I had Mutti at home with the girls, because I was barely there. When I did have time, I was visiting Erich in the hospital.

About a month after the accident, I finally faced the inevitable. Visiting hours were almost over and we'd exhausted the small talk. Erich knew how dire our financial situation was but I felt we couldn't delay making a decision any longer. After all the hard work we'd done to get ahead, we were almost back to where we started.

I shifted restlessly in my chair and took a deep breath in then blew out a long sigh. 'We have some decisions to make,' I said quietly. None of the options we had were good.

'We'll get through this, I promise you.' Erich's hand rested on my forearm, warm and solid, but the anguish in his eyes was heartbreaking. 'I will make this right.'

'I know.' I picked at the fluff on the cotton blanket uneasily.

'We can sell the farm. It will give us some flexibility until I can return to work.'

I glanced up in surprise to find his face impassive, his resolute eyes the colour of the ocean, watching me. The farm and what we could do with it meant so much to him – and to me too, I'd realised, once we'd started going out every Sunday. To give it up before we'd even lived there meant sacrificing yet another of our dreams.

'Are you sure?' I placed my hand over his, still resting on my arm. 'You love the farm . . . It's what you really wanted.'

'I won't put you under any more stress than I already have. We'll just have to start saving again when we can.' He sighed, shifting slightly on the bed. 'We can't go back to those days in Germany of not being able to put food on the table. I won't have you and our children in that situation ever again. It defeats the purpose of coming to Australia and I won't have it.' His jaw muscles clenched and tightened, the fierce emotions warring with cool logic. He'd had time to think about our choices and although I didn't like it, selling the farm was probably the best way forward. But now that it had been said out loud, it didn't feel right.

There was another option I'd been considering, one I knew that Erich would never think of himself. It would make life more difficult rather than better in the short term, but perhaps we could keep our dream alive.

'Let's move out to the farm the way it is.'

'No.' Erich jerked his hand free. 'No. That's not a possibility.'

I leant forward, my elbows on the bed. 'Why not? The garage is liveable. When you come home you can do more to it, make it comfortable until we can build the house. I can make do, you know that.' To me, this choice felt like hope and not failure.

'But I don't want you to.' He frowned at me. 'You deserve more. Besides, it's too hard to travel into Liverpool every day.'

I only stared back, unflappable. 'It'll be fine. I'll go in on the bus in the morning with the girls. They can either wait for me at the studio of an afternoon or do their homework with Anna and Peter until I can collect them. I know Claudia and Franz won't mind. Or they can come home on their own. They're old enough, after all. And it won't be much longer until we have the money from the insurance for another car.'

'It sounds like you've thought this through.' He sat rigid against the pillows, as if he was made of glass and would shatter at any moment.

'This feels right – all our hard work won't have gone to waste.'

'But we have no electricity or water out there. You can't live like that. How would your mother ever cope?'

Erich was intent on dissuading me, sure that this was a silly fancy he could put to rest without too much trouble. But I knew it could work. I took his hand in mine. It felt stiff and unyielding.

'I know you want to protect me and the children. I know you feel terribly guilty for putting us in this situation, but none of it's your fault. Now we have to make the best of it and if that means we suffer a little discomfort while you're suffering from your injuries in this hospital room, well, so be it.' Erich opened his mouth to disagree but I didn't let him get a word in, squeezing his hand as I continued. 'It'll only be for a while and won't hurt any of us. Once you're back on your feet, I know you'll make it comfortable with all the amenities we need and then we can look at building the house. I'm sure we'll have a lovely home then and maybe the children will appreciate it more for having to live through its building.' I wanted to show him that I could look after our family too and make decisions that would benefit us all. Unfortunately, it required Erich to swallow his pride and let go of his guilt.

'No, I can't do this to you.' He shook his head, pulling his hand away again.

'I'm thirty-five next week. I think by now I can decide what I can and can't manage.' I was trying not to be angry with him. I had expected his resistance, after all, and losing my temper wouldn't get me what I wanted.

'This is a decision we make together and I don't like it. It won't work.'

'How do you know it won't work until you look at what we have to do to make it work? You've always taken care of me and protected me but now it's time for you to let me do this for you and our family. It makes no sense to sell the farm. You light up when you go out there, you come home happy and smiling after a day working on the block. It's the right place for the children to grow up, in the fresh air and with plenty of space to run around . . . And you must know

I like it too. It's peaceful and tranquil. I think we'll be very happy there.' I smiled smugly. It would be hard for him to argue against that.

'This,' he viciously gestured to his leg, trying to keep his voice down, 'changes everything. It's a fact of life now and any amount of dreaming and wishful thinking won't change our situation. The hard truth remains that what you're suggesting is an impossibility.'

I blinked back tears. His words broke my heart, because there was no doubt as to how deeply he was suffering. In his eyes, the accident had made him useless and, worse still, a burden.

'Besides, you wouldn't manage out there on your own. There's too much to do and it's all hard work, not something I want you to do. No, it won't be happening.' He was breathing heavily, trying to keep a lid on his fury. He was a stubborn man but I understood how devastated he felt, placing us in this position, unable to give me the life he thought I wanted. I knew Erich harboured guilt about being unable to give me the life I was accustomed to after the war. But the truth was that all I had ever wanted was him.

Now I wanted him home with me and I wanted him to be happy. A beautiful home and household goods were wonderful but paled into insignificance after the accident. I could've lost him and my gorgeous girl that day. Nothing could ever make such a loss right, not all the money in the world. I could be just as stubborn as him and he was about to discover that I wasn't going to give in to his damaged pride. This was best for our family and I knew it.

'I want to do it.'

'The garage isn't finished and we need a kitchen, running water and a toilet, for a start. You wouldn't put our children in those conditions.'

'You've got the time to work out what we need to do,' I said icily. 'When I come in without the children next, we can talk about how to make it happen.'

'You'll be sorely disappointed,' Erich growled. If he could have got out of that bed, he would have. 'There's nothing to think about.'

'You're a stubborn man. If you think about it, you'll see that it can be done. Stop trying to shelter me. I'm the one who has to do it and it's what I want to do.'

The following week we all visited Erich, bringing the cake Mutti had made for my birthday, so we could celebrate together. By the time we were finished it was late and nearing the end of visiting hours, so Mutti took the girls home while I stayed a while longer. I was a regular now and the nursing staff turned a blind eye to my presence after visiting hours.

'Have you thought any more about the farm?' I asked casually, moving the vase of flowers the girls had picked for him to one side of his bedside table. The small bunch of asters and white daisies made the cubicle feel more cheery and less impersonal. There were also vases of deep purple, orange and yellow dahlias mixed with pastel roses, and a couple of magnificent red gladioli in a vase. Flowers he had planted himself that were now blooming with a riot of colour.

'I have,' he said gruffly.

'And?' I sat in the chair by the bed.

'If you refuse to stop being so stubborn, I suppose I might have to see how we can make it work.' Just like a man to take his wife's idea and call it his own. At least the spiced apple cake had done its job and Erich was in a more amiable mood.

'How would we go about that?'

'Enough problems for today.' he said. 'Let's not discuss it tonight. It's your birthday after all.'

I stared into his eyes and saw this was not the time to push him.

'All right,' I said. 'I suppose you need some time to work out the details.' I smiled prettily back at him and he laughed.

He pulled me closer to him. 'So it's like that, is it?'

We were interrupted by the nurse sliding open the curtain. 'Everything all right, Mr Drescher?'

'Yes, thank you.'

'Here's your medication for the night.' She placed four fat tablets onto Erich's palm, handing him a cup of water. Erich dutifully popped them in his mouth and took a sip of water. She bustled around the bed, checking on his leg and the traction and writing in his notes while Erich waited calmly for her to leave, his gaze sliding across to me from time to time.

'Visiting hours are over soon, Mrs Drescher,' the nurse said, smiling at me. Her white hat sat stiffly upon her head and her starched apron crinkled as she moved. 'Just close the curtains as you go. There's always activity on the ward at night. See you both tomorrow.'

'Thank you, Sister Evans,' Erich said. He shuffled a little to get more comfortable before resting back on the pillows. He took my hand and brought it to his lips. 'Happy birthday, my *liebling*.'

My pulse began to race. Weeks of being cooped up in a hospital bed hadn't dampened his ardour. If anything, it had increased.

'I'm sorry I can't give you the present I wanted to give you,' he whispered.

I leant in, kissing him on the mouth, and his hand reached behind my head, drawing me closer as he responded with a passionate kiss of his own, one that dispelled any doubt I might have had about his meaning. He released me slowly, a smile spreading across his face.

'What?' I murmured, wishing we were at home in the privacy of our bedroom.

'I have something else in mind for you.' He patted the bed beside him. 'Come a little closer so I can show you.'

It took a second for me to realise what he meant.

'No!' I whispered, horrified. 'What if the nurse comes in?'

'She won't. I've had my medication. They won't come in unless they have to. They're busy with more demanding patients than me.' He took my arm, pulling me towards him. 'It'll give me something to think about to break the tedium until I see you next.'

'Don't be so ridiculous,' I said, mortified, but I didn't pull away. I couldn't resist those magnetic eyes, even after all of these years, and I sat on the bed beside him.

'Now, I can't move much,' he whispered into my ear, 'but I still have the full use of my fingers.' He pulled the blanket over me, his hand reaching under the covers. I gasped as his palm grazed my nipples and caressed the curves of my body, moving lower until he had found his mark. I gritted my teeth. I couldn't make a sound. It had been so long and he knew exactly what I needed. I closed my eyes and suddenly I didn't care where I was as my body arched and I surrendered to his loving touch. I was molten liquid, as though my body had been heated until fire sang through my veins and I had dissolved.

Gradually I felt reason return to me, my body solid upon the bed.

'I can't believe you did that here,' I muttered, trying to sit upright, smoothing my dishevelled clothes.

'Why not? Nobody disturbed us. Maybe we should make this a regular thing? Mmm?' Erich's hands were resting behind his head and he wore a look of satisfaction on his face. 'I need to entertain myself, after all . . . Unless you didn't like it, of course.'

'You know I did.' I glared at him, not sure how to feel. Shock, embarrassment and excitement all warred within me, as well as relief that nobody had discovered us. I slid off the bed and back onto the chair like a pool of honey, eyes trained on the curtain in case someone walked in.

'Well then, I think that's settled.' Erich's green eyes sparkled with a brightness I hadn't seen for some time. Maybe it had been worth the risk, just to see the light in his eyes.

Erich and I continued to fight over the idea of moving to the farm. I wouldn't budge and, in the end, the fact that we couldn't continue to pay the rent and the mortgage on the block forced Erich to yield. It wasn't ideal, but eventually our plans consolidated until I realised it was really going to happen.

The girls loved coming to the hospital and, after exhausting the conversation of what they'd been doing since last they saw him, they'd leave me to go over the details of the move with their father. Greta was intrigued by the injuries of the various men on the ward, and followed the nurses around like a puppy, asking questions, or sitting quietly watching their routine. She and Johanna both enjoyed watching the television on the ward. It was a luxury and novelty to them, and this was the only place they could watch the shows they talked about with their friends at school But between working and what we needed to do on the farm so that we could live there, the time I could manage at the hospital was getting shorter and shorter.

Mutti insisted on taking some of the load off my shoulders by doing the shopping during the week. It was one less thing for me to think about. I tried to make sure one of the girls was able to go with her most days, but sometimes she was on her own. At first I was worried, her English wasn't good, but she promised to stick to the list I made for her and assured me that she would show the list to the shop assistant if she was unsure.

I thought no more about it until some weeks later.

'Do you think you could come with me to the delicatessen during your lunch break?' said Mutti.

'Why?' I was rushing out the door to get to work on time.

'I want to make a special meal for you and the girls but I can't find the right cheese. Maybe you can help me find one that's similar.'

'Can't the shop assistant do that for you?' I picked up my handbag from the table.

'No, I can't explain it properly.' I glanced across to Mutti and frowned. I really didn't have time but I knew how she worried about being misunderstood.

'All right.'

At the delicatessen, Mutti explained to me what she was after, which I translated to the shopkeeper behind the counter. He was patient enough, allowing Mutti to try a few different cheeses until she found what she wanted. But I did notice the woman waiting behind us begin to get restless, muttering under her breath.

Finally we made our purchases and the woman rushed to the counter, glaring at us. It was then that I saw a man waiting by the door, staring. I ushered Mutti out, hoping she hadn't noticed his expression. Something about him reminded me of the man I'd encountered at the train station when the girls and I had travelled from Bonegilla to Sydney. It was hatred, I realised with a flash of recognition, and I had no desire to become the target of his anger.

'Hey!' shouted a voice behind us. I slipped my arm around Mutti's waist.

'Keep walking,' I said to her.

The man from the deli caught up with us. He stopped in front of us and caught a whiff of odour from the cheese Mutti had bought.

'You stinking Krauts,' he said with disgust. Mutti flinched as if she'd been slapped and I could feel my cheeks flame with colour

'You come here and think you own the place but you can't even speak English,' he snarled. People hurried past on the other side of the road, ignoring the angry outburst. 'My wife shouldn't have to wait while you talk amongst yourselves and make up your mind. Show some respect or go back to your Nazi-loving country.'

'Leave us alone,' I said, white-hot anger coursing through me. 'We're decent, hardworking people and we deserve to be here as much as you do.'

He glowered at me, turned on his heel and returned to the delicatessen while Mutti stared in shock.

'Are you all right, Mutti?'

She nodded, shaking like a leaf. I was feeling rather light-headed myself.

'Come on, I'll take you home.'

We were nearly home before she was able to speak.

'How can people be so cruel? What's wrong with this country?'

'The same thing happened to me not long after we arrived, but there are narrow-minded bigots wherever you go.'

The terrible encounter of three years earlier had come flooding back and with it the feelings of disbelief and utter humiliation. I couldn't protect myself or my children from that vicious verbal attack but now I could stand up for myself. I thought about how far I'd come since that time. My English was good now and I was managing on my own with Erich in hospital, something I'd never envisaged back then.

'Only ignorant, primitive people behave this way,' she said, her outrage taking over. At least she was getting over the shock.

'Don't take it to heart. Australians are mostly kind and friendly. The stationmaster's wife helped me that day and look at how Suzanne loves you.'

'I never thought it would be this difficult.'

'It will get easier but I think that until you feel confident on your own, one of us will come shopping with you.'

'I'm sorry, Lotte. All I wanted to do was help.'

I squeezed her hand, swallowing the lump in my throat. 'But you do.'

After Erich's accident there had been little time to even think about what was happening on the farm, let alone head out there to do anything.

It was past harvest time when we finally got out there. The corn crop had been destroyed. The cobs were mouldy, shoots sticking out from the sprouted seeds, and some were fermenting and rotting in their husks. I was told by one of the neighbours, a farmer, that it was because of all the rain we'd had. It was such a waste and I berated myself for allowing it to become ruined. All Erich's hard work had been for nothing and any extra income we were hoping for was lost. All the crop was good for now was pig and cow fodder. I debated whether to leave it in the field to rot as I had so little time or to find a local farmer who would buy it for feed.

It was Reinhardt who once again saved the day. A friend of his who had a dairy near Cobbitty would take the corn – not just the cobs but the stalks too – for his cows and pigs. Reinhardt arranged for someone to cut the corn and trans-port it for a small fee. We didn't make a great amount but at least the paddock was cleared, the corn gone and not wasted.

We wouldn't have managed if it hadn't been for Franz, Claudia and Ernst. Franz, although he had so little time himself between work and studying for his law degree, insisted on driving out to the farm with us on Sundays so we could begin making preparations to move. Franz and Ernst finished off the garage, installing the glass door and two panes of fixed glass where the garage doors would have been. I felt a glow of pride seeing it completed. Erich had made sure it was solidly built on a concrete slab and it looked neat and tidy, white fibro with wood panelling at the apex of the pitched corrugated iron roof to meet the door frame below.

'It's not very big,' said Claudia. We were standing inside the garage. It was enough for a single car and a small workshop and I wondered how we'd fit everything in the space.

'It's not for long,' I said, putting on a brave face. 'We'll put the lounge and dining area at the front where you come in the door. I'll partition off the bedroom at the back with the wardrobes and we'll have a small kitchen area next to it.'

'One bedroom for all of you?' Claudia looked at me dubiously.

I shrugged. 'It will have to do for now. We'll fit bunks for the girls and a bed for Mutti.'

'What about you?'

'I'll sleep on the lounge. It's a fold-out and it'll do the job until we can build the house.'

'You're a braver woman than me,' she said, shaking her head.

Franz and Ernst also erected two small sheds at the back of the garage, one around the toilet – a bucket with a toilet seat and lid – and the other to house a bathroom and laundry. Together with Claudia and the children, and even Mutti, we tidied up around the property and prepared the ground to start a small garden to grow as many vegetables as we could to cut down our costs.

The frost in those early mornings of winter made the grass white and it crunched under our feet as we walked across the paddock. It reminded me a little of Germany and made me surprisingly wistful for the days of the first snows, when winter really arrived. Although after the war they'd been our most difficult days, they were also our most treasured. When the snows came, we spent more time indoors as a family. Those days seemed a lifetime ago.

'How are you such an expert at all this work?' I asked Franz and Ernst as I handed them cups of steaming coffee from the thermos. 'Surely there wasn't much call for such skills living in Berlin?'

Franz leant on the shovel, white puffs of mist from his mouth punctuating the still morning air as he held the cup in leather-gloved hands. 'I learnt a great variety of skills and did many different things over the years,' he said loftily, his eyes sparkling.

'Don't listen to him,' said Ernst, sipping the hot liquid. 'I had a farm back in Germany and Franz helped me during many of his holidays.'

'He insisted that I learn the value of manual labour,' said Franz.

'I couldn't let his hands become soft and useless while studying law.'

'No, that would've been a tragedy,' said Franz, rolling his eyes.

'You have no idea what a tragedy it might have been,' Ernst said softly.

Franz shook his head in frustration. 'Leave it be,' he said, glaring at his uncle. There was an undercurrent of bitterness between the two men and I wondered about their relationship. Ernst was good to us, helping get the farm ready to move in, but I knew Claudia didn't care for him. I wondered if he was controlling, like my mother could be.

'Good coffee?' I asked.

'Very good, thank you, Lotte,' said Ernst, 'but at my age, drinking too much of it means I need to visit the trees. Excuse me. I'll be back in a moment.' He put his cup down on a stump and walked towards the tree line.

Franz blew on the surface of the coffee, steam rising into his face, and took a cautious sip. 'Ahh, lovely.' He smiled at me, blue eyes creased into triangles, blond hair falling over his forehead. 'Watch that husband of yours when he gets home.'

The sudden change of subject surprised me. 'What do you mean?' I asked more sharply than I intended. 'He won't be able to do much.'

Franz shook his head. 'No, I didn't mean that, although you'll have to watch that he doesn't do too much too quickly. He'll want to have this place built and organised to perfection before he's in any condition to do it. What I'm talking about is the union. While he's recovering at home, he'll have plenty of time to think about all the injustices still to fight and the best way to fix them. The union won't leave him alone and I know how much the work he can do through them means to him. But I'm worried about some of his associates.' He put his cup on the ground and paused as if unsure what to say next.

I placed my hand on his arm, which was damp with sweat. 'What is it, Franz?'

'I don't want to worry you, but I think it's best that you know. I've spoken to Erich before about this, but there's a risk in him being associated with these men. Not only are they affiliated with the Communist Party, but some of them are members. I'm sure these men are being watched by the government.'

'But Erich isn't doing anything wrong!'

'I know that, but look what happened when he was threatened. It's about who's perceived to be a troublemaker, who pushes the boundaries of established order.'

'Even when those boundaries no longer apply,' I said. 'All Erich wants to do is make equality a reality for everyone, not just those who've lived here for generations.'

'Change comes slowly, Lotte. We're all proud of the things he's pushed for and succeeded in implementing already, but I'd hate to see him in danger and you in any more difficulty than you have already experienced.'

'Thank you, Franz, for your honesty,' I said, not certain if I should feel reassured or worried. I was lucky to have friends who cared enough to tell me the truth. It was a rare commodity that I treasured deeply.

'On that note, I'd better get back to work.' He handed me the cup and smiled before lifting the shovel and digging once more.

Bewildered, I walked away slowly, wondering what to think about Franz's warning. I was proud that Erich was standing up for injustice and doing something about it. He cared and took his responsibility to improve the lives of those less fortunate seriously. I couldn't understand how that made him a threat to anyone.

*

Over lunch one day, Reinhardt invited us to his home for the Queen's Birthday celebrations on the long weekend in June.

'I'll be visiting Erich, packing or at the farm,' I said, lighting up a cigarette. Everyone in the studio smoked and, much to my disgust, I'd finally succumbed to the habit. It helped enormously with my constant state of exhaustion, allowing me to keep going with more energy than I thought I had.

'You're not doing Cracker Night?' Otto looked like there was no greater outrage. 'I know it's an Australian tradition, but it's great fun. We've been doing it for years.'

'No,' I said, sipping my tepid coffee. I had no time or money to waste on frivolities.

'Have you or the children ever been?' Sabine asked. She was working fewer hours at the moment, as she was pregnant again after suffering a miscarriage.

'We've never had the chance,' I said. 'We missed any fireworks display at Villawood the first year we were here and since then . . . we've been too busy.' I couldn't say that we hadn't known any Australians who had hosted Cracker Night. I suddenly felt that we hadn't made enough effort to get to know people socially because we'd been working so hard.

'Your children haven't been to a Cracker Night!' Reinhardt repeated, incredulous, shaking his head.

'Vati has a huge pile of wood ready for the largest bonfire we've ever had,' said Sabine, her eyes shining with enthusiasm. 'Karl can't wait to light the fire and see how big it'll get. He's just a boy at heart.'

'Yes, and we've ordered the best firecrackers,' added Otto, his sandwich forgotten. 'Roman candles, skyrockets and

Catherine wheels. It's going to be loud and smoky but lots of fun.'

'You must bring the children and your mother, of course,' said Reinhardt. 'We're doing it on Sunday evening because of the Saturday weddings and it won't be a late night. We'll have a barbecue and we can stand around the bonfire to keep warm.'

'There's so much to do before we move. I don't know if I'll have time.'

'You'll have all day to do what you have to,' said Otto. 'I'll come and pick you all up around four o'clock. The kids will love it!'

'Yes, you have to come,' said Sabine. 'It's not as much fun without children. Please come.'

She looked at me with such hope that I couldn't say no. Reinhardt and his children were becoming like family to me. And after the last few months, the girls deserved a little treat.

'All right,' I said.

As Reinhardt had promised, the bonfire blazed tall, tiny embers floating golden into the inky sky. We ate Bratwurst sausages cooked on the grill of a barbecue, served so hot they burnt the tips of my fingers, steaming jacket potatoes cooked in the coals and topped with melted butter, and dark bread and sauerkraut, the perfect accompaniments to the crisp night air. Mutti and I were happy enough, full, warm and relaxed, a glass of wine in our hands. The girls were running and laughing, playing tip with the children of the other families that Reinhardt had invited. How long had it been since Erich and I had done something like this? I was determined to make more of our life; there was so much on offer, all we had to do was take it with both hands and enjoy. I wished he were with us.

A bustle of activity intruded on my reverie – Otto, Karl and Reinhardt were making their way to the bonfire, carrying large boxes.

'Time for the fireworks!' shouted Sabine. She laughed as the children rushed to swamp the men as they placed their boxes on the ground.

'Wait a minute,' said Otto, rummaging in one of the boxes. 'Let me put some Catherine wheels on the post while Vati sets up the skyrockets.'

'I'll get the Roman candles ready,' said Karl, just as excited as the children.

Reinhardt set the long sticks attached to the skyrockets into old milk and beer bottles on the ground, a distance away from the fire. 'Not too close, children,' he said, lighting the first skyrocket. Mothers clasped small children to their chests, ready for the loud noises that might scare them, and pulled away older children who wandered too close.

The firecracker flew high through the sky and emitted a loud bang and crackling sound. I jumped at the noise, my heart racing, even though I was expecting it, taken straight back to the war and the gunfire that had become a part of life. Golden stars shot out of the cracker, eliciting oohs and ahhs from the crowd below. I breathed out slowly, pressing my shaking hands to my thighs. Mutti stood rigidly beside me, her eyes staring into the distance, and I knew that she had relived the same memories. I took her arm and felt the tiny vibrations that racked her body begin to ease. We weren't in a warzone but in the Australian countryside, celebrating life and our good fortune to live in this peaceful land, far from the chaos of Europe.

Otto lit a Catherine wheel. It began to whizz and spin, a sparkling circle of silver and gold. Karl handed Sabine the first Roman candle, planted a kiss on her mouth and whispered in her ear. Hand over her belly, Sabine looked tenderly at her husband. The children were silent with anticipation, all eyes resting on the cracker, as she positioned it away from her while Karl lit it. A shower of red sparkles streamed from the top and Sabine laughed with joy.

The men continued to light one firecracker at a time, waiting just long enough between them to get the maximum anticipation out of the crowd. I looked forward to telling Erich about the night when I saw him next, although I knew the children would be fighting to tell him first.

'Look at the children.' I leant in to Mutti so she could hear me above the noise. 'They're loving it.'

She smiled broadly. 'What a wonderful way to grow up. They're very lucky.' She squeezed my hand. 'I can see why you and Erich came here. They're so happy and healthy and don't have a worry in the world.'

Tears sprang to my eyes as I watched my girls, the firelight illuminating Johanna's face, turned to the sky in rapture, Greta, standing nearby, was just as mesmerised. We'd done the right thing. I'd always hoped we had, but here was the proof. Australia was home for the girls now and I realised that it was beginning to feel like home for me, too.

11

'**C**an't you wait until I can help you?' Erich said, banging his hand on the bed. He was in a foul mood.

'No, you know we can't,' I snapped back, glaring at him. 'Do you really think I want to do this now and without you? Nobody knows when you'll be able to come home. We have to move, otherwise we sell and we're back to square one.'

The doctors suggested that Erich would require another three months or so of healing and rehabilitation to learn to walk again before they would think about his return home.

'I'll check myself out and come home now, then. I can't do anything useful from here.'

'Don't be preposterous,' I hissed. 'What good are you if your leg doesn't heal properly? If you can't walk, what will you do then?'

'I'll walk, don't you worry. I'll find a way to manage.' Although he kept his voice low, he was furious now, at me, at the situation, at his helplessness. 'Nobody can tell me what I can or can't do.'

I turned away, my hands over my face, grief and anger coursing through my body like a river, hot tears springing from my eyes. I had had enough. I understood Erich's agony, the constant pain, his helplessness. Not only couldn't he help me and his family, he couldn't help himself until the bones in his leg had healed. The only way to make that happen was to remain bedbound, unable to move.

On the other hand, I was exhausted from working long hours, trying to keep our heads above water financially, preparing for the move and ensuring we had everything on Erich's list. I'd ticked off the endless number of chores required to make this move happen and I felt stretched to breaking point – I had no patience left with anyone. I'd begun to resent the fact that I was moving with the children out into the country-side without a car and that we'd be living in primitive conditions without heating, electricity and plumbing. It reminded me – more often than I liked – of the terrible days after the war and the old, dilapidated farm cottage we lived in. We'd left Germany for a better life and here we were, about to live in similar conditions. I was surprised to discover how much it bothered me, since I had been the one who'd suggested it.

'I'm sorry, *liebling*. I didn't mean to upset you.'

Wiping the tears from my face, I turned back to him. My heart seized at the look of remorse on his face. I couldn't imagine how hard this was for him, a man who could never sit still. It was cruel.

'I know. But you have to do whatever you must to get better. I want you back home with us more than anything, but not at the expense of your health.'

'Come here.' He took my hand and drew me to him, so I sat on the bed next to him. 'I know you're doing this for us. I can never thank you enough.'

I kissed him lightly on the lips. 'You can thank me when you come home. We're doing this together, whatever you think ... I could never do it without you. Soon we'll be enjoying our own place, our own home, and this time will be behind us.'

'That's what I love about you – you're the eternal optimist. All right, I'll be good now and trust that you're right.'

'You know I am.'

It was July when we were ready to move in. Franz, Ernst, Otto and Reinhardt helped us. We used Otto's ute and Franz's car to transport our belongings.

It had been hard to say goodbye to Tommy, Suzanne and little Joan but we'd still see them: Suzanne insisted that Mutti come to visit one day a week, and that the girls come after school and do homework, and we stay for dinner whenever we visited Erich. Although I wasn't used to being offered help, her offer would make a great difference to how we'd manage and I was happy to agree. Suzanne and I had become friends despite the age difference. She and Mutti had become close too, and Suzanne valued her advice with managing Joan.

The weekly outing would be good for Mutti. Although she could go in to Liverpool on the bus whenever she wanted,

Mutti wasn't confident yet with her language skills and needed a push to get out on her own. She would really feel the isolation out on the farm. I was pleased that Suzanne would continue to go shopping with Mutti and spend the day conversing in English with her. It was one less thing to worry about.

Moving day was long and filled with backbreaking work. Mutti, Claudia and the children helped move the smaller pieces. I'd spent hours working out the configuration of the space with Erich, so it was relatively easy to divide it into our rooms with wardrobes. But it was going to be tight.

'How are you going to manage?' asked Claudia.

'We'll be okay,' I said. I moved a box of the children's things onto their bunk beds.

She glanced around at the unlined walls and concrete slab, her brows knitted into a worried frown. 'How will you stay warm? It's freezing. You have no electricity.'

'We have a kerosene heater. It'll do a good job. I've made thick curtains for the two windows and we still have our warm eiderdowns from Germany. You watch, it will be homely by the time I'm finished with it,' I said, opening a box that I knew contained a floor rug. I rummaged round in it and pulled out the fluffy orange and red rug. I shook it out and placed it on the floor in the front area. 'See, that looks better already, doesn't it?'

I knew exactly what she was saying but I was trying my hardest to be upbeat, so I couldn't tell her my misgivings. I felt as if that would be a betrayal of Erich. I had to be positive, otherwise we might slide into despair.

Claudia put her hand on my arm. 'Any time you feel like it's too much, please just come to us. You can stay with us for a while if you need to, at least until it's warm enough for you to manage out here.'

'We'll be fine.'

'The children are welcome to stay any time. They get on so well with Anna and Peter that they're just like family. As are you and Erich.'

I nodded, touched by her heartfelt words, and clasped her hand in thanks. They were wonderful friends, perhaps the best we'd ever had. We had been through so much together and they understood what it was like, but I would make this situation work. I wouldn't make Erich feel any worse than he already did.

'Thank you, Claudia. It means a lot to me. I'll keep it in mind.'

'How will you cook and wash? And the clothes? You have no running water.'

I sighed. She wasn't going to let this go. I supposed I wouldn't either if it was my friend. 'We have a camp stove that we'll use for now. Our neighbour has agreed to let us use water from the hose in his yard until we get the water connected, which will be soon, and once the insurance money comes through we can begin on the house. It will all be worth it.' The washing itself would be backbreaking work in buckets and hung out dripping on a line strung between two poles, but I would manage – I had to.

'What if Erich can't return to work? You've said yourself that his leg isn't mending as it should and he's still in a lot of pain. What will you do then?'

This took the wind from my sails and I fell into a chair, my hands over my face. 'I don't know. I can't think too much about that or I'll go mad and won't have the strength to keep going.' I looked up at her. 'I have to do this. The farm will be a good place for Erich to recover and regain his strength. The girls love it here and I feel calm and happy. I *can't* and *won't* let everything we've worked so hard for just slip away.'

Claudia nodded. 'I understand. Just promise me you'll come for dinner every week until Erich comes home. That's one day less you have to cook on that stove.'

'All right.' I smiled. Claudia was a good cook and I would enjoy her meals and her company.

I was touched by the thoughtfulness of our friends and acquaintances. Our move made me aware that we had developed a network of friends, people who were willing to support us and help us through the tough times. This was a new experience for me. Erich and I had always managed on our own, in spite of the odds, and had learnt to rely on each other, strong and independent. We were becoming part of a community and the ties felt good. I began to understand that we were stronger for it.

By the end of the day, the fold-out lounge and armchairs sat in our makeshift living room, a little cramped around the coffee table. Thick beige curtains hung to each side of the glass panels and door, allowing sunlight to stream in, and the orange and red rug covered the cold, grey concrete and added warmth to the room. A small table and chairs intruded into the back half of the space, separated from the small kitchen by a couple of small bookshelves. The bedroom was partitioned off next to the kitchen, the wardrobes giving some privacy from the lounge room and kitchen areas.

Over the following week we emptied the boxes and stacked the bookshelves with things that made a place home: books, photos and ornaments such as the elephant we had bought in Colombo. The radio held pride of place on one shelf and a vase stood on the coffee table. I filled it with wattle, clusters of fluffy yellow blooms bright against the soft bottle green of the vase. I was quite proud of our efforts.

In the kitchen, the stove perched on top of the cupboard where we stored the utensils and crockery. A small esky filled with ice sat on the floor to one side of the cupboard, containing milk, butter and cheese. The small shed that Franz and Ernst had finished building housed the laundry and bathroom. When we had the electricity and plumbing hooked up we would have proper facilities, but for now it would do.

It was October before Erich was discharged from hospital.

'I'll work on my leg at home,' he told everyone convincingly. He used a walking stick to travel short distances and crutches to get around outside. It was wonderful to finally see him out of traction and on his feet but my blood ran cold to see how wasted, thin and disfigured his leg was, even after the constant exercises he did and the long sessions of rehabilitation that totally drained him.

'When can I return to work?' he asked the doctor before leaving hospital.

The doctor looked hesitantly at the physiotherapist, who was arranging a time for Erich's weekly sessions. 'Mr Drescher, you've surprised us all with how well you've done and while your leg is now healed, the bones haven't set as straight as we'd like. You have a shorter right leg, and a knee bent in flexion. This may affect the time it takes for you to gain full function in your leg.'

'How long?'

'It'll be many months before you can stand or walk for longer periods. Only time will tell whether your knee stiffness improves and whether you can walk or use your leg normally again.'

This was the moment I'd been waiting for and my world tilted drunkenly. Thank God I was sitting. Although I knew in my heart that Erich's leg didn't look good, I could never admit to myself that there was a chance he would never use it properly again. What were we going to do? I grasped Erich's hand and squeezed it tightly.

Doubt flickered in his eyes. He had been sure he'd walk normally again. He'd been so determined to prove everyone wrong.

'What about my old job?'

'At the factory?' said the physiotherapist.

'That's right,' said Erich.

'I doubt you'll be able to return to that type of work,' the doctor said. 'The long periods of standing, manoeuvring heavy objects . . . Returning to any work is a long way off. Sitting without support for your leg's still painful, so it may be six months to a year, and even then it will be a graduated return. Maybe you should consider a line of work that doesn't involve manual labour, one that's less stressful on your body.'

Erich's face was pale but no emotion showed on it besides mild interest. 'Thank you, doctor, for your advice.'

That night, as we lay down together on the fold-out lounge burrowed under our eiderdown, I sighed as my toes began to thaw. I'd missed Erich sleeping next to me, but I'd forgotten how he radiated heat like a fire. I was blissfully warm for the first time since we'd moved to the farm.

He tossed and turned, unable to get comfortable. The medication never really gave him good relief, it only took the edge off his pain. We had tried rolled-up towels and pillows to support his leg with varying degrees of success, but now he pushed them to one side.

'What's wrong?' I murmured, sleep tugging at my body.

'Nothing. I just want to be near you.' He wriggled towards me again until we were touching, moving his leg carefully.

The feel of him beside me, the sound of his breath next to my ear, made me realise once again how close I'd come to losing him.

'I missed you. I'm so glad you're home.'

'I've missed you too. I went to sleep every night dreaming about the day I'd be home and lying next to you.' Erich embraced me, his leg awkwardly out to the side.

'There were some days I wondered if this was ever going to happen, but we did it.'

Erich shifted slightly to get comfortable. 'We did, thanks to you. All your hard work's paid off. Everyone's happy.'

'Better than a single bed and a curtain, isn't it?'

I expected a grin but instead he sighed. 'That was the hardest thing, you know. Being apart from you, not being able to touch you and hold you . . .'

I held his face between my hands. 'Don't ever do that to me again.'

'Do what?'

'Don't ever scare me like that again . . . don't ever leave me like that again,' I said, my voice cracking. The pent up emotion of the last few months came rushing out and I wept in his arms, relieved that he was finally home.

He squeezed me tight, making my ribs creak in protest. 'Oh, my *liebling*, if I could take that day back, I would.' He kissed away my tears and we held each other until I fell into an easy sleep.

It was a long, painstaking recovery for Erich. It was wonderful to have him home but it broke my heart to see how slow and difficult his movements were. I knew how determined he was to get back to normal. He never let it stop him, however. He was stubborn like that, pushing himself until he couldn't any longer, his muscles quivering and his face white with pain. It was frustrating for him to see things that needed doing that he couldn't manage. But he was able to chase up the council about getting the utilities connected, and finally we had electricity and hot and cold water. Life was still rudimentary but it was a huge improvement on what we'd had.

Leading up to Christmas, work was busier than ever with studio shoots and weddings as Sabine prepared for the birth of her first child. Even Reinhardt was forced back behind the camera most days, a situation he was willing to put up with until he found a new photographer. I didn't mind the work. It had become routine and standard, not very exciting or creative, but I loved improving my skills and taking the best photographs I could. My dream of one day opening a studio and exercising my creative flair still lurked at the back of my mind, but for now I was happy enough.

That was until Erich received a letter from his oldest child, Eva, just before Christmas. This time of year was always difficult for him with his family still on the other side of the world. Eva had written to us while Erich was in hospital to tell us about her engagement. We were both thrilled for her but it worried me that Erich had time to think about how far away he was from his other children and how unlikely it was that he'd get to her wedding.

'She's getting married in April,' he said softly, as I watched him lower himself carefully into the lounge with the assistance of his walking stick, eyes glued to the page. 'She'd like me to be there.'

'A spring wedding, then.' I left the dining table, where I was colouring photographs, and joined him. 'I know how much you want to be there.' I rubbed his back gently before picking up the jar of ointment to begin the nightly ritual of massaging the tightness from his leg.

I remembered the days when Eva and Walter had lived with us. Despite the awkward situation, they'd adored their new sisters. I was grateful for how wonderful they were with the girls, drawing and singing songs, allowing themselves to be dragged around and even cuddling them on their laps. Eva was already almost a woman then, helpful and kind, and Walter had taken his role as big brother seriously. Now they were grown up and living lives of their own.

'I'd hoped that maybe by some miracle I'd be able to make the trip or that maybe she'd set the date for later in the year but now . . .' He shrugged. 'There's no possible way I can go the way I am.'

'Maybe we can plan a trip once your leg has healed,' I said soothingly. I knew how much he missed them.

'Who knows when that will be?' He pushed hard on his knee, trying to force it to straighten but it was stuck in the same position like a block of concrete.

'It'll happen,' I said, a little alarmed by his heavy-handedness, 'but it's going to take time.' My fingers were greasy and I wiped the excess ointment gently on his knee.

'Let's face it, I'm not much good for anything now.'

'Don't be ridiculous—'

'I couldn't get anything more than factory work before, and now I can't even manage that.' He shifted to get more comfortable and let out a sigh of frustration. 'I don't think I can do this any more.'

I frowned, feeling my heart beat rapidly in my chest. 'What are you talking about? Of course you can, look how far you've come with your leg.'

'No, I can work on my leg but I can't begin again, I'm too old to have to try something new. I think I'm out of options.'

I watched as the fight went out of him, like the air from a balloon. It was true, he was getting older, his fiftieth birthday loomed on the horizon, but to me he was the same as ever: strong, capable and able to adapt to any situation.

'You've managed far worse than this,' I said. 'You're in pain, frustrated and not thinking straight. You'll find the right thing, I know you will, but it's early days. You should be concentrating on getting mobile and strong again.'

He seized my arm. 'We have to face reality, Lotte. I may never get much better than this. You might end up with an invalid on your hands.'

The doctors had warned us shortly after Erich's accident that he might never walk again, but that had been nearly a year ago. The fact that he could was a miracle, a testament to his iron will and determination. But we both realised that it would be a long time before his leg was normal again, if ever. He had to find another job that was less physically demanding.

Blinking tears away, I grabbed him by the shoulders. 'You're not an invalid. The doctors are already amazed by your progress. You'll prove everyone wrong and show them what you're made of.'

I dropped my hands to my lap. I always felt capable of finding a solution to a problem, always knew what to say to inspire hope, but now I didn't know what else to say to him. In the face of his despair, I had no answers.

'Don't cry, Lotte. All I mean is that the promises I made you before we came to Australia have come to nothing. This is all my fault. I haven't given you the life you wanted and I can't give you another child while I'm like this.' He gazed at me with regret. 'I don't want to disappoint you any more.'

I'd had lingering doubt that we would ever have another child, but Erich's accident had made this a reality. It would be hard to accept at first, but I knew the pain and loss would soften to a dull ache. I would cope. I put my arms around him. 'You could never disappoint me.'

'Maybe we'd be better off going back to Germany. I know that's what you wanted.'

'You want to go back? After everything?'

'Nothing's worked out here for us, maybe it's for the best.' His voice was flat and dispassionate.

'But look what we've done here. We've bought a farm, we live in our own house and although it's not much at the moment it's ours . . . The children are happy and thriving and I love my work as a photographer. We didn't have any of that in Germany. We've laid roots, finally.'

'But we need my income and I'm not fit for anything right now and I have no idea what kind of job I'll ever be able to get.'

'We'll cope until you're able to work and you find something, even if you have to go back to study and get some qualifications.'

He ran his hands through his hair. 'I don't want to do that to you. I'm supposed to be the breadwinner and I feel like I'm no man at all, just a broken-down horse who needs to be put out to pasture.' He choked on those last words and my heart broke for him. He couldn't cope with being a kept man. He'd always prided himself on doing whatever he had to, to keep his family fed, comfortable and happy.

'One last time, my darling. Promise me you'll try one more time.'

He stared into the distance and then nodded. 'All right, I'll try.'

12

1961

Erich kept his word and worked hard to improve the flexibility and strength of his leg. He continued his rehabilitation sessions at the hospital, insisting on going to Liverpool on the bus one or two days a week, although his walking was slow and laboured and he struggled to get up and down the steps. During the warm weather, he took advantage of swimming at the public pool. He was doing everything he could, to the point where I wondered if he was pushing his leg too hard, but he was stubborn. All I could do was support him.

Sometimes he'd call in to have a coffee with me during my break or he'd walk around the shops for a short while, talking to shopkeepers he knew, especially those who'd come from Germany or Europe, before catching the bus home.

'What've you been doing?' I asked him one hot February day. I was adjusting the lens of my camera in the lunchroom while we waited for the water to boil. I'd noticed that his sessions always fell on a day that Mutti was home. She came into Liverpool two days a week, spending one day with Suzanne and another day with Claudia's cousin Hildegard, a widowed woman in her forties who had just immigrated and was staying with Claudia and Franz until she was on her feet. They were good company for each other. Mutti's mood was always more cheerful when she returned home after a day out.

Erich gave me a strange look and then shrugged. 'I've been to the library looking for something stimulating to read but I think I prefer to read in German. Then I got talking to another German man at the library. It started with books and jobs and ended up with our childhood and where we grew up.' He smiled. 'And he got me thinking.'

'About what?'

'About something I could do as a new business.'

My head jerked up in surprise and I stared into his eyes. He was serious. My mind began to race at a million miles an hour. I was so focused on work, keeping us afloat and on Erich's recovery that I hadn't considered him going into business for himself, but it made perfect sense. He was driven, methodical and good with people, and he could find something that wouldn't tax his leg.

'What are you thinking?'

Erich looked pleased with himself. 'I've got a few ideas that I have to research. Don't worry, I'll let you know when I have something more concrete.'

*

We were having breakfast at the table one Sunday about six weeks later, the sun streaming in through the glass door. Mutti and the girls had gone into Liverpool. The girls were helping Claudia and her children make Easter ornaments from eggshells while Mutti visited Hilde. It was lovely not to be rushing for a change. The house was quiet and peaceful except for the warbling of magpies over the background chirping of the birds outside. I loved it here surrounded by gum trees and space – our sanctuary.

I looked out the window at the patches of vibrant colour between the soft green of the eucalypts. I missed the riot of red, gold and purple that was everywhere you looked in Germany and the piles of dry leaves crunching underfoot as winter approached, but there were still some signs of the changing seasons here, enough to make me smile when I saw them. It made me realise how much I'd grown to love the evergreen gum and the steady and peaceful flow from one season to the next. I felt that peace in myself now – and I know it showed in the way I looked and held myself. I felt happy and confident. I knew Erich could see it, too, in those moments I caught him looking at me with pride and love in his eyes.

'We'll have been in Australia for five years soon,' I said casually.

'It's gone so fast,' said Erich.

'What do you think about applying for Australian citizenship?' I said, taking a bite of my jam and bread, although now that I had started the conversation I'd wanted to have, I could barely get the mouthful down. My heart began to pound.

Erich stared at me. 'What?'

I took a deep breath. 'We can apply six months before the qualifying residency period of five years. I think we should.'

He put the newspaper down. 'What's brought this on?'

'I think it'll be good for us – for the children. They speak English like Australians and they've lost their accents. With each passing year, they become more Australian. At the very least we have to do it for them, but I think it's right for us too.' I didn't tell him that I thought it would be good for him; he seemed lost now that he was out of work, gravitating to anything German, to what he'd always known.

The truth was that my past life in Germany was becoming a distant and hazy memory as my present took over, demanding all of my attention. I was feeling settled and had begun to fall in love with Australia. The move to the farm had unexpectedly made me realise that I wanted to stay.

Erich was watching me intently, his green eyes narrowed, jaw tight with tension. 'I don't see why we need citizenship. We can do all the things we want without that. What if we want to go back to Germany?'

It was my turn to stare at him. 'The children's future is here and it's the next step for us.'

'But what if I can't get a business off the ground? I won't become another unemployment statistic, I won't become a burden.' The frustration rolled off him in waves as the anxiety of the last year finally came to a head. At least he was talking to me about it rather than bottling it up.

'You'd never be a burden.' I squeezed his hand, still strong and capable. But I knew there was something more. Eva's wedding was the following week, on Easter Sunday. 'You want to go back to see Eva, Walter and your mother.' Germany's pull was strong for him and had been getting stronger since the accident.

'Of course I miss them. I'd love nothing more than to see them. I wanted to walk Eva down the aisle on her wedding day . . .' He hesitated, gazing wistfully out the glass door to the marigolds and daisies lining the dirt path. 'But I know I can't. I know that Greta and Johanna's futures are here. Maybe you're right about citizenship.' He smiled sadly.

'We'll go back one day and see them all.'

'I've had a lot of time to think after everything that's happened and I've only recently realised how much I've struggled to fit in here, to belong. I know that I've promised to find a way to make it work and I honestly think that a business is the best choice for me, for us. I've been making enquiries, putting a plan in place for our future . . .' He sighed deeply, sadness settling into his face.

'Part of me imagines a life back in Germany. The money we'd get for this farm would be enough to build our dream house in the mountains. We could run a guesthouse and even have someone work for us. That way, we'd have an income and we wouldn't have to work so hard. We could enjoy life a little more until we're both ready to retire.'

'You want to retire in Germany?' I'd never expected this, never entertained the notion of what we might do when we were older.

'I want us to live out our old age content and peaceful and I want to die on German soil.' He met my eye then, and his vulnerability hit me in the chest like a physical blow.

'I never knew you felt this way.'

'Neither did I. I know it doesn't make much sense, but I can't get the idea out of my head.'

'Retirement's a long way off,' I said automatically. 'The children would have to be settled in their own lives . . .' I didn't want to go back to Germany to live. I could never leave my girls behind, no matter how old they were, but if Erich didn't begin to feel settled here, how could I deny him? 'Maybe we could plan a trip back to Germany to see everyone when Eva starts having children of her own.'

'Maybe . . . but I suppose that citizenship doesn't prevent us from going back at any time. Go ahead and get the application forms and paperwork together.'

About a month later, I arrived home to find Erich sitting on the edge of the lounge, staring at a sheet of paper in his hands. I'd worked late after a full day of studio sittings, helping Reinhardt and Otto put together the final selection of negatives and prints for a promotional shoot we'd done for one of our biggest clients. We were very proud of the final product and I was sure the client would be happy.

I was managing the studio shoots on my own now without Otto's supervision. Although they weren't the high profile customers, I went to work each day excited to be behind the camera. I loved interacting with people, even the children who didn't want to sit in a particular pose or the babies who squirmed on their mothers' laps.

'Lotte, can you stay late after your sittings?' Otto had asked. 'Vati and I can't agree on the shots for the client and we have to make a decision by tomorrow. You've got a good sense of what works. We could really use your help.'

They had wanted my professional opinion. I couldn't help but smile whenever I replayed that conversation over in my mind. I was becoming a respected photographer and I couldn't have been any happier.

I noticed paperwork on the coffee table as I walked to the kitchen, where I hoped Mutti had left me something for dinner. I was starving and my feet ached. I checked the pots on the stove. Boiled potatoes and fried kidney and onions – it would do.

'That's better,' I said, dropping onto the lounge next to Erich after I'd eaten, kicking my shoes off. 'Everyone in bed?'

'Uh-huh, we have the house to ourselves for a change,' he said. 'Here, give me your feet.'

'It's all right. It's late and you look tired too.'

'No, come on.'

I shuffled on the lounge so that my feet were in his lap. I closed my eyes in bliss as he began to massage, working on the pressure points. When I was so busy, it was easy to forget that I wasn't as young as I used to be. It was when I stopped that I noticed the aches and pains and how tired I was. I wondered how much longer I'd have to work this hard. 'How did you know this is exactly what I needed?' I groaned.

'I'm a mind reader,' he said softly. 'Didn't you know?'

I smiled at that. He was so thoughtful, often surprising me with little acts of kindness and appreciation that always made me feel special and loved.

'Are they the citizenship forms?' I asked. I'd been expecting them in the post for the past fortnight and didn't want to chase them up yet again.

He nodded. 'I only just opened the letter when you came in the door. I haven't read them yet.' He stopped massaging my feet and passed me some pages.

'There's a bit of work, but they look fine.'

Erich picked up another page from the table and put on his reading glasses. I glanced at him – his shoulders had stiffened and he was engrossed in what he was reading.

'What is it?' I swung my legs down and sat next to him.

He put the paper on the coffee table and looked at me, his brows furrowed with concern. If we apply for Australian citizenship, we renounce our German nationality.'

'What?'

'We can't hold dual citizenship. On becoming Australian citizens, our German citizenship's revoked.'

'You sure? It can't be right. We were never told of this before.'

'No, there's no mistake,' he said, passing me the papers. I quickly scanned them and found the offending paragraph.

'I can't believe it. Germany's our homeland. It's our identity. We shouldn't have to choose!' I was furious now, but there was nothing we could do about it.

'No, we shouldn't, but remember we're doing this for the girls, for their future and for ours . . .'

'But haven't we given up enough?' Erich's arm was around me, his lips soothing against my hot temple as he tried to comfort me.

'Nobody can take away how we feel about Germany, and the girls will always remember where they've come from. I don't like this any more than you, but we have to decide what's best for our family.'

'Australia's our home now,' I said, decisively.

'Yes, it is,' replied Erich, picking up a pen from the coffee table and writing his name on the form.

Filling out the applications took time and I spent quite a few nights working on getting all the information together, leaving papers scattered across the dining table.

'Why do you want to become a citizen?' asked my mother one evening as she brought me a cup of coffee. 'It's not like this country has done you any favours. Besides, I thought you wanted to go back to Germany some day.'

'I did once, but not now.' I was tired and it was late. The children were asleep and Erich was at his first union meeting since the accident – our decision to become Australian citizens had reignited his interest in their work. 'This is good for our family, especially the children. We want to be part of this country, and becoming citizens will cement our future here.'

'It's one thing to live here but another to become a citizen. You're German first. How can you give up your heritage and tie yourself to a people who have no culture, no history?' said Mutti irritably.

'It doesn't matter what you think. Nobody's asked you to become a citizen, so don't worry about what we're doing,' I snapped.

'Do what you want. You always do. I don't know why I bother saying anything to you. I'm just good enough to look after your children but not to have an opinion on whatever happens in this household.' She waved her hand and turned away quickly, but I'd seen the tears in her eyes and I knew that I'd hurt her.

'Mutti!'

'I'm going to bed. I'm tired.'

I watched her walk away, my guilt warring with my anger. I understood that Mutti was upset because, to her, citizenship symbolised a rejection of everything important she'd instilled in me, but perhaps Mutti felt as though I was rejecting her too. But it wasn't about her: it was about creating a future for my family. Leaving the past behind didn't mean that I rejected my culture and nationality – it was part of who I was – but I had to decide how to give my children the best life possible, just as she had when she decided to divorce my real father when I was a child.

The house was quiet and empty. I'd slept in. I'd heard Erich come home in the early hours, tip-toeing not to wake us, but he was up again some time before me, most likely because of the pain and stiffness in his leg. I had no idea where Mutti and the girls had gone. It was rare for me not to hear the morning clatter of breakfast, the shuffling of feet and closing of doors, but I had slept through it all. I was exhausted, bleary-eyed and dull-headed. *Any wonder*, I thought, as I padded to the kitchen to make myself a coffee, noticing that the bread, butter and jam had been left out.

The previous day's wedding had gone late and I had stayed until the end, taking photos of the bride and groom as they left the reception as a favour to Reinhardt – he was in Europe and they were family friends of his. With part of the compensation money, we'd managed to buy a little second-hand Volkswagen Beetle for me through the contacts Erich had kept at Lanock Motors. The treks into Liverpool, Campbelltown and Camden became short and pleasant drives and it was great to be able to use my own car for work on Saturdays, going straight to the appointments from home, rather than picking up a car from the studio.

Normally Erich and I would walk together on a Sunday morning but the sun was high in the sky. I assumed he had let me sleep and had been out already. He walked twice a day like clockwork, pushing himself further each time to strengthen muscles that had withered after so many months of convalescence. He still had a bad limp but he was moving around with greater ease and could walk for longer with a stick. It wasn't just about the physical, I knew, but the mental toughness and determination to not let his injuries get the better of him, as well as about dealing with the raw emotions he'd been experiencing since the accident. That was the beauty of the bush, it gave him the space to think and reflect, as well as exercise. I felt disappointed that I'd missed out on our time together walking down the back. We always returned to the house laughing or smiling, our cares and worries soothed, content and ready to begin the day.

He was most likely working on a coffee table he was making as a surprise for Franz and Claudia. Ernst had brought him the timber after Claudia had been telling him about how much she admired the table Erich had made for our lounge room. He would be busy working all day. I didn't mind. It kept him occupied and kept his mind off the pain, a form of rehabilitation in its own way. Something had changed in him since the decision to file our citizenship papers and he'd returned to the things that brought him joy and purpose.

Sipping my coffee, I walked back to the front room and opened the curtains, wanting to feel the sunshine on my face. I stretched languorously like a cat, lapping up the rays of the sun, and closed my eyes, relishing the quiet and grateful for a few moments to myself.

I decided to get a start on my ironing for the week. Mutti did a reasonable job on the children's uniforms but I preferred to do my own and Erich's clothes. Besides, I loved using the new iron that Erich had bought me. He insisted that I have the best he could give me. It was a Westinghouse steam iron that took out the wrinkles with ease and had a separate spray button to dampen the cloth where there were tough creases. I set up the ironing table.

Erich opened the door and came inside, his face lined with exhaustion and pain. 'You're up,' he said. 'Late night?'

'It was long. I couldn't wait to get into bed and off my aching feet. Coffee?'

'I'd love one.'

I went to the kitchen to boil the kettle. 'What about you? You came in very late.' I heard the chair scrape across the floor. He was tired because normally he'd berate the girls for doing that.

'Yes, sorry about that. I had to wait till George was ready to drive me home.' I heard the sigh of relief as he took the weight off his leg. Although he could now drive short distances, I used the car most of the time and we couldn't afford a second car as yet.

'There were big celebrations last night. It looks like the nationwide union support's made all the difference.'

The month before, German and Italian migrants at Bonegilla had staged a demonstration against unemployment and migrant discrimination that had lasted for a week. They called for the right to work and demanded employment. Eleven people were arrested for rioting. Erich had joined the efforts to lobby support from unions across the country for those arrested men and increase the political pressure on the government until they were released, but also for the rights they were defending.

'What was the result?'

'A call's been made to end the misleading information on employment and wages that migrants are fed before they leave their homelands. Finally, there's some understanding of the difficulty they encounter when they arrive.'

'That's wonderful! Congratulations,' I said, remembering how devastating it had been for us to find no work and little support when we arrived. I set his coffee on the table and kissed him lightly before returning to the ironing table.

'All they wanted was a chance to work. It was what they'd been promised before they immigrated.'

A niggle of doubt wormed its way through me. 'Do you worry about the association of communist elements with the union?' I asked, Franz's conversation with me echoing in my mind.

He sipped his coffee before he answered. 'The Communist Party supported the call of the unions. It's the only party that's against the White Australia Policy, so that makes them popular with migrant workers. They've been fighting for its dissolution for years. I have to say, I like some of the things they stand for, and the way they speak out against racism and discrimination against migrants.'

'You're not about to join, are you?' I asked nervously, running the iron too quickly over the edge of the skirt where I held it taut and burning my finger. From what I'd heard, belonging to the Communist Party would only damage our chances at a good life here in Australia.

'No, as much as I agree with their ideals, I don't agree with their politics. The Communist Party spells trouble.'

'And the communists in the union?' I remembered what Franz had told me.

'It's nothing to worry about. There's no communist threat here. It's all a figment of people's imaginations,' he said stiffly. 'I just wish that Australians understood how lucky they are to be living in such isolation. They take their freedom and democracy for granted.'

'Most Europeans understand how precious those things are.' Many of us who had endured under single-party regimes and dictatorships knew the value of democracy very well. But I wasn't utterly convinced that the danger of being associated with communists didn't exist, be they figments and shadows or not, however, all I could do for now was watch and see.

'There's something else I wanted to talk to you about,' Erich said. He looked suddenly wary. 'I've decided I want to make timber furniture.'

'Really?' I carefully placed the iron upright on the table. We'd talked through a number of options earlier and making timber furniture was the most physically demanding. 'Are you sure you can manage that with your leg?'

'I'll manage just fine.'

'But you don't have trade qualifications. The work you do is beautiful, but surely there's more to learn than what your father taught you? Will it make a decent living?' The frustration and worry I'd held back for months bubbled over like boiling oil, searing and scalding, my tone harder than I could control.

'Are you finished?' he asked quietly.

I nodded, too wound up to say any more.

'I know everything I need to get started. Anything extra, I'll learn as I go. I'm resourceful, remember.'

Of course he was, and I was treating him like a child who didn't know anything.

'I made many of the pieces for my father, pieces that were of a standard with his work, and he was a master craftsman.'

'But who will buy your furniture? Pieces are so cheap now.'

'You're right, but those pieces are made with inferior materials and won't last as long. Mine will be handcrafted, solid timber that will last for generations. There's always a market for quality craftsmanship. Ernst has some new contacts at the factory, timber merchants who are willing to sell to me at a reasonable price. All I have to do is expand my workshop and find my first clients.'

'Is it what you really want to do? Are you sure?'

'I'm sure. I've researched thoroughly and I know I can make a successful business.' He squeezed my hand. I could feel the vibration of excitement running through him. 'It's something I know and understand. A niche business like this could do very well, and I can't wait to use some of these Australian timbers. This is the chance we've been waiting for.'

'Well, I'm happy then,' I said, relief and concern swirling through me so I didn't quite know how to feel. It made Erich happy, that was for sure, and he was definitely gifted, but I worried how he'd manage with his leg and whether we could survive on the income from this business. Then I let my doubts go. We had a way forward and I had to trust him.

Erich took my face in his hands and kissed me soundly. 'We'll have to celebrate later, then.'

13

We joined Franz and Claudia for a picnic at the beach at Bulli. It was November and finally warm enough for the children to swim.

Erich was enjoying the sunshine, too full to move, drinking beer with Ernst and talking about timber, while Hilde and Mutti sat chatting on a blanket on the edge of the sand under the shade of a Norfolk pine tree. Franz was searching for something among the bags. There were plenty of eyes on the children, so Claudia and I took advantage of the extra adult supervision to walk along the beach.

We'd walked a couple of hundred metres along the shoreline, talking about our daily lives, Erich's business, work at the studio, the difficulties living with Ernst, and the trouble Hilde and Mutti were having settling into Australian life, when Franz jogged up behind us.

'Mind if I join you, ladies?' he asked, panting. 'I had to move after that big lunch but I can't run any more, I'm puffed.'

Claudia looked at me and I shrugged. 'Fine,' I said. 'We always enjoy your company.' Claudia snorted. 'Well, most of the time anyway.'

'I won't outstay my welcome then,' he said, breathing heavily. 'I'll walk with you part of the way and then when I get up the courage or energy, I'll try to run a bit more.'

'He's trying to get fit, now that he's sitting behind a desk all day,' said Claudia from the corner of her mouth. 'Just so long as he doesn't drop dead of a heart attack.'

I tried to hide my smirk, sneaking a look at the small pot belly Franz had developed.

'I heard that,' he said with mock outrage, 'but I'll be trim and back to my old self by the end of summer, just you see.'

'Yes, we will see,' said Claudia, frowning slightly. His face did look very red and I wasn't sure it was just sunburn.

We walked in silence for a few minutes. I found the pounding of the surf soothing and energising at the same time. I drifted onto the soft sand, my feet sinking in, burning. 'Oh, that's hot!' I exclaimed and quickly tip-toed back to the firm, wet sand. The cool water rippling over my feet was a welcome relief.

Franz now walked between us. 'So, what are you talking about?' he asked politely.

'Nothing important,' said Claudia, kicking water at him.

'Thank you, my sweetheart. That's lovely. Shall I return the favour?'

She stepped back immediately, staying out of range.

'We're so lucky to be able to enjoy such beautiful beaches,' I said.

'Speaking of which, have you heard back about your citizenship application?' Franz asked.

I shook my head. 'No, still nothing. I've rung a couple of times to find out how much longer it's going to be and all I'm ever told is that it's being processed, that it will take as long as it needs and to be patient. Erich's tried as well but he received the same answer.'

'Has he now?' Franz's eyes were piercing blue and razor sharp.

'How long since you lodged the applications?' asked Claudia, her frizzy hair flying around her round face.

'Since the end of May.'

'Over five months?' Franz's eyebrows rose in surprise. 'Ours only took three months.' Franz and Claudia had been naturalised in July.

'I know that look. What are you thinking?' asked Claudia sharply.

'You know that the firm I work for often deals with political activists and has contacts in high places.'

Claudia and I glanced at each other and I could see that she was worried too. Franz worked in civil rights law. He and Erich had had many heated discussions on the best way to tackle the problems they saw on a day-to-day basis.

'One of Erich's union colleagues has been denied citizenship, and his family back in Greece were questioned about his communist activities in Australia. He's been refused a re-entry visa back into Australia if he wants to visit his sick mother in Greece.'

'Surely he must be involved in illegal activities to be treated like this?' said Claudia.

Franz shook his head, blond hair falling across his brow in the gentle breeze. 'He's done nothing illegal as far as we can tell. He's a passionate advocate for migrant rights, just like Erich. The only difference is that he's a member of the Communist Party.'

'Reds under the bed,' I whispered. I found it hard to reconcile what Franz had just told me about withholding the freedoms of a man whose only crime was to fight for the rights of others that were as synonymous with Australia and its reputation as the land of opportunity as the sand, ocean and blue sky around us.

'What's this got to do with Erich?' asked Claudia.

'He'll be tarred with the same brush, just by association. We know of another activist who's been denied citizenship repeatedly and we fear it's because of his known links to communist members. Migrants are the ones who are most at risk, who have the most to lose.'

'Does Erich know?'

Franz stopped walking, looking apologetic as he placed his hand on my shoulder. 'He didn't until I told him, but he refuses to listen.'

'Surely you can understand?' I said. 'You know what it means to him to try to make a difference and he feels that he's finally making headway. He's so proud of the role he played in the Bonegilla incident.'

'I know, but with that success comes exposure.'

'So you're saying that their citizenship applications might be held up while Erich's investigated,' said Claudia.

'It's possible.'

'But Erich's done nothing wrong,' I said.

'I know, Lotte, but it's not worth the risk,' said Franz. 'You have to tell Erich to step away from this, at least for a while . . . if not for himself, then for you and the children.'

I nodded, fear swirling in my belly. 'I'll talk to him.'

'I don't feel like going any further,' said Claudia. 'You go for another run and I'll walk back with Lotte.' She grasped my hand and glared at her husband. 'Off you go.'

'I'm sorry, Lotte, but I had to say something.' He looked at his wife's thunderous expression. 'All right, I'm going.'

We watched him run back towards our picnic spot.

'He means well, but sometimes I wonder if he thinks he's still in wartime Germany, surrounded by intrigue and deception. The way he and Onkel Ernst behave at times, you'd think that they were spies or something. It makes me cross.'

'Maybe he's right. What if Erich's really in danger and putting our life here in jeopardy?'

'All you can do is talk to him and trust him to make the right decision. He'll know if the risk is real.'

A few days later, I decided it was time to talk Erich.

It was cool in the workshop, the sound of repetitive buffing soothing. Fluorescent light illuminated the furniture sitting on the shed floor in various stages of completion. Stacks of timber lay to one side, the resinous perfume of freshly cut wood filling the air. Erich had shown me how each timber had a distinctive fragrance when I accompanied him to the timber yard. My favourite was red cedar, which he told me was often used for panelling and decorative features.

Erich's business was in its infancy but at least it was up and running. The insurance money from the accident had made it possible to buy the tools and equipment he needed for the specialist work he was doing – a variety of handsaws, planes, chisels, hand drills, carving tools and lathes and an old station wagon, a 1956 Holden FE Special, to transport timber, equipment and small furniture pieces. The work was labour intensive but well worth the effort. It didn't take me long to discover that this was what he should be doing and I was so relieved. He was happy, his body was getting stronger by the day, and he was occupied. He walked without a stick now, although he'd always have a limp and stiffness in his knee. It was remarkable, really. Nobody had expected him to walk properly again.

It was his eye for detail and design, and his practical and analytical skills combined with his creative flair, that made his pieces unique. The timber's grain was always the feature, the surprising array of rich, luxurious hues of the wood enhancing each piece so that it not only served a practical purpose but was also a work of art.

Reinhardt had kindly commissioned pieces that I knew he loved and he quickly spread the word of Erich's superior craftsmanship among his well-heeled friends, associates and clients. Many of these were Erich's first customers and now the small shed we'd erected was crammed with tools, equipment, partly finished items and various timber slabs and pieces.

However, I wondered how long it would take for Erich's business to make the kind of money we needed so that I could cut back on my work and spend some time with the children. They were growing up, and in a blink of an eye they would be adults.

The sight of Erich stopped me in my tracks. He had his back to me and he was magnificent – shirt straining at his shoulders, the muscles of his arms rippling with each stroke across the timber table top, legs planted firmly on the concrete floor, strong and solid below the shorts that accentuated his shapely behind. My fingers itched for the camera, to capture him in this moment . . . but then I remembered my task.

'We have to talk,' I said.

Erich stilled and all I could hear were the sounds of small animals rooting through the underbrush, perhaps a possum or two hopeful for a few mouthfuls of tender greens from our vegetable garden. The slight sighing of the wind through the gum trees was punctuated by a distant bark from a dog on one of the neighbouring farms. Our German Shepherd puppy, Wolfie, was asleep in his kennel.

Erich turned towards me. He looked tired, dark shadows lining his face in the harsh light, but his eyes were peaceful. 'What is it, *liebling*?' He smiled and wiped his hands on a small piece of terry towelling.

I almost lost my nerve then. I didn't want to fight but to say nothing would be burying my head in the sand.

'I know Franz has spoken to you about the union. He tells me it's not safe for you to continue your activism.'

Erich closed his eyes and took a deep breath before opening them again. He dropped the towel on the bench and came to me. 'He's a lawyer, Lotte. He sees things differently.'

'That's not true. He works towards the same cause as you. He knows what's going on, but he also hears things that you don't. He knows about the communist links to the union, he's told me about the risk to those associated with Communist Party members. Franz thinks that it's affected our citizenship application, and that may only be the tip of the iceberg. You're not safe and we're not safe unless you keep a low profile. I don't want to come home from work one day to find you gone, to hear that you've been deported and can never return to us.'

Erich gently took hold of my wrists. 'Do you really think I'd put you and the children in danger? How can you say such things after everything we've been through? Have you forgotten how we've struggled?'

'Of course not! But why does it always have to be you? You've done so much for others and it's time to look after your own family. Maybe you've forgotten about us.'

'You know me better than that. I would *never* put anything before my family. Everything I do is for you.'

'Then quit the union.'

'You know I can't do that.'

My heart dropped like a stone. This was what I had been dreading. 'But surely it's time for someone else to take over the lobbying and activism,' I pleaded.

Erich gripped my wrists more tightly, giving them a shake. 'Don't you want an Australia that values the voice of all people, no matter where they've come from? Don't you want a future for our girls where freedom of speech and equal rights is accepted as normal? That's why we came here, isn't it?'

He dropped his hands and took a step away from me. 'If I stop now, it will all have been for nothing. I'll be worth nothing, undeserving of you and the children, and I couldn't bear that.'

I stood there stunned. I knew Erich was racked with guilt about the position he'd put us in. Nothing had gone to plan since we'd arrived in Australia, but how could he believe that the union was his only chance at redemption? Why couldn't he see how our family was thriving despite the setbacks? And that by remaining on his path, he was threatening all he and I had worked so hard for?

*

The letter informing us that our applications to be made Australian citizens had been approved finally arrived a few weeks after our conversation. I was overjoyed, relieved and guilt-ridden at the same time. Maybe there had been nothing to worry about after all, and everything I'd said to Erich had been unnecessary, but I couldn't take it back.

The citizenship ceremony was held in the Liverpool Town Hall on a warm summer's day in 1962 – January 26th, Australia Day. I was surprised to see how many people were being naturalised: the hall was full of citizens-to-be and their friends and family, everyone dressed in their Sunday best. Streamers hung from the lights and across the ornate ceiling.

Despite her objections, Mutti had come to watch the ceremony, and she and I followed Erich and the girls down the central aisle, pushing our way through the crowd to find our seats. I held the small bible I'd been handed on entering the hall tightly, trying to still my shaking hands and ignore the rush of nerves. Were we doing the right thing, giving up German citizenship to be Australian? It was too late to change my mind – the official paperwork had already been done. I shifted in my seat, restless.

Then I glanced at the girls sitting quietly between Erich and me, dressed in their best and looking beautiful. We were doing this for them. They were thriving in a way I couldn't have imagined possible in Germany. Their future – and so our future – was here, and nothing else mattered.

The mayor, recognisable by the chain of office that hung across his ermine robes, and the town clerk stood at the front next to the podium draped with the Australian flag, ready for the ceremony to begin. City officials and dignitaries sat in a row along the front of the stage, stiff-backed and solemn.

Erich caught my eye and smiled, shining with pride. 'Are you ready for this?'

'Yes,' I said.

He reached over the children and took my hand. His was firm and warm, his touch secure and grounding. 'This is a new beginning,' he told the girls and me. 'Soon we'll be Australians.'

'I don't know why you have to do this and give up who you are and where you've come from,' Mutti huffed, more to herself than us. We'd had this discussion with her many times but she believed we were wiping out our past, the glorious past of our family and our homeland. That was unforgivable in her eyes.

'She'll be right, mate,' said Greta louder than she needed to, grinning cheekily, as much for the occasion as to bedevil her grandmother.

Mutti huffed again and turned to look the other way.

Johanna decided to join in with the fun. 'G'day, mate.'

'Enough, girls,' I whispered. 'This is a serious occasion. Behave yourselves.'

Both girls nodded dutifully, although I could still see the smiles on their faces.

The mayor stood at the podium welcoming us and speaking about what it was to be an Australian citizen. I tried to pay attention but my focus wandered. Then it was time to stand and take the Oath of Allegiance. Hand on my bible, I read the oath from a sheet of paper, although Erich and I had already memorised it.

And it was done. We were officially Australian citizens.

Erich's name was called and then my own and I followed my husband to the podium where the mayor handed me my certificate of naturalisation and shook my hand with his white-gloved one. Back in my seat, I stared at the piece of paper that made my daughters Australian citizens – that made them *Australian*. As minors, they were naturalised now because I was. Any children they had here would be automatically Australian. It was what Erich and I had wanted: a home for our children and particularly our grandchildren, where freedom of choice and the wide open spaces of this land were their birthright.

We had a little celebration after. Franz, Claudia, Ernst, Anna, Peter and the twins, Suzanne, Tommy and little Joan, Reinhardt, Sabine and Karl, and Otto and his new girlfriend Cherie all joined us at home for coffee and cake. We were all Australians now, besides Mutti and Ernst. It was time to move forward and secure the future, not only for ourselves but for our children and their children. However, I knew the pull of Germany was still strong for Erich. He'd often pick up the framed photos of Walter and Eva on her wedding day and, more recently, photos of his new grandson. It made me sad to know that we would never have any more children and how Erich was missing out on being a grandfather. He'd missed out on so much with his oldest children. The months that we all lived under the same roof, although fraught with difficulty, had been precious for him.

Erich's mother was well into her seventies and he was sure he'd never see her again. Although he said nothing, I believed that upset him the most, especially watching me with my own mother. Karoline had lived with us in Germany and, although I didn't always see eye to eye with her, we'd developed a good relationship. She'd gone to live with Inga, Erich's ex-wife, helping her with the children. I knew Karoline was trying to make up for the years she lost while in a Russian work camp after the war but Eva and Walter were grown now, and she'd written to Erich, telling him that she felt lost. She'd decided it was time to come to us, to spend the twilight years of her life with her only child and her younger grandchildren.

It was unexpected news but I was pleased for Erich. I understood how he felt about seeing her again, to be able to hold her in his arms. I begrudgingly admired the courage it must have taken for her to make the decision to travel to the other side of the world at her age, to a country so different from what she knew, without speaking the language. Erich and I both had our concerns about how she would cope, but we were especially worried about how our mothers would get on – they were polar opposites: Mutti vivacious and social while Karoline was quiet and kept to herself.

But Erich soon became excited and full of energy once more, working on plans to extend our house; it was too small as it was but with an extra person it would be impossible. Karoline's application to immigrate would take months to process but they were months we needed. The money we had wasn't going to cover the cost of building a new house as we'd originally planned, but our situation would be unmanageable without more space. We needed a room for Karoline, preferably at the opposite end of the house from Mutti, a proper kitchen and dining area, a bathroom with a shower, a bedroom for Erich and me, and separate rooms for the girls. Erich wanted to build a carport to protect the cars from the extremes of temperature but also so that I didn't get wet bringing groceries in when it rained. We decided it was time to build a larger workshop off the carport for Erich's business too. He needed more space, somewhere to work properly and somewhere presentable to meet his customers. Extending the garage seemed to be our only option.

I knew his pride was on the line with his mother arriving soon. It was bad enough that he had to endure Mutti's glares. Now that she had settled into Australian life and made friends, meeting them for coffee and cake, going out to the occasional concert with our family doctor, Dr Rodsky, and keeping her weekly lunch with Suzanne, she had become more vocal in her disapproval of our living conditions.

'We don't have to build all of it now,' I said to him late one night, adding up the figures while looking at the plans strewn across the coffee table. 'As long as your mother has a room and maybe we tidy up the kitchen, we'll manage.'

'No. If we're going to do it, we may as well do it all now. We've lived like gypsies long enough.' He put his half-smoked cigarette on the edge of the ashtray.

'But I can't see how we're going to afford it all,' I said, rubbing my temples. I felt a headache coming on.

'I know I can't build you a new house just yet, but you deserve a proper working kitchen and laundry and I want the privacy of a bedroom so I can have you all to myself again.'

I looked into his eyes and saw the yearning there despite the exhaustion. Erich was the only one home most of the time. The girls were more often at school or with their friends than at home, Mutti was out visiting the majority of the time and I was working.

This was probably our only opportunity to make the house as functional as we could. I didn't want to admit that I was tired of living like this too, crammed on top of each other. We now had an electric stove and refrigerator in the kitchen and a copper to do the washing, but conditions were still difficult.

'The numbers don't add up,' I said, disheartened. 'See for yourself.' I pushed the notebook filled with his meticulous notes and costs across to him.

'Well, we haven't factored in our other incomes,' he said. 'I know it's only a little extra but it all helps.' Erich was trying to supplement our income in other ways while he was establishing his business. We'd started with pigs but they'd been too much work, smelly, and left the paddocks disfigured with bare, scarred earth. Then we'd tried turkeys and sold them at Christmas, making a modest profit. This year, Erich had been earmarking turpentine trees across the farm for sale as electricity poles.

But there was no need for me to tell him what he already knew but was trying desperately to avoid – it still wouldn't be enough. He pored over the numbers, reconfiguring and recalculating. The frustration made his body stiffen until he was as tightly coiled as a spring. He shifted and stretched his leg, rubbing the thigh where the worst break had been. Restless, I went to the kitchen to boil the kettle. It was going to be a long night and we could both do with a coffee.

'We can't do it,' he said finally.

I returned and draped my arms around him, kissing his neck. I knew the guilt he carried, the feeling that he'd let me down. 'It doesn't matter. We've managed this long, we'll manage a little longer.'

In the end, all we could do was sell part of the land to finance the build. It went against what we wanted, but we had no choice. So we picked five acres to sell.

14

The five acres sold within a couple of months and we could begin building shortly after. But it was a difficult few months, living among the building – draughty, dirty, dusty and chaotic. Thank God in heaven Erich was there to oversee all the work, because I would have lost my patience. I sighed every morning as I slipped into the driver's seat of my little car, happy to be going somewhere that wasn't gritty and noisy.

Not only that, but all the activity had disturbed the local population of reptiles. It was a dry year and we were on constant lookout for lizards and snakes. One day, we heard a terrible screech out the back. My blood ran cold as I raced out of the laundry, my hands still sudsy, to see what had happened.

Mutti was standing between the toilet and the house, frozen, staring at the grass near her feet, face white with fear.

'What's wrong?' I asked then stopped. Slithering away, heading for the safety of the trees, was a long black snake. I saw a flash of pink on its underside.

Erich came around the side of the house in time to see it. Without missing a beat, he grabbed the canvas bag he'd left hanging on a hook, darted towards the snake, picked it up and stuffed it into the bag, head first, before it could reach back to bite him.

'What in God's name are you doing?' I screamed.

'It's a red-belly black snake,' said Erich, grinning widely and holding the bag tightly closed at arm's length.

'It could've bitten you,' I said, my voice tight with anger. 'What were you thinking?'

'It's all right. It's not as venomous as the brown snake and I've been shown how to handle them properly.' One of his friends from the door factory was now a budding taxidermist and regularly dealt with reptiles.

He moved towards the kitchen.

I eyed the bulging bag nervously. 'Where do you think you're going with that?'

'I'm putting it in the freezer. Hermann will want this. It's a lovely specimen.'

'Not in the house!' said Mutti, outraged.

'It's all right. It'll be dead before long. Snakes don't like the cold and it won't be able to move in the freezer.'

'Erich, no!'

'I promise you, it's safe.' He opened the door, his eyes darting to the bag. 'Just to be sure, don't open the freezer,' he said, after seeing the horror on our faces.

Hermann did a beautiful job on the snake and gave it to us as a gift. Erich displayed it in pride of place on our bookshelf, next to photos of Johanna hugging Wolfie and Greta dressed in the knee-length lemon brocade dress I'd made for the school dance. The girls were fascinated by it but Mutti and I shivered whenever we looked at it.

'How can you let him do such things?' Mutti hissed. 'It's bad enough he put a live snake in your freezer and now this?'

'It's dead, Mutti,' I said.

'Don't you defend him,' she said, clearly exasperated. 'After all your husband's promises of a new life, luring you away from me and your family, it's come to this.' She spread her arms.

'What? What do you mean by that?' I stared at her, mortified. I couldn't help myself, the old habit of reacting to her barbs coming back as if it had never left me. The old Mutti had returned with a vengeance.

'We live in a hovel, surrounded by dangerous creatures, filth and dirt, in the middle of nowhere while you work your fingers to the bone day in and day out, and for what? To live worse off than when you were in Germany. You were going to have more children, but now look at you. With Erich injured and deciding to build furniture, you'll have to continue working just as hard until you're past childbearing age. There's no money in furniture making. Besides, he's never home when you are. He's always off wasting his time with that union nonsense. He should be out there working two jobs if he has to, to provide for his family like a real man, rather than playing politics, something he has no business being involved in.'

Mutti held my deepest fears and anxieties up in front of me so I couldn't hide from them. How could she be so cruel?

'You know nothing about Erich and me,' I said in a low voice, trying not to tremble.

'I can see you have no future with him. Why didn't you listen to me all those years ago? Why didn't you marry Heinrich? All I wanted for you was to have a good life, but you threw it all away.'

'Stop it, Mutti! Stop dredging up the past! You know this wasn't Erich's fault. He's done everything to make our lives manageable and after all that's happened, we're still standing and we have our own home, something we could never have afforded in Germany.' I knew how protective Mutti was of me, I was all she had left and she didn't want me to suffer the way she did before she married Vati. But she had to understand that this was my life to live.

'He still asks after you, you know. He writes to me at Christmas.' Her eyes glittered with sadness and regret.

'I don't want to know, Mutti. Heinrich's living his life and I'm living mine. I chose Erich and we're staying together. I love him more than ever and I'm grateful for him every day of my life. So don't you dare speak about him that way. You don't have to like what he does, but for my sake, just keep your mouth shut. Do you understand me?'

Mutti glared at me, furious. She'd expected me to back down but I'd had enough – there was plenty on my shoulders without her complaints and reminders of the past.

She spun away from me and left the room. I heard her throw herself onto her bed and burst into tears. I stood there a moment, tempted to go to her and apologise, but then

I remembered: this was my new life and I wasn't going to be dragged back to my old one, caught in the controlling web of my mother's whims. None of us enjoyed the mess we were living in, so my mother could put up with it too.

The snake was gone the following day. Nobody made mention of it and I didn't bother to ask who had moved it. But when I went out to the workshop, I discovered it sitting on one of the finished cabinets and I knew that Erich had heard our argument. My heart sank and I made a vow to keep the peace with my mother, no matter how much effort it took.

There were other things I worried about, lurking at the edge of my mind. From time to time I'd noticed that some of our mail arrived unsealed, but I thought nothing of it at first. Then I realised that the odd letter or bill had been placed in the envelopes upside down or back to front.

'I think someone's opening our mail,' I said to Claudia one Sunday when I couldn't stand the dust and dirt any longer and had taken Mutti and the girls into Liverpool.

'What makes you say that?' she asked, her brows drawn into a deep frown. I told her what I'd found.

'It's only every now and then,' I said as we walked to the café where the girls liked to go. We'd left the twins with Hilde and Mutti, and Anna and Peter had joined my girls, walking ahead of us so it looked like they were on their own and not with adults.

They loved to get a milkshake and listen to songs on the jukebox, particularly those of Elvis Presley and the Beatles, especially Greta. It was something all their friends liked to do after school and I allowed them to go on a Friday afternoon. They met me after I finished work and we'd come home together. I had to let them have some social life now they were teenagers. Greta was sixteen already and quite gregarious and social, while at fourteen, Johanna was quieter and more studious. Although they had boys as friends, I was pleased that there was no talk of boyfriends just yet.

'Have you noticed anything strange? Has Erich told you about anything unusual happening perhaps with the union?'

'No. Mind you, he hasn't got time for too much with the building work going on. He's doing most of it himself even though his leg gives him terrible trouble by the end of the day. Then he's short-tempered and grumpy and he tosses and turns so much at night that some mornings I think I've barely slept.'

'He's stubborn, that's for sure.'

'To his own detriment sometimes.'

Claudia smiled and nodded but she looked thoughtful. 'Well, I don't know . . . Do you think someone's reading your mail?'

I looked sharply at her. 'Why would anyone want to do that?'

She shrugged. 'It's the only explanation. Have you told Erich?'

'No. I didn't want to fight with him over something that might be nothing.' Erich and I hadn't spoken again about me asking him to quit the union, but it was a point of tension between us, though there was an uneasy truce since that emotional night.

Claudia shook her head again, fine strands of hair slipping free from its pins. 'I really don't know, Lotte. Franz can have a wild imagination but what if it's true, and Erich – and by extension all of you – are being watched?'

'That's ludicrous,' I said, but my heart clutched with fear. 'It's nothing.'

'If you say so,' said Claudia, though I could see that she wasn't convinced.

For a while everything seemed fine and I wondered if I'd imagined it all. Between work and the extensions, teenage daughters and a cranky husband and mother, I had little time or energy to waste on shadows. I wasn't getting any younger and by the end of some days all I wanted was to put my aching feet up and a little time to myself. I'd never pictured being in this situation in my late thirties, still working so hard to get ahead. Yet I could see that it was finally coming together for us, there was light at the end of the tunnel. I wouldn't let my exhausted worries take over. Anyway, everyone was distracted by Australia's involvement in the Vietnam War, with the government sending military advisers and planes to the region.

'Surely the Australian government has more sense than that?' said Mutti as we listened to the late-night news on the radio.

'Apparently not,' I said, looking up from the colouring work I was still doing for the Sydney studio. 'But I have to say that I'm shocked by the decision.'

'I don't understand,' said Mutti, putting down the book she'd been reading. 'I always thought that Australia was a peace-loving country, and the last war's still so fresh in people's memories, even here. What must all those poor people who left Europe for what they thought was an isolated country, sheltered from war, be thinking now?'

It was true. None of us ever imagined Australia would become involved in a war far beyond its borders.

'Australia's had no choice,' said Erich, putting his pen down with a sigh. He was writing up a report for the union. 'It has to do with our obligations to the treaties we have. America's become involved so now we have to. But Menzies has only agreed to a small advisory team joining the forces in South Vietnam.'

'So there's nothing to worry about?' I asked.

'As long as the military isn't committed and the war stays on foreign soil, I'm sure the public will forget about our involvement within the month,' he said. 'I know the unions will protest if our commitment increases.'

'At least some people have some sense,' said Mutti, taking off her reading glasses. 'How can anyone condone and promote war after what we've seen with the last two world wars?' She tapped the heavy frame on the wooden arm of the chair. 'It defies logic that we haven't learnt from those devastating years.'

'I doubt it will go any further than this,' said Erich, trying to reassure both my mother and me. I hoped he was right.

However, the threat of war came to our attention again two months later with the Cuban Missile Crisis: America blockaded Cuba after discovering that the Russians were building missile sites in the communist country. Many feared that we were once again on the brink of war, not only that but a nuclear war that would be so catastrophic it would devastate humanity. I shivered, remembering the shocking news about the devastation wreaked on Japan at the end of the war. I wondered why world leaders hadn't had enough and thought seriously about joining the Peace Movement. Somebody had to take a stand. The world had to say no. Thank God Kennedy and Khrushchev had negotiated a diplomatic solution.

Karoline arrived in December. Waiting for her in the arrivals hall at Sydney Airport, I felt as nervous as I had been all those years ago when she came to live with us in Germany.

When she appeared, she seemed tinier than I remembered, but she still moved with a vibrancy and strength that belied her years. She wore a simple dress, her grey hair nearly white but still plaited and pinned to her head in the style she had worn for as long as I had known her. She looked eagerly around the hall for Erich and her hazel eyes lit up with joy when she found him. Then she was in his arms, crying softly.

'I've waited so long to see you,' she said, while Erich clasped her to him like she was precious porcelain. 'I was worried that I'd die before I saw you again. Just to touch you makes me feel that everything was worth the wait.'

'You're here now, Mutti,' was all he could say, his emotions held tightly in check. I knew that when we got home, he would take a walk in the bush and allow the tide of emotion to wash over him so he could return to the house composed and calm.

Then Karoline embraced me. 'Lotte, it's good to see you.'

'And you too. The children can't wait to see you. They're a bit bigger than when you last saw them.'

Karoline laughed. 'Yes, I know it's been too long, but I'm glad to be here at last.' She touched my face. 'It looks like Australia suits you, my dear.'

*

Karoline settled in well. I soon discovered that although she still doted on Erich, she no longer felt like a threat to me. Inga and Erich's other children were on the opposite side of the world and she accepted me as Erich's wife, accepted that I was the one who made him happy.

She now occupied the new front bedroom off the lounge room with a lovely view out over the garden. Erich had ensured that the fibro additions to both sides of the garage with their flat iron roofs blended in well so it now looked like more of a home than a garage and it gave us the four new bedrooms we desperately needed. We finally had a bedroom too on the opposite side of the lounge room and both girls had a room of their own for the first time, large enough for a desk each to do their homework. Mutti was able to keep her room, more spacious without the girls' beds. The kitchen was extended out the back, making it bigger and allowing more space for a dining area and the bathroom shed was made part of the house. Erich even managed to build a workshop next to the carport for his furniture business. With carpet laid throughout and fresh curtains Mutti and I had made, the house felt a lot more comfortable and homely, a place I thought we all wanted to come home to.

However, Karoline loved the garden most of all and she pottered about for much of the day, tending to the vegetable plot and the flower garden with such dedication that both flourished. Erich and I had planted the garden with the best of intentions but between building the extension and all the work we were both doing it had been sadly neglected. Now we had juicy tomatoes plucked off their vines at just the right time, salad greens, beans, celery, corn and potatoes. And patches of colour exploded around the house, the clusters of abundant blossoms making me smile whenever I drove up the driveway or looked out the windows.

Although Karoline loved to be involved in whatever the girls were doing, they had their own lives now and didn't spend so much time with either grandmother. Karoline and Mutti kept away from each other as much as possible. They understood that if the current living arrangements were going to work, they would need to employ restraint. They had never been friends and now living on top of each other only seemed to accentuate their differences. But Mutti was out most days of the week for at least a few hours and that seemed to remedy the situation.

Karoline spoilt Erich, making him lunch and bringing him cups of coffee at regular intervals throughout the day. She saw how stubborn he was, refusing to let his leg stop him from doing the things he wanted and how the pain wore him down, often making him gruff and uncommunicative by the end of the day. I knew he didn't mind the small intrusions as it made him rest his leg and relax his iron will. Besides, they had a common interest in furniture making – his mother had worked in her husband's store and had watched him make furniture on many occasions. It must have been poignant for her, watching her son take on the same occupation as his father.

Karoline's presence was good for Erich. He was able to reminisce with her, and although I knew how much he wanted to return to Germany, he seemed to accept that it wouldn't be possible for a long while and took comfort in hearing every little detail about Eva's and Walter's lives from his mother. Sharing his experiences with her reminded him how much we'd achieved since arriving in Australia and how our family was thriving. And that could only be a good thing.

But it didn't stop Erich's quest for change. Since the success he'd had with the Bonegilla incident eighteen months earlier, he'd become more politically active, lobbying government departments and determined to help push for new legislation to make discrimination against migrants more difficult to perpetrate. He was like a dog with a bone. The nature of his crusading had changed, putting him further in the way of the government, and my anxiety grew and grew.

I knew I couldn't stop him. His desire to help those unable to help themselves was driven by something much deeper than ego, pride and a man's unerring belief in his own freedom and right to do as he pleased. It was something already within him, perhaps from what he'd witnessed through the war and fuelled by the helplessness and guilt he'd felt since we'd arrived.

Rather than resent him for the time he gave to his cause and for the worry that always lurked in the back of my mind, I decided to join Sabine at her art class one night a week. If Erich could spend time pursuing his passion, then so could I. From the way she spoke of it at work, it sounded like a lot of fun, nothing too serious, but something new I'd enjoy. Once she saw I was interested, she encouraged me to come. A light-hearted atmosphere would give me space to breathe and bring me some much needed laughter. I could leave the household in the capable hands of the mothers for a few hours. When I told Karoline, she nearly pushed me out the door.

'Go, have fun. Do something for yourself,' she said. 'It will be good for you.'

'I don't know why I didn't do this sooner,' I said to Sabine as I stood at the easel, sketching the bottle, glasses and fruit on the table and thirsty for more knowledge. I found that I understood the techniques the teacher was explaining to us and implicitly knew how to apply what I'd learnt to the paper beneath my hand.

'You're a natural,' she said, gazing at my sketch. I'd quickly drawn in with some detail the figure of one of the women who sat waiting at the table. It seemed a good likeness of her. 'You're coming every week until you're better than the teacher and I won't take no for an answer.'

'Don't be silly.'

'I mean it, Lotte. Promise me you'll keep coming. You have real talent and you have to see where this takes you.'

Perhaps it was something I could be good at, something that was just for me. I nodded slowly. 'All right, I promise.'

'Maybe one day I'll be able to say that I knew you before you were famous,' she said grinning. I dismissed her comment with a wave of my hand but something inside of me had ignited and I couldn't wait until the next week's lesson.

Reading the newspaper in my lunchbreak one Friday in early February, I was shocked to see that another diplomatic incident was unfolding in Canberra. The First Secretary of the Russian Embassy, a man named Skripov, was being expelled after it was discovered that he'd been involved in espionage. My thoughts immediately went to Erich. Claudia and Franz's warnings and the opened mail came flooding back to me. Evidence of Russian intelligence and espionage on Australian soil would only heighten the watchful eyes of ASIO, tightening the net around any suspected of dealings or association with communists.

That newspaper article fermented in the back of my mind for the rest of the day while I smiled and calmly guided clients into the right position for that perfect photo shoot, so my blood was boiling when I finally got into the car, readying myself for a confrontation with Erich.

He was in his workshop, sawing timber for a telephone table he was making.

'Have you seen the newspaper today?' I asked, standing in the doorway.

He straightened, laying the handsaw on the bench beside him before turning to look at me. 'No, what is it?'

'A diplomatic incident with the Russian Embassy. The government's deported one of the senior diplomats.' I thrust the newspaper at him.

Erich glanced at the front page. 'Espionage?'

'That's right, and there's hard evidence: photos, letters, packages, a transmitting device and testimony from an Australian agent Skripov cultivated. What would they want from Australia? We're not exactly the centre of the world.'

'Most likely anything to do with Australia's military program and its projects with the British and Americans. There's been a lot of opposition to the testing of long-range missiles at Woomera.'

'That kind of information in Russian hands will only bring the world one step closer to outright war!' The Peace Movement was against the missile project at Woomera and I understood that opposition – those of us who'd experienced the devas-tation of bombing raids could never condone the escalation of weapons development, but I'd never thought of Russian interest – communist interest – in such Australian projects.

'That's right,' said Erich. 'Who'd ever have imagined the state of the world this soon after the last war? The money that's spent on these programs would be better spent improving the lives of ordinary people. It's madness.'

'It'll be high alert now. Anyone at all associated with known communists will be scrutinised. Erich, you can't afford to be anywhere near them.' I loved him for his passion – he'd make a good politician and an honest one – but his fight against injustice was becoming dangerous.

He frowned and I seized his arms, panic overwhelming me.

'I think someone's reading our mail,' I blurted. 'If you can't listen to Franz or to me, then please listen to reason. What if you're already being followed?'

'Lotte, Franz is well-meaning but he's overreacting. Ernst told me Franz was a junior law clerk during the war. He was involved with the cases of people associated with the White Rose movement and in the 1944 assassination attempt on Hitler. According to Ernst, the hunting down and prosecution of those people has haunted him ever since.'

I sagged, deflated for a moment, understanding what that might mean to Franz. I remembered the conversations Heinrich and I had had about the White Rose. He'd known some of them – medical students like him working together on the Eastern Front and studying at the University of Munich, good people – and understood their disillusionment with the Nazi regime. He had mourned their loss when they were executed by the Gestapo. How could our past, our history, not influence our future, who we were? Any of us who had lived under tyranny felt deeply about justice and freedom and many of us continued that fight here in Australia.

'That explains a lot about his passion for civil rights.'

Erich nodded. 'The firm he works with now deals with a lot of backhanded negotiations, political manoeuvring and intrigue. Although the men they represent speak up about injustice and try to force change, they don't work in the background: they're openly defiant and make themselves targets for the government. After what he's seen, of course he's going to imagine the worst.'

'And *you're* not openly defiant? Don't you openly oppose the treatment of migrant workers? Don't you lobby for fair and equal rights and an end to discrimination?'

He slammed the newspaper down on the bench. 'I'll never back down from these injustices, you know that, but I make sure that I'm smart about it. I don't flaunt myself and I don't agree with violence as a means of gaining attention. I'm only exercising my rights as an Australian citizen by using my voice to speak for those who can't be heard. I'm in no danger. I know how to stay out of trouble.'

'The communists—'

'They have no real power in Australia, Lotte. Besides, the Communist Party is a legal political party that I have no affiliation with.'

He stepped towards me and cupped my cheek. 'Don't worry, my darling. Nothing will happen to me, I promise. Our family is safe. Just trust me.'

I only hoped that he was right, that he was careful enough. All I could do now was put my faith in him.

15

It was a cold autumn evening, the first that heralded the coming of winter, when I came home to find Erich sitting in the kitchen with a strange expression on his face, somewhere between thoughtfulness and bewilderment. The beer he had opened sat untouched on the laminate table, beads of condensation trickling down the bottle.

'What's wrong?' I asked. *This is it*, I thought. The government had finally cornered him. 'Has something happened?'

Erich nodded. 'What is it?' I put my handbag down on the kitchen counter and slid across the lime vinyl of the bench seat, feeling sick to my stomach. I glanced at the electric cooktop and oven surrounded by a row of new white cupboards. There was dinner still to cook but it didn't matter for now.

'I received my biggest commission today. I've been asked to make a dining suite: chairs, table and buffet; all in top-grade timber, with possibly more commissions to come.'

It wasn't his union activities. I took a deep breath and let it out slowly. My heart resumed its regular beat and my vision became sharp and clear again.

'That's wonderful. How did you get it?' I was thirsty and took a sip of his beer.

'Word of mouth . . . It's a new customer but when I met him today, I realised I knew him.'

He reached for the bottle and took a long swallow then looked at me, his green eyes round and misty with memory. 'From my days in Silesia. I never thought I'd see him or his family again. In fact, I didn't know if they'd survived.'

'Did something happen?'

He tipped the bottle to his mouth. 'They're Jews, Lotte.' He let that comment hang in the air for a moment. Then he sighed and pushed his hand through his hair. 'Vati was involved with a network that helped to get them out of Germany safely. He'd been helping local families to emigrate while I was still studying. It was only when I returned home to manage the furniture shop when he was ill with pneumonia that I discovered what he was doing and how deep his involvement was. I took over from him until he was well again and we worked together until I left Grottkau. As far as I know he continued long into the war.'

'What? Why have you never told me this before?' I whispered. I had never known Erich's father. He'd disappeared in those final days of the war, fighting in Breslau with the Volkssturm.

'At first it was dangerous for you to know and I wanted to protect you. Afterwards, we were struggling to survive. When we decided to make a fresh start in Australia, stories of our past seemed best left behind, along with those years we'd rather forget. We've been working so hard to secure our future since that I never thought to bring it up.'

A sudden surge of irritation rippled through me. We'd been married for nearly eighteen years and this was an important part of his life that he'd kept from me. I had always been strong enough to hear the truth and had never shied away from it. I had told him everything.

'But it's no small thing.'

Erich shrugged. 'Vati considered it his duty, what any decent human being would do to help a fellow neighbour. But we had no idea how far things would go . . . It's remarkable how many families my father and his acquaintances helped, families that still live and breathe today.' This was a part of Erich's life I knew so little about, but he didn't see how his omission might have upset me. It was just something that he had done many years ago, before he had known me. As much as it annoyed me, it wasn't worth arguing about now.

He leant forward, his elbows on the table, frowning. 'Julius Berlowitz and his family had been planning to leave Germany before my father fell ill. But before their travel plans could be finalised, the Nuremberg Race Laws came into effect and travel became a dangerous and difficult thing. We were finally able to get them safe passage to Switzerland, where the next stage of their travel plans would be made. He told me that they finally made it to Australia in 1937 . . . He asked after my father, of course.'

'That's unbelievable.' A hot flame of pride coursed through me. I had always known that Erich was a compassionate man, courageous, a man of principle who felt called to protect not just those he loved but those who were unable to protect themselves. Now I understood where these traits had come from and a sudden realisation slotted into place like the final piece of a puzzle. This was why he was fighting so hard for migrants. It was personal for him. I wished I had known him then. I wished I had known his father, who had put the needs of others above his own safety.

He passed me the bottle and I took another sip, enjoying the bitterness lingering on my tongue.

'Berlowitz is retired now. He went back to university to get his law degree and eventually set up his own firm in the city, which his son now runs. He's just built a new house looking out over the bush in Killara and wants to furnish it with handcrafted items.' His expression turned wistful again. 'Apparently he had some of my father's pieces in his home in Grottkau. He told me that he had never seen a finer craftsman than my father but that my furniture not only shows expert craftsmanship but artistic flair. I did learn from the best.'

'How did he hear about you?'

'Through Franz, of all people. Franz works for his firm and told him about my work and Julius put two and two together . . .'

'Really? Isn't it a strange world?'

'Yes. He's promised me more work, more commissions in fact, and knows a number of people who would be interested in my pieces who are prepared to pay for quality craftsmanship and original design.' He looked at me with wonder. 'I think our fortunes have just improved. If this eventuates, we can start to make a good living and you won't have to work so hard.'

I kissed him and his arms enfolded me as he held me tight.

'That's so wonderful, my darling,' I said. So often, the long arm of our past touched us with cold fingers and the harsh reality of what had been came flooding back, but today it brought a golden light and a happy ending.

Work was busier than ever for me. Business at the studio was growing and Reinhardt had to employ another photographer. Marion was young and relatively inexperienced and it often fell to me to supervise and mentor her. With appointments so crammed through the day, the few minutes I could spare with her here and there never seemed enough. I remembered how it had been for me when I'd started and made time after work to instruct her on the finer points of the European training I'd received.

'Hi, Otto.' The sound of what I knew was a school bag, thudded on the floor in the lunchroom. Another followed close behind.

'Hi, girls. How was school?'

'All right.' It was Greta. I heard her slam her books on the table. She still had homework even after spending the afternoon in the school library while Johanna was at athletics training.

'Your mother's going to be a little while yet. Do you want some toast?'

'Yes, I'm starved.' I smiled before turning my attention back to Marion. Johanna was always hungry these days. She was slim and willowy but I was sure she had hollow legs. At fifteen she was as tall as me but still growing. The girls were growing up and time was passing us by. All I wanted to do was spend the evening with them, to capture the very ordinary moments of a school night before they were gone.

'That will do for today, Marion. Practise these techniques as much as possible to improve your skills. You've come a long way already.'

'Thanks for taking the time to help me, Lotte,' she said, packing up her equipment.

'I'm glad to help. See you tomorrow.'

I went to the lunchroom to find Johanna munching on hot buttered toast, Otto smoking a cigarette while waiting for the kettle to boil and Greta's dark head bent over her school books.

'Thank you, Otto,' I murmured as I cupped Johanna's cheek in greeting and gazed over Greta's shoulder at her work. He was like family to us and often looked in on the girls on the days that they stayed late with me, feeding them or helping with homework when he could.

I kissed her silky hair. 'How are you, my darling?'

'Not good, Mutti,' she muttered. 'I've got an essay due tomorrow and I haven't started.'

'Why have you left it to the last minute? What were you doing this afternoon?'

'She was with her friends,' said Johanna with a mouth full of toast. 'She went down to the café to play the jukebox with them.'

Greta's head jerked up, her face contorted with outrage. 'How would you know?'

'Amanda's sister told us when she came to pick her up,' she said smugly.

I glanced at Otto, who raised an eyebrow wryly. He'd seen enough to understand teenage girls by now. Instead of getting upset, I took a deep breath. Even moments like these were times to treasure.

'Enough, girls,' I said in my sternest tone. 'Johanna, don't tell tales on your sister. You know she's allowed to go to the café once a week with her friends – she is nearly seventeen after all.' I could see Greta smile from the corner of my eye. 'Greta, I know you enjoy your socialising but if you have homework that has to come first.'

She nodded, looking worried again. 'Sorry, Mutti.'

'Come on, let's go home early and leave Otto in peace. I'll help you with your assignment, Greta, and Johanna, you can tell us all about your athletics over dinner.'

Both girls looked so pleased that I felt a stab of guilt. They needed me more than ever I realised. Even with both grand-mothers at home, they still needed me, wanted my attention. I reached for Johanna with one arm, pulled Greta to me as she rose from the chair, and hugged them tightly.

'I love you both.'

'We love you too,' whispered Greta.

'Come on, Mutti, let's go home. I've got so much to tell you,' said Johanna, beaming.

I was sitting at the big dining table opening the mail one evening when I came across a plain envelope, its front blank – it had been hand-delivered. Karoline was in the kitchen with the girls cleaning up after dinner, Mutti was reading on the lounge and Erich was in the workshop. I opened the envelope.

GO BACK TO WHERE YOU CAME FROM, YOU COMMIE NAZI BASTARD, was written on the page in the envelope in large, black capitals.

'Dear God!' I whispered. I pushed the chair back, barely making a noise on the lino. Greta's head appeared in the kitchen doorway.

'What's wrong, Mutti?'

I stared up at her, my heart thumping. 'Nothing,' I said in a strangled voice. 'I have to talk to Vati about something, that's all. Go and help Omi in the kitchen.'

She nodded dubiously.

'Now, Greta,' I snapped.

Her face turned from concern to anger as she disappeared from the doorway in a huff.

I picked up the letter with shaking hands and took it to the workshop.

Erich was at my side in an instant. 'What is it? You're white as a ghost. Here, sit before you fall down.' He helped me into the chair and crouched beside me.

'This came today,' I said.

Erich frowned and pulled the letter from my grasp. '*Scheisse!*'

'What are you going to do?'

'It's all right. Don't worry. I'll take care of it.'

'What do you mean? Do you know who's done this? What kind of crazy person out there wants to do us harm? Our children—'

'I'll fix this, I promise.'

'How can you fix it? It's too late.'

'It's just someone trying to get to me by scaring you,' he whispered, kissing my forehead.

I pushed him away. 'Why? What haven't you been telling me?'

He sat quite suddenly on an upturned bucket, his shoulders hunched. Then he sighed, rubbing his face with his hands. 'There are a few union members who think I'm a bit too vocal . . . narrow-minded bigots. They promised to make my life difficult if I didn't stay away from migrant matters.'

'And you didn't think to tell me that? After all my concerns?'

'I didn't want to worry you and I never thought it would amount to anything.'

I stood, knocking the chair over in my haste, breathing heavily. Erich rose too, eyes wary. 'I don't feel safe,' I said. 'Do I have to constantly look over my shoulder now and worry about strangers walking towards me or the children?'

'It's me they're trying to intimidate. You know I'll make sure nothing happens to you.'

'So you'll resign from the union? Surely that's all they really want from you.' My voice was low and tight with anger.

He shook his head. 'No. It's time to take this matter to the police.'

'What if it doesn't stop?'

'Then I'll follow it up with the proper authorities until it does. It's just standover tactics. I've seen it before, but I'll do everything to make sure our family is safe.'

I realised then he wasn't going to stop, even with this threat and the potential risk to our family. On the other hand, I didn't know if I'd respect him if he did. I was furious that men were trying to manipulate and intimidate Erich, determined to quiet the voice of vulnerable people in search of a better life and to keep the status quo. Should I support him – or walk away for the sake of my family?

I stumbled back to the house and to the inky blackness of our bedroom.

But my troubles were far from over. Mutti had had enough. It had been nearly a year since the arrival of Karoline and tensions between them had reached boiling point.

'She doesn't even acknowledge me,' hissed Mutti one Sunday afternoon, flipping through the pages of *Woman's Day*. Erich had taken his mother and the girls on a drive to the other side of Sydney to inspect the timber supplies of a merchant on the Northern Beaches. He'd promised the girls an ice cream and a walk along the beach.

'Well, if you made more effort with her, maybe she would. You're never home as it is.'

Mutti had developed a number of friendships among the German community but Claudia's cousin Hilde, our old neighbour Suzanne, and Dr Rodsky, Rudi as she now called him, were among her closest friends. Mutti was even working now, helping Dr Rodsky in his surgery three days a week. As a consequence, Mutti was hardly home and, whenever she was, it didn't take much for her to become irritated and annoyed.

'Why would I spend my days here? You and the girls aren't home and I don't need to watch your mother-in-law pander to her son while throwing me dirty looks when I've not done a thing. When she's had enough, she has her own room to go to, while I still have the tiny area next to the kitchen.

Even you and your children have your own rooms now. I had to put up with living in the middle of nowhere with no plumbing, electricity or hot water, sleeping in the same room as your children for months – which I did happily to support you. I kept an eye on your husband after the accident until he was independent again, which I also didn't mind. But when news of his mother coming arrived, there was suddenly talk of building plans. I lived through the dirt and chaos of the extensions without complaint but when Karoline arrived, it was she who got the new bedroom.' Mutti scowled at me, her blue eyes bright with anger. 'I hardly think it's fair.'

'We've been over this a thousand times, Mutti,' I said, banging down the iron more heavily than I needed to. I was tired after a full week and a wedding the night before. The last thing I needed was Mutti whingeing and stirring up trouble. 'I know your room is smaller and noisy but at least it's your own private space. Karoline's much older than you and frail. She sleeps in the afternoon and her room is quieter and there's less chance of her having a fall. You're hardly home anyway. One day, when we can afford it, we'll extend some more and give you a bigger room.'

'I know she doesn't approve of my social life or the fact that I'm working. She thinks I should stay home, look after you all and serve you hand and foot. As far as she's concerned, my life's over now. I should kiss her son's feet and be grateful to be living here in squalor and isolation. If only I could change that day when I lost everything on the ship . . . Things would be so different now. Look at what I've come to.'

'Stop, Mutti! It's not that bad. You're exaggerating now. She never said those things.' I picked up a pair of slacks and placed them on the ironing table, wondering how much more of this I needed to put up with until Dr Rodsky arrived to pick her up. He was taking her to the movies to see *Cleopatra*.

'Neither of us would be in this situation if you'd married Heinrich. He's doing well in Germany, an important and influential man within the new Ministry of Health.'

'I don't care about Heinrich. But have you thought that maybe neither of us would be in this situation if you'd insured your belongings?' I said hotly, pulling savagely at the waistband of the slacks. I hated when she mentioned him. He was ancient history and best left in the past where he belonged.

'How dare you throw that in my face after everything I've done for you! Your husband still can't support you like you deserve and rather than finding another job, he spends his time off talking about improving the lives of others, migrants like us, but here you are, his own wife, still working like a slave. You've been propping him up for years. Tell me how that's right?'

I hadn't told Mutti about our troubles with the anonymous letter and thank God I hadn't, because I would never have heard the end of it. I wanted to throw the iron at her but I placed it carefully down on the table. I wasn't happy about our situation and I was still terribly angry about the danger Erich had put us in, but that was nobody's concern but ours.

'Everything Erich does is for this family. Keep your nose out of our affairs.'

'Oh, but it is my business,' said Mutti icily, rising from her chair. 'You are my daughter. I know about the risk your husband's putting you and the children in.'

I stared at her, horrified.

'Yes, that's right. Hilde told me. She overheard Franz talking about it to Erich. For his own gratification, his own chest-beating, he's putting his family in danger.'

'It's not like that,' I said, moving calmly away from the ironing table, although I could feel the panic building inside me. 'You know he wouldn't do anything that would put us in harm's way and I'm proud of what he's doing. He's the one ensuring a better future for all of us.' I couldn't help myself. I had to defend him.

'All he'll be remembered for is being a Nazi and a communist!'

'Look who's cavorting with a Russian!' I shouted, losing control. 'Have you ever thought that maybe you're the one bringing danger down on our heads? You and Rudi frequent the Russian Club and I've heard that it's a hotbed of communist activity. Why can't you go to the Concordia Club instead?'

'Cavorting?' Mutti and I were nose to nose. 'I don't cavort and Rudi would never do anything to place me or you in any danger, unlike your selfish husband.'

'If you can't keep your nasty opinions to yourself, I don't want you here. You can go and find somewhere else.'

'You wouldn't dare throw me out!' bellowed Mutti.

'You just try me!'

'You know, you're right. I don't know why I've put up with this for so long.' She was breathing heavily, her face red and blotchy with fury. 'You want me out of your business? Well, that can definitely be arranged. I'll start looking for my own place tomorrow.' She turned on her heel and strode to her bedroom, slamming the door behind her.

I was livid, but mortified by what I'd just done. I had to get out of the house before the situation had a chance to escalate any further, if that was at all possible. I jumped in my car and went into the studio to do some work but all I could think about was the past and the tumultuous relationship I'd always had with my mother. Even when I was a young girl, she'd constantly remind me of our rigid social traditions, impressing on me the importance of upholding our family name, but she didn't see me, the person I was and so desperately wanted to express. Erich had understood that about me almost immediately. My mother's interference nearly destroyed our relationship once, but I was damned if she would have the chance again. Whatever I chose to do, it was my decision to make and nobody else's, and although Mutti's words had forced me to make the choice, I chose to stand by Erich's side as he'd always done for me.

When I'd cooled down enough to come home, my mother's belongings were gone.

16

Later that week, I met Claudia at one of the few coffee shops that sold continental cakes. Mutti hadn't returned home since our fight but Suzanne had rung me to tell me that she was staying with her until she found her own place. I was conflicted about the situation – I felt guilty and heartless, but I knew I had to be strong and stand my ground. I had decided not to tell Erich about it, only that Mutti was helping Suzanne out for a few days. I didn't want him to feel responsible for the rift between my mother and me, and besides, some of what Mutti had said rang true, although I could hardly admit it to myself. She had put niggling doubts into my head about the wisdom of supporting Erich's activities and staying with him. I still hadn't forgiven him. Claudia was the one person I could tell who would understand.

'I told my mother to move out on Sunday. I'm tired of her blaming Erich for everything that isn't to her satisfaction.

I know she finds it difficult with Karoline, but she's hardly home to worry about it.'

'She's been spending a lot of time with Hilde this week. I overheard them talking about finding an apartment to rent together. Hilde's ready to go too. She's had enough of Onkel Ernst. As have I, to be honest.'

'You've had to put up with a lot. Maybe we should leave them all to their own devices and you and I move out and enjoy ourselves for a change.'

Claudia laughed. 'Your mother told Hilde that since you don't need her to look after the children any more, it made sense to move back into Liverpool, closer to work.'

'Really?' I sat there flabbergasted that my mother could turn this to her advantage. 'She might think that this is a great adventure but I'm not so sure how she'll manage on her small income. You know how much she loves the high life.'

Mutti was desperate to make a new life for herself. She missed the cultural hub of Munich and having everything within walking distance. It was a city thrumming with energy, and there was always something new and exciting to keep her interested. She missed her friends and her old life. She and Rudi had attended the few cultural pursuits that were available in Sydney, such as opera or symphonies, but I worried that it only made her miss what she'd left behind even more. She was never going to try to become Australian, to really forge a new life for herself here. Instead she surrounded herself with her German and European friends, those who enjoyed the finer things in life, who could reminisce about the old days with her. It felt as if she was living in the shadows of her old life.

'She told Hilde that she and Dr Rodsky were more than friends.' Hilde worked as a pharmacist's assistant at the chemist and had introduced Mutti to Rudi, who was now the doctor for both families. Claudia leant conspiratorially across the table. 'Do you think she loves him?'

I sighed again. How did life get so complicated? 'All I know is that since they've become friends and Mutti's been making a little money, she's become a lot more comfortable and confident here. That's when she started showing her true colours again – she has money and a man behind her and she thinks she can tell me whatever she likes, meddle in my affairs and my marriage. But she tried that once. Never again.'

Claudia grasped my hand across the table and squeezed it in sympathy.

'I know my mother blames Erich for her being here at all. She misses my father and I understand her frustrations, but she went one step too far . . .' I leant in towards Claudia. 'She called him a Nazi and a communist,' I whispered. 'I saw red.'

'He's neither of those things,' said Claudia quietly.

'No, he's not, and I know she didn't mean it, but she's got it in her head that he's putting us in danger.' The waitress placed a slice of dark chocolate cake with a luscious dollop of whipped cream in front of me. I stared at it longingly, waiting for our coffee to arrive.

'And you don't agree? I know what Franz has been telling you and Erich. Everyone seems to be whipped into a frenzy over the supposed communist invasion of this country.'

I nodded to the waitress as she placed my coffee in front of me. I inhaled, taking in the delicious smell of the dark brew before adding a dash of milk. I thought about how to answer Claudia as I watched her fork cut into the flaky pastry of the apple strudel she'd ordered. It was strange to believe that simple food like this had been impossible to find in the suburbs a few years earlier.

'All right. I'm worried that Erich's in deeper than he realises. He's not Martin Luther King, for goodness sake. What if he steps over some invisible line again? Who's to say that the consequences won't be more serious next time?'

'Franz's activities during the war haunt him, you know.' I glanced at Claudia in surprise and she nodded. 'Since joining the firm, he's begun to tell me about his job as a law clerk during those years. He was helpless to save good people from Nazi prosecution and I think maybe now he can't bear to see anyone in a precarious and dangerous position as a result of them speaking out against injustice.' She patted her mouth daintily with the linen serviette. 'If anything, I think he's more single-minded than ever since his uncle's arrived. It's as if having Onkel Ernst around is a constant reminder of that time. I know that he was Franz's mentor and found him work after law school, but Franz refuses to say any more than that.' She looked into the distance. 'You know, there are times when he seems so on edge that the children and I walk on eggshells around them both.'

'I've noticed it sometimes too. It's like Franz loves Ernst but hates him at the same time.'

'That's exactly what it is. I don't know how long we can go on like this before Franz reaches breaking point.'

'Maybe Ernst should move in with Mutti. She'd sort him out quick smart.'

Claudia laughed and I smirked, thinking it was actually a good idea. I tried a mouthful of the cake. It was velvety smooth and sweet with a hint of bitter dark chocolate. Almost as good as the ones back in Germany.

'Instead, your mother is taking Hilde with her. I don't blame Hilde for wanting to go. The children are always underfoot, noisy and messy, while Franz and Onkel Ernst constantly try to outdo each other to show who's in charge. Franz religiously plays an hour of piano every night, it's his way to relax, and gives each of the children lessons, which only seems to anger his uncle. It's his only real act of defiance, because we both know that the piano, the house and the law degree were all only possible because of Ernst. I don't want to ask how, but I know that he could take it all away in a heartbeat. He seems harmless, but if he doesn't get what he wants . . .'

'We came here to start over, to have a new life, but it seems that our controlling family members are intent on dragging us all back to the restrictions of our past. He has to go too, Claudia.'

'I know,' she said sadly. She was trapped and could do nothing about it except stand by her husband's side and support him. Franz, like Erich, would do what he thought was best but it didn't make it any easier on us. It seemed that we were the strong ones who held up our husbands and families. Despite their best intentions, they were the ones causing us to suffer. I thought about Mutti, seeking her freedom, and for a moment I wished I were in her shoes.

'I thought I was coming here today to ease my conscience about asking my mother to leave. I haven't been able to sleep, worried I've done the wrong thing – been too harsh on her.'

'And now?'

'Mutti has to find her own place in this country, just as you and I do. I almost envy the freedom she has to choose what she wants but I also know that asking her to go was the only decision that would allow me to find my place. I have to manage the troubles I'm having with Erich on my own.' Since our confrontation about the threatening letter and Erich's refusal to quit, the safety of my family only seemed possible if I left and took the girls with me. It was a horrific thought, one I could barely contemplate. But I knew I had to try everything I could before I walked away.

'You don't mean that your marriage is in real trouble, do you? You belong together.'

'What if love isn't enough, Claudia? What if Mutti's right? If the danger to my family doesn't stop? That's Erich's doing. He put us through that, he put us at risk.' I shut my eyes briefly, swallowing my tears, trying to pull myself together. 'I still don't feel safe. I can't stop looking over my shoulder, I jump every time there's a knock at the door. I have to put my children first.'

'Lotte, you're getting ahead of yourself. Go home and tell Erich that your mother's decided to live in town with Hilde. I'm sure without your mother constantly looking over your shoulders, you'll find that things settle down. Give yourselves some time to breathe. You can find each other again.'

I nodded, overwhelmed. 'Maybe you're right. I'm just drained. I never imagined doing something like asking my mother to leave. Suddenly everything seems unmanageable.'

'We understand each other, Lotte. Maybe we should do this more regularly or maybe even see a movie once in a while? It might do those men some good to see what it's like without us for an evening.'

I laughed shakily. 'Let's do that.'

We were watching the news on our new television a month before Christmas when we learnt that the American president, John F Kennedy, had been assassinated.

'This will cause shockwaves across the globe,' said Erich, leaning back on the lounge, legs stretched out on the carpet square under the coffee table, as if he still relished the extra space and calm since Mutti had left.

But I wasn't really listening. I was watching Jackie Kennedy in her blood-smeared dress, her expression of uncomprehending horror and shock. She had lost her husband and the father of her children. None of us knew when our time was up and although Mutti was fit as an ox, she wasn't getting any younger. Maybe it was time to patch things up with her.

I went to see Mutti at her flat. It was lunchtime and my mother's day off.

'What are you doing here?'

'Can I come in?' She stared at me a moment, her blue eyes like ice.

'All right. For a moment. I have to go to work.' I nodded and bit back my retort, following her into the tiny lounge area.

'Coffee?'

'Yes please.' Mutti's good manners to a guest were automatic, even to me.

She moved to the kitchen and put on the kettle. 'What do you want? Don't ask me to come back to your place, because

I won't.' She put two cups and saucers on the bench, refusing to look at me.

'I know, and I'm not here to ask you to. I just wanted to see you . . . I miss you.' Her stony expression softened. 'Did you see Jackie Kennedy after her husband was assassinated?'

Mutti nodded and frowned, placing a teaspoon of instant coffee into each cup.

'Life's too short, Mutti. We've been through so much together and always come out the other end. I don't want to fight with you any more.'

Her shoulders sagged. 'What you did was unforgivable. I've only ever wanted the best for you yet you disregard and ignore me.' She sighed. 'You did me a favour really. It was time to stand on my own two feet.'

'I'm sorry. Really I am . . . but you pushed me too far. You have to let me stand on my own two feet too.'

'I know. We're too much alike.' She smiled wearily and poured the water into the cups.

'Can we try again? Maybe the distance is good for us. If we can respect each other's lives, we can start talking.'

'Maybe.' She handed me my coffee. 'Come and sit down then.'

Slowly Mutti and I began talking once more. We gave each other the space that we needed and met once a week only for coffee at first. I was pleased to learn that Mutti was doing well on her own. Hilde was pefect company for her but she was spending a lot more time with Rudi. He was good to her and it made me happy to see her moving past the loss of Vati.

I was more than a little envious when she told me that they had attended a special performance by the Australian

Ballet where Margot Fonteyn and Rudolf Nureyev appeared together. Nureyev was Russian and had defected while on tour in Paris in 1961, causing an international sensation. The Soviet government kept a tight rein on its national icons.

I sat, mesmerised, as Mutti described the once-in-a-life-time performance and hoped that one day I could enjoy such things again.

I told her about Johanna who was desperate to see the Beatles when they began their Australian concert tour. She had pictures of the English group plastered on the wall of her bedroom and begged me to let her go, but I'd seen the images of girls screaming and swooning at the sight of the four young men in Sydney, crushed against barricades and being trampled by the surging crowd. She was too young, only sixteen, and I refused. She was crushed and resorted to playing her one Beatles record over and over, and sat glued to our small television whenever the evening news was broadcast. I felt bad, but I was too busy to take her and there was no way she was going on her own. I realised that the older my daughters got, the more I understood my mother.

The fight with Mutti had reminded me what I loved about Erich and in forcing me to defend him, it now made me realise I had to put any thoughts of leaving him out of my head and make things work. I still didn't know from day to day if I was doing the right thing but, since the anonymous letter, he'd been making the effort to spend more time with us and that was a start.

One Sunday we visited the famous blowhole in Kiama. Karoline had decided to stay home this time, making the excuse that she had a headache. I suspected that she wanted

Erich and I to have some time together. Her hazel eyes were becoming cloudy with age but they missed nothing. She'd seen the distance between us and the frosty interactions that took place whenever Erich attended public rallies or spoke at large gatherings, especially with the recent Mount Isa strikes, where a significant number of migrants were involved in the fight for better wages and conditions for the first time. The worry that we'd be targeted again and our life made unbearable was constantly in the back of my mind.

The girls were already at the viewing area, looking out over the sparkling ocean, waiting for the blowhole to erupt. The stiff breeze buffeted us as we walked past the lighthouse to join them and I pulled my coat closed, tying the belt tight. It was soft and warm, made from fine Australian wool and expensive. Erich had bought it for me as a surprise and had even made sure the colour was right, a fashionable pale blue. I adored it and wore it every opportunity I got. It wasn't something we could afford but it was a little bit of luxury he could give me.

'Let's see if this blowhole is as good as everyone says,' Erich said, smiling. 'Then we'll take the girls for fish and chips.'

It was wonderful to see him so relaxed. The drive down the coast had been breathtaking, emerging from the windy road of the mountain pass cocooned by the lush green of the rainforest to the rugged cliffs and sandy beaches against the blue expanse of the Pacific Ocean. We had stopped along the way at the lookouts to catch and photograph the snatches of the coastline through the trees.

'It's such a beautiful day. We could sit in the park and have a picnic.'

'That's what I was thinking. It looks like there are some

good rock pools too. Maybe after lunch we can go for a walk along the beach and let the girls wander through them.'

I put my arm around his waist. 'They'd love that.'

The blowhole was as good as expected. The excitement on the girls' faces as they waited for the swell to build and enter the cavern below us was priceless and I couldn't help but pull out the camera and get some good close-ups of them. The shrieks of delight and surprise as the blowhole erupted with a deafening boom, showering us with icy cold sea spray, warmed my heart as I jumped back quickly to keep my camera and coat from becoming soaked with my eye still to the viewfinder and clicking furiously away. There were bound to be a few perfect shots among them to remind us of a perfect morning.

We were all laughing, Erich and the girls' damp hair plastered to their faces, cheeks red from the cool breeze, eyes bright with joy.

'That was fantastic,' said Johanna. 'Can we do it again?'

'Maybe later,' I said, putting the camera away. 'There's so much more to see. Let's walk around and explore.'

'I'm hungry. It's lunchtime isn't it?' Johanna shot me a cheeky grin while Greta rolled her eyes in mock disgust.

'Come on then,' said Erich, clutching Johanna tightly to him. 'You seem a bit scrawny. I suppose we'd better feed you up and not let you fade away to a shadow.'

We sat on the grass under the tall Norfolk pines that overlooked the beach.

'There's nothing better than freshly caught and cooked fish, is there?' Erich sighed in pleasure, shifting on the blanket to stretch out his stiff knee.

He was right. The batter was light and crisp and the white fish soft, delicate and juicy. Even the hot chips were good, salty and crisp. White and grey seagulls crowded around, waiting for crumbs to drop, the more brazen ones venturing closer, trying to steal from the pile of chips at the edge of the blanket. Greta threw a chip across the grass and the flock of birds chased after the morsel, squawking and fighting for the prize until the victor flew away with the chip in its beak.

'Give them another one,' said Johanna, amused by the entertainment. Greta obliged and they took it in turn to see which seagull would claim the chip they threw, enticing the birds down onto the yellow sand.

'They're happy,' I said, gazing across the beach.

'They are. Are you?'

'I am, sitting here with you and watching them laugh and have fun.' I looked across to him, leaning back on his elbows. His face was clear of worry, the creases smooth and his eyes a brilliant green. I was suddenly transported back to the meadow on the day the war had ended when we'd stopped and embraced the moment, allowing our problems to drop away for just a little while. I had wanted to photograph him then, to capture the look on his face, the same expression on his face now. This was the man I had married. 'What about you?'

'I'm happy. I have you and the girls and your happiness means everything to me. I see now what you mean. These days are special, they remind me of what's truly important and why we came to Australia in the first place.' He leant across and kissed me. The salt on his lips and taste of fish in his mouth mingled with the wind sighing through the dark green branches of the trees and the gentle pounding of the surf. This felt like home. If only we could stay like this forever. Perhaps if we could remember this feeling whenever we felt adrift we would be all right.

1965

My newfound resolve wavered with the fierce government backlash to the Mount Isa strikes. The Queensland government declared a state of emergency. Picketing was outlawed and the use of banners and distribution of pamphlets had been restricted. This only made the unions more determined to fight for what they believed in. The government retaliated by giving the police unlimited power and the right to disperse any meetings, clamping down on protesters with further arrests. The environment was becoming more volatile by the week.

'How can we live with a government that allows authoritative state rule, giving the police unlimited power to target whoever they like?' Erich's brows were low over eyes that glowed like coals. 'It's not too much of a stretch to that swastika the strikers painted. We left all that behind us, and I'll be damned if I sit and do nothing.'

'I know it's what you have to do – but I worry for your safety.' The usual conflict warred within me. Were we making any headway or was I wasting my time?

He kissed the top of my head. 'Finally migrant voices are heard at a national level but I have to continue the fight until this crisis is resolved for the sake of everything I've worked towards. I promise you that, when it's over, I'll step down from the union.'

'Do you mean it?' It was what I had wanted to hear for so long, I had to be sure.

'I swear to you,' he said, and I began to cry.

It was late afternoon and I was at Claudia's waiting for Greta to finish studying with Anna. They were in their final year of school. Peter was practising the piano, the twins were watching television in the back room and I was chatting to Claudia in the kitchen while she prepared dinner.

'He promised me he'd stop after Mount Isa and I know he will,' I said, 'but it's been dragging on for weeks. Every time he goes out, I wonder if he'll come back in one piece or if I'll get a phone call to tell me he's in hospital, and I worry about the girls too. There's only so much the police can do—'

'Stop that infernal racket!' I stared at Claudia in shock.

'Don't worry. It's just Onkel Ernst. Sometimes he comes in from work cranky and all he wants is quiet. He'll settle down in a minute.' Her smile was half-hearted.

Peter continued at the piano.

'I said quiet!' shouted Ernst in the next room. 'I'll push that blasted piano out the window if I hear another sound.'

Claudia dropped the wooden spoon on the bench and hurried into the lounge room. I stopped in the doorway to see Ernst hovering over a cowering Peter.

'Enough,' said Claudia, getting between Ernst and her son. 'You know Peter has to practise. He wants to be a musician one day.'

'It's bad enough he plays the cello, but does he have to play this, too? Didn't your husband learn his lesson from his father? Music is nothing more than a hobby, not something you can make a decent livelihood out of. If the boy spent more time at his studies maybe he could be a lawyer like his father and me.' Ernst glared at Claudia, swaying as he stepped away.

'You're drunk. Go and sleep it off and leave Peter alone. It's none of your business what he does.'

'Is that so?' He stared at them a moment and then caught sight of me in the doorway. He shrugged and turned away. 'I'm just an old man. What would I know? Knock on my door when dinner's ready.' I watched Ernst walk down the hallway and heard the heavy thud of his door as it shut. Claudia had her arms around Peter, who looked shaken but not surprised.

'It's all right, Mutti,' he said. 'Sometimes the piano sets Onkel Ernst off. Vati said it's because of something that happened during the war when Onkel Ernst made Opa stop being a pianist and Vati had to go to law school instead of the Conservatorium.'

'It doesn't matter. He has no right to treat you that way.' She brushed the blond hair from his forehead.

'Nobody's going to stop me doing what I love.' His blue eyes were defiant and determined.

She kissed his head. 'I know. Finish your practice and wash up for dinner.'

Back in the kitchen, I watched Claudia return to her cooking for a minute.

'Is he always like that?'

'He's worse when he's drunk, which seems to be more often these days.' Her hands were shaking but I sensed that it was with anger rather than fear.

'Do you want me to stay until Franz gets home?'

'No, he's on his way.'

'What did Peter mean about Franz's father?'

'He was a concert pianist. All I know was that he stopped performing rather than abandon the Jewish musicians and conductors he worked with. Ernst convinced him that it was better for Franz to do law and took him under his wing. His father only ever taught after that and the family was nearly destitute. Franz supplemented the family's income until well after the war. As for the rest, I don't know. There's more to it but Franz won't speak about it to me.'

I touched her on the arm. 'I'm sorry, Claudia.'

She smiled sadly. 'Me too.'

Claudia's troubles made me pensive. She was also in a difficult situation. I was sure neither of us had ever imagined our lives being this way and I began to wonder when Erich and I had started drifting apart.

'I can see how upset you are,' Karoline said to me one day while Erich was away on union business.

I looked up. She had been sitting quietly in the corner reading a German classic for her book club, *Effi Briest* by Theodor Fontane. Karoline couldn't speak English very well and was reticent to go out on her own. We'd finally persuaded her to become involved in a club that discussed novels written in German. She felt at home there, speaking with women like herself, and having a particular book to read each month and sharing her views on it gave her an interest outside the house. Besides, I think she was also pleased to give us time to ourselves.

The corner lamp created a halo around her head, long silver braids still coiled neatly at the back. *Just like an angel,*

I thought, my brain automatically seeking photographic opportunities.

'It's nothing,' I said, lighting another cigarette with a quivering hand. I tried to smoke only at work but lately I'd started to smoke at night when Erich was away.

'Erich's a stubborn man, but surely you know he does what he does because he believes it's right.'

'I know,' I said dully, looking out the window into the inky blackness.

'I see how the two of you are together. You're a true partnership. This brings you into conflict at times, but the honesty gives you the means to work through it. Don't give up on him. You have a rare thing: a deep and abiding love for each other.'

I nodded, tears filling my eyes. I put the cigarette out in the ashtray.

'These men of ours will always cause us worry and trouble, but they're men of principle, of passion, and that's what we love about them.'

'I know, but sometimes it's such a struggle.'

Her eyes narrowed. 'You know he can look after himself. He's always thinking one step ahead. He's done it before and in much more dire circumstances.'

'He promised me that it would be over after this Mount Isa crisis.'

'Then trust him and know that the time will come when he'll turn his focus back to home. When he returns fully to you, he'll return empowered and whole, a man who feels he deserves the woman he loves. My husband never had the chance to return to me, and not a day goes by when I wonder what that would have been like.' She smiled sadly.

'You really believe it's as simple as that?'

'I do, and I have every faith in the two of you. You've raised two wonderful daughters who will grow to become strong women just like us, and they will have children who will only know the good life that this country will give them. Their future is beyond anything we could ever have imagined.'

'I know that's what Erich's doing, trying to make things better for our children.'

'You both are, in your own way. Don't forget, I'm always here and you can talk to me.'

'Thank you, Karoline,' I said. Maybe it really was that simple. I felt like I could breathe for the first time in months and I couldn't wait for Erich to come home.

Work was good for me. Keeping busy stopped the thoughts going round and round in my head, I was much requested for studio shoots and weddings and I found that I enjoyed teaching the new photographers what I had learnt during my training and through my years of experience. Sabine worked only occasionally now she had two small children, and Otto split his time between working with his father and working in Europe. I had given up the work at the Sydney studio as it had become too much to manage with the extra hours I was working.

'Lotte, can I see you in my office for a moment?' Reinhardt popped his head around the lunchroom door where I'd been making a coffee and finalising the roster for the weekend while waiting to talk to our newest girl about her photographic skills.

'Of course.' I'd been on my feet all day with back to back studio shoots made more difficult and prolonged by the sudden departure of one of the photographers going home sick and a few crying babies and toddlers that wouldn't settle for their pictures. I stubbed out my cigarette and followed him into the office. 'Is everything all right?'

'Yes, yes. Sit down.' He was still formal when it came to business and I sat across from him at the desk. 'I wanted to talk to you about your duties. You've taken on a lot of extra responsibility these last months, really helping me out when I've been overseas with Otto.'

'I've enjoyed it.'

'I see that. Otto's not here enough to run things efficiently like you can. I think he's more interested in taking his photography in a creative direction but the studio work and weddings are our bread and butter.'

I nodded, thinking about the conversations I'd had with Otto about the perspective of beauty. It was a subjective thing, something not easily translated from the eye of the beholder to the finished photograph. Painting was an interesting medium to explore this desire to express what I found beautiful. I had progressed from the basic classes in drawing to the more complex art of creating a lifelike scene using watercolours and oil paint. It was one thing to draw well, another to paint realistically. I enjoyed experimenting with colour, shading, perspectives in the fore, mid and background, something I couldn't do with film. My background in photography helped, but I wondered if it also made it more difficult as I strove for the perfect finished canvas that was all too elusive. I had many conversations with my teacher about technique and style but I realised that the problem was that I wasn't sure what I was trying to create or what I was trying to express.

'We really wouldn't manage without you and now I want to make it official. I'm promoting you to senior photographer. It comes with a substantial pay increase. You'll be doing everything that you already have been – managing the junior staff, running the studio shoots and drawing up the roster for the weekend weddings.'

My mouth dropped open in shock, and then all of a sudden I couldn't stop smiling. 'Thank you, Reinhardt. I won't let you down.' Finally I was being recognised for all the work I'd been doing and getting a pay rise. 'Senior photographer' had a lovely ring to it, too. It meant that I now had the top pick of the studio work and would attend only the highest profile or exclusive weddings on the weekends. After all the years of doubting that I'd ever work in the industry, here I was, virtually running the studio.

'You deserve it. You're a very fine photographer and you have a good head for business. We're lucky to have you.'

I reached across the desk and squeezed his hand. 'You're like family to us. Over the years we wouldn't have managed without you, Otto and Sabine.'

'Well it's good to see that you're finally on your feet and your family is doing well.' He brushed his thick grey moustache with his hand. 'I sometimes wonder that if my wife was still alive, whether Otto would have found a wife and settled down by now.'

'Don't worry. He's still young. Maybe he hasn't found the right girl yet.'

'Time will tell.' He nodded and smiled. 'Well, I have two grandchildren waiting for me. Sabine's invited me for dinner.'

It was April by the time there was some resolution of the Mount Isa situation.

'I've done what I set out to do. I'm happy with that. Migrants have the same rights as Australian workers now, and there are enough delegates to fight for better wages and conditions for all workers,' said Erich as we came up the driveway from our walk.

'I'm very proud of you. You've made a difference, a better place for our children and for our grandchildren to grow up in.' Wolfie came charging towards us, overjoyed that we were home.

'It's time for me to spend more time with you and the children before they grow up.'

'There's nothing more you want to do?' I braced myself as the German Shepherd jumped up, large paws on my chest. I pushed Wolfie down and scratched behind his ear, his fur soft and warm, waiting for Erich's reply.

'I'm done, like I promised.'

'Are you sure?' I stared into his face but all I could see was determination and relief in his eyes.

He nodded. 'I am.'

I hugged him, the fear I'd been holding on to for years draining away making me light-headed and giddy. He had seen his fight through and had returned to me.

Now it was time to see if we could repair the rift between us.

17

Even with all the positive changes we'd witnessed, none of us were prepared for what was to come: Australia had officially committed itself to the Vietnam War. Civilian medical teams had already departed and military personnel were to follow. But what truly shocked us was the announcement by Prime Minister Menzies in November 1964 that compulsory National Service was to be introduced. Apparently, Australia was no longer safe from the 'aggressive communism' that was trying to take hold in Southeast Asia and it needed more men to defend our shores. The idea that all young men would be subject to a ballot in the year they turned twenty and be bound for two years of military service – with an additional three years' service with the Army Reserves – sparked wide-spread outrage.

Not long after Erich had withdrawn from the union, Claudia and I were discussing the first results of the ballot in disbelief. The first group of conscripts would be sent to training camps by June.

'We came here to protect our children,' said Claudia, banging her coffee cup on the laminate table. She wore a cheery floral dress that showed off her ample bosom and a bright cardigan, perfect for the April weather, but she was anything but cheerful.

'I never wanted my children to ever have anything to do with war, yet here we are.' I couldn't believe it. After all our efforts to come to a country that valued peace and our desire to become Australian citizens, now we'd sentenced our children to participate in a war that had nothing to do with us.

'It's like we're back in Germany at the beginning of the war. These boys are called up against their will, but they're not even old enough to vote. They're still minors under our protection but we can't protect them. How is that right?'

'It's not.' What else could I say? These were boys, only nineteen years old. I was furious, feeling betrayed by the country I now called my own.

'Peter's only a child,' she whispered, tears filling her eyes. 'If this war isn't over in two years, he could be called up.'

I grasped her hand. 'It has to be over by then. The Americans will make sure of that. And the conscripts aren't being sent overseas – they're being trained in the defence of our shores.' I had to believe that this was where it would end, but a cold tendril of fear coiled in my belly. More troops had just been sent to Vietnam, so it certainly looked like Australia was scaling up its commitment to the Vietnam War, not just to prevent communism from reaching our shores but also to improve the relationship with America. By bringing us closer and making us an important ally, it seemed that Australia was losing its innocence. Everything we had come to love, the relaxed and laid-back atmosphere, the peace-loving attitude, its isolation from world troubles, was at risk of disappearing for good.

'I know, but what if he has to go? It's not like any war we've seen before. Nobody really knows what to expect. Even if Peter comes home alive, he'll never be the same.' Her eyes were wide with horror. We had both sent brothers off to war and knew the terrible reality young soldiers faced. Both my brothers had died, while Claudia's brother had returned, only to die of his injuries. We had been fortunate not to watch brothers or husbands waste away in a sanitarium. My mother had had to watch my real father self-destruct after distinguished service in the Great War.

'Surely it won't come to that. If nothing else, the protests will give the government pause, once they see how opposed people are to conscription.'

Claudia nodded. 'I hope you're right. Franz tells me not to worry too, but I hear how his uncle mutters under his breath that the army would do Peter the world of good, make him a man, and my anxiety soars again. You've seen what he's like. Sometimes I want to kill that man with my bare hands.' Her eyes narrowed. 'I know he's manipulated Franz, has him under his control somehow. I know something terrible happened to Franz during the war. He won't talk about it, of course, but the nightmares have never stopped. In fact, they're only getting worse. If I don't get to the bottom of it, I'm afraid it will tear us apart.' Tears filled her eyes.

'Surely Ernst can't hurt him now? He's an old man, living on your generosity.'

'Everything Ernst does is calculated, I can see it in his eyes. He's almost indifferent to me and has very little to do with the children now, thankfully, but he does whatever he wants and continually gets his way, trying to sway Franz to his way of thinking.'

'Franz doesn't strike me as a man who gives in easily.'

'He has a backbone of steel, even against Ernst when it really matters to him. They had an enormous argument when Franz went to work for the Berlowitz firm. "They're Jews and known for their agitator and activist clients and their intrusion into international affairs," Ernst told him. "Why don't you work for one of the more prestigious established firms and focus on commercial law?" He certainly doesn't like the civil rights principles that Franz feels so strongly about.'

She smiled. 'I might come across as the mild-mannered wife, but you know that my family is everything. I'll fight for my husband and children, for our life here. Ernst's presence constantly reminds Franz of his pain. Of that I'm sure. I'm determined to find out what's happened between them, and I will. When I do, I'll look for a way to get Ernst out of our lives once and for all.'

'Is it that serious?'

'It is. I can see my husband slowly withering in front of my eyes, torment eating away at him.'

'Well, if there's anything we can do to help you . . .'

'I know, but I don't think there's anything you can do. Franz has to start talking to me. Otherwise I worry what will happen to him.'

'Just remember that we're here for you.'

Why couldn't things be easy for a change? We'd all tried so hard to escape the shackles of our past, the ghosts of wartime, but inevitably that past stayed with us, catching up with us when we least expected it.

Erich's ghosts, however, seemed to be laid to rest. He seemed more at ease having accomplished what he'd set out to do with the union. He'd even stopped talking about returning to Germany to live, although I knew how much he wanted to see his children and grandchildren. We would visit them as soon as we were able, but I was sure that Erich now considered Australia home. He was happy crafting furniture using many Australian timbers, and had settled easily into a routine without the interruptions of his union work. The furniture business was starting to do well, and he now had a constant stream of work and money coming in. My relief was enormous. It paved the way for an easier relationship and the return of honest, open communication that I'd previously taken for granted.

Erich had his back to me, leaning over the work bench. He'd been cutting timber and I could smell the rich, resinous perfume of the wood. I took a deep breath in. The sight in front of me was wonderful: Erich's back muscles taut cords against the thin white cotton of his shirt as he worked to perfectly match the contrasting timbers he was using in the front of a cocktail cabinet. My eye was drawn down the graceful line of his back. Booted feet planted squarely on the floor supported strong, muscular bare legs. He was a man who had a solid connection to the earth, both grounded in reality and linked to the creativity of nature. I admired and envied this gift he had.

He turned, aware of my eyes on him, and smiled.

'How are you going?' I asked. 'Are you ready for lunch?'

'Give me another fifteen minutes. I just want to finish these front panels.' He straightened up, bending back a few times to take the stiffness out of his spine. I kissed his neck, which smelled of wood shavings, and peered over his shoulder at the design taking shape on the bench.

'Cedar?' I enquired. I loved the rich red lustre of the timber Erich often used as a contrast.

Erich nodded. 'I've decided to use the Australian red cedar. It's more durable than the western red.'

My gaze drifted to the partially completed cabinet made from silver ash. Erich's sense of precision was what made the differing patterns of timber so breathtaking. He enjoyed making pieces that were stylish and elegant, eye-catching in their own way, but still functional and made to last a lifetime. 'It'll be exquisite when you've finished,' I murmured.

'I hope the client likes it.' He sighed, rubbing his thigh and knee. 'It's a fine balance to walk, especially when you throw in the client's requirements.' He smiled ruefully, but I could see the pride in his eyes.

Erich deserved success and the accolades that came with it. There weren't many furniture makers like him.

'I have no doubt they'll love it,' I replied. 'The girls are out and your mother is being picked up after lunch to go to her book club. We'll have the house to ourselves for the afternoon.'

Erich put his arms around me and kissed me. 'That sounds promising. I think I might have to take the afternoon off.' His voice was throaty with desire and I shivered with anticipation at the rare delight of an afternoon on our own.

*

Later that afternoon, lying in bed next to Erich, languid and replete, I was aware of simple pleasures: my arm resting lazily across his chest, feeling its rhythmic rise and fall; the soft breeze from the open windows caressing my naked skin; the mellow glow of the afternoon sun as it fell dappled against the bedroom wall. We were suspended in a state of grace, far removed from the ordinary world. It was wonderful to look at him at leisure and in the daylight, taking in the lines of his body, the hard planes and smooth skin, the creases and folds that told a thousand words and the scars that reminded me of his accident and hard-won recovery.

We were both getting older. I slid my hand over my belly, wondering about the possibilities of falling pregnant and having a child at my age. At forty, I knew the chances were remote, and if I were honest with myself, I'd moved past the stage of nappies and bottles – and yet that desire hadn't completely diminished. Now that we had found our feet, I knew Erich would accept another child with joy, but I wasn't sure it was the right thing for me any more.

'I'm glad we can be close like this again,' I said. 'I wondered if we'd ever get back to what we were.' He had always been the only one for me – my best friend and my lover.

'I don't know what I would have done if I'd lost you.' A spasm of pain crossed his face, catching my breath.

'At least now I understand why you felt compelled to do what you did.'

'And I understand what I put you through. Proving myself worthy of you nearly drove you away. Can you ever forgive me?' His eyes sparkled with unshed tears.

I cupped his cheek. 'You know I already have, but I'm not the same woman that I was. Too much has happened.'

We had been through so much after twenty years of marriage and were still together but we had to accept how close we'd come to losing each other. It had forced us to talk about all that had happened since arriving in Australia openly and honestly, how we had drifted from one another. Slowly the rift between us was closing.

'I know. I couldn't expect you to be . . . but where do we go from here?' He pushed away the rumpled sheets with his feet.

'I think we keep talking, rediscover each other.'

'Like this?' He caressed the line of my hip and thigh, a slight smile playing on his lips.

'Uh huh. We could be stronger than we ever were.'

Staring into the brilliant green eyes that gazed adoringly at me, I silently thanked God for this man, the one I was blessed to share my life with.

It was walking along the bush track at dusk later that day that I remembered my conversation with Claudia.

'Claudia and Franz are still having trouble,' I said.

Erich's brow creased with concern. 'What do you mean?'

I told him of Claudia's concerns and her vow to discover the reason for Ernst's hold on her husband.

'Surely it's best left in the past?' said Erich, holding a branch out of the way for me.

That was what we had all believed when we came to Australia, but now I realised that the past never stayed in the past, especially when unfinished business was concerned. Most of us had unresolved issues, complicated truths that we thought we had left behind in Europe, things too painful for us to dwell on or acknowledge. But these were the demons that drove us forward and shaped our actions, that created our future in this new land, and I now understood that sooner or later we would all have to confront what we'd left behind.

'She can't take much more.'

'Is it really that bad?'

'I think so. Claudia's seen another side to him and I saw it too when he lashed out at Peter.' I stopped and looked up at the pink blush fading into the purple sky. His hand slid across my shoulder and down my arm, the calluses on his palm rough against my skin, and I leant towards him.

'We have to help them. Claudia's worried about Franz too. He's been having episodes of deep melancholy where he plays the piano for hours and won't respond to anyone.'

'Perhaps he needs professional help,' said Erich quietly. We'd both seen men and women disappear into the depths of despair after the things they'd experienced during the war. Many never returned.

'Maybe he just needs Ernst to go.'

Erich shuffled uneasily beside me. 'It's not our business.'

I understood his reluctance to get involved in such situations. 'Erich, they're our best friends. Perhaps you can talk to Franz.'

'All right. I know he wants to set up his own law practice. I'll go and talk to him, ask him how he's going.'

I smiled at him, the branches behind him forming delicate silhouettes in the dying light. The first stars twinkled in the velvety darkness like the first rays of hope. I clasped his hand in mine.

'Let's go home.'

*

The girls and I were having lunch at Mutti's one Saturday. I was doing fewer weddings and had more free time. Hilde was out visiting Claudia. It was a good opportunity for us all to get together. Mutti and I were getting along much better, but she refused to come to the house or to see Erich.

'How's school, Greta?' asked Mutti, passing the mashed potato across the tiny table to Johanna. She still cooked a hot meal at lunch on the days she didn't work and had a light, cold dinner at night. Some habits die hard, but with Mutti I was sure it was pure stubbornness to keep as many traditions from Germany as possible.

'Good, Grossmama. I'm studying hard.'

'Do you know what you want to do when you finish?'

'I want to become a nurse.' The time Erich had spent in hospital had opened her eyes to the medical world and ignited her interest.

'Where do you do that?'

'I want to try for one of the big Sydney hospitals. The training and lectures are run through them.'

Mutti put down her knife and fork. 'What do you mean try? If you study hard, surely you'll have your pick of the best hospitals. You're a clever girl, after all. In fact, why not consider something like law? I know girls these days can do anything they want. Surely it's better paying and better on your body. All that lifting and wiping bottoms. You don't need that.'

'But she doesn't like law, she likes anything medical,' said Johanna with a slight tone of defiance. Mutti stared at her for a second with steely eyes.

'What about medicine then? I'm sure Doctor Rodsky could help you if you were interested.' She and Rudi were almost inseparable these days. Erich was disapproving at first, since they weren't married, but when Greta told him that he was a fossil and living in the dark ages, he tactfully kept his opinions to himself.

'I don't want to be a doctor. I want to look after the whole person.' She had a deeply caring nature that was essential to nursing.

'It's a good profession, one she can continue with anywhere,' I said, interrupting before Mutti could say more.

'All right then. If that's what you want to do.' She looked down at her plate. 'I suppose your mother knows best. You'll do well at whatever you decide to do.'

If anything, her beloved grandmother's criticism pushed Greta to work harder than ever to be accepted for nursing.

'Let's go somewhere this weekend,' said Erich one night while we were having dinner.

'Haven't you got work to do?' I asked absently, trying to go over the weekend work roster in my mind, making sure I had the right photographers on the right jobs.

'It can wait until next week.'

'Do you have to study?' I asked Greta.

'Yes. I have too much to do,' she said. 'And I have to prepare for my interview at the hospital.'

'Which one is this?' asked Karoline.

'The one I want to get into, Royal Prince Alfred.'

'I'm sure you'll be fine. They'd be lucky to have you,' said Karoline, smiling proudly.

'Thank you, Omi.'

'But that's not for a few weeks yet,' I said. A weekend away with all of us together would be wonderful. 'What about you, Johanna? Any homework you have to finish?'

Johanna shook her head, gingerly chewing the lamb's fry I'd cooked, then swallowed heavily. She still didn't enjoy liver but I continued to cook it with mashed potatoes because I knew that Erich and Karoline loved it and it was packed with goodness.

'We're all going to take a little trip. It's settled,' said Erich. 'You can bring your books, Greta. You'll come too, Mutti, won't you?' He looked across to Karoline. Apart from outings with the women from the book club and our Sunday drives, she rarely went out unless Erich or I took her somewhere.

'Where are we going?' asked Karoline, her cutlery placed across her plate. There was still some food left, even though I'd served her a small amount. She ate so little these days. I would have berated my children for leaving anything on their plates but I now just wondered how well Karoline was feeling. Maybe Johanna and I should bake some biscuits or a cake to entice her to eat a little more.

'The Abercrombie River,' said Erich.

I looked at Johanna, Greta and Karoline. Their faces were as blank as I'm sure mine was. 'Where? I've never heard of it.'

'It's out past Goulburn. One of my customers has a caravan there that we can stay in. It's pristine and untouched bushland, he said. We'll see all sorts of wildlife. You never know what we might find.'

'So it's a work trip to find timber,' said Greta flatly. 'How far away is this place? It doesn't sound very exciting.' Greta's face had gone from blank to annoyed but Johanna's eyes were sparkling with interest. She loved the outdoors.

'A few hours' drive and, no, it's not a work trip.'

'Why don't you and Mutti go? It's been forever since the two of you had a weekend together.' Greta glanced at me to gauge my reaction.

My heart fell. We'd left this too late. Greta was nineteen and getting too old to want to spend the weekend with us. Johanna wouldn't be far behind.

'No, we're all going. There's no more to it. We're spending the weekend together as a family.'

I smiled but Greta's face was stony.

'I thought we could all explore a little bit. If it's warm enough you can swim in the river. Besides, I thought you might like to come trout fishing with me.' He looked at Greta and Johanna with an injured expression. The girls used to love fishing with their father but fishing trips had been far and few between for some time. 'Come on, it will be fun, like old times.'

Johanna looked pleadingly at Greta, who shrugged. 'All right, Vati, we'll go,' she said and Johanna smiled gratefully.

He sat back in his chair as though he was the magnanimous lord of his castle and people but I could see the twinkle in his eyes – he was very excited, and I shared that feeling. This was our first weekend away and I loved the Australian bush.

'Wonderful,' I said, smiling. 'Our first holiday!'

18

I had no idea that our trip to the Abercrombie would leave such a lasting impression on me. We had been on day trips often with Franz and Claudia and Reinhardt to the Blue Mountains, Kiama and the beach at Bulli and I had loved everything I'd seen and experienced, but they didn't prepare me for this. My reaction was visceral – I fell in love with the place immediately and, to my amazement, so did Erich.

I read the map and Erich drove. Once we left the Hume Highway after Mittagong, civilisation fell away as farms were gradually replaced by bushland. Sections of the Wombeyan Caves road were unsealed, narrow, rugged and winding, making the journey slow, but I didn't mind. It was beautiful, breathtaking really, coming down to the Wollondilly River, great sandstone cliffs shining yellow in the sunlight and standing like guardians over the glittering river that flowed between them. I couldn't stop smiling. Then, coming up the other side, spectacular views of the surrounding forest and mountain peaks in muted tones of green met us with each turn in the road. At one point I feared that we were lost in the middle of nowhere, but suddenly we reached the Abercrombie River, driving along a narrow road, the river just below us down a very steep slope on the right hand side of the car. Erich's client had given us directions to his caravan, which was parked on a stretch of flat, grassed land by the river.

As I stepped out of the car, I felt the spirit of the bush embrace us. It was alive, the peace punctuated by birdcalls, the burble of the river and the gentle sighing of the breeze in the trees.

Erich climbed stiffly out of the car, groaning softly.

'All right?' I asked.

'Just my leg,' he said, rubbing his knee. 'I'm not used to sitting in the car for so long.' He tried bending it a few times, like he was oiling the joint, then he straightened and placed weight gingerly on his foot, taking in his surroundings. 'I have a good feeling about this weekend,' he said.

I took his arm and kissed him on the neck. 'Mmm, so do I.'

Karoline came to stand beside us, but Greta and Johanna wasted no time heading to the river's edge.

The caravan was adequate: a double bed for Erich and me, a single pull-out sofa for Karoline and cushions on the floor with eiderdowns and blankets for the girls. A little table and bench made the whole arrangement quite civilised. I knew Erich would have loved to go camping in tents but it was too hard on his leg and too much for Karoline. At the end of the war Erich and I had slept out in the open, under bushes and on rough ground with nothing more than our coats, but we were twenty years younger. One of the benefits of getting older, I realised, was that I didn't have to punish my body unnecessarily. I could still enjoy the outdoors with the comfort of a caravan.

After we had unpacked and eaten the sandwiches I'd brought, the girls went exploring while Erich prepared the fishing rods to hopefully catch us some dinner. Karoline and I went for a walk to collect firewood.

'You seem happy,' she said. There was no one else on the little dirt track and it was as if we were the only people in the world.

'I am,' I said, somehow surprised now that I'd said it out loud. 'I love the river and the bush. Who wouldn't be happy in such a beautiful place as this? It's so peaceful, so healing.'

'It's home for you,' said Karoline, looking curiously at me, the gold in her hazel eyes gleaming in the sunlight.

We kept walking while I thought about that. We were surrounded by green, soft against the stark, sculptural white of limbs and trunks, delicate ribbons of bark twisting down their lengths in shades of grey and brown.

'Yes, it is,' I said after a while. 'There's something about the Australian bush that I feel very drawn to.'

'I can see Erich feels that way too,' she said. 'His fascination shows in the way he brings Australian timbers to life in his furniture. His father would have been so proud of him. I understand why he wanted to come out here. He wants to see how it all fits together.'

'What do you mean?'

'The river, the bush and the animals, the plants and flowers . . . there's oneness here – it's untouched.'

'I know what you mean – the spirit of this place,' I said. 'I felt it when I got out of the car.'

'You and Erich have found your place in the world. Australia is where you're both meant to be. I didn't understand that for a long time, even when I first arrived here, but I can see it now.'

'Things are finally coming together for us. It's taken a long time but I think Erich's accident was a blessing in disguise. He loves his work and he's doing well.'

'What about you? Do you love what you're doing?'

I stared down the track, the red-brown dirt leading us to who knew where. 'I do. In fact, I'm almost running the business, but I have to say that I've often thought about the creative work that Otto does and watching Erich work with timber has made me realise that I want to photograph the Australian landscape and its animals as well as its people.' I had brought my camera and couldn't wait to take some photos. There were perfect shots everywhere I looked.

'Have you ever considered painting the landscape rather than photographing it?'

I stopped walking and looked at her. She was frowning.

'I've seen you paint and draw, Lotte. You're very talented. Erich's finally using his talents, and see what he's capable of. Maybe you should try while he's fishing. This is the place to feel inspiration if ever there was one.'

'I wouldn't know how to start.'

'I'm sure that won't stop you. Promise me you'll think about it.'

'OK, I'll think about it,' I said to appease her. But the seed was sown. 'We'd better head back now and see what they've caught for dinner,' I said reluctantly, wondering what I would have found further down the track.

Erich and the girls had caught plenty of fish and Karoline and I had brought back enough wood to make a good camp fire that would keep us warm as the sun began to set. I left them to scale and gut the fish while I wandered along the bank of the river with my camera, watching the reflection of the trees and the sky change colour.

A rustle of dry grass behind me made me turn.

Erich approached. 'How's it going?'

'I'm getting some wonderful shots.'

'The fish are ready to cook.' He wrapped his arms around me as we watched the sun begin to sink behind the trees. The world changed once again, the inky black shadows beginning to lengthen, and a stillness settled on the bush. The soft breeze carried in it a chill and a kookaburra punctuated the silence with its raucous laugh. I felt at one with the coming night.

Erich pulled me closer. 'We might have to send the others to find more firewood, I think. That fish will need a lot of cooking.'

'Maybe we have to go and find firewood,' I murmured. 'Who knows, we might get lost for a while.'

Erich jerked. 'What, out in the open?'

'Why not? Nobody's around, and it's not like we haven't done it before.'

He kissed my temple. 'That was a very long time ago. I was young and fit back then.'

I looked at him, but he only shrugged and glanced at his leg.

'You mean to say that you're not up to it any more?'

His eyes levelled with mine, still bright green in the fading light and full of promise. 'If you're game, then so am I.'

After that trip to the Abercrombie, we bought a caravan and Erich and I spent weekends at the river whenever we could. Between Johanna studying for her final exams and Greta studying nursing at the hospital, they couldn't manage to join us often. Karoline was happy to stay at home to keep one or both of them company; the trip was too long and tiring for her. But she insisted I paint while I was there, and even took the girls shopping for supplies. She wanted to see the countryside through my eyes, she said. There was only so much walking and reading I could do while Erich fished, so I obliged.

Even with my weekly art classes, my first attempts were terrible but slowly, the more I practised and experimented, the more my paintings resembled the landscape. I tried watercolour and oils in my attempt to recreate the beauty of the gum trees and the way the light played across the river snaking through the bushland. The colours were hardest to get right, because the river constantly shifted: silver in the early morning light, still as a mirror, reflecting the blue sky and leafy hills, other times slow and ponderous, dark and mysterious, and softly golden at sunset.

As I got into the rhythm of painting, I lost myself in the creative process, often bringing photos of the scenery home so I could continue whenever I had time. I found it very therapeutic, and all my worries dropped away as I focused my energy on solving the problems in front of me.

'I can see what you've painted,' Karoline said, squinting at the canvas, 'and the detail is beautiful, but it looks flat.' She was brutally honest but somehow encouraging at the same time.

'I know,' I said, huffing in exasperation. 'I'm trying to convey depth in the picture while capturing the changing colour due to how the light falls.'

'What is it that you want the audience to see?'

'What I see, not just what's in the photo,' I said, pointing to the image lying on the table, 'but how I remember that scene, what struck me as beautiful, how it made me feel.'

'How it made you feel.' Realisation hit me as I stared at her. 'You can have the technique but if you don't paint from your heart, from your feelings, your painting won't have that soul you're looking for.'

It was exactly what I needed to do.

As painting became more than a hobby to me, I found myself wondering about my work. I loved photography, but the management of the studio and the repetitive nature of the shoots had begun to wear me down. I wanted something more creative.

'How's your painting going?' asked Sabine one day. 'I haven't done anything for ages.'

It was a rare day when both Sabine and Otto were in the studio. I had called them both in to cover the absence of two photographers, one with a sick child and the other who was away attending to a family emergency. I seemed to spend more and more of my day in the office keeping on top of the business side of things rather than behind the camera.

'I'm working on my landscapes. Our trips to the Abercrombie have inspired me but I can't quite do justice to the bush.' I pushed the proofs I was looking at to one side for a moment.

'What seems to be the problem?' asked Otto, bringing in a cup of coffee for us both. He was going to go over the proofs with me with a fresh pair of eyes. I often envied him, able to work occasionally in the studio and spend the majority of his time on his creative projects, often freelancing for magazine location shoots and cutting-edge fashion photography.

'I think it's getting the play of light right in a bush setting,' I said sipping at the hot liquid.

'Have you thought about taking the focus off the bush and on a subject in that setting? Sometimes I find that works for me in my photo shoots.'

I nodded, contemplating his idea. 'That's a good suggestion, it might help.'

'I know you'll work it out,' said Sabine. 'You're a natural. I'll have to come by and take a look what you've done one of these days.'

'Whenever you like,' I said, smiling warmly. 'I know you've got your hands full with the boys but it will be nice to see you. In the meantime, we'd better get back to work or none of us will ever get home tonight.'

The National Service law had been amended to allow conscripts to serve overseas, and it was only a matter of time before these young men were sent to Vietnam, so Claudia had joined a group of Sydney women who'd begun protesting against conscription. They called themselves the Save Our Sons movement and were the mothers of boys who had been already conscripted or were eligible for conscription. The women argued that it was morally wrong to send minors to serve overseas, and sending them to Vietnam as part of a military force would be breaking the Geneva Accords of 1954. Not only would their intent be to kill or take away the basic freedoms of other human beings, but to do so was against the wishes of their parents. And they were right – until they were twenty-one, these boys had to seek their parents' permission to marry, buy a car or obtain a passport to travel overseas. Claudia was petrified that Peter would be called up.

I agreed that conscription was wrong and I attended some of the meetings with her, to give my support. But it wasn't only that. I'd never forgotten my feelings of helplessness when the dressmaker who'd made my wedding gown was dragged away by the Gestapo in Munich. I was powerless to do anything then, but now I would help stand up for these young men and their families.

It must have been strange to see middle-aged, respectable women finding ways to protest peacefully against the establishment. We were a far cry from anything seen in the newspaper and on TV of the more vocal, less peaceful student movement. We were instructed in the laws surrounding conscription and conscientious objection and quickly learnt everything there was to know about Vietnam, the war that raged there and Australia's commitment to it. Most of us had no experience in political activism but were open to trying ideas that had previously worked to ensure our voices were heard by the public and to apply pressure to the government to force it to review its legislation. Petitions to the prime minister, and press, radio and television interviews were arranged, as were interviews with federal ministers, to spread the anti-conscription message. Before long, our group had learnt how to efficiently raise funds, publish and distribute information and organise public meetings, teach-ins, rallies and protest marches.

Claudia and I attended at a silent protest in Martin Place in the centre of Sydney in January 1966. It was my first big public protest and, although we'd been told there was nothing to worry about, I was nervous. What if those who objected to our stance became violent and it got out of hand? Blue and white sashes emblazoned with the words WOMEN FOR PEACE had been distributed to us. As I slipped one on, I noticed that I wasn't the only one who was anxious and it hit me then how serious this was.

'This is it,' I whispered to Claudia.

She nodded. 'It feels good to do something, doesn't it?'

Like Erich, Franz had supported Claudia's decision to become involved with the group, but Ernst had only ridiculed her. Despite her digging, she was no closer to understanding what was between her husband and his uncle.

'It does. I just hope that the cameras and reporters see more than a group of desperate mothers and portray what we stand for, what we're trying to achieve.' I meant it. I glanced down the orderly row of women lining Martin Place, all holding handbags, most wearing gloves and many with hats and sensible shoes. There was not a skirt higher than mid-calf. We certainly couldn't be mistaken for trouble-making anti-war protesters. It was good to stand up for what we believed in but I wasn't sure what the Australian public would make of us. Would we be a laughing stock?

Now I began to really understand Erich and his union activities. I wondered if he had felt like this when he'd first become involved, worried his voice wouldn't be heard, and that he and his group would be seen as ineffectual and impotent.

I glanced at the enormous SAVE OUR SONS banner and then at the placards. PARENTS ABOLISH CONSCRIPTION NOW, MAKE ASIAN FRIENDS NOT ASIAN FOES, NOT OUR SONS NOT YOUR SONS NOT THEIR SONS, DON'T DRAFT OUR SONS TO BOMB AND DESTROY, NO CONSCRIPTION WITHOUT REFERENDUM and simply NO CONSCRIPTION OF YOUTH.

'Well, we are a group of desperate mothers, but it doesn't make what we have to say any less important. If anything, we're the ones who should be listened to – we're fighting on behalf of our sons,' said Claudia, holding her poster firmly with both hands.

She was right. It was time for women and mothers to have their say and be heard, but the only way to do it was peaceably. The flash from cameras drew my attention to the group of journalists nearby.

'The newpapers are here,' I said. 'We should get some good coverage. Maybe even front page.' The changes that were sweeping the nation altered the way Australians lived and how they were perceived by the world.

'As long as we're being noticed, any article or photo will be useful whether it's positive or negative press,' said Claudia pragmatically.

There were photos and articles in all the major newspapers but we weren't front page news. There was no excitement in our silent protest, holding our signs and handing out pamphlets. I hoped that we'd be seen favourably, as respectful citizens, but most of all that we'd be taken seriously. In many cases we were, but some papers painted the SOS as communist inciters and 'rabble rousers'. But Claudia was right, at least people would read about us and our concerns could only encourage the conscription debate in ordinary households across the country. When we arrived here, I never imagined that we'd play a part in promoting Australia as the land of freedom and opportunity, but it was liberating to take a stand, something I'd never been able to do in Nazi Germany.

It was a time to embrace the new opportunities for women. Johanna completed her Leaving Certificate in November, which meant both girls had now finished school. Greta had just finished her first year of nursing at Royal Prince Alfred Hospital in the inner city. She loved it. Her face lit up when she talked about her work. We saw her from time to time, when she had a few days off and was allowed to leave the nurses' home to come for a visit. She always looked tired, dark smudges under her eyes, but she told us she was happy and had made new friends. Erich and I were immensely proud of her.

'We've done it,' I said to Erich one Saturday afternoon about a month before Christmas, when Johanna had some friends over to celebrate the end of their schooling. I'd served them coffee and cake and watched with pride from the kitchen as the girls talked excitedly about the future.

'We have,' replied Erich. 'Both our girls have done very well. They're smart and take after their mother.'

'You're the smart one who was determined to get a good education,' I said, wiping the benchtop down. 'Look at all the courses you did.'

'Mmm, well, where did that get me?'

'We wouldn't have met, for one thing.'

'No, you're right.'

'And look where we are now,' I said. 'Happy, healthy and doing well. Soon we'll be able to think about bigger premises for your business and that trip back to Germany to see your family.'

He brushed the hair from my face, caressing my cheek and unable to hide a sudden surge of emotion. 'I know much of that is due to you and everything you've had to endure. I'm a lucky man to have you.'

I held back my surprise at his words. Our trouble had made him more aware, I realised. It was good to be recognised for all I had done for our family. 'We're lucky to have each other,' I said.

'Mmm. I'm only glad that the girls have the opportunity to do whatever they like. I think that's what we both wanted, isn't it?'

'It is and I'm very grateful for that.' I opened the refrigerator, pulling out the pitcher of cordial and filling two glasses.

The raucous laughter of teenage girls echoed from the lounge room.

'So, Jo,' one of the girls said, 'what are you going to do with yourself?'

They called her Jo, not Johanna. It wasn't a girl's name and yet it was what she called herself these days. Even Greta called her Jo. 'Get with the times,' Greta had told me. 'This is Australia after all, not Germany.'

'I'm going to do some work at the vet's in Camden over the holidays and then I hope to get into Sydney University to do veterinary science.'

Johanna had tossed up between becoming a teacher or a vet. Teaching was a good career, Erich had told her. One she could return to after having children if she wanted. In the end we agreed that she should do something she was passionate about. She was aware that the work would be hard, sometimes physically exhausting, but she was young, strong and determined.

'You'll make a great vet,' said someone. It sounded like Beth, Johanna's best friend. She would too. Like her father, Johanna loved animals. She looked after Wolfie, fed Moshi, who was now an old cat, and she rode and exercised the neighbour's horses every weekend.

'Are there any female vets?' asked another girl dubiously.

'There are a few,' said Johanna. 'But who says women can't be as good vets as men? Besides, it's what I really want to do.'

'She reminds me of someone,' said Erich softly.

I smiled. I was a similar age to Johanna when my mother crushed my dream of becoming a professional photographer. I had been adamant that I wanted to work for the military as a photojournalist on the front. 'She has so much of both of us in her.'

'I pity the man who ends up with her, then,' said Erich.

I nudged him in the ribs. 'He should be so lucky.' But it got me thinking. Johanna had been spending a lot more time at Claudia's place and I wondered if the reason was Peter. I thought I might ask Greta if she knew anything.

As far as I knew, Greta had no boyfriend. She was too busy for one, constantly working and studying. Besides, there were strict rules for young nurses – they were only allowed to marry in their fourth year, which was a great deterrent. Greta was still so young and yet to make her mark upon the world. There'd be plenty of time for boyfriends once she was well established.

Erich sighed. 'That's years away anyhow. Right now, I'm content. The girls are happy and doing well and so are we. What more could we ask for?'

What more indeed, I thought, smiling at him as I joined him at the table. I held my glass up to him.

'To our family,' I said, clinking glasses with him.

19

1967

There was huge uproar over the visit to Australia of the premier of South Vietnam. Air Vice-Marshal Ky was beginning his tour in Canberra, then going to Brisbane, Sydney and finally Melbourne before heading to New Zealand.

'I can't believe he's been invited here!' hissed Claudia. She was overwrought and I understood why. Peter had recently registered for the ballot as this was the year he was turning twenty. He could be called up within months. Like Johanna, he'd only just finished school.

'It looks like there are a few protests planned,' I said, scanning the SOS newsletter.

'Will you come to the Canberra protest? I'll make sure I'm going.'

I checked the dates. 'No, I can't, it's mid-week, but I

see there's a protest organised for Sydney too and it's on a Saturday. I can make that one.'

Claudia nodded. 'That'll be great.' She stared out the window for a moment. 'You know what this man said during an interview?'

I shook my head but I could guess. Ky was seen as a pro-fascist leader, only marginally better than the communists he was fighting against.

'He said his hero was Hitler. We travelled halfway around the world to get away from the memory of Hitler and all that he did to Germany! I don't know what country we're in any more.'

I was shocked, holding my cup centimetres from my lips. That someone who idolised Hitler would be welcomed here seemed outrageous.

'If nothing else, it's made people more aware of this war we're fighting. Many of these young conscripts' fathers fought Hitler, but I think it's worse for those of us who happened to fight for him. I know lots of young ones think our troops are doing a good thing in Vietnam, protecting Australia and the world from communism, but they haven't seen what our generation has seen, what war does.'

A young waitress walked past our table and frowned as she overheard a snippet of our conversation.

'After what we went through, we vowed to keep our children safe and to ensure they never had to fight in a war in their lifetime,' I whispered. I put my coffee down, feeling sick at the thought of our children marching off to war.

'Now here they are, being forced to go to war against their will to uphold a fascist leader who aspires to be like Hitler. Is this a nightmare? Can you shake me now so that I'll wake up and find that Australia is the country we believed it to be?'

She was furious, and rightly so. My heart broke for her – Peter was just a boy – and for the Australia we'd believed in. There was no turning back now, no return to innocence. All we could do was remind the public of the inherent wrongs that were being perpetrated and highlight the terrible path this country had embarked upon.

'This visit might not be a bad thing,' I said. 'They're expecting huge crowds at the protests and it might be what we need to make people see. Mr Calwell's called for widespread demonstrations against the visit and he'll be leading the marches.' Calwell was the federal opposition leader and leader of the Labor Party. Vehemently opposed to Australia's role in Vietnam and to conscription, he was a passionate speaker, an effective contributor and a wonderful asset to our cause.

'We can only hope the government listens,' Claudia said grimly.

Peter played the cello in a number of string groups and youth orchestras and taught cello to school children, and was hoping to gain selection to the Australian Youth Orchestra. He'd decided to follow a career in music, something his father had been denied. When his number was drawn in the March ballot, we all hoped that he could secure an exemption or even a deferment based on conscientious objection and proof of his acceptance to the Conservatorium of Music in Sydney.

Claudia and Franz were devastated, but Onkel Ernst had told them that it was just as well he'd been drafted.

'It will make him a man,' he'd said, 'and not a sissy, pretending that playing music is a serious career and hiding behind women's skirts.'

Claudia repeated that conversation to me in a tremulous voice, trying hard not to dissolve into tears. 'It nearly brought Ernst and Franz to blows, and Franz threatened to throw him out. They were both so close to losing control – I was so frightened – but then Ernst left in a dark silence, which scared me even more. Franz went straight to the piano and the whiskey bottle. I couldn't stay there with the children. We had to get out.' She clasped her hands together to stop shaking. She, Anna and the twins were visiting us, and Johanna was helping Anna get the twins to sleep in Greta's room. I knew the girls would be up for hours talking and consoling each other. Peter's conscription was a shock to us all. Thank God that he was on tour with one of the orchestras.

Apparently Ernst returned the following day as if nothing had happened and, with his son safely away, Franz did nothing further. But Claudia could see that he was close to breaking and she had no idea how to help him. He continued working long hours, continued preparing to open a small practice in Liverpool and played the piano until late in the night.

Ernst was away during the day and mostly kept to his room at night but Claudia told me she could feel his eyes on her while she cooked dinner, and he would casually appear in the room when she was taking a phone call or trying to talk to Franz. The only real privacy she felt she had was in bed with her husband. Erich and I were horrified, but felt helpless. All we could do was continue to see them regularly and offer them our support.

Greta was upset when she heard that Peter was being drafted. She spent time with Anna, who was across the street from the hospital at Sydney University studying law, whenever she could. But I worried about Johanna. Although she and Peter had been close since childhood, it seemed that their friendship had deepened in spite of the different lives they now lived. I didn't know how I would console her if anything happened to him, how I would ease her pain. I began to pray for Peter and all the young men in Vietnam and redoubled my efforts with Save Our Sons, writing letters to members of parliament, drafting petitions and supporting Claudia at the meetings and demonstrations I could attend.

Erich was wonderful with his practical advice but his work had become busier than ever. He had crafted a number of furniture pieces to be included in the Australian pavilion, themed 'Spirit of Adventure', at the international expo in Montreal and had received a number of large commissions as a result. It felt like our troubles were finally behind us. But there was a little voice within me that reminded me of my discontent at work. I had always thought it would be more satisfying running a business but I'd realised Reinhardt's studio would never be *my* business. Reinhardt deferred to me more often than not, but I'd never found that sense of fulfilment I'd been after.

'You're not happy, are you?' asked Karoline one Sunday morning as I accompanied her on a walk.

'What are you talking about?'

'Are you doing what you love?'

I sighed. I didn't really want to have this conversation. I had no intention of upsetting the finely balanced calm I had discovered. But Karoline was intent on getting answers.

'I don't know any more. You know how I love photography but . . .' I thought for a moment, trying to articulate what I'd been feeling for a while. 'Somehow the artificial settings and positions day after day have worn me down. So often it feels soulless.'

'So when do you feel the joy?'

'Natural settings,' I said. 'Among people going about what they do . . . out in nature. So much of the photography I do is staged and I do see the value of it, but I want something more.'

'Have you ever thought that maybe you just need to balance the two? Surely you can drop back to part-time work at the studio and perhaps begin a small business on the side for yourself, taking photos of what you love, showing the soul and spirit of this country just as your husband does with his furniture? You're so very much alike.'

'Nobody would buy them,' I said flatly. I knew how hard Otto had worked to find success with his photography and he didn't have a family to feed.

'What about Erich's contacts, the ones who buy his furniture? Wouldn't they be interested in Australian scenes, photographs or paintings?'

'I don't know.'

'It's your perspective that's unique, how you see things behind the lens of the camera. That's what makes you special.

The sooner you realise that, the sooner you'll find your happiness.'

'How can you be so sure?'

'My dear,' she said, laughing. 'I'm an old woman and I've seen enough of the world to understand these things.' She squeezed my arm. 'You're the daughter I never had and I'm as proud of you as I am of my son.'

Emotions welled up inside me and tears rolled down my cheeks unchecked. I only wished my own mother had been able to tell me these things.

'Just promise me you won't forget my words. When the time is right and you're ready, what I've said will resonate with you.'

I took her hand in mine and held it tightly. 'I promise.'

Peter was refused his exemption and deferral.

It was a blow to us all. There was talk about hiding him in a network of safe houses that kept drafted boys from serving, but in the end Peter decided that he had to do his duty. Claudia and Franz could do nothing to sway him, and rather than lose him, because he promised never to speak to them again if they persisted, they let him go. I wondered if Ernst had been an influence in Peter's decision.

Of course we were all there at Marrickville Army Barracks when his time came. We knew he'd be away at the training camp for about five or six months before he was deployed, probably at Kapooka near Wagga Wagga. Peter was a strapping young man, his blond hair cut neatly. He wore a suit jacket and his shoes had been polished until they gleamed.

He was a good boy, respectful, hard-working and driven. It didn't seem right to send him into war like this, with his life ahead of him, but perhaps he would do well.

I watched Johanna say goodbye to him. The tight embrace, the deep kiss and the longing gazes were all I needed to see what it meant for them to be parted.

Keep him safe and whole, I prayed. *Bring him back to his family and my Johanna.*

The memory of my two brothers and Heinrich leaving for war at a similar age all those years ago came to me like it had been yesterday. Emotions overwhelmed me so I reached for Erich's arm to steady myself as my vision swam. War changed everything. Both my brothers had died and Heinrich and I – well, our lives had been irreversibly altered.

Loved ones milled around the new recruits, bursts of tears or nervous laughter accentuating the low murmur of goodbyes. The ever-respectable women of the SOS held a silent vigil, lining the street outside the barracks, brandishing their placards and posters like avenging angels in long coats and gloves to ward off the wintry cold of the July morning. Something made me glance across the street and I spotted men carrying cameras, taking photos of the event and the SOS. Some were journalists but others were not. I shook my head in amazement.

'There are men across the street who think we're a security risk,' I whispered to Erich.

'Oh yes, I see them. They're clear as day, aren't they?'

'If you know what to look for. Were they the same at your rallies and demonstrations?'

'They were. I always knew when they were there, trying to catch us out.'

'I can't believe they think that a group of mothers concerned for their sons and the youth of this country could be a risk. I mean, for God's sake, take a look at them! Have you ever seen a more benign-looking group?'

'It means you're making headway, making waves, and that's a good thing.'

'We get spat on, shoved, pushed and called all the names under the sun by people who don't like what we stand for. As much as that is horrifying and humiliating, I suppose it shows that we're being noticed and heard.'

'You should be proud. Your group's getting under the skin of the government and the public.'

I leant against him, as much to ward off the blast of icy wind as to feel his solid strength beside me. 'Thank you. I'm sorry I made it so hard for you when you were out there. I was so afraid for you.'

'I know.' He kissed my forehead and pulled me closer to him. 'I think we'll have some tears when we get home – it looks like we need to get Peter back as quickly as possible before Johanna falls away to nothing pining after him. I know she's got a sensible head on her shoulders but I'd forgotten how much the young ones think they know it all.'

'First love,' I murmured, remembering my engagement to Heinrich, and when I'd first met Erich.

'As long as he hasn't touched her,' he said darkly. 'If anything happens to him . . .'

'She's smart enough not to have done that,' I said with confidence, but I remembered that cold March day with Erich twenty-two years earlier and suddenly I wasn't so sure.

*

Nineteen sixty-eight started with uncertainty and change.

'I can't believe the prime minister just disappeared like that,' I said to Claudia, over an iced coffee.

'They never even found his body. How can such a thing happen?' she whispered, horrified, scooping ice cream through the thick layer of cream. The disappearance of Harold Holt while swimming off a beach in Victoria had been the talk for weeks.

'It's not like anything's changed with Gorton as prime minister.'

'No,' said Claudia, her face falling. 'Public support for the war in Vietnam is dropping with the casualties and deaths of our soldiers but there's still no end in sight to the fighting.'

'I'm sorry, Claudia.' I placed my hand on her arm. 'How are you and Franz? How's Peter?' Peter had recently been deployed to Vietnam with the infantry.

'It's all right,' she said, nodding, her pale blue eyes bright with tears. 'Peter's fine with it. He wants to do his duty to his country and prove his worth as a man.'

'Of course, he'll make us all proud. And you?'

'We don't talk about it, especially whenever Onkel Ernst is in earshot, which is most of the time since he's retired, but I know Franz is as worried as I am. He stares at Peter's photograph when he plays the piano, the one you took before he left. At least Peter's writing to us – it's the only way we know he's alive and safe.'

My heart clutched at her words. I had a sudden memory of the portrait I'd taken of my brother Willi before he'd been deployed to war and how I'd stared at it for hours after we'd learnt that he'd been killed in action.

'I'll pray for his safe return,' I whispered.

'We just have to get our boys home,' she replied, steel in her voice, and I knew that Save Our Sons was all that was keeping her going and holding her together.

Peter wrote regularly to Johanna too. Sometimes she would read parts of his letters after dinner. I only ever heard her read out one full letter, behind her bedroom door as I passed, to Greta when she was home one evening.

9th June, 1968

My dearest Johanna,

I'm so sorry it's taken me so long to write back to you. It sounds like another busy year at university but I know you'll be wonderful as ever and the best (and most gorgeous) veterinary student of your year! Good to hear that Mutti, Vati and the girls are holding up.

I haven't had much time to miss the cello or music, but when there's a lull in the constant noise of aircraft (mostly helicopters and jet air strikes) or the noise of artillery and gun fire, I can imagine playing Bach, Beethoven or Dvorak. If I'm telling the truth, what I most imagine is playing Bach's Suite No 1 – Prelude *in a private performance just for you, but I won't get into that right now in case your parents see this letter. When the ground shakes from the bombs and leaves fall from the trees like confetti or when we're lying in the pits and we hear the whiz of bullets too close for comfort, I fantasise about having you in my arms to chase away the bone-numbing fear, and about becoming a world-class cellist like Pablo Casals, using my music to spread a message of peace around the globe.*

In the meantime, I keep myself busy. Since arriving in Nui Dat in April, it's been crazy. As I'm sure you're well aware from the papers, everyone's been on high alert since the Tet Offensive. One day often blurs into the next as we move through the jungles in the humid heat and often in the pouring rain and dig pits at every position we reach. We only get a few hours' sleep in between. Sometimes when a rainstorm hits we have to sleep sitting up as the bottoms of our pits get flooded.

We were redeployed to a new operation last month, following the withdrawal of the Viet Cong and North Vietnamese forces. We offer support at a couple of the fire bases. One of the bases was attacked with the most intense fighting we'd seen while we've been here. It was there that I saw death first hand when one of our own was hit by shrapnel from a mortar. It was a frightening but sobering moment, and made me more determined than ever to get back home to you alive and in one piece.

I think the worst is over now. We're back in Nui Dat, continuing with our regular tasks, and I'm very happy to have dry feet, warm food and somewhere safe to sleep. I'm so glad I have you to tell my private thoughts and feelings to. It eases my mind to know that I can tell you anything. Nobody else would understand.

I have to go now but I look forward to your next letter.

Love,

Peter

War was war anywhere, and I couldn't stop the tears falling as I rushed to my bedroom. I understood the innocence Peter and these young men had lost and I knew that they would never be the same again. I wept for them all, and for Johanna. Peter could never return as the boy he had been.

About this time, it was announced that those trying to evade National Service would be prosecuted with jail time equivalent to the period of National Service – up to two years. Massive demonstrations erupted across the country. Clashes with police became more common and violent, leading to many arrests. But the tide had turned against the war in Vietnam and the demonstrations didn't stop. Various anti-war and anti-conscription groups began to work together, applying further pressure on the government. With the opposition even greater in the United States, many agreed that it was only a matter of time before both governments called for an end to the war.

Amid the madness that surrounded us, our family was going from strength to strength. Johanna submerged her anxiety for Peter by working hard at university. Greta had one more year of nursing to go and was doing well. She was in charge of the night duty on one of the surgical wards and often in charge on weekends. She was extremely busy and we only occasionally got to see her, but we were happy that she was doing what she loved. She couldn't stop talking about Australia's first heart transplant, which had just been performed at St Vincent's Hospital, and she told me she was interested in completing further studies in intensive care.

Erich had outgrown his work space and it was with heavy hearts that we decided to sell the farm and buy a block with a new home and space for a larger shed and display room.

My conversation with Karoline had got me thinking and I had discussed the possibility of my own part-time business with Erich. He insisted that we make room for a small studio and darkroom for me.

We found what we were looking for at Ingleburn, not far from where we were. Erich and I were smitten when we discovered that it backed onto rugged bushland and the Georges River – a sanctuary right at our door. Any reservations we held about leaving a home that we had invested so much in and which held so many memories were dispelled. We bought the property immediately and began building the shed before we'd even moved in.

I shared our good news with Mutti over lunch.

'I have some good news for you too,' she said smiling. 'Rudi and I have decided to get married.'

I flushed with pleasure. 'Mutti, that's wonderful. We've all been wondering if you were ever going to do it. Why have you waited so long?'

Despite my initial reservations about their relationship, I could see how Mutti blossomed when she was with Rudi. There was a bounce in her step and a sparkle in her eye. He was a lovely man with grown-up children and a total gentleman. And since I didn't see Mutti as much as I would've liked after her move to Liverpool, I was glad she had someone to care for her. I could even say that our relationship was so much better since she was with him. Even Erich couldn't begrudge Mutti her happiness.

A shadow passed over her face. 'Rudi's wanted this for some time but it's been so hard after Vati. I've never really been able to let him go.' I squeezed her hand and nodded.

Losing Vati had seemed to drain the life from her. He had been her true love.

'What changed your mind?'

'We're not getting any younger and neither of us wants to waste any more time.' Mutti was beaming. It was wonderful to see her so happy and finally settled.

'I'm so happy for you both. Have you set a date?'

'Not yet. We have a few things to organise and Rudi wants to wait until his daughter returns from Europe.' She patted my hand. 'Don't worry. You'll be the first to know.'

But on the heels of happy news came terrible news. We were at Claudia and Franz's place, the house they'd built themselves on two acres at Cobbitty, celebrating the opening of Franz's new law practice. It was October and the first warm day we'd had that spring. Greta had joined us to visit Anna before a party she was going to. She was gorgeous in a sleeveless dress of sheer fabric over a strapless bodice, pointy-toed heels that were all the fashion and her dark hair constructed into a bouffant roll called a beehive. She looked glamorous and vibrant like Audrey Hepburn. Johanna was at home with Karoline, studying for her exams. Anna hadn't yet returned from picking the twins up from a birthday party in Camden.

'Can you get that, Franz?' called Claudia from the kitchen when the phone rang.

We heard the low tones of his voice coming from the hallway as Claudia returned to the lounge room with pretzels and nuts.

'Claudia, can you come here please?' yelled Franz.

Claudia frowned and looked towards the doorway. 'Sorry, I won't be a moment.' She gave us an apologetic look before heading out to the hallway.

Erich, Greta and I were looking at each other, not sure what to expect, when Claudia stumbled into the lounge room, pale-faced, Franz following, not looking much better.

'Peter's been injured – gunshot wounds to his chest, abdomen and thigh,' he said shakily. 'He's being airlifted from the medical facility at Nui Dat to the military hospital at Vung Tau.'

'It's all right, Tante Claudia,' said Greta, taking Claudia by the arm and helping her into a chair. 'It's the best medical facility we have. We've heard good things about the unit there from those who have already been to Vietnam. One of our top nurses joined the military and she's at Vung Tau.' She kissed Claudia's cheek. 'Peter's in good hands.'

Franz slumped into an armchair, his skin ashen. 'Are you sure?'

'I'm sure, Onkel Franz. She writes regularly and she's told us about the team and the work they do. In fact, maybe I can ask after Peter at the hospital, find out his prognosis and treatment.'

'Would you do that?' The hope on Claudia's face nearly broke my heart.

'Of course. I'll do it tomorrow.' Greta squeezed Claudia's hand.

I sat beside Claudia, putting my arm around her. She was cold as ice and shivering. 'He's alive and that's good news,' I said, shooting a concerned look to Erich.

'That's right,' said Erich. 'If Greta says they're the best, then they are.'

'Who's alive?' Ernst stood in the doorway of the lounge room, stooped and older than when I'd last seen him. His eyes and apparently his ears still missed nothing as he scrutinised the room.

'Peter's been shot,' said Franz softly.

'Hmph,' said Ernst. 'The boy will either live or die and if he lives, he'll be a better man for it.'

'Stop it!' shouted Claudia. 'Don't speak about him like that!'

'You're just a woman who knows nothing about war.' Ernst waved his hand dismissively, his face a mask of disgust and derision.

'You have no right to speak to my wife like that. Apologise!'

Franz hadn't moved but I sensed that he would fly from his chair in an instant and kill his uncle if he uttered one more word. Greta was still standing next to me and I grasped her hand, wanting somehow to protect her from what I knew was coming.

'I'll do no such thing. I'm only stating the truth.' Ernst looked smug, as if he knew that Franz would back down.

'It's true she doesn't know about the war – and I thank God every day for that. I only wish that I could've protected all my family from its ugly reality. Now my son, fighting in another country's war, is lying on a stretcher far from his family. He knows what war is now and maybe it's time my wife knows too.'

'What are you talking about?' Claudia asked, bewildered.

'You wouldn't dare!' bellowed Ernst, his eyes blazing, striding towards Franz.

'Stop.' Erich stood in front of the old man and placed a hand on his arm. 'They've just received a terrible blow. Whatever you need to settle, it can wait. Come on, let's you and me go and get a drink down at the club.'

I tightened my grip on Greta's hand. I could feel her trembling. 'It's time for you to go, my darling,' I whispered to her. 'Leave quietly, take my car and just go. We'll pick it up later.'

She looked at me, her disbelief turning to anxiety for us.

'It'll be all right. Vati and I will deal with this, but it's not something you should see.' I squeezed her hand and she hurried from the room without a backwards glance.

'He's not going anywhere until I've said my piece!' shouted Franz, jumping from his seat.

'You've got more to lose than I have,' growled Ernst. He reminded me of a guard dog ready to attack.

'I've had enough of your disrespect and controlling ways.'

They were nose to nose, Franz's face beetroot red with fury while Erich tried to hold Ernst back.

'After everything I've done for you!' cried Ernst, side-stepping Erich. 'You're the most ungrateful creature I've ever come across. If it wasn't for me, you'd be long dead and your parents and siblings destitute and homeless.'

'If it wasn't for you, my father would have attained the acclaim of the music world that he deserved and I'd be a musician just like him. If it wasn't for you I'd never have been forced to work with the Nazis! If it wasn't for you, I'd never have had to watch good people I wanted to protect executed for their fight against oppression.' Franz's voice cracked. 'Faces I've seen in my dreams every night of my life.' His fists were clenched tightly at his sides, ready to throw the first punch.

Although Ernst was still a big man, he was not as secure on his feet as he once was and I was concerned that a single punch could knock him to the ground – perhaps even kill him.

'Your stupidity nearly cost you not only your life but that of your family!' Ernst snarled.

'You were only protecting your own neck! That's why you dragged me to those camps to show me what became of those who defied Hitler and the Nazis. I can still smell the oily stench of burning bodies—' The breath caught in Franz's throat, face frozen in horror. 'The only way I can try to drown out the gunshots and terrified screams is by playing the piano until I feel like I no longer exist. I was too afraid to say or do anything except what I was supposed to after that,' Franz whispered, the fight going out of him as he sank back into his chair. 'I couldn't bear to have my family or even your death on my conscience.'

The old man's lip curled into a sneer. 'It was the only way to bring you to heel.'

'You were involved in these atrocities?' Erich stared at Ernst in disbelief.

'I was a public prosecutor. I had my orders from the ministry, nothing more.'

'But then you became a judge. You had a choice. You could have saved lives.' Franz's voice was cold as ice.

'I had no choice!' barked Ernst. 'I did what I had to.'

'You were Nazis?' Claudia's voice was thin and breathless.

'That's right, my dear,' said Ernst, standing straight and tall. 'It was the only way to survive in those times. My position was the only thing that kept your husband and his family safe.'

'What about you, Franz?' I couldn't bear the heartbreak in her voice.

Franz nodded, distress etched in the features of his grey face. 'Like all lawyers, I had to join the Party to be able to practise, and like most, I had nothing to do with Nazi politics or party workings. I worked with the public prosecutors where Onkel Ernst found me an appointment, but I saw more than enough . . . more than I ever wanted to. The fact that I did nothing about such injustice has weighed on my conscience ever since.'

'But you couldn't,' Claudia said. 'You tried and then were threatened with your family by your own uncle.' Coiled as tight as a spring with the fury she'd been holding, she turned to Ernst. 'No wonder you disappeared after the war, leaving Franz to the mercy of the occupied forces. He spent time in prison for his Nazi membership and wartime work, because of *you*. He seemed a broken man when I met him and I assumed it was because of his treatment by the allies.'

I remembered denazification well. My aunt and uncle were torn from their family and flung into prison for being members of the Nazi Party, leaving their children without a mother and father. Erich and I had looked after their boys, schooling them, caring for them and loving them until their parents returned home, exonerated. But Claudia used the right words – they seemed broken and things were never the same between us again.

Ernst just stared at her defiantly but rather than quailing under his glare, she continued with the questions she'd wanted answers to for so long.

'How did you find him after all those years? Why did you ever make contact with him again? Why didn't you just leave him alone?'

Ernst shrugged. 'He was like a son to me. He's all the family I have left.'

'Only because you couldn't go back to Germany. Or maybe because nobody there wanted to know you,' Claudia spat scornfully. 'How did you even get into this country?'

She sat on the edge of her seat now and I readied myself to intervene if she launched herself at the old man. I wasn't worried about what she might do to him, but what he could do to her.

'I'm a Spanish citizen and was for many years even before the war.' He turned to walk away.

'I doubt that very much,' said Claudia softly.

Franz had his head in his hands. 'The threat has always been that he would expose me and link me to those terrible cases I was involved in, even here in Australia. I had no choice but to allow him to come and I prayed that his financial help would be enough to compensate, to make a good life for us and to make a difference in this country, but of course it never was.'

Claudia was up more quickly than I imagined possible, to slap Ernst across the face. 'I should hand you in,' she hissed. 'You'd be extradited back to Germany for your crimes.'

'What, and bring your husband down with me?' Ernst obviously still thought he had the upper hand. He rubbed his face absently and I wondered how long it had been since someone had dared to hit him or confront him about his past.

'No, we won't be handing him in,' said Franz slowly. He rose from his chair and went to his wife's side, taking her hand in his and looking Ernst in the eye. 'But from this moment you're no longer welcome in my house and I never want to speak to you as long as you live. You're a spiteful old man who's lost his mind and you can't hurt me or my family any more. We've more important things to attend to now, so leave and don't waste another minute of my time.'

Ernst's face went slack with shock and he suddenly seemed small and wizened. He nodded and walked through the lounge room door without a word. He knew he'd lost everything – his family.

20

Karoline died peacefully in her sleep in May 1969. Rudi said that it was most likely that she'd had a stroke. We knew that one day we'd have to face this moment but it was still a shock when it came. She was in her mid-eighties after all. Erich was calm and composed but I knew how much he was hurting. His mother was his last link to his family, his last link to Germany. They had been reminiscing in the days prior to her death, as if she knew what was coming and wanted to impart to him all she could before she went.

Her funeral was attended by all our friends and associates, even some of Erich's closest customers, including Julius Berlowitz, and Mutti and Rudi of course. However, I knew Erich missed his other children on the other side of the world.

'They should be here with their children,' he said sadly as we walked towards the burial site. There was nothing I could do except make sure Greta and Johanna were on either side of him to give him the support he needed. We'd have to book that trip back to Germany soon, I realised.

I took comfort in having our girls with us, all together for the first time in a while. They were sad and spoke in low whispers about their childhood memories of Karoline. I was surprised that they remembered as much as they did – the loft room she'd had in Illesheim; the way the girls used to snuggle under the eiderdown with her; the walks to and from school with her; the prayers she had taught them to recite.

I couldn't help but smile as the girls' memories took me back to those days. Karoline and I hadn't always been on good terms and for the longest time I had wondered how much she blamed me for the loss of his family.

But when she'd joined us in Australia, I came to appreciate her insights, her wisdom and her calm strength.

'I want the best for you,' she'd told me one bright afternoon after she'd come to inspect my painting. 'You've got so much to give to the world. Don't hide your light under a bushel.'

I hadn't known what to say, overcome with emotion as I was, and so I had hugged her and kissed the top of her head.

I was going to miss her. To honour her I vowed not to be discouraged by the early attempts at my new style of realistic photography. I would continue with my painting, improve upon it and see how far I could take it.

As Erich and I walked back to the car, arm in arm, I felt him shiver.

'What's wrong?'

'Nothing,' he said quickly. He glanced back at his mother's burial plot. 'It's just this place.'

I kissed his cheek. It was cold as ice. 'Come on, let's go and celebrate your mother's life.'

It was quiet in the new house without Karoline, despite Erich's business flourishing and the constant activity at the back of the house. The work shed was complete, with a display room for Erich's furniture pieces where customers often came, and there seemed endless deliveries of timber coming in and furniture going out. I spent much of my spare time in my small studio and darkroom, where Erich had ensured I had everything I needed to get started: easels, canvases, brushes, paper, painting supplies and basic photo-developing equipment. No expense had been spared.

Despite our busy life, I knew that thoughts of Germany rested heavily on Erich's mind since the passing of his mother.

'Let's plan that trip back to Germany,' I said lightly one afternoon as we sat on the back verandah.

'We will.' He stared into the gathering shadows, drinking beer from the bottle. I had some in a glass on the small circular table next to me.

'I mean it, Erich. We can afford it now. Let's go after our twenty-fifth anniversary – just you and me.'

He looked at me then, brows furrowed. 'I don't know. That's too far in the future to plan. Who knows what I'll have on?'

'These things need planning in advance. We can figure out the cost and begin saving. Besides, you can work around it. We don't have to be away too long.' I placed my hand on his sun-kissed arm. 'I know you've wanted to do this for so long and now with your mother gone and the girls settled, I think it's time. You've got five grandchildren that you've never seen and they're growing up too fast.'

He seemed to deflate, as if a valve had been released, letting go of a worry he'd been holding for so long. 'It's never been the right time . . . and I've missed so much.' The light sparkled in his eyes once again. I could almost see his brain ticking over, racing through the plans he wanted to make. 'All right, let's do it. Maybe we could look at house prices while we're there. I wouldn't mind buying something when the market's right, so we can go and visit whenever we want and bring the girls, without inconveniencing anyone.'

I couldn't help but grin. It wasn't a bad idea and his excitement was infectious.

'We could take the girls, remind them of their cultural heritage . . . and their children too, one day, to show them where we all came from.'

'Exactly! Look into going to Paris and France on the way home. I always wanted to take you there. Call it a late anniversary celebration.'

'Really?'

'We deserve a romantic holiday, and I know how much you love Paris.'

'You do?' I looked at him in surprise.

'I remember you telling me during the war, and I gave you that scarf from Paris for Christmas.'

'My last Christmas at home,' I said, thinking of that Christmas Eve at my parents' apartment. My parents had done their best to make it special, using their connections and saving rations to bring the Christmas spirit to our table. That was when he had presented me with the blue silk scarf and I couldn't deny to myself any longer how in love I was with him.

'I know. A scarf was all I could give you then but now I can finally take you there.'

'I love you.' I leant in to kiss him.

Erich and I were on our own much of the time these days. We had this beautiful new home with enough bedrooms for everyone, an indoor bathroom with shower and bath, thick carpet throughout except for the kitchen, which had lovely slate floor tiles, and a spacious lounge and dining area. But there was nobody to enjoy it except for us. Johanna still lived at home but she was hardly there, either at university or with Peter. He was back in Australia, recuperating from his injuries and soon to be discharged from the army. He wasn't going back to Vietnam. Although his condition had been life-threatening with a collapsed lung and terrible abdominal injuries as well as a shattered thigh, he had recovered well and talked now about returning to music.

Greta had kept Claudia and Franz informed of every development and even now visited Peter whenever she could, reminding him to take deep breaths and pushing him to slowly increase his gentle exercise regime. She was a very good nurse but more than that, she was compassionate and caring and understood how the trauma and healing process might affect him. I'd been so worried about Johanna and it was Greta who'd buoyed her during those weeks before Peter returned home, prepared her for what she would find. I was never so proud of my girls as I was during that crisis.

Occasionally I accompanied Johanna and Peter on their daily walks along the country lanes, fennel fronds tickling my ankles as we looked over the calm green pastures of the surrounding farms. It must have seemed strange to Peter after what he'd seen, another world perhaps, but he seemed content enough. He and Johanna were companionable and comfortable with each other as always but I didn't see the spark that had been there before he left for Vietnam. Perhaps it was too soon after his injuries and the trauma he'd suffered, but I feared that the war had changed him and neither of them knew how to deal with that. My heart ached. A painful path lay ahead of them.

Franz's deep melancholy had lifted with Ernst's departure and Peter's return. His law practice was doing well and he was excited that Anna planned to join him when she'd finished her studies and gained a little experience. Claudia helped Franz in the office, but she was more passionate than ever about bringing our soldiers home from Vietnam, fighting to end conscription and the destruction of young lives. She spent much of her time speaking about her experiences with Peter, lobbying and helping plan demonstrations with Save Our Sons. Much to her relief, Ernst had not made contact. They'd heard that he was staying with an old colleague from the factory but that he'd been unwell.

I called into Mutti's the day that man landed on the moon. We'd had the radio on at the studio all day, hearing progress reports of the Apollo 11 mission, but I wanted to share this incredible moment with someone special. I didn't have time to go all the way home and Mutti was just down the street. She prepared a light lunch for us but we were soon glued to the screen of her small black and white TV. I sat on the edge of the lounge, rigid with anticipation, while Mutti fidgeted in her seat. Finally we saw images of Neil Armstrong climbing down the ladder of the *Eagle*.

'Look, Mutti, here he comes!' I said, clutching her hand with excitement. I was surprised at the clarity of the pictures, considering how far they'd come.

'Who'd ever have thought?' whispered Mutti. 'As a child we were told stories about the man in the moon but now we'll know what's really up there.'

Armstrong reached the surface of the moon and took a step forward. I squeezed Mutti's hand. The world had just entered a new age and we'd witnessed perhaps the most significant event of all time.

'How incredible!'

'But there's nothing there. It's desolate.' Mutti looked bemused, her eyes wide with astonishment.

'It's a new world, Mutti, with new possibilities. Who knows what they'll discover? It's only the beginning.'

She nodded but I could see that she wasn't so sure. I was glad I was with Mutti but I knew she didn't understand what this moment really represented to me. I couldn't wait to see Erich. He'd have watched the moon walk on TV and I knew that he'd share my view of the event, the optimism I felt that humankind could achieve anything.

'Did you see it?' I asked as I took off my coat, slung it over a chair and put my handbag on the kitchen counter. I loved those counters, white laminate that contrasted so beautifully with the floor-to-ceiling timber cupboards. Erich was sitting at the kitchen table with a cup of coffee and a cigarette. He smiled when he saw me, my excitement transferring to him.

'It was spectacular,' he said. 'I loved Armstrong's words, so inspiring, but I particularly liked what Aldrin called the surface of the moon: "magnificent desolation".'

I boiled the electric kettle and spooned instant coffee into a cup. 'Yes, that was such a perfect description. It does have its own type of beauty. You know, Mutti didn't understand the point of going to the moon, because there's nothing there.'

'What did you expect? Your mother thought coming to Australia was the end of the earth.'

'I suppose the moon landing was much like coming to Australia.'

'How's that?'

'We didn't know what to expect, coming to a new world. It was a fresh beginning for us.' I sat opposite him with my coffee, moving the small vase of wattle to one side. 'We wanted a better world and life for our family and were prepared to find something new. When we arrived, the place was so totally alien to us, and so very far away from home, far from help. We had to rely on each other and work things out on our own.' I sipped my coffee.

'You're absolutely right. It did feel like we were going to the moon.'

'That first step onto the moon by Armstrong reminded me of our first step off the *Skaubryn* in Fremantle. The first time we stood on Australian soil. I was terrified and excited all at the same time.'

'We both were,' said Erich. 'And look at us now. After everything we've been through, we've prevailed.'

'We have endless possibilities now that we never had before. And after what happened today, the world will never be the same again.'

'Would you change it?' asked Erich softly.

I stared into his luminous green eyes and a surge of love threatened to bring tears to my eyes. 'Not a single thing.'

The My Lai Massacre received widespread media coverage in November, with articles describing the event and horrific, grisly photographs printed in newspapers and magazines and shown on television.

South Vietnamese civilians, mainly women, children and old men, had been shot dead as suspected Viet Cong guerrillas in their villages by US troops just over eighteen months earlier. The US Army had attempted a cover-up but the soldiers and photographers who saw the attack and its aftermath had been trying to bring this atrocity to the eyes of the world ever since. The photos showed bodies strewn on dirt roadways, thrown in irrigation ditches, children dead outside the doors to their homes; women and children crying and in distress, apparently seconds before they were killed. Villages burning to the ground. Hundreds were slaughtered in cold blood.

'I can't believe something like that can happen in this day and age,' I said.

Erich and I were sitting at the kitchen table reading the papers, Wolfie flopped on the verandah at the sliding door, taking in the morning sun. 'After everything that happened during the last war . . . How can human beings do this to each other?'

'War's the same anywhere,' said Erich. 'A pack mentality prevails when men in those circumstances are living with constant fear. I've seen it before. War can bring out the worst in people but it can also bring out the best. Think about the bravery of those men who tried to help the villagers, the men who brought these horrendous crimes to light.'

I wondered if he was thinking about the terrible massacres in Lemberg that had occurred before he arrived as a young technical inspector for the Luftwaffe. I kissed his hand then nodded.

'This war has to stop.'

Erich and I celebrated twenty-five years of marriage in 1970 and I spent a lot of time planning a silver anniversary party for us, to celebrate the good life we had been blessed with.

We had the party at home, inviting family and close friends, with finger food and drinks, followed by coffee and cake. Mutti asked Hilde to make the anniversary cake; she had begun a cake-decorating business from home and was preparing to expand into Mutti's room once she left to marry Rudi. The cake was glorious, two tiers covered in white fondant icing and decorated with edible red roses, silver satin ribbon and beautiful icing lacework, with ERICH AND LOTTE, 25TH ANNIVERSARY written in thick silver lettering. It far overshadowed anything we'd had for either of our wedding parties.

Greta and Johanna came shopping with me for a new dress. I was excited and nervous at the same time. I hadn't shopped for clothes like this since I was a girl. In fact the last time was trying wedding gowns in the fashionable salon in Munich when Heinrich and I had been engaged. Mutti had criticised everything I'd tried but I had known when I put on the perfect gown. It had made me feel beautiful. All I wanted was to find that again.

The girls single-mindedly sorted through the rows of clothing until we had a pile draped over my arm.

'This will be fun,' said Johanna, leading the way to the fitting rooms, grinning widely. They waited on the seats outside for me to parade past them like a model on the catwalk.

'No, too boring,' said Johanna as I twirled in front of her in one dress and I had to agree.

'You can do better,' they said after a few more fittings. Some dresses were lovely and certainly flattering but we all knew they weren't quite right.

'Definitely not me,' I said about another dress.

'Try on the next on,' ordered Greta handing me a dress. 'I know it doesn't look much but it might be nice on.'

I burst into laughter after squeezing myself into the outfit. 'I look ridiculous,' I called out. 'I'm forty-five, not fifteen.'

'Come on, you have to show us,' pleaded Greta but I could hear the laughter in her voice.

'All right.' I walked back out to them still giggling, like a teenage girl in fact. The girls immediately broke down in laughter too.

'Maybe not,' said Johanna.

'Too modern,' said Greta, still laughing.

'How does anyone fit into this scrap of material?' I said, gazing down at the mini skirt and the bright lime and pink patterns. 'Just looking at it gives me a headache.'

Johanna wiped the tears from her eyes.

'Give me the black sleeveless one,' I said, shaking my head in mock disgust.

It fitted perfectly – simple, elegant and modern. The black velvet hugged my figure in all the right places.

Both girls stood as soon as I came out.

'It's gorgeous on you,' said Greta, nodding.

'I love it, Mutti,' said Johanna. 'I thought it would be too plain and ordinary but the velvet just makes it.'

'Do you know that my wedding dress was black velvet? We couldn't get material after the war, let alone white bridal fabric. Your Vati wanted me to have something new and found the velvet for me.'

'That makes this dress all the more special,' said Johanna. 'Vati will be surprised. You have to get it.'

I stared into the mirror. I wanted Erich to be amazed. I didn't think I looked too different from the way I had on our wedding day. I was more curvaceous now, not thin as we all had been at the end of the war. My blue eyes were bright and my face was still smooth, but my features were softer like I'd settled into my body. I'd taken to wearing my blonde hair in a short bob with soft bangs that fell to my cheekbones. It was easy to manage and suited my face quite well but silver streaks were becoming noticeable, particularly around my temples. There was one big difference, I decided. Age had given me life experience and confidence and this was what I saw in the mirror. That's what made me feel beautiful and sexy, not only the dress.

'It only needs one thing,' I said, turning as I looked in the mirror. 'A splash of colour.'

'Maybe a red silk flower on the bodice,' said Greta, frowning slightly. 'I know where we can go.'

'Vati won't know what's hit him when he sees you,' said Johanna, grinning.

'Thank you both for helping me with this. The dress is perfect.' I clasped both their hands. 'I've loved shopping with you. We'll have to do it more often.'

Johanna's eyes were sparkling with excitement. She was enjoying the day as much as I was. 'We're not finished with you yet. You need shoes and we're going to make you an appointment at the hairdresser's.'

'Then we're going to take you to lunch,' said Greta, kissing my cheek and smiling.

Erich looked suave and elegant like James Bond, wearing a dinner suit and bow tie, his salt and pepper hair slicked back from his face.

'My God, you're breathtaking,' he said to me when I emerged from the bedroom. He pulled me to him and whispered, 'Let's forget the party.'

It was just the reaction I'd hoped for. 'You don't look so bad yourself,' I said.

Greta called out impatiently from the kitchen and I sighed. There was still a lot to do before everyone arrived.

'Well, you'll just have to find me at the end of the night.'

'Wait! Don't go yet. I have something for you.'

'What is it?'

'Come and you'll see.'

I let him take my hand and lead me into the lounge room, where Johanna was adding the final touches to the decorations and placing a vase of native Australian flowers on the table as the centrepiece. I saw her grin before she left the room.

He reached into his jacket pocket. 'I wanted to give you this before the guests arrive. It's something I've wanted to do for years but was never able to. You deserve this and so much more.' He pulled out a small jewellery box. He opened the box and presented it to me. 'To show you how much I love you now . . . and for eternity.'

'God in heaven!' I looked up at him in amazement. It was a diamond-encrusted ring, the stones set in yellow gold. 'It's so beautiful. It must have cost you a fortune.'

'I had it made for you . . . I couldn't give you much when we married.'

'Erich, I was happy. My wedding ring was a symbol of our union but this – this is exquisite.' I blinked furiously, refusing to allow my eyes to fill with tears after all the effort I'd put in to my makeup.

'Try it on.' He gently prised the ring from its case and slipped it onto my finger, next to my wedding band.

'It's a good fit,' I murmured as I lifted my hand, both of us mesmerised by how the diamonds caught the light and sparkled brilliantly.

'I used your ring size but you can never be sure until it's on,' he said, smiling at the delight and shock on my face. 'Do you like it?'

He'd gone to so much effort and expense and put so much thought into what he thought I'd like. And he was right, I adored it. I kissed him and threw my arms around him.

'It's perfect. I love you.'

'Happy anniversary, my darling,' he said, holding me tight.

It was a wonderful evening, filled with sparkling conversation, delicious food, wine, champagne, spirits and everyone we loved around us. Among the noise and laughter, Erich and I found each other for a moment, and sat unnoticed in the corner while we took the evening in.

'Aren't our daughters gorgeous?' I said, sipping my Southern Comfort, watching Greta and Johanna offering food to the guests. 'Such perfect hostesses.' They'd refused to allow me to help, telling me it was my night with their father. The girls looked like models in their short dresses, Greta with her dramatic eye makeup and dark hair swept high off her face and cascading down her back. Johanna's blonde locks were piled on her head, curls falling elegantly over her shoulders.

'They take after their mother,' Erich said, his eyes shining with pride. He kissed me lightly on the lips and ran his finger across the fabric of my dress. 'Black velvet. My favourite.'

'You remembered.'

'Of course, and I want you just as much now as the first time I saw you in your wedding dress.'

I blushed at the memory of our wedding night and how he'd made me feel.

Twenty-five years on and I still thought he was the most handsome man. Now it was the more intimate and small nuances that made him so beautiful to me: the creases at his eyes, the way his mouth curved in silent amusement, the faraway look in his eyes when he was deep in thought and the way he strode across a room with total self-assurance, comfortable with who he'd become.

'I see you remember that night too. I think we'll have to have an encore performance later. I want to see your soft white skin against that velvet again.'

'Do you now? We'd better get on with our party then, so our guests can go home full, drunk and happy.'

He sighed with mock exasperation and got to his feet, helping me up, and we were the centre of attention again.

It was just Greta, Erich and me for breakfast the next morning. Johanna had gone out early to the university farm at Cobbitty. As tired and fuzzy-headed as I was, I could feel the tension in Greta as she joined us at the table. She seemed nervous, sitting on the edge of the chair, her back stiff, eyes darting between Erich and myself.

'I've decided to apply to join the medical team the hospital's putting together for next year's tour,' she said without preamble. She'd finished her nursing course the year before and was now completing further studies in emergency nursing and surgical care, all while continuing to work on the surgical wards.

Bleary-eyed, I put my coffee cup down and frowned. 'What are you talking about? What tour?'

'The hospital's recruiting nurses to apply for the medical team to go to Vietnam.'

'You want to go there?' Erich asked, incredulous.

'To Vietnam? Where the war is?' I had to clarify, sure I hadn't heard right.

She nodded, her lips tight. 'I want to help look after the casualties of the war, people who are injured from the fighting.'

'The soldiers?' I wondered if it had to do with what had happened to Peter.

'No, the South Vietnamese people. Civilian surgical teams go to the provincial hospitals, help take on the load of local casualties, teach Western medical techniques to local Vietnamese doctors and nurses, and provide help to local communities and villages. The military medical teams work in the military hospitals.'

'Tell me if I'm wrong, but aren't these hospitals within the battle zones?' Erich's tone made it quite clear that Greta was skating on thin ice.

She only shrugged, choosing to ignore her father's rising anger. 'It's where the work needs to be done. These people are suffering and have less access to medical treatment than our soldiers. Any injuries they sustain could destroy not only their livelihoods but the lives of their families. The letters that've come back to the hospital talk not just about terrible casualties but health problems, malnutrition, young children starving and suffering from preventable diseases.' She looked at the embroidered tablecloth, one we'd brought from Germany, unable to meet either of us in the eye.

I glanced at Erich helplessly, shock preventing me from gathering my thoughts.

'No, you're not going. Your mother and I didn't leave a war-torn country and travel to the other side of the world for you to place yourself in harm's way. You know how we both feel about this war – about any war.'

'Vati, you can't protect me forever. I'm grown up now and I can make my own decisions. I wanted to do this sooner, but I won't be considered until I turn twenty-five and I've had enough experience.' She stared at her father defiantly. 'Besides, I'm not supporting the war – I'm helping the innocent victims of it. Isn't that what you've taught us to do, what you do? Help those less fortunate, stand up for those who can't help themselves?'

I took Greta's hand. 'It's too dangerous. What if something happens to you?'

'I'll be all right, Mutti. I'm Australian and have access to all the security and medical care I need.'

I could see the burning determination in her eyes, the same as I'd seen in her father's eyes. She was right. She was old enough to decide. I was married with two children at her age. And yet she was so innocent; she didn't know what war did to a person. I'd prayed that she and Johanna would never find out.

There was a battle ahead of us and I didn't know which side I'd be on. I was terrified of what might happen to her, how she'd come back traumatised and scarred. But growing up in Australia meant that she had opportunities to do anything and the freedom and confidence to pursue them. The world had changed and women were demanding their place by the side of men as equals, as it should be. By denying her this opportunity, I was denying Greta her place in the world, I was denying her expression of who she was – as my mother had denied me. Just like her father and me, Greta was passionate about helping others, fighting for those who couldn't fight for themselves.

'You're not going and that's final,' said Erich.

'We'll see about that,' said Greta, her face red with fury. She pushed back her chair, scraping it against the slate and left the house without a backwards glance, slamming the door.

*

With Greta's announcement fresh in my mind, I put the plans of our trip to Germany on hold, but I kept the itinerary so that I could book it when we were ready. I'd had the idea to try to plan the trip around Erich's sixtieth birthday, but postponing turned out to be a wise move, because Mutti moved back in with us not long after the party.

Rudi had passed away suddenly from a massive heart attack. Mutti was devastated. She'd delayed the wedding and now they would never get the chance to live together as husband and wife. Hilde insisted that Mutti stay with her but Mutti was already packed in preparation to go to Rudi's, so, at my suggestion, she came to live with us again. Erich wasn't excited about the idea but I could hardly deny my mother. She was barely able to function as memories of Vati's passing merged with her fresh grief, and she spent days at a time in bed. Her behaviour reminded me of when we'd received news of Willi's death, when Vati and I had to coax Mutti from her bed and slowly back into life. Those days had been very dark for us all. At least now I wasn't grieving too and I had Erich and the girls to support and help me.

Unpacking Mutti's boxes for her while she slept one Sunday afternoon, I came across a photo of Heinrich. It was the last photo I'd taken of him during the war. I'd carried it with me during the months he'd been on the Eastern Front. It was a good photo, one of my best. It had been taken in spring, the new blossoms hanging like jewels on the delicate branches. We were engaged then.

As I gazed at his boyish grin in the faded photo, that day in the Englischer Garten came back to me. He was lying on his side, resting on his elbow among the meadow's spring

336

flowers, casual in dark slacks and white shirt, sleeves rolled up and collar open at the neck, revealing the smooth hollow at the base of his throat. His blond hair fell over his forehead, and his face was relaxed, though his blue eyes were intense, the grin loosening the tightness I had seen for weeks in his square jaw.

'Don't move,' I'd said, bringing the camera to my eye, making the adjustments automatically. Capturing the true essence of him was a miracle of the moment.

I shook my head and sighed at the memory. They were carefree days that were long gone, but I sent a swift thank you to God for them and my time with Heinrich. He had been a dear friend and my first love.

I knew Mutti corresponded with him at Christmas but I never asked after him. Some things were best left in the past, and ours was a complicated history. Looking at the young man in the picture with hope in his eyes, I prayed that life had treated him well. I put the photo back in the box and decided to leave the rest of the unpacking to my mother. It would be good to have something for her to do . . . And I had no desire to disturb the ghosts of the past.

21

Greta had her way in the end. Despite the government beginning to withdraw Australian troops from Vietnam in November, civilian surgical teams still moved in to support the local population. It didn't make sense to me that civilians were sent in to a deteriorating situation as their support and security were leaving. Erich and I argued at length with Greta about the folly of her decision, about the risk she was taking, but it made no difference.

After a rigorous screening process, she was selected for the team. She had the courtesy to come home and tell us. Erich was irate, forbidding her from going and telling her she wasn't welcome at home if she went.

'How could you say that to her?' I yelled at him after Greta had left. 'Now she won't want to come home.'

'Maybe she'll wake up to herself,' he said stiffly.

'Don't you see that it'll make no difference? She's just like you, passionate and focused on what she believes she has to do. She'll go anyway, and all you've done is push her away.'

'I'm nothing like that! I've always put those I love ahead of my own agenda, ahead of my own needs. You, of all people, should know that.' He pushed past me, stalking out the door to the shed.

I sank to the chair. He didn't see it, *wouldn't* see it, because if he did, he'd have to accept how painful it was to be on the other side and acknowledge the pain he'd caused me.

Mutti didn't help. 'How can you let her go and throw away her life? Remember when you wanted to go to the front and work as a military photographer? I forbade you, and Vati arranged for you to work as an office girl. We made the decision for you and kept you safe. Now it's your turn.'

But Mutti still didn't understand the anguish I'd experienced from being denied the opportunity to follow my dream and my passion – how that decision she'd made for me changed the course of my life forever.

Greta was very much like me too, I realised. We didn't stand a chance against the force of her will.

I understood Mutti's fear, but it was pointless to argue with her, I'd learnt that much. Greta had to make her own way. All I could hope for was reconciliation between her and her father, and that she remained safe and came home to us whole and not traumatised.

It was a chilly spring day when we farewelled our eldest daughter at the new international terminal at Sydney Airport.

Johanna, Mutti and I shed tears of sadness and worry, but also of pride. Greta's matron had explained to us what an honour it was for her to be selected because only five or six nurses were chosen nationally for each team.

I hugged Greta tight, not wanting to let go, memorising the feel of her, the sound of her voice, in case this was the last time I'd ever see her.

'I understand why you're going,' I whispered to her. 'You have do what you have to do – what makes you happy. I'm so very proud of the strong, caring woman you've become, but keep yourself safe, don't let the things you see get to you, and you come home to me.'

'I know, Mutti. Grossmama told me all about you and wanting to work on the front and about Onkel Ludwig and Onkel Willi. I'll be careful, I promise, and come home in one piece. I've got too much living to do.' She hugged me tighter. 'I'll see you soon, Mutti,' she whispered, tears running down her cheeks. 'Look after Vati.'

Erich had come to the airport under sufferance, giving in to the constant pleas and demands from Johanna, Mutti and me. I knew in his heart that he was proud of Greta's achievement, but their farewell was terse, the pair of them frosty with each other. He still hadn't forgiven her for her decision to go and she hadn't returned to the house in the months since her father's ultimatum. He was still angry that she'd not budged – and I was angry that he'd deprived me of the chance to spend time with Greta at home before she left.

'I hope you're pleased with yourself,' I said disdainfully a few days later when I could bring myself to speak to him again. We were preparing for bed and I couldn't hold it in

uitcase of Dreams*

any longer. 'How could you leave things like that with your daughter? What if something happens to her?' My voice caught in my throat.

He was buttoning his pyjama shirt and turned to me. 'I can't do a thing to help her over there,' he said softly. 'She's so young. What does she know about the world? I'm her father and I've done everything to protect her from harm, to prevent her from knowing war, to give her a future we could never have dreamed of, the opportunity to have a life of comfort and joy.' He sank to the bed, distraught. 'For Christ's sake, we left our families and all we knew for that. I left my other children behind to give her and Johanna a future. How can she have such little regard for that and throw it all away?'

He looked at me with anguish but I refused to comfort him – my own pain was too great.

'My God, Erich, she's a product of both of us! How can you have expected her to do anything else? She's all grown up. We were living our own lives and making our own decisions at her age. You have to let her make her own choices and believe that we've taught her enough. And I hope she can forgive you and that you get to see her again so you can apologise for your stupid and thoughtless behaviour.'

Erich jerked as if he'd been slapped, then left the room without another word.

I heard the back door close and knew he was going to the workshop. Good. He would think about what I'd said while he worked.

*

Greta was stationed at Bien Hoa for a nine-month posting. She sent us letters regularly. It became our ritual for me to read them out over the breakfast table.

'It's chaotic here but it's the smells that remind me that I'm far from home – the incense, the diesel from cars and machinery, the rubbish on the streets and open sewers,' I read one morning in October. *'The hospital is near an American airbase and the soldiers there are our godsend, helping us with supplies, taking care of the security of the hospital compound and anything else we might need. It can get pretty noisy here with the aircraft taking off and landing nearby, shaking the buildings, but we're getting used to it.*

'I'm learning Vietnamese as I go. The training at home was far from adequate and often we communicate with the locals with a few words and hand gestures, although we have an interpreter we use for the more important exchanges of information.'

'Well, it sounds like she's managing,' I said brightly, lowering the page to look at Erich, Johanna and Mutti over my new reading glasses.

Erich's face was stony as he drank his coffee.

'She doesn't need to be there,' muttered Mutti. 'If she wants to nurse, there's plenty to do here, right under her nose.' I knew it was only fear for Greta that was making her grumble and that beneath it she was proud of her granddaughter and her bravery.

'Well, I could never have imagined Greta going off and doing something like this,' said Johanna, shaking her head in amazement.

I nodded and looked at the letter again. *'We see endless cases of injury from the war, of local civilians from the town and outlying villages as well as refugees from further north. They often require immediate and drastic surgery to save their lives. These people are often poor women and children surviving without their menfolk, who are fighting in this bloody war. Some we can patch up, but others' lives will never be the same again and I wonder what will happen to them, unable to work, some requiring help to just manage their basic activities. It's heart-wrenching but makes me more determined than ever to do what I can to help.*

My emotions were in conflict. I was horrified by what Greta had to deal with. Although I wasn't a nurse, I had some idea of what she was talking about – I'd seen things like this before, during and after the war. This wasn't the life I wanted for her. On the other hand, I was enormously proud of her having the courage to stand up for what she believes in, the endurance to continue day after day and the optimism and passion for never-ending and often thankless hard work. She was a strong young woman, and I prayed that she stayed that way and didn't become disillusioned.

'I know she'll be great after how she helped Peter,' said Johanna. 'Those people are lucky to have her. Don't worry, Mutti, she'll be fine.' She put her hand on my shoulder and kissed my cheek. Then she stared at Erich reading the newspaper and pushed her chair back without saying any more.

Greta kept up with the letter writing. Sometimes the letters were hard to read – she had experienced such terrible things – but at least I knew she was alive and well. And I was overjoyed that she still believed in what she was doing after what she'd seen, grateful that she'd learnt so much about how other people live and also about herself. Of course I worried about her safety but I also worried about what this experience would do to her when she got home and settled back into ordinary life, how the trauma might come back to haunt her.

'She's working herself to the bone,' said Mutti, one morning after I'd finished reading Greta's latest letter, her breakfast untouched in front of her.

The back door was open and I could hear a kookaburra laughing in the distance. It was warm and the sun streaming into the kitchen made the room bright but still I shivered.

'She's doing what she has to do,' snapped Erich.

Mutti glared at him. He'd made no comment about Greta's letters before now but at least this was something. I wanted desperately to heal the dissent that had come between Erich and Greta and consequently between us. Maybe I could talk to him.

'I'm sure she's learning a lot,' I said.' I looked at Erich, hopeful of another reaction or comment. He nodded grimly and said no more.

Johanna was subdued too, sipping her tea and staring out the window to the bush beyond. I knew she was thinking not only of her sister but also of what Peter had been through. It had been a tough road to recovery for him and although he'd returned to music, playing in an orchestra and finishing his course at the conservatorium, he was often withdrawn and moody.

Johanna had just finished her degree and had decided to apply for a veterinary position in the country. One of her lecturers knew about an opening in a reputable practice in Yass, specialising in the large animals she loved working with. It was about four hours away but an easy drive down the Hume Highway. She was due to start in January. It was a decision that surprised many, especially Mutti – but not me. I knew that, just like her sister, Johanna was never going to follow the conventional road. I was going to miss her but I was so very proud of her. She'd worked hard and done well in a male-dominated course. I knew she'd have her challenges in the country, where attitudes towards women were even more old-fashioned than in the city. It might take people a while to accept a female vet, especially on the farms, but she'd show them that she was equal to the task and as good as any man at the job.

'What about you and Peter?' I'd asked softly when she'd told us of her plans.

'It's over between us.'

I'd opened my mouth to reply but she hadn't let me get a word out.

'It wasn't Vietnam, Mutti. Things were never going to work out between us, we're too different,' she'd said, looking sad, but I'd wondered, as I did still.

Claudia had told me how Peter would wake screaming in the night from nightmares. She'd had plenty of experience dealing with Franz and his trauma but this on top of it all was wearing her down. Peter just wasn't doing well. At least Onkel Ernst's passing a couple of months earlier gave her one less worry. Franz had seen him before he died but Claudia had refused to go. She'd worried about Franz, but he'd come home calm and at peace.

'How's Peter coping with the breakup?' I asked her over our regular coffee.

'At first he wouldn't talk about it. Franz has been good with him, though. He seems to understand what he's going through. I'm very proud that Peter's finished his course and has been working. Nobody would know that he's any different.' She stirred her coffee absently. The strands of grey were more noticeable in her hair. 'Franz told me that Peter doesn't want Johanna to have to go through what I've gone through with him.' Her voice caught. 'He's well aware that he's damaged and refuses to let Johanna in. He doesn't want her to get hurt. He wants her to lead her own life, to *have* a life ... He loves her that much.' Tears spilled down her face.

I fumbled in my handbag to find a clean handkerchief and gave it to her while blinking my own tears back.

'Is there anything we can do?' We both knew that only time would heal Peter and he'd let someone in to see the person he'd become when he was ready.

'No. Please tell Johanna how sorry we are. We were looking forward to her becoming part of our family one day.' Claudia dabbed at her face again. 'I hope she understands.'

I nodded. 'She hasn't said much but I think she knows. They'll always be friends.'

'I'm sure they'll always be there to support each other.'

We smiled.

'How are things with the SOS?' I asked suddenly, feeling guilty that I hadn't been able to make the last few meetings. Between the studio and the effort I'd been putting into my fledgling business, perfecting my style so I'd been able to sell a small number of paintings and photographs mainly to clients of Erich, I could hardly keep up.

'As busy as ever. As you know, most of the troops have been returning from Vietnam but they're being brought home often in the dead of night. There's no ticker tape parades for them, no huge hero's welcome. I know that the public backlash against the war has been strong of late and the public reception to our soldiers' coming home has become more hostile, but this is ludicrous.'

'The government sent these boys to war,' I said, indignant. 'They should welcome them home as war heroes, proud that they've been fighting for their country, keeping us all safe.'

'That's the thing. Many people don't see it as our war at all. It's a war to be ashamed of, a war we shouldn't have got involved with, a war that's still continuing despite our best efforts. All people see on the news and in the paper is bloodshed – the destruction of Vietnam, dead civilians. All we have to show for this are our dead and maimed soldiers, traumatised boys who will never be the same again.'

'What those soldiers have endured . . .'

'Peter's told me a little of what it was like. He said that they dream of coming home after their tour, proud of their service to their country. Most didn't like what they had to do and will never forget the terrible things they saw, but it was what their country asked of them. All of that could be eased by the love and support of not only their families but the Australian public and government, who should also be proud of their brave and courageous service to their country. Instead, they're whisked away at night like fugitives, criminals, for fear of being seen. All they feel is shame and what they suffered was for nothing.'

'Peter told you that?' The noise of the café had dropped away to a distant hum.

She nodded sadly. 'It's a widespread problem. Peter's stayed in touch with many of the boys he served with. Some of them have been told that they can't join the RSL because they didn't fight in a "real" war.'

'What, like our war?'

She nodded again. 'It's disgraceful. So while our work with the SOS isn't done until conscription is banned, I think someone needs to do something to help these soldiers be accepted for their service and settle back into civilian life.'

'I wonder who that might be,' I said, raising my eyebrows.

Claudia laughed. 'I'm not the only one. There's a group of us wanting to set things in motion and Peter and some of his army friends want to get involved too.'

'Maybe it's a good way for him to heal,' I said.

'I think so,' she said softly. 'Now, tell me about Greta. How's she going in Bien Hoa? When are they bringing her home?'

The day before Christmas I found Erich down by the river. He was sitting on a sandstone boulder overlooking the water, a letter from Greta in his hands. It was quiet and serene here, the perfect place to think, to become whole again. You wouldn't know that houses existed just over the rise. We rarely had time to go to the Abercrombie these days with the amount of work we had.

'I wondered where you got to,' I said lightly, sitting beside him.

'Just clearing my head.'

'Everything's done for tonight. Johanna and Mutti have just put up the tree. Tommy and Suzanne and the children will be here at half-past six.'

He nodded absently.

'It'll be strange not to have Greta home at all over Christmas.' I listened to the rustle of leaves as the breeze gently caressed the tops of the trees. I held my breath, hoping he'd talk to me.

'It won't be the same without her,' he murmured.

I kissed his shoulder and leant against him. 'She'll be home for next Christmas.' I had to believe that, believe that no harm would come to her. She hadn't managed to write recently, but given how busy she'd sounded, I didn't really expect she'd be able to.

Erich grasped my hand then, hard, like he was hanging on to a lifeline. 'You were right. I can't protect her any more. She has to make her own decisions, but I still don't like it.'

'Neither do I,' I said. 'I'm not only worried about her safety but . . . we both know what war can do.'

'It'll change her forever. I know that for a fact.'

'You couldn't have stopped her. She has that same fire burning in her that you have – she has to help people in need. Both the girls do, they just express it in different ways.'

'Why couldn't she have found another way to express it? Something closer to home, something less dangerous?'

'She's her father's daughter.'

Erich's head was bowed, his face contorted with the pain and grief he'd been holding on to for the last few months. 'I never wanted this for her.'

'I know, my darling, neither of us did.'

He broke then, racked with silent sobs as I wrapped my arms around him and cried too, for him, and for Greta.

22

Five months later, we finally received the letter that gave us hope that Greta would soon be home, but it wasn't the letter I'd been expecting, or a letter I'd wanted to read.

16th May, 1972
Dearest Mutti, Vati and Grossmama,

It was so good to hear that you're all well. I can't believe that Johanna's working in the country now! But she's always been a country girl at heart. Just watch that some farmer doesn't sweep her off her feet! I'm sorry that she and Peter didn't work out. Maybe it's for the best.

Nothing's really changed here and yet everything has. The fighting is on our doorstep, with the American base nearby being a major target of the Viet Cong. It's harder than ever to get supplies after the withdrawal of US and Australian troops.

There are fewer soldiers than before and our security measures have been tightened considerably.

We've been given M16 assault rifles and other weapons to use to defend the hospital, if it comes to that. I was told that I was a natural by the American soldier who was training us to use them.

There's a curfew in place and we've been advised to stay off the highway to Saigon at night and during the afternoon siesta period. Our accommodation has moved nearer the American base and we're taken to and from work in armoured personnel carriers. Apparently, time-delay rockets have been placed in strategic positions by the Viet Cong targeting the US base and we've been woken early in the morning to the sound of them detonating, the walls around us shaking and pulling us out of our beds in panic. We've heard explosions near the hospital too – some of the hospital windows have been shattered by the blasts.

None of this stops us from doing our work. If anything, we have more patients than ever as the battles rage so close by. We're all afraid of when and where the next explosion will be, but we know the hospital won't be targeted as we treat any who walk through our doors, including the Viet Cong and their sympathisers. All we can do is keep together and focus on the injured in front of us – the people who need us – and this brings us the strength and coolheadedness that we need to keep going.

I skipped ahead to the end, not wanting to know any more details of the danger she was in.

If all goes well, I'll be coming home soon but none of us knows when that will be.

The lights are out tonight and my candle has burnt to a stub. It's time for me to say goodnight.

All my love,

Greta xxx

Erich pulled me tight to him. We were sitting in bed. It was late but neither of us could have waited to read her letter.

'We both knew it would probably come to this,' I whispered. I couldn't stop shaking.

'We both survived the war, my *liebling*, and she will too. It won't be long before she's home again.'

I nodded, praying that he was right. I leant against him, the soft flannelette of his pyjamas and the warmth of his body soothing me.

'Let's plan a party for her return, a few weeks after she arrives. We'll make sure Johanna can come home.'

'That sounds nice,' I said, trying to pull myself together. I knew how much Erich missed his daughters. He'd been writing regularly to them both. It was strange to have an empty house without laughter, loud voices, music blaring from the bedroom and even, dare I say, arguing.

Greta arrived home in June. It was the most wonderful moment when I held her in my arms.

'Welcome home, my darling,' I whispered, not wanting to let go. Our tears mingled, wet on our cheeks.

'It's so good to see you, Mutti.'

Then she was in her father's arms. Erich hugged her tight, fierce pride shining in his eyes, and she sagged against him, drawing comfort from his touch. She knew things were good between them again. Mutti embraced Greta and kissed her multiple times, and I noticed how tiny she was compared to her granddaughter. She was getting older, in her seventies now, and was home on her own too much, but I'd been taking her into Liverpool with me some days. She had gradually re-established the friendships she'd made and, in this way, began to face the loss of Rudi. She'd even started helping Hilde in her cake-decorating business, doing her accounts and administrative work.

'Come on, let's get you home,' I said, taking Greta's arm. 'Johanna will be waiting for us by the time we get back. I know she's dying to see you.' I kissed her on the cheek and hugged her again. She was thin and angular from the long hours of hard work and the stress, but she was real. I wanted to feed her up with the foods she loved and hold her hand while she told the stories I knew she had to tell.

I'd roasted a duck and a leg of pork and served them with baked vegetables, potato gratin, peas with bacon and cauliflower with white sauce. For dessert, we had trifle. The girls regaled us with stories of their time away and it was just like it had always been. It was wonderful to have both our daughters under the same roof again.

'So, any man in your life?' Greta asked cheekily, her face flushed from the wine and her dessert bowl scraped clean.

'Greta, is that any question to ask in front of your parents?' admonished Mutti, although I could see that she was just teasing.

'Oh, I didn't mean you, Grossmama,' replied Greta with a look of horrified innocence on her face. 'I was asking Johanna. Although if you've got something to tell me, you'd better come out with it. Obviously I've been away for too long.' She grinned mischievously at her grandmother. We all laughed. Nobody else could have gotten away with saying something like that to Mutti.

Mutti slapped Greta playfully with her serviette. 'A lady never divulges her secrets,' she said with as much dignity as she could. 'You know I'm past it now. I just live for the details of the love lives of my granddaughters!'

'There, there, Grossmama,' crooned Greta, patting her grandmother's hand. 'We'd better give you something exciting to keep you going, then. Come on, Johanna, give us all the gory details.'

I held my breath for a second, watching Mutti's face, but she continued to smile, indulging Greta's wicked humour. It had been difficult for her since Rudi's death and I knew that she missed him terribly. She had almost always had a man by her side and now she was on her own, I had noticed some of the spark had gone out of her.

Johanna had turned beetroot red. She squirmed uncomfortably in her chair, all eyes on her. She and Peter had broken up about eight months earlier but remained close friends. I knew she continued to support him by going to his concerts when she could and helping with his veterans work. Now I suspected she'd moved on a lot more quickly than I'd thought she might.

'Well, actually, I have met someone.' She twisted the serviette in her hands. 'He's a farmer and his name is James. His parents own a big property not far from where I work.'

Erich looked at me in surprise, his wine glass to his mouth, and I shook my head imperceptibly. I didn't know either.

'So when are we going to meet him?' asked Mutti.

'Maybe next time I come home,' Johanna said, smiling radiantly. Ah, there it was. This was no ordinary romance. I had never seen her glow like this with Peter.

'We look forward to meeting him when the time comes,' I said, passing the trifle to Greta.

'What about you?' asked Mutti, watching her oldest granddaughter add another spoonful to her bowl. 'There was a young man at the airport when you left and there again when you returned.' She raised her eyebrow, taking the trifle from Greta. Johanna hadn't been able to tell us much about him after Greta left, except that his name was Jonathan, he was a doctor at the hospital and that they'd been friends for some time.

'We'll have to see,' said Greta. 'I'll let you know if there's anything to tell.' She was suddenly very interested in her bowl.

Erich held my hand under the table, hiding his smile behind his serviette while pretending to wipe his mouth. It was as it should be. Our girls were grown up, we both knew that, but I hoped these young men were worthy of them both.

Greta spent some time with us at home. Generally, she slept long into the morning after a late night and restless sleep. She and Mutti walked and talked until midday, when Erich made sure he'd come in to have lunch with them. In the afternoon, Greta would help her father in the workshop, bonding with him again and finding familiar and comfortable territory after the way things had been left between them. I got home as soon as I could after an early morning start and often the two of us would walk down to the river before dinner.

Slowly Greta lost the haggardness in her face, her eyes began to sparkle and the haunted expression came less frequently. She was jumpy, starting violently at loud noises and bangs, and one day she dived to the floor, hiding behind the solid protection of the timber-framed lounge after a car backfired down the road. It was distressing, but it was behaviour Erich, Mutti and I had seen before and had experienced ourselves.

'I have to go back to work,' she said one afternoon after being home about a month. We were on the verandah about to go down to the river.

'You don't have to do that yet, my darling,' I said, smoothing the wisps of dark hair from her face.

'I can't mope around here all day. It doesn't help.'

'It's too soon. Give yourself time. After the experience you've had, you need time to heal.'

'Mutti, I don't think any amount of time will make this go away.' Her eyes were dark with trouble.

'Nightmares?' I'd heard her call out in the night a number of times. Mothers were always light sleepers when their children were nearby.

She nodded.

'You can always come in and wake me,' I said.

'I know, but it's not only that. You see how I jump at any little noise.' She shook her head as if frustrated by her own reactions. 'It takes me straight back to those moments.'

'It's normal.' I took her arm and we walked across the gravel driveway to the dirt track. Cockatoos squawked as they flew overhead, no doubt on their way to join the others decimating the tops of our pine trees.

'I know, Mutti, but sometimes even knowing that doesn't help. You and Vati and Grossmama understand, she told me about your real father . . .' She looked at me from the corner of her eye.

I smiled sadly and shrugged. 'It was a long time ago, but Grossmama was right to tell you. He suffered after the war, and maybe it was the reason my parents divorced, but that kind of trauma wasn't talked about then and wasn't accepted – it's different now. That's why if you can talk about it, perhaps we can help.'

We were surrounded by eucalypt green like the sanctuary of a Catholic confessional. I kissed her cheek. I wanted so desperately to protect her and help her through her pain.

'It's hard. So overwhelming. Now all I want to do is get back to normal, live my life and forget, at least for a while . . . let the horrors recede. Maybe then it won't be so painful, so difficult to bear.'

She looked at me with such a look of despair that my heart clenched. This was what I'd been afraid of. I didn't want her to withdraw from us because we kept pushing her. How could we help her? I didn't want to lose her.

'Maybe you're right. A normal life might be what you need right now. Just remember that Vati and I are here for you. We won't ask questions but you can talk to us about anything, any time.' Erich and I had seen the best and worst of humans as well. We understood how she might be suffering. The experiences were still painful to remember, but we hoped that the knowledge would help her realise she wasn't alone.

Greta nodded and sighed. 'Thanks, Mutti. I've spoken to the hospital. I can start there in a couple of weeks.'

I tried to smile brightly. 'Then we'd better have that welcome home party before you leave.'

'That would be nice.' She hesitated. 'I know that you and Vati delayed your trip to Europe because of me—'

'It's all right, darling.'

'No, let me finish.' She put her hands on my shoulders, the look of earnestness on her face breaking my heart. 'I want you to go. Do it before the weather turns cold over there. I'm going back to work. I'll manage fine, and Grossmama and Johanna are here if I need them. You won't be gone long anyway.'

'Greta, I don't think—'

'Mutti, please. You and Vati have waited long enough. If there's something I've learnt, it's that life's too short. Go and see Eva, Walter and the kids. You know how happy it will make Vati. Go and have a romantic few days in Paris with him. You both deserve it and it will lift my spirits to know that you've gone. Promise me.'

Her brown eyes were so filled with determination, just like her father's, that I couldn't say no.

'All right, I promise.'

'Good, I'll hold you to it.' She smiled sweetly and I kissed her on the forehead.

'We have a bit of organising to do. Let's work out what we need for your party first of all.'

Johanna came home with James for the party and Greta was in high spirits, mingling with her friends, including the mysterious Jonathan, and with old family friends too. It was as if now she could celebrate being home, alive, safe and in one piece, as if what she'd experienced had taught her to live life to the fullest and appreciate any opportunity for joy. I remembered how that felt and I knew that Erich did too, because I caught him watching her with an odd gleam in his eye.

'Do you remember throwing caution to the wind and living life with such abandon because tomorrow might never come?' he whispered in my ear at the end of the night as we walked to the river in the moonlight, leaving the young ones to continue to celebrate.

'I remember,' I said, the memory of it inflaming my desire. Erich let go of my hand and his arm snaked around my waist, pulling me tight.

The truth was that I still felt that way about Erich – it was how we both felt about each other. There was a bond between us, as if we were two parts of one whole, always better when we were together. We were unstoppable and could even make what seemed impossible, possible.

'I think we're better now than we were back then.'

He was right. Everything we'd been through had brought us to this point. Our love was so much deeper and richer than I could ever have imagined. He kissed my throat and I melted in his arms.

'I think we should go back,' I whispered, feeling his need against my belly.

'No, it's closer to the river.' He grabbed my hand again and led me, laughing, to our boulder.

The river below was a sinuous ribbon of silver. The gums on the opposite bank stood like ghostly sentinels in the moonlight, whispering their lullaby to the river, weaving the magic of the night around us.

'It's beautiful.' I wanted to capture this scene in my mind so I could remember how to paint it.

'Just like you,' said Erich, staring at me as though he wanted to remember me like this forever. His eyes gleamed in the faint light and he took my face in his hands and kissed me.

As he spread the blanket we'd forgotten to take back to the house the day before on the sandy surface below the rocks, memories of the first time he'd placed his coat down for me to lie on came to me. The same fire erupted within me at the touch of his hands.

We ended up in a jumble of clothes, the breeze caressing our skin, cooling the heat of our bodies. I told myself that it was the magical night that surrounded us, but whatever the reason, it was the best night we'd ever had together. We were uninhibited and free, as if we had really become one, as our boundaries gave way and we fell into oblivion. The perfect conclusion to a perfect evening.

'You're the love of my life,' I said as I lay in his arms.

'It's only ever been you,' he replied, 'from that first moment you came into my office, unsure and nervous.'

I smiled at the memory. He'd reminded me of a Greek god and I'd been almost dumbstruck by him. 'It was love at first sight.'

Erich kissed me again. 'And there was nothing either of us could do about it. Here we are, nearly thirty years later, and you still have that effect on me.'

'I've never been so happy. Do you know how lucky we are to have this? It's something everybody wants but very few people ever experience.'

'I know.' He held me closer. 'I don't know what I did to deserve you but I thank God for you every day.'

'So do I.' I closed my eyes, knowing I was loved – safe and warm in his arms.

I kept my promise to Greta. We were leaving for Germany soon but there was still so much to do before we went, so I'd begun arriving at the studio early.

'Lotte,' called Otto from the office one Friday morning. 'Phone call.'

'Who is it?' I asked impatiently, preparing for an important shoot that I'd moved forward.

'It's your mother.'

I looked at my watch. It was a quarter to nine already. 'Tell her I'll call her back when I'm finished with this sitting.'

'She says it's urgent.'

'Oh, really!' I said, exasperated. I had a million things to do and didn't need any interruptions. 'All right, I'm coming.'

I took the call in Reinhardt's office. 'What's wrong, Mutti? I'm busy,' I snapped.

'*Schatz*, you have to come home.' There was something not right in her voice.

'What is it, Mutti?' Fear began to stir in my belly, making my neck prickle.

'There's been a car accident. It's Erich.'

A loud roaring began in my ears and for a minute I was confused and couldn't respond. 'What? What are you talking about?' I said eventually.

'You have to come home.'

'Why – is he all right? Do I have to go to the hospital?'

'Lotte, I'm so sorry.' Her voice trembled. 'He's been declared dead at the scene.'

The room was spinning and the telephone receiver crashed to the floor. I heard a scream somewhere in the distance. Suddenly Otto was there. *Otto was there before, too*, I thought vaguely, before everything went black.

23

'There was no other vehicle involved. It looks like he drifted off the road and hit the tree. The impact likely killed him.'

'How's that possible? He's driven that stretch of road more times than I can count. He was only one hundred metres from home.' It was Mutti, sitting beside me, holding my hand, firing the questions at the police officer, who watched us with compassion.

Through my haze, I remembered that Erich had worked through the night on his latest commission. He had a number of furniture pieces he wanted to have delivered to the clients before we left for Europe. He'd still been in the workshop when I left for work at dawn. We were going with Greta to Yass later in the day, to see Johanna for the weekend. But he'd gone out for some reason. All I could think was that he'd needed something to complete the piece.

'I'm nearly finished,' he'd told me when I scolded him for being up all night. 'It's my best piece yet.' He'd looked grey with exhaustion but was exuberant and happy.

I'd kissed him goodbye and told him to get some rest before Greta arrived at lunchtime.

'I will,' he'd promised. 'See you when you get home.'

I hadn't lingered, desperate to get to work. I hadn't known it would be the last time we'd speak. The last time I'd see him and touch him. Maybe if I'd stayed a little longer I could have stopped him from going.

It was only in the clinical viewing room, standing in front of Erich's body, that reality hit like the pain of our first child being ripped from my body, already dead. I doubled over as if I'd been punched in the stomach, and gasped for air. I clung to the edge of the cold metal table, not sure if I wanted oxygen to fill my lungs or to die alongside him, but breath came anyway and with it the pain of the truth.

Otto and Suzanne supported me on either side. Erich looked so peaceful, as if he was sleeping and any moment would wake up and smile at me. Everything in me screamed out that he couldn't be dead . . . But then I realised that there was no rise and fall of his chest. I reached out to touch his cheek, to reassure myself that it was a dream, but his skin was stiff under my hand and I recoiled in horror.

I broke down then, great sobs racking my body. Otto and Suzanne tried to draw me away but I couldn't leave him. I kissed his lips, cold on mine, and I knew. He was gone. The man I loved wasn't there any more. His broken body was an empty vessel.

I didn't know if I could survive the pain of his loss. What made it worse was knowing that he'd realised what was happening in his last seconds. The police report surmised that he'd fallen asleep at the wheel for a second. There was evidence in the tyre markings that he'd attempted to swing the car back onto the bitumen but it was too late and he'd slammed into a tree. I couldn't begin to think what his last thoughts had been.

By the day of the funeral, I was numb. I couldn't allow myself to feel anything as Erich's coffin was lowered into the ground beside his mother's. It was too soon. He was too young, cut down just as the rewards for the years of hard work were finally coming. Part of me wanted nothing more than to hurl myself onto the smooth wooden lid of his coffin – to bury myself with him. How could I live without him? How could I go on? And yet I knew I had to, for the sake of our daughters.

I moved like a zombie, each step excruciating, answering questions automatically. It was cool and calm in my bubble, like the sterile, steel-covered environment of an operating theatre. Like the morgue.

It was the only way I could survive. Without my protection, I knew I'd die. My heart would be wrenched from my body and the shock and pain would be unendurable.

Johanna and Greta were by my side, and Mutti too, but I could barely acknowledge their presence. Nothing could intrude into my space, nothing could burst my bubble. I went through the motions, did what I had to do until the funeral was over. Then I was home, surrounded by familiarity, Mutti and the girls hovering, but I was utterly alone and it nearly drove me mad.

Everywhere I turned, memories haunted me. Sleep eluded me. When finally I succumbed to exhaustion or took one of the sleeping pills Greta had asked Jonathan to prescribe me, I'd wake full of hope of a normal day, only to have my illusions shattered when I realised that Erich was not lying beside me.

I did anything I could think of to remain close to him. I had to do something to keep the panic at bay. I spent hours in the shed, sliding my hands over the polished surfaces of the furniture pieces that still sat there, surfaces that he'd work so hard to perfect, surfaces he'd touched. I couldn't even keep his business going – I knew nothing about furniture making. In the end, I called in one of Erich's colleagues, who'd offered to finish off the items that remained and deliver them to the customers. It broke my heart to see the final cabinet loaded into the truck, but each of the customers was aware of what had happened – some had even come to his funeral – and I hoped that they'd treasure those pieces the way I would have.

With the help of Reinhardt and Julius, I sold Erich's equipment and disassembled his business. The money would come in handy to help pay off the house. But I couldn't bring myself to sell his display models. There was so much of his soul in them, a piece of him I couldn't bear to part with. Maybe one day the girls would want them for their homes. I kept his leather tool belt and his hand tools, too. How could I part with them, remembering the belt at his waist, his stance as he used the saw, the total focus as he chiselled the fine details . . .

I still felt close to Erich in the workshop, among the small piles of timber that remained. The resinous smell of the western red cedar would always remind me of him. I kept a few pieces in my workroom to conjure his spirit whenever I entered.

All I wanted was to stay home, close to where Erich had been. I didn't care if I turned into a hermit.

'Mutti, the bills are piling up,' said Greta one afternoon about six weeks after Erich's death. She'd taken a few days off to spend with me. We sat on the boulder overlooking the river, listening to the cicadas and kookaburras, as burnished gold tinted the river below. It was my favourite place to watch the sunset and think of him.

I closed my eyes. I didn't want to think of bills.

'Vati's money won't last forever,' she said, 'and I think it'll do you good to go back to work.'

'I can't,' I said, my voice cracking.

'Reinhardt needs you at the studio. He looked terrible yesterday. He's not coping without you. Neither is Grossmama.'

'I don't think I'll be any good to anyone.'

She put her arm around me. 'You need to go back. You need a purpose, a reason to keep putting one foot in front of the other until it feels natural again. I understand what you're going through – it's hard for me too, and for Johanna.'

Tears filled my eyes. 'I'm so sorry, my darling. What have I been thinking? Of course it's hard on you too.'

'It's all my fault, Mutti,' she whispered, suddenly trembling.

I wiped my cheeks and looked into her face. It was filled with despair. 'What are you talking about?'

'I was the one who pushed you into going to Germany so soon and it was my idea to leave on that Friday to visit

Johanna. We could have waited until Saturday and maybe Vati would still be with us. Jo blames herself too. She could have come up to Sydney that weekend.' She was crying now, her arms around me.

'No, no, no.' I rubbed her back, trying to soothe her. 'It wasn't your fault at all, either of you. It was what Vati and I wanted to do. Neither of you forced us to do anything. He was so stubborn, he wouldn't listen. He thought he had super-human powers, that he was invincible.'

Greta laughed, a strangled sound, but the idea brought a smile to her face all the same. 'I can't believe he's gone.' Then tears were running down her face unchecked. 'I think about all the times I disappointed him but most of all how upset he was that I went to Vietnam.'

'You're so very like him, you know. Your father only had to admit that to himself to understand why you went. When he did, he was so terribly proud of you. We both were.' I smoothed the dark hair from her face and wiped her tears with my thumbs.

She sighed, leaning against me like she had as a little girl. I put my arm around her, remembering that it was me who was supposed to protect her from pain and hurt. 'I told him how it had been for me in Vietnam. I think he understood.'

'I know he did.'

'It was the closest I'd felt to him for a long time.'

'Well, hold on to that and know how proud he was of you.'

She nodded. 'You have to talk to Johanna. She's hurting too, and she can't get the accident she had with Vati out of her head . . .'

'I will.' I blinked my tears away and held her tight. My beautiful, wonderful daughter was still here with me and I'd neglected her when she needed me most. I vowed to return to the land of the living and count each precious moment with the ones still here, the ones I loved most.

I returned to work and was surprised to find that it helped me to gradually return to my life again. The ice surrounding my heart began to thaw as I realised what I'd been putting the girls and Mutti through. I had to find the inner strength to ensure I was there for each of them. I had to help the girls understand that their father's death wasn't their fault, only a terrible accident. It had been his time. As I came out of the haze of my mourning, I was relieved to find that they could turn to their friends, especially Jonathan and James; at times I didn't feel like I had enough of what they needed to help them heal.

I resumed a normal life, yet nothing was ever going to be the same again. I ran the studio in my usual efficient style, I worked long hours, spent time with Mutti and the girls, cooked and cleaned and visited friends and continued my regular coffee meetings with Claudia.

At night, when there were no distractions, my demons sought to escape. I remembered the poetry I used to write to my father and revisited writing to ease my pain. It helped a little, but I couldn't show my words to a single person, they were the ravings of a tormented soul. Inevitably, I would find myself in my workroom next to Erich's workshop, spending the hours until dawn drawing and painting, covering canvas after canvas. Some of my work was awful but some was inspired: raw and bold, sad and dark, light and graceful; but all drawn from the depths of my suffering and despair. Sometimes I felt like Karoline was standing behind me, whispering encouragement over my shoulder, telling me that everything would be all right. At other times, I was sure I could feel Erich's caress on my cheek.

Then it was Christmas. Our first without Erich and over three months since his death. Johanna was home and her boyfriend James was joining us for Christmas Eve before heading back to the farm on Christmas Day. Greta was home too and Mutti had insisted that she bring Jonathan. I decided that we'd have a quiet evening this year. I didn't think I was ready to have friends around me.

The candles were burning and all the food Erich would have enjoyed lay steaming in the centre of the table. Despite their loss, the girls' faces glowed with happiness to have brought their boys to this special family event.

'Vati would be proud of you,' I said, holding my daughters' hands as we sat around the dinner table. The tightness in my chest began to ease. The girls were my rock, the reason I got up every day, my joy, the only part of Erich I had left.

'As he would be of you,' said Johanna, her voice only faltering a little as she squeezed my hand gently.

'It's the next chapter for each of us now,' I said, trying to smile. 'And it's wonderful to welcome you boys to our home.' I raised my glass to each of them in turn, wondering if these young men were my future sons-in-law. Especially since Erich had met them both and given his preliminary approval.

'Has Greta mentioned what the next chapter is for her?' Jonathon enquired casually, nervously pushing the wavy brown hair from his forehead.

'No.' I looked at my daughter sitting by his side, her dark eyes meeting mine.

'I'll talk to you about it tomorrow, Mutti,' she said. 'It's something I'm excited about.'

'I look forward to hearing about it then.' I didn't miss the look of apology from Jonathan and gathered that it involved them both. All I prayed was that she wasn't pregnant. I didn't think she'd be able to cope with that just yet, after everything she'd been through.

After a lazy start to Christmas morning and an indulgent breakfast of biscuits, fruit cake, stollen and lots of coffee, I found out. James had left early and Johanna had gone with Mutti to feed Wolfie the leftovers from dinner, so Jonathan and Greta sat with me at the kitchen table, the sun streaming in through the sliding door.

'Mutti, I've decided to do some further studies,' Greta said, the tight line of her jaw betraying her nervousness. Jonathan was holding her hand, I noticed, lending his support even as his face betrayed his worry.

'That sounds good,' I said, pleased she was moving forward but waiting for what was coming. I sipped my coffee, trying to play it cool and relaxed. 'What do you want to do?'

'Postgraduate studies in cardiac medicine and nursing.' Her eyes were sparkling. This was something she was passionate about.

'Will you stay at RPA?' Wolfie barked in the background.

Greta shifted in her seat, avoiding looking at Jonathan, who sat quietly by her side, gazing at Greta with admiration and love. 'No, I'm going to London to train at the National Heart Hospital. Jon's going there to begin his specialist training and I'm going with him.'

'What?' I had not expected this. Perhaps a move inter-state, I'd thought, maybe Melbourne, but not to the other side of the world. I put down my cup, my pretence over.

'Cardiac medicine's the field we both want a career in. We've each been offered a position at the heart hospital,' said Jonathan, attempting to explain. Greta had told me how they had met while working on the cardiac ward, so it was no real surprise.

'So you're going to London?' I repeated, still stunned. I shivered and instinctively looked out the door, expecting to see the sun behind a cloud, but it was still shining as brightly as ever.

'Yes, Mutti. It's a prestigious placement at a specialist hospital at the cutting edge of coronary care and research. I'll learn so much more there than I can here. I'll come home with experience and knowledge I wouldn't get in Australia.' She reached for her glass of orange juice and drank, trying to affect nonchalance.

My self-control was slowly slipping and I blinked away tears. I didn't know if I could let her go. 'How long will you be gone?'

'At least a couple of years, maybe more,' she said, her brown eyes soft. 'I know it's terrible timing with Vati, but I couldn't turn down the opportunity. Besides, I need a change, a new environment and new challenges . . . after Vietnam.

I'm hoping it'll give me the chance I need to start fresh and heal away from the people who remind me of what I've done and where I've been.' She looked at her hands, trembling on her lap. 'I want to forget, Mutti.'

I jumped up from my seat, throwing my arms around her to hug her tight. 'Go, my darling, and be happy. You're too young to refuse opportunity and later regret it. Live your life to the fullest. That's what Vati would want you to do.' I drew away and smoothed the hair from her face.

'Are you sure, Mutti?'

'I'm sure. Just stay in touch, and write or call me as often as you can. I want to know how you are – how you're going.'

Greta nodded, wiping her tears with the back of her hand. 'Maybe you can come and visit us next Christmas,' she said.

'That sounds like a good idea,' I said, kissing the top of her head. I turned to Jonathan and saw the anxiety easing from his features. 'You'd better look after my daughter and treat her right or you'll have to deal with me.' I was sure they would live together, but after everything we'd each been through, I had no quarrel with them living unmarried. They were adults and they were happy. The rest would come if it was meant to.

'Of course,' said Jonathan quietly. 'I love Greta and I can't imagine my life without her. I waited for her to come back from Vietnam and I'll never let her out of my sight again.'

'Good,' I said. 'Now, you'd better go and tell Johanna and Grossmama your plans.'

I was happy for them but all I could think about was how Erich must have felt to have his two children on the other side of the world. They never got to see their father again, nor he them. We would've been with them on the day of his funeral.

Although I'd written brief letters to them, I knew I had to sit down to write something more. I'd collected some of their father's things and, one day when I was ready, I wanted to take that trip we'd planned, see his children and grandchildren and give them those few precious mementoes. Maybe Greta's decision and my promise to visit her would be just the push I'd need to go.

1973

It was April and I was restless. With Greta gone and Johanna in the country, Mutti and I rattled around the house. A number of her boxes remained unpacked in the corner of the spare bedroom, so we finally opened them one Sunday afternoon. Mutti was ready to face her memories and past.

'Look,' she said, pulling out Heinrich's photo, as I opened the beige curtains. 'I'd forgotten I had that.' She smiled. 'It's one of my favourite photos, one that you took in Germany. You really captured Heinrich's essence.'

'Yes, it is a good one,' I agreed, looking over her shoulder. 'I carried that photo around with me after he left for Poland the last time.'

'Why don't you get back in touch with him?' she suggested. 'I'm sure he'd love to hear from you. He always asks after you at Christmas.'

'No, I don't think so,' I said quickly. 'It was so long ago . . .' I turned, hearing steps on the back verandah and then a knock at the back door, feeling grateful for the interruption.

I was delighted to discover Johanna and James at the door.

'What a surprise!' I exclaimed, hugging Johanna tightly and kissing James on the cheek. 'What brings you up to Sydney?'

'Some of our clients have cattle and sheep coming up to the Easter Show and I've been given the job to check that they arrive safely and settle in before judging. But they don't arrive until tomorrow and James and I managed to get a few days to look around the show before we head home.'

'We've got some of our merino sheep coming up tomorrow as well,' said James, smiling. 'It was perfect timing and I can give Jo a hand.' He was beaming, large green eyes lit up with excitement.

'Sit down and I'll make you some coffee and I'll tell Grossmama that you're here.'

They insisted on helping with the last of the furniture that Mutti and I were moving to make space for a few of Erich's pieces, and found the old photo albums I had tucked away in the bottom of the buffet.

'When were these taken?' asked Johanna, settling into the soft fabric of the lounge and opening the ageing book carefully.

Bittersweet emotions washed over me. I sat next to her, not sure my legs would hold me up, and placed my arm on the timber armrest. I gazed at the images of a relaxed, younger Erich smiling back at me, lying in a meadow of wildflowers. It was a day I'd never forget.

'I took these the day that the war ended. Your father and I were on our way to Grossmama's sister's house.'

'I remember the stories you've told Greta and me about those days and how tough things were after the war . . . Why don't you tell James about how you met Vati and had to run away from Munich and the Americans?'

I hesitated in answering, not sure if I was ready to speak about Erich.

Johanna took my arm and kissed my cheek. 'Come on, Mutti, you love telling those stories, and I know James would love to hear. I want to hear them again too,' she said softly.

My gaze drifted across to the wood and chrome standing ashtray that still graced the side of the lounge Erich used to sit in. The nest of side tables that he'd made stood in front of it, topped with a single red grevillea in a tiny frosted vase.

'It's all right, Jo,' said James, placing his hand on Johanna's shoulder. 'Maybe your mother doesn't want to talk about it now.'

She nodded, blinking tears away, but the disappointment showed on her face as she gazed at the photos. I knew that she needed to hear those stories again, to bring her closer to her father and to help James understand her family and where she came from. I just had to bring myself to tell them without ripping open wounds that were still so fresh.

'Of course I'll tell you,' I said slowly, leaning back on the cushions and praying that I would hold it together.

'Amazing,' said James softly when I was done. 'I could never have imagined what you and Erich went through. Things are tough on the land but that is something else entirely.'

'I know – it's hard to imagine, isn't it? Vati only occasionally spoke about life in Germany but one story he used to always tell was the day I was born. What's really stayed with me is how difficult things were.'

'I don't know what your father told you, but your birth was one of the best days of my life,' I said, smoothing the blonde strands from her face as I used to do when she was a child.

'You would say that, Mutti, but how Vati told it was that it was the coldest winter day of the year, with heavy snow falls. He was at work when you went into labour and you had nobody to fetch the midwife.'

'That's right. It was so cold that ice formed on top of the milk. I didn't even have time to start the fire, that's how quickly you came.' I smiled at the memory, but at the time I was alone and had Greta to care for and had been worried that something would go wrong. 'All I could do was bundle Greta up in warm clothes and put her in the playpen. She wouldn't stop crying and eventually cried herself to sleep. Then Vati arrived home just after you were born. You were an angel, perfect and no trouble.' I cupped her cheek. 'And you still are.'

'Who's perfect?' asked Mutti, coming into the room.

'Jo, apparently,' said James, teasing her.

'Ah, well, she's always been the sensible and quiet one,' said Mutti, sitting on a lounge chair. 'Greta's the one who needed watching, Johanna was easy.'

'I'm so proud of you both,' I said. 'You had the courage to follow your dream of becoming a vet in a country practice and what about the work you've been doing with war veterans? I know I say that Greta's so much like your father, but you are too. He was so proud.'

'And like you, Mutti.' Johanna grasped my hand. 'You've both always been so passionate and worked hard towards what you believed in, no matter what anyone else thinks. That's all I've ever wanted to do.'

'I'm so lucky to have you.'

'See? I *am* perfect.' She smiled sweetly at James before turning to my mother. 'Mutti was just telling us about the day I was born.'

'She was on her own,' said Mutti, regret flitting across her face.

I reached across and squeezed her hand. 'It all worked out well in the end, Mutti.'

'Vati told the story differently,' persisted Johanna. 'He said that you managed everything on your own and it was because of your level head that everything went well. If you hadn't brought the wood in to start the fire, there would have been no fire because the logs outside were too damp to get one going.'

I shrugged. 'Something took over and I knew what I had to do.'

'Not only that, but when Vati arrived home, it was quiet and he tip-toed into the bedroom, thinking Greta and you were both sleeping, and found you sitting up in bed just like you'd had an afternoon nap. He didn't see me at first, wrapped up in the crib, and when he did, he was shocked that it'd happened so fast and that you were alone.'

'After it was over and you were safely in my arms, I felt like the tallest woman in the world, that I could do anything.'

'Vati said much the same thing. He'd always known what a strong and capable woman you were but in that moment he realised that you could do anything you set your mind to. He said that he'd never been so proud to have you by his side— '
Her voice broke and she bent her head.

Tears filled my eyes too. It was a memory I'd treasure forever, the four of us together in that room, my family safe and well, a moment of total bliss.

'He said that he thanked God every day for you.'

'Oh, Johanna,' I said, my trembling hand across my mouth and tears running freely down my face.

'I miss him so much, Mutti,' she whispered.

I pulled her to me and hugged her tight. 'I do too.'

'He was a good man,' said Mutti.

I glanced at her. It wasn't an admission that came easily to her and something I'd heard only a handful of times. I realised that Erich's loss had affected her too. She looked older, more worn, and sadder. She'd known so much loss. And I'd put her though more worry than I should have.

'Grosspapa had a saying about your father. He said that even if he only had the dirt under his fingernails, he would make something of that. Your Vati always found a way to make the best of what he had. He only ever wanted the best for you and your sister and your mother.' Mutti looked at me, blue eyes filled with remorse. 'He loved you all with his whole being. In the end, he was able to give you the life he'd always wanted to and he'd found the real success that he deserved.'

'I know, Grossmama.' Johanna looked at Mutti with an expression of mingled pride and sadness. 'It's because of Vati and Mutti that Greta and I've been able to do the things we want.' She took James's hand and interlaced her fingers with his, smiling at him wistfully. 'I remember living in Germany in a little village where life was very simple. My parents came to Australia to give us a better life, with nothing but determination, their dreams and hopes. When they first arrived and found that everything they'd been told was a lie, they stood up for what they saw were injustices. They really believed in the future of this country – see what they've accomplished?

Despite their misfortune, they educated Greta and me, we have a beautiful home and both of them have been successful in business.'

'Why you stayed, I'll never know,' said Mutti, shaking her head. 'But you did.'

'It's all been worth it. Both of you girls are happy and have the world at your feet. That's all Vati and I wanted for you.'

'I love your stories,' said James. 'Thank you for sharing them with me.'

I could see that he understood how hard it had been for us to talk about Erich. He was perceptive and sensitive – a good match for Johanna.

'Don't worry,' said Johanna. 'I've heard them a thousand times and I'm sure Mutti will tell my children too. If you stick around, you might be lucky enough to hear them again.' She grinned, pushing against him with her shoulder, but he just grinned back. They were definitely smitten.

24

October 1973

Mutti was meeting one of Rudi's sisters in the city and begged me to join her, because she was feeling a little unwell with a headache but didn't want to cancel. Although they had a good relationship, I knew she was nervous. She still struggled with anything connected with Rudi but now I sympathised with her, understanding how hard it could be – it was a little over a year since Erich's death.

They'd decided to meet at the café in the Botanic Gardens in the city. Mutti and I arrived first, taking a table with a lovely view out over the gardens. It was a glorious day, warm enough for short sleeves, and I was looking forward to wandering through the grounds afterwards and along the harbour to view the Opera House at Bennelong Point.

As I fiddled with my eternity ring, wondering what Erich would have thought about the new Opera House, I noticed a man walk in. He was tall, tanned and blond, and something about him seemed familiar. Turning my head to look at him properly, I froze.

I stared at the man as he approached us. He looked worried, as if he was searching for someone, then his eyes fell on Mutti and he frowned as if trying to place her, before his face cleared and he smiled with recognition.

'Amelia?'

Mutti looked up at the man in astonishment. 'Heinrich? Is it really you?'

The man nodded.

'Fancy seeing you here!' She stood and they hugged.

I felt sick to my stomach and beads of perspiration broke out on my forehead, despite the cool breeze coming in through the open windows. Time stood still as the murmur of conversation and clatter of crockery and cutlery faded into the background.

'What a coincidence! Please sit and join us,' said Mutti, gesturing to the empty chair.

'All right. Just for a minute. I can't stay long.'

'What brings you here?' asked Mutti.

'I'm in Sydney for a few days of meetings before flying to Canberra to meet with the Minister for Health.'

Heinrich looked into my eyes and I was transported back thirty years. He was older, fine lines creasing the corners of his eyes when he smiled, worry lines on his forehead and around his mouth and his blond hair streaked with grey, but his eyes were the same bright blue and with the twinkle that I remembered.

'Hello, Lotte,' he said softly. 'It's been a long time.'

'Hello, Heinrich,' I replied, my mouth as dry as the sands of the outback. I felt hot too, my cheeks burning with embarrassment, and I wanted nothing more than to shrivel up and disappear. I didn't like to be surprised like this.

'Sydney's a beautiful city,' he said.

'Your first time here?' I managed to say. My shock aside, good manners demanded that I speak.

'Yes and I was very excited to come. Your mother's told me so much about Australia.' He smiled and Mutti patted his hand affectionately. 'I look forward to a little sight-seeing around Sydney. Maybe you can suggest where to go and what to see?'

'Don't you have people to organise all that for you?' I asked, smiling sweetly, controlling the surge of anger that raced through me. I doubted this was a coincidental meeting at all. I was furious with Mutti for her deception, and with Heinrich too. Part of me wanted to get up and leave immediately but another part of me was curious about him and what his life had been like since we last parted.

'Of course, but I thought that a local like yourself would have a much better idea of what's worthwhile to see in the limited time that I have.'

'I'll have to put some serious thought into it and let you know,' I said somewhat ungraciously.

'Thank you, Lotte,' said Heinrich easily, ignoring my tone. 'Anything will be a help.'

I stared at the view, trying to take in its serenity.

'Let's order some coffee,' said Mutti. 'Natalia can order when she arrives.' She didn't meet my eye, and I wondered if Rudi's sister was meeting us at all.

The coffee and cake helped, giving me something to do other than twisting the serviette in my lap, as well as the energy I needed to get over my shock.

We stayed talking for about an hour, catching each other up on the main events of our lives, filling the awkward gaps with small talk. Heinrich had three children, two boys and a girl, all either working or at university. He lived on his own after going through a divorce and there was nobody special in his life. It was strange, at times it felt like the years apart had disappeared and at others it felt like the distance of time and events made us total strangers.

'I'm so sorry to hear about Erich,' said Heinrich quietly after Mutti got up to go to the bathroom. I stiffened in my seat. 'I always admired you as a couple. I know how much you loved each other. I suppose I always wanted the kind of love you shared, but I never had that with my wife . . . In the end, it wasn't enough for either of us. I regretted not being able to give her what she wanted and the years we lost trying to make it work, but she's finally happy now.'

'Thank you. I'm sorry that you've had such a difficult time too.' I was surprised that he was opening up to me like this, unsure if I felt flattered or uncomfortable. Heinrich and Erich had always been jealous of each other.

'It was my own fault, I suppose. Besides, I have three beautiful children. Here, I have a photo of them.' He pulled out his wallet and found the photo. It wasn't recent but showed three children smiling happily in a studio shoot.

'It's lovely,' I said, kindly. 'Whoever took this did a good job of getting them all to smile and make it look natural.'

'Yes, it was taken just after my wife and I separated, so the children weren't particularly happy at that time. They've struggled with the divorce and it's been a challenge to help them cope, to find a way to make it easier on them ... My daughter's been the hardest, being the youngest.'

Mutti returned. 'Natalia's been caught up. She rang the café to let me know. Her grand-daughter's sick and she had to pick her up from school and look after her while her daughter's at work. She won't be coming.'

I nodded. I wasn't surprised. Mutti was back to her meddling best.

'Well, I'm going to enjoy these gardens and see what the fuss is all about with this new Opera House,' I said.

'Would you like to join us, Heinrich?' asked Mutti.

'I'm sure he's busy. He's got a meeting to get to this afternoon.' I had to stop this before it began but I felt my control of the situation slipping away.

'No, it's all right. How often do I run into old friends on the other side of the world? I can manage without extra preparation. As long as I turn up to the meeting, I'll be fine.' He stood and offered Mutti his arm. 'Let's go and have a look around. I've been dying to see the harbour.'

I had to go along with it since I had suggested it, but I was fuming.

Heinrich spent a couple of hours with us, walking around the gardens, admiring the magnificent harbour and walking past the imposing white sails of the Opera House. The magnificent building was worth the wait and all the controversy, I decided.

'It's more beautiful than I imagined,' Heinrich said. Mutti was walking a little behind us. 'No wonder you want to live here.'

I inhaled the smell of salt water, feeling surprisingly relaxed. The midday sun was warm on my skin and seagulls cried as they soared overhead then came in to land, jostling for morsels of the leftover chips a generous person had thrown to them. It really was a wonderful place to live. I had to admit that I'd enjoyed showing Heinrich what I thought was the most stunning part of the city. Anyone who viewed the harbour couldn't help but be impressed, and I was feeling smug. The choice Erich and I had made to come here to live all those years ago that many thought dubious probably looked like a very good decision to someone like Heinrich now.

He smiled at me. 'The lifestyle suits you. You haven't really changed in the twenty years since I last saw you.'

'Don't be silly. Of course I have.' For a start, I wasn't a girl who could be affected by honeyed words any more.

He laughed. 'We both have. But what I mean is that I still see you, the girl I used to know and the woman who left me, who was strong, vibrant and independent.'

A ferry out on the harbour announced its arrival at the pier at Circular Quay by sounding its horn.

'I have to go now,' I said, blushing and slowing to a stop. I hadn't blushed in years and now twice in one day. 'Unlike you, I've got a lot of work to get through this afternoon.' As much as I'd unexpectedly enjoyed showing Heinrich around the harbour, I now felt uncomfortable near him – and with his flattery.

'Didn't you want to look around the Opera House?'

I waved my hand impatiently. 'Another time.' I turned to my mother. 'We have to go, Mutti.'

Heinrich grasped my hand and I started as a shot of electricity passed between us. Memories of his touch many years earlier confused me for a moment.

'Please promise me that I can see you one more time before I leave for Canberra. Perhaps we can see the inside of the Opera House together, maybe a concert?'

I stared at him and then gazed at the striking stairway that led to the top level and grand façade of the building.

'I'll think about it,' I said finally. 'I'll call you at your hotel tomorrow.'

'I look forward to it,' he said, kissing my cheek. 'Until next time.'

'Goodbye, Heinrich,' I said coolly. Then I turned and walked away, dazed by the conflicting emotions warring inside me.

It was World War Three when Mutti and I got home.

'How could you?' I shouted as I slammed the door. 'You went behind my back and arranged that meeting with Heinrich. There was nothing coincidental about it!'

Mutti shrugged as she put her handbag on the kitchen table, calm and cool. 'He was coming to Sydney anyway and you were never going to agree to meet him on your own. I just gave you a helping hand. Heinrich always wanted to see you, even just for the sake of an old friendship.'

'Yours or mine?' I yelled, becoming more furious because she remained so unruffled.

'Both, *schätzchen*. Where's the harm in reconnecting with old friends?' She spread her hands, palms up. 'Besides, you're both adults. You can choose how far your relationship develops.'

'That's it, isn't it? You can't help yourself! You just have to push us together again. Don't you remember the havoc you caused last time? The suffering you caused me, Erich, Heinrich and his family?'

'Erich's gone,' she said softly, touching my arm. 'I'm sorry for that, truly I am. I know how much you loved him – like I loved Vati. But now you're on your own. I'm not saying you have to fall into Heinrich's arms, but I am saying there's no reason for the two of you not to be friends now.'

'Stay out of it, Mutti!' I stormed out the door and strode to the shed, ready to bury myself in my work.

But I couldn't concentrate. Images of Heinrich as a young man kept coming to me, like the water rushing from opened floodgates. Despite all our differences and the pain we'd put each other through, there was still so much to like about him. The little I'd seen of Heinrich in the gardens had shown me that time had tempered him, matured him, softening the hard edges. What had comforted me, however, was his familiarity. We had a long history as children and young adults and although I'd been through so much and changed, like he had, we remembered who we had once been.

After much soul searching, it was the thought of comforting my bleeding heart and wounded soul that made me decide to join Heinrich for dinner. As twisted as it seemed, Heinrich provided a connection to Erich, to those heady days when we'd first met and married. It would do me good to talk about the old days.

I didn't think that letting down my guard, even a little, would be dangerous. We'd be old friends having dinner with polite, friendly conversation, like colleagues meeting socially for a meal. I saw no harm in that. All the same, I was nervous on the night, taking care with my outfit, finding something suitably flattering without being overtly enticing. It had been over a year since I'd really cared about how I looked. I turned my body and looked in the mirror, adjusting straps and smoothing fabric until I was satisfied. An extra mist of hairspray kept my shoulder-length hair in place before I finished my makeup, applying a final touch of lipstick and subtly dabbing Chanel No. 5, Erich's favourite perfume, at my throat and wrists.

Heinrich was staying at the Sydney Boulevarde. He surprised me – he was a total gentleman and that formality put me at ease. It wasn't until we were laughing about our antics as children, drinking expensive wine and savouring each morsel of the tiny but flavoursome offerings from huge plates that I began to relax. I realised I was enjoying myself. Perhaps that was the mistake. He really was good company. We were having such a lovely time reminiscing that we left the restaurant after our meal and went to a club for cocktails.

Somehow we ended up dancing. The physical contact felt like a shock at first, my nerves buzzing, but my body remembered and before I knew it, we were cheek to cheek, our bodies fitted together and moving as one. We had spent endless balls dancing together in our youth, but this was different. I saw the yearning in his eyes but it was controlled. He would never touch me unless I allowed it, no matter how much he wanted me.

The kiss on the dancefloor made everything fall away. Heinrich's lips were soft, his hands strong, and for the first time since Erich's death, I felt safe to let go. The memory of our last encounter came back to me, the intensity and desperation. Perhaps it was because nobody but Erich had looked at me like that in twenty years. Perhaps it was because it had been over a year since I had been touched by a man and my body responded to that physical need. There was no desperation now, only free choice. Whatever we did, we did as mature adults, with no impact on anyone else but ourselves. That was liberating.

Somehow we ended up back in his hotel room. The taxi ride only heightened my longing, Heinrich's hand in mine, bodies barely touching, driving me crazy. Once the suite door closed behind us, we lost control. Shoes and clothes were strewn across the room in a bid to feel skin against skin. He was fit, strong, powerful – more than I remembered – and I allowed the waves of desire to overtake me. We had never made love before. I'd been waiting until our wedding night, which never came.

There was no slaking our thirst, our need for each other, until the night changed to soft grey and the early morning rays peeked around the edges of the block-out curtains. Then we slept in a tangle of arms, legs and sheets. He was a good lover – considerate, I decided when I woke and discovered him still sleeping by my side. The activities of the night before were more than enough to satisfy my needs but I was surprised and a little dismayed to find that it was his thoughtfulness and vulnerability that touched my heart – something I'd never expected.

'Good morning.' His voice was husky from sleep. 'I wasn't sure if you'd still be here.'

'Do you want me to go?' I asked.

'Absolutely not,' he said, wrapping his arms around me.

I felt safe and secure, protected, and it was such a relief to have the burden I'd been carrying lifted from my shoulders for a little while.

'Well, then,' I said smiling. He kissed me and I became soft like marshmallow.

'You're a tigress,' he whispered. 'I always imagined . . . but now I understand that no man could ever control you.'

'Is that so?' I said, my nerve endings beginning to hum again. I couldn't tell him that last night had outstripped what I had fantasised about decades earlier. 'You'd better tell me more.' I nibbled his earlobe, not gently, and felt his intake of breath.

'A breathtakingly beautiful, wild woman . . .'

I didn't need to hear any more. I rolled and sat astride him in a single fluid motion. His hands rested on my hips and slid up my torso, caressing my breasts.

'Sweet Jesus in heaven,' he groaned.

Heinrich had to leave for Canberra and I had to get home to work. I hadn't planned on seeing him again, even on contacting him while he remained in Australia. Now, we both knew we'd started something we couldn't stop, but I wouldn't promise him anything.

'Call me when you get back to Sydney,' I said as I kissed him goodbye. His blue eyes were dark with desire but he let me leave.

The next three weeks were awful. I couldn't stop thinking about Heinrich, about our night together. It was like I was a teenager again, like the first time I'd fallen for him. My paintings took a new turn, becoming soft and sensual. I focused on the image of a naked woman sitting on a stool with her back to the viewer, head turned, as if she knew someone was watching. To me, it represented a woman who understood her own power, who was comfortable in her own skin, who had the confidence to be who she was and not hide from the world or pretend she was something other than herself.

Mutti knew Heinrich and I had met without being told. She saw me smiling and humming to myself, distracted and distant.

'He's good for you,' she said, one evening as she dried the dishes. 'I always knew you were right for each other.'

I opened my mouth to tell her to mind her own business but she continued.

'But I was wrong. Sometimes there isn't just one person who can be the one, sometimes there are two. I was blessed to find that out with Rudi and I think that maybe you might be too. Give Heinrich a chance to prove himself to you. Don't be quick to dismiss him.'

'Don't be ridiculous, Mutti. We're just friends. Besides, he lives on the other side of the world.' I sloshed soapy water over the edge of the sink in my exasperation.

'And what's holding you here?' She flapped the tea-towel in my direction, equally frustrated. 'Johanna could come with you, she's not married, and if she decided to stay, you could come and visit. You'd be closer to Greta, you'd be back with family and relatives, back in your homeland, where you belong . . . and so would I.' Mutti sagged suddenly. 'I'm not getting any younger and the thought of dying in Germany soothes my soul.'

'Stop it, Mutti,' I said, banging a pot on the sink. 'Don't talk to me about Germany! There's no future with Heinrich. Leave it alone.'

She'd struck a nerve. Erich had said he wanted to die in Germany too. Although that had been after his accident and I knew how happy and settled he was before he died, I wondered if a part of him had still carried that longing. Looking for a house in Germany had probably meant more to him than just being able to visit whenever he wanted. He never had the chance to set foot on German soil again. I couldn't take the guilt of bearing the responsibility for Mutti's wishes as well.

'All right then,' said Mutti, but I could see by the determination on her face that she wasn't finished with me.

'I hear you and Grossmama met your old fiancé when he came to Sydney recently,' Greta said casually over the phone, when she was done talking about work and how she and Jonathan had moved into a bigger, more comfortable apartment.

'Yes, but he's an old friend, nothing more,' I said forcefully. 'Your grandmother's keen for me to find someone.'

'She's just worried about you being on your own and she knows how well you two used to get on.'

'It's not her business to meddle in. I'm sure you wouldn't like it if I tried to organise your love life.'

'I suppose not.'

'Then let it be – please. I'm fine. I don't need any help.'

'All right, Mutti, if you're sure. Now, we have to talk about your plans to come over Christmas. You can stay with us, of course.'

The change of topic was a breath of fresh air. 'That sounds wonderful, darling. Let me work out what's happening here and what dates we're looking at before I check flights. I'll see if Grossmama wants to come too, otherwise she'll stay with Johanna while I'm gone.'

After the phone call, I sat at the telephone table for some time, thinking, gently chewing on my bottom lip and twisting my eternity ring around my finger. Maybe it was time for me to extend my visit and make that trip back to Germany. I didn't know when I'd be able to visit Greta next. Perhaps she'd be already home before I had the chance to get back to Europe and this was my best chance of honouring what Erich had always wanted to do, maybe of even looking at buying that house he'd wanted. I still wanted to take my daughters back one day, and their children too . . .

Heinrich called when he arrived in Sydney. The sound of his voice made me weak at the knees. We spent an hour on the phone, laughing, leaving me breathless before he had to go to a dinner meeting.

'I have to see you,' he said. 'I'm sorry I can't do tonight. I'd get out of this if I could. What about tomorrow night? Are you free?'

I wanted to say no. It was best to leave what we'd had as a foolish and indulgent mistake and not complicate things further, but the echoes of that night stayed with me. A little harmless fun was fine, surely? It didn't have to mean anything more than that. He was going home in a couple of weeks.

'Yes, I'm free. I'll come to you, shall I?'

'Perfect. I'll see you then.'

I hung up, grinning like an idiot.

We spent every spare minute of the next two weeks together. I tried to sneak out of the house without Mutti seeing me or calling out as I was going, telling her when I'd return. I shook my head ruefully when I thought about it – not even Greta and Johanna had behaved like this as teenagers. But they didn't have a mother like Mutti, relentless in her determination to ensure Heinrich and I stayed together. The less she knew, the better.

I played tourist with Heinrich: a sunset cruise around the harbour drinking champagne and eating lobster tail; fish and chips and ice cream at Manly; a picnic in the Botanic Gardens; and dinner and dancing until the small hours of the morning.

I wondered if I'd become addicted to the distraction of him. When I was with Heinrich, I didn't have to think, only exist in the moment. With him, the pain of Erich's loss was muted for a little while and I felt like I could breathe again – like I was alive again. What made these weeks special was that apart from being giddy with love or physical desire – I wasn't sure where one ended and the other began – Heinrich made me feel safe and secure enough to allow myself to explore my desires and dreams once more.

On the last night, Heinrich surprised me with tickets to a performance in the concert hall at the Sydney Opera House. I'd told him that I'd always wanted to go, ever since those early days of the building's construction when Erich and I were struggling so much and I'd dreamed of the day when we could afford to watch a performance there. We could now, but Erich was gone. I thought of him as Heinrich and I made our way into the auditorium and wished he was by my side. Although Erich hadn't liked Heinrich, I felt sure that he'd be happy that I was doing something I enjoyed with someone who would treat me well.

Claudia had told me that Peter was back in Australia after studying overseas and was touring with one of the orchestras he'd played with, but I never imagined I would be at the Opera House to see him. I only wished Johanna was there, not just for Peter, but to see how he'd succeeded after all they'd both been through. She would have been proud of him.

'Do you know that the first performance here in September was a selection of Wagner pieces?' I told Heinrich. We were in our seats, listening to the chaotic tuning and warming up of instruments before the performance started that always made my skin tingle with anticipation.

'Even here in Australia, German culture is recognised as superior,' he replied.

I frowned in the gathering darkness. That wasn't what I'd meant. I made a noncommittal noise that he took as agreement.

'Australia has its charms, but it's still a provincial backwater. You'll have to come back to Munich and I'll take you to the opera, ballet, symphonies, whatever you like. Maybe we can talk about it later,' he whispered, squeezing my hand.

Australia isn't a provincial backwater, I thought, annoyed, but the start of the music saved my response. Maybe a few weeks here weren't enough for him to see the incredible country Australia was, free from the ties of an ancient European past, free to determine and shape its own future. Wild and free, like he thought I was.

I brushed his comments off. Perhaps they had been off-the-cuff remarks made without thinking. I wanted to enjoy this night.

The concert was magnificent, taking me to other worlds and making me feel euphoria and blood-boiling passion then heart-wrenching sadness and the depths of despair. Heinrich sat beside me, steadfast and solid.

Supper after the concert was dreamlike. It was our last night together and we both wanted to make memories we wouldn't forget. Vintage Bollinger champagne and seafood were an exquisite first course to the main meal we hungered for, and we couldn't keep our hands off each other when we finally made it to the privacy of Heinrich's suite.

Afterwards, in a haze of satisfaction, Heinrich rolled onto his side to look me in the eye.

'We have to talk.'

'Mmm?' Limp and languid, I wasn't in any fit state to be thinking, let alone talking.

'I want to see you again.'

His frank blue gaze forced the cogs of my mind to turn lazily.

'But you're going home in a few hours.'

'I know. Come with me.'

Now I was quite awake and alert.

He held my hand and kissed it. 'Come home with me. Maybe not tomorrow, but what about after Christmas?'

I stretched, trying to think straight. 'I could possibly do that – on my way home from Greta in London.'

Another interlude after Christmas sounded tempting, I had to admit, and I was thinking about going back . . . I squeezed my eyes shut. I had to keep Erich and Heinrich separate. Maybe it wasn't such a good idea after all.

When I opened my eyes, Heinrich was shaking his head, blond locks falling over his eyes. I automatically threaded my fingers through his hair and combed it back from his forehead – just like I used to do with Erich. I removed my hand.

'No, I mean to stay. Come back to Germany.'

I stilled. 'I can't do that,' I said, frowning with irritation. 'I have Mutti and Johanna here, the studio and my business. Besides, I have nowhere to go. Mutti sold everything before she came.'

He grasped me by the shoulders, his eyes filled with intensity and excitement. 'You can set up your own studio in Germany. I know that's what you always wanted and it will accommodate your new business too. We'll find the right place together. Your mother and Johanna can join us, of course.'

I pulled away, angry blood surging through my body, making my head throb. 'Have you been talking to my mother? Has she put you up to this? Because if she has, I want you to know that I'm fine. I can manage on my own.'

Heinrich's face bloomed red with outrage and the look of hurt in his eyes made me regret my hasty words. 'I don't know what you're talking about. I haven't spoken to your mother since the day after I arrived.' He sighed and shook his head, attempting to calm down. 'I know you're capable of doing anything on your own. That's not the point. Why manage on your own if you don't have to? You don't have to work if you don't want to. I have a good income and I still have my inheritance. There's plenty for us to do whatever we want.'

'Heinrich, I—'

'I have an apartment, but if you don't like it, we can find something you'd prefer.'

After everything, I was being offered a way to go back to my old life and to realise my dream of a photography studio. Then there was the thought that Erich had imagined living out his old age in his homeland, perhaps even to his dying day, which tormented me. Maybe I could return with Mutti and fulfil her wish, give my children somewhere to visit and live Erich's dream. But I'd be doing it with Heinrich.

I shook my head to clear it of the thoughts that tumbled over each other.

'Are you asking me to move in with you?' I asked, taken aback by the swift and unexpected direction this evening was taking.

'Yes, to start with.' He caressed my cheek, his hand warm against my skin. 'We can take it slowly and see how we go. I don't want to push you.'

I turned my head away so he wouldn't see the tears prickle my eyes. The irony was more than I could bear. 'What are you asking me, Heinrich?' I had to hear all of it, know exactly what it was I was considering.

He took a deep breath. 'I'm asking you to marry me, Lotte.'

This was the third proposal I'd received from him and he was as serious as I'd ever seen him. I could hear Mutti's voice in my head, rejoicing. 'Third time lucky!' she would've told me. I was mute. I couldn't believe this was happening – again.

'Look how good we are together. You make me happy, and the truth is that I've never stopped loving you. But I'm a realist. Don't give me an answer now. Let's move in together and see how that works. Rent out your home here until you decide if it's what you really want. Then we can take the next step.' He'd obviously learnt over the years how to be practical and pragmatic.

'What about if you move out here?' I watched him carefully.

'You know I can't do that.' There was regret in his eyes but stubborn determination too. 'My children are there, my career is there, my home and my family. It's impossible.'

I stared at the boldly patterned wallpaper on the wall opposite and said nothing. How much did he love me if he wouldn't consider my obligations and what I might really want? There had been no discussion and he hadn't even asked me if moving to Germany was what I wanted. It seemed that nothing had really changed after all. He was the same man I had left for Erich.

'Come on, Lotte, would you rather stay here, in this backward place? Remember the life you used to have: the culture, arts, fashion; our glorious history. You could have all that again, regain the social status you were born with . . . We could be like this all the time.' He was persuasive, trailing his fingers down my body and watching me gasp, smiling with supreme self-confidence. He kissed me lightly. 'Promise me you'll think about it. Once you've decided, I'll organise the rest so we can be together as soon as possible. I can't imagine you out of my life ever again.'

'I'll think about it,' I murmured. But I couldn't think straight with him so near. The offer was tempting in some ways, allowing me to run away and forget all the hardship and heart-ache I'd endured, leave behind everything that reminded me of Erich and that only brought me fresh waves of pain. Back to a life of luxury and ease, a life my mother so desperately missed.

Heinrich kissed me again with such passion that the past and the future dropped away and I let everything else go.

I was a mess after. I couldn't eat or sleep. I missed the touch of him, the security he'd wrapped around me when I was with him. It was like a cocoon that allowed me to grow and develop free from other influences. Now I felt fragile, vulnerable and conflicted.

In the end, I spoke to Mutti about it at breakfast after another sleepless night. I was spent, my constant thoughts giving me no rest. I couldn't take it much longer.

'Why is this such a hard decision?' she asked, toast with cherry jam lying untouched on her plate. 'He loves you and wants to give you a good life. What's so wrong with that?'

'It's not that simple.' I dragged my hands through my unkempt hair. I felt as rudderless and directionless as I had after Erich died.

She shrugged. 'From what I've seen, you don't dislike him. Perhaps you even love him, although you can't admit it to yourself. Don't waste your opportunity to be happy like I did with Rudi.'

'I don't know if he's right for me. He was only supposed to be a distraction.' I stared into my coffee cup, finding no inspiration there. I knew the answer in my bones, yet I craved security and an end to my struggles. Was that so wrong?

'How can you say that? He's offering you everything. You wouldn't have stayed in Sydney with him for days at a time if he didn't make you feel something.'

Her exasperation made no difference to me. 'I don't know if it's what I want.' My eyes felt hot and dry, as if I'd cried all the moisture from my body.

She banged the table hard, her eyes blazing, making me wince. 'I thought it's exactly what you wanted. You and Erich were going back. Maybe even to stay one day. What's changed?'

'I was doing it with him and for him. Now he's gone.' I put my head in my hands. I felt like I was breaking in two.

'What about for your children and grandchildren? You'll be able to show them where they come from, show them our traditions.'

'I can do that without living there, without marrying Heinrich,' I said through my fingers. Something fell into place and I looked up. 'These are different times, Mutti, not like when Heinrich and I were first engaged. I can make decisions for myself and not have someone else who thinks they know better make them for me. I can do the things I want to do on my own, as an independent woman.'

Mutti's eyes filled with tears. 'I push you because all I want is to see you happy, financially secure and settled, to know you're well looked after and having a good life. You're still so young. You're my darling girl.' She was trembling like a leaf but there was determination on her face. 'I only ever wanted the best for you, now as always, and whatever that happens to be – Heinrich or not. I want to give you the world but I can't. I want to see you happy and comfortable before I die. Otherwise I'll have failed as a mother.' She looked beseechingly at me and it tore at my already ragged heart.

I broke then, tears falling silently down my face. I reached for her, hugging her tiny frame tight.

'Oh, Mutti! I love you.' I felt as I had as a little child, when I'd run to my mother for comfort. Somehow everything felt better when I was in her embrace.

She drew away after a few moments and wiped my cheeks with a handkerchief she pulled from her sleeve. She smoothed the hair from my face and brow, like I was eight years old again. 'Think about what makes you truly happy. That's your answer.'

'But I don't know—'

'I want to see the girl who shone like a light from the inside out. The girl who knew the world was at her feet and that she could do anything. You had so much to give . . .' She sighed. 'Vati and I always knew that you were strong and independent and that you'd do whatever you wanted. I was like that too, once.'

'But the war changed everything,' I said, thinking not only of what had happened to me but also what had happened to Mutti, who'd lived through two wars.

She nodded and cupped my face in her hands. 'Now, for the first time, you have nobody to answer to, no small children who need you, and you live in a time of peace. It's time for you. Do what makes you happy and show the world and your daughters what you're made of.' She kissed my forehead like a blessing, a benediction.

'Really?' I frowned because she made sense – my controlling, rigid mother made perfect sense.

'Maybe I was wrong to have pushed you so hard all those years. Rudi helped me understand. But maybe it's old age too. From my perspective, things look different, and I see what seemed so important when I was younger now isn't. Just go and be happy and I'll be happy too.'

I kissed her cheek, a rush of gratitude threatening to make me sob like a child. 'Thank you.'

Erich was with me as I walked to our boulder by the river, Mutti's wise words refusing to leave my mind. *Be happy.* Staring out at the water, I remembered the last time he and I had been here. We were one then, and happy. Now I felt broken, a part of my soul missing, and I didn't know how to be happy again.

'How could you have left me?' I whispered. 'After everything we'd been through. We were ready for the good times. These should've been our best years.'

I crumpled to the ground, fingers clawing at the sandstone until they bled. The pain flowed with my sorrow, powerful sobs racking my frame. I hadn't allowed myself to really cry after Erich's death, fearing that the release of my uncontrollable anguish would destroy me completely. But I couldn't hold it in any longer, and my grief poured out of me. Suddenly I didn't care if I dissolved to nothing under the weight of my pain or if I was reduced to an empty husk. Anything would be better than keeping my torment locked in my heart for a second longer.

'How can I do this without you?' I said to the open air when my sobs had subsided. 'You were my world and my life, now I'm spinning like a top, and I'm afraid I'll never be able to put my shattered heart together again.'

I don't know how long it was until I raised my head, the rock beneath me warm from my body and soaked with my tears and my despair, but my skin was stippled with gooseflesh and the sun had dropped close to the horizon. I wasn't empty at all. It was as if the bush around me had absorbed my grief and heartache so they were no longer overwhelming. Hope and light had filled the spaces darkness had left within me. I could now see that it was possible to put the pieces of my heart, my soul and my life back together. It felt good to remember that I had the strength and the support around me to do it.

I no longer felt stuck in limbo. I could see with a clear eye now. The echoes of our past always remained with us but didn't have to determine our future. Heinrich was my past, but I'd changed so much from the girl he'd known. He was still part of the old world I'd left behind and he'd only stifle me. Finally I was willing to admit to myself that he'd never been the real problem, only a distraction from my pain, from what I knew I needed to do.

I had never doubted Erich's love but he'd never been able to change like I had. It had caused conflict between us as I struggled to find my place in this new country, where anything was possible. Maybe it was because he was so much older than me and couldn't shake the deeply ingrained belief that he had to protect me, prove he was worthy of me. But his life in Germany had left an indelible mark on him and he couldn't walk away from his desire to help others and make Australia a better place.

I loved him anyway. He had been my everything. But now it was time to let him go.

I remembered back to the first time our circumstances had parted us. I had been terrified, alone in this country with its foreign ways and language, left to find my way with the girls, to join him in Sydney. Then there had been the accident and I had to shoulder the responsibility of our family's survival. I had managed on my own and my family had thrived because of what I'd done. I'd come so far since that day I'd first set foot on Australian soil.

Now the girls were grown and doing well. It was time to stand on my own two feet and live the life I wanted for myself. It was time to look to my future.

'I love you, Erich,' I whispered into the sky. I noticed a lone eagle wheeling over the trees, coasting on the currents of air. I wondered where its mate was. Eagles mated for life and pined if their partner died. I knew I wouldn't die; I had our daughters to guide and love, and Erich wasn't really far away. I saw him in them.

'Watch over us, my darling.'

We were Australians. This was my home. Erich and I had fought hard for our place here. Now our children could thrive, their futures bright with opportunity, and they and their children could be and do anything their hearts desired.

The bush and the river were my sanctuary. The smells of the timber, the laugh of the kookaburra and the dazzling beauty of the eucalyptus flowers were part of me and reminded me that I was home. I wasn't going anywhere. Mutti was right. It was time for me, time to find what made me shine. Whatever difficulties were ahead, I owed it to myself to work out what the next part of my life held. This was what Karoline had tried to get me to understand.

I thought of the naked woman I'd painted only weeks earlier. It was my favourite work and now I realised why: I was her. I had painted her wanting to become her, and now I had.

'Thank you,' I whispered.

I felt as free as the eagle and imagined myself soaring high through the air, over my domain. I was where I belonged.

Epilogue

1976
Canberra

I perched on the edge of the white leather and chrome lounge suite, twirling my eternity ring around my finger and glued to the news on the colour television, mixed emotions washing over me.

I was dressed in a figure-hugging, full-length gown of royal blue jersey silk for the opening night of my first exhibition, photographs and paintings of Australian landscapes and Australians at work, rest and play. I'd closed the photography studio in Manuka early so I could prepare, and we were off to Marco's restaurant in Barton after to celebrate and share the good news that Johanna and James, now six months married, had been sitting on for a few weeks. They were picking up Mutti, who lived a couple of streets from Marco and me, on their way from the property at Yass. Greta and Jonathan were due to arrive at any moment, having flown in to Sydney from London. I couldn't wait to have all my family with me under one roof. And Claudia and Franz were meeting us at the gallery along with many of our friends.

'Are you ready, *amore mio*?' Marco, impeccably dressed in suit and tie, his shiny black shoes clicking loudly across the timber floors, stopped at the sight of me and frowned. I'd met him about eighteen months earlier, through Marissa, a friend I'd made at art class. I hadn't expected to fall in love again, but the loss of Erich and my interlude with Heinrich had taught me to open myself to living life fully. Life was too short, as the girls and Mutti had reminded me.

'Look, more Vietnamese boat people,' I said as he joined me on the lounge. Saigon had fallen to the communist regime a year earlier. Finally the war was over but thousands of civilians had fled the country, refugees risking their lives in tiny fishing boats, looking for sanctuary wherever they could find it. Many had reached Australian shores, looking for safety and security, and a future for their families.

'Remember what it was like when we came out?'

'I remember, *tesero mio*,' he said softly, grasping my hand. 'I think it'll be difficult for these new people to find their place here.'

'It's a multicultural country now, different to what it was back then, and people are a lot more accepting and inclusive,' I said, remembering how doggedly Erich had fought. 'Perhaps it'll just take time.'

I stared out the floor-to-ceiling windows over the shadows gathering on Lake Burley Griffin, the setting sun casting a golden glow over the white façade of Parliament House and the Brindabella Mountains beyond. I loved living in the nation's capital, at the centre of it all, and I knew that Erich would be proud of the life I'd made for myself.

'Like it did for us,' agreed Marco, kissing my hand and threading his arm around my waist.

I looked at him adoringly, hardly able to believe that we were this happy.

'It was hard for a long time but I wouldn't want to be anywhere else,' I said, smiling, 'Australia has given us everything – and no matter where we go, this is home.'

Author's note

Suitcase of Dreams is inspired by a true story—my grandparents' story.

Many of you may wonder how much is truth and how much is fiction, so I wanted to share the true stories and historical background that has lent authenticity to the migrant experience of the 1950s and 60s and has brought *Suitcase of Dreams* to life.

My grandparents arrived from Germany on the *Skaubryn* in 1956. They docked in Fremantle before disembarking in Melbourne and taking the train to Bonegilla, near Albury on the Victoria–New South Wales border. My grandfather was an aeronautic engineer and was also promised work in Australia, but like so many educated and professional migrants, he found out that his qualifications weren't recognised once he arrived. He travelled up to Sydney to find work and my grandmother and their children later joined him in the Villawood hostel where they stayed for about nine months. He worked as a mechanic and in factories, including the disastrous stint with the engineering firm.

My grandmother was trained as a photographer in Europe, but didn't work professionally in that field until she arrived in Australia. She began painting while at the Abercrombie River— she loved the Australian bush, the flora and fauna, and the landscapes. She was a talented painter, and I have some of her works on my walls at home. She later also began painting on fabric, adorning tablecloths, table runners, scarves, T-shirts and even umbrellas with Australian animals and plants.

Her mother did in fact travel on the ill-fated last journey of the *Skaubryn*. She, like all the passengers, lost everything on that voyage, including the valuables she kept in the captain's safe. Not long after, my grandfather's mother came to Australia, to spend her twilight years with her son and grandchildren – a courageous thing to do so late in life.

After my grandfather was involved in the terrible car accident described in the story, my grandmother and the children moved from their rented semi-detached house to the garage he had built at the 'farm'. The injuries he sustained were extensive enough that the doctors believed he'd never have full use of that leg again – and yet he did.

My grandfather did start up his own business after the accident but although his father had a furniture shop and made furniture in Germany and my grandfather could do woodwork, he turned his hand to taxidermy – a specialised craft he had seen as a young man surrounded by the mountains and forests of his youth. He learnt the art from scratch and built up a successful business which my grandmother learnt and continued for a time after his death.

While I had family stories, photographs, letters and first-hand accounts to draw on, I wanted to research further to understand what Australia would have been like for them when they arrived. I discovered that it was a fascinating time in history. Up until the period of post-war migration, the Australia culture and way of life had been predominantly British. As Europeans began to arrive in Australia, the cultural landscape slowly changed, but this change didn't come without resistance and its challenges. 'New Australians' were the engine room of the economic growth stimulated after the war, but they were often discriminated against and taken advantage of.

That was no surprise to me, but when I began researching communism and the union movement of the 1950s and 1960s, I was amazed to discover what a hothouse of intrigue this period was. Communism was rearing its head across the globe, threatening western democracies and instigating the widespread fear of 'Reds under the bed'. In Australia, diplomatic scandals like the Petrov affair and the Skripov incident rocked the belief that Australia was far from such problems of the world. Suddenly we were thrust into this global crisis. And with our involvement in the Vietnam War and our increasing ties to the United States, we were no longer seen as a provincial backwater but embedded fully in world politics. The time of Australia's innocence was over and with this came the massive social changes of the 1960s. The fight for civil rights for all people, especially minority groups, took centre stage and political and social awareness grew rapidly across the general population. Women discovered that they had a voice, too, and the feminist movement was born. This turbulent time of change touched all people and Lotte and her family were no exception.

Migrants certainly played a vital role in the changes sweeping Australia. Researching the role of migrants in the union movement proved how important they were in pushing for a fair and equal nation. They were prominent in this fight, determined that their voices should be heard. The Bonegilla Riots of 1952 and 1961 were prime examples of the discontent many were experiencing. Some joined the unions as a way of speaking up and fostering change and many also joined the Communist Party, which promoted equality, freedom of speech and anti-discrimination. I was fascinated to learn that some of these people became known to the government as suspected or known communist troublemakers and were placed on a secret migrant blacklist. They were often placed under surveillance, photographed at political or union meetings, rallies, protests and even social gatherings. In some cases, mail was censored and citizenship denied for years.

Research helped me place the lives of migrants into this fascinating period of history and also gave context to my own grandparents' story. I couldn't help but use what I had learned, and through Lotte and Erich's association with the union movement and activism, it helped me illuminate the struggles many migrants encountered in their quest to make Australia a better place and the multicultural nation it's now become.

Like most migrants, my grandparents had many ups and downs but they never gave up and they continued to push on towards better times. I'm grateful that my grandmother saw me grow up, go to university, have a career, get married and have my own children. She watched my life unfold and must have marvelled at the endless opportunities that being Australian and living in this country offered all her grand-children and great-grandchildren. It was home for her and, despite all the difficulties, she would have been proud of the decision they made to come to Australia.

Reading group questions

1. Lotte has lived a big life – surviving wartime and postwar Germany and then forging a new life on the other side of the world with her young family. How common do you think stories like Lotte's are in multicultural Australia?

2. Does your own family have a story that might match the trials and tribulations of Lotte's as she struggles to find her place as an Australian?

3. What kind of memories of past trauma do Lotte and Erich carry with them from their experiences in the war, and do you think they are able to fully shake them off?

4. Lotte and Erich's relationship is put through a lot as they move from one side of the world to the other. Do you think they were as happy as they could be?

5. There is so much social and political change that Lotte must absorb and respond to in her life journey from Germany to Australia. What are some of the big movements that help shape her identity?

6. How do you think Lotte's life would have been different if Erich had lived a longer life?

7. Lotte tries to provide a better future for her family in Australia, but works long hours to get ahead. How do you think the girls felt about Lotte always working?

8. Do you think Greta and Johanna consider themselves Australian? Do you think it's different for each of them? What events do you think might have shaped their sense of identity?

9. Lotte has a very complicated relationship with her mother. Do you think the war or the experience of migration affected their relationship, or is it a common mother–daughter relationship?

10. What is it about Lotte's friendship with Claudia that is so important to her? What makes it an enduring friendship?

11. Both grandmothers were very different from each other and carried very different values and attitudes. What do you think the relationship was like between Amelia and the girls? What about between Karoline and the girls?

12. Do you think Lotte's daughters knew much about her past in Germany, and how do you think they might have felt about it? What about their father's past? How might they think differently about his experiences?

13. Lotte's attitudes and values are shaped by the privileged upbringing she's had as well as her own life experiences, and Erich's were shaped by his own background and what he saw in the war. How do you think Lotte and Erich's attitudes and values shape the lives of their daughters? Do they accept or reject them, or mould them to their own needs?

14. Many of Lotte's generation were indoctrinated by Nazi teachings as children during school and through the activities of the Hitler Youth or League of German Girls. With Germany's defeat, they were forced to acknowledge that these teachings were lies and that Hitler had betrayed his people. How do you think this background may have affected them in adulthood and in their relationships with their families? How might someone who has migrated to a new country deal with their past?

Acknowledgements

Since this is Lotte's story, the first person I have to thank is my grandmother – Oma. Without her stories and her careful keeping of detailed documents, letters and photos that chronicled her life in Australia, I couldn't have written *Suitcase of Dreams*. She has been the source of my inspiration, the one who always supported my writing journey even when I was a child. She was my very first reader.

My grandfather passed away when I was little and I only have vague flashes of memory of him. However, I came to know him again through the letters and writings he left behind and by following his story here in Australia. I was delighted to find his writing style so familiar – it's just like mine. I feel very blessed to have had the opportunity to reconnect with him and learn about the man that he was.

Without my grandparents taking the brave step of coming to Australia in the 1950s to make a better life for their family,

I would not be here. Through their example and through my parents, both child migrants, I have understood the value of determination, hard work, perseverance and courage. Because of them, I've been able to follow my dreams and do what I love – write. I can never be thankful enough for the gifts they've given me.

As always, my brilliant team at Simon & Schuster Australia has elevated this story to the next level and transformed it into the book it's become. Their support and belief in me is precious and I can't thank them enough for that. Special thanks to Dan Ruffino, Fiona Henderson, Kirsty Noffke, the amazing sales and marketing team, Kylie Mason, Michelle Swainson and most especially to my publisher Roberta Ivers, who helps me strive to be the best writer I can be. Her support and guidance means a lot to me.

Thank you to my agent Selwa Anthony for her encouragement and wisdom. I'm very lucky to have her friendship.

This journey wouldn't have been complete without my mother, Giselle Brame. It was very special to follow my grandparents' story in Australia with her. She's the one who has helped fill in the blanks for me; translated letters, brought details to my attention, retold stories, delved back into memories of those early days in Australia. Her insights have helped this story remain authentic and through her I was able to see her parents with new eyes. I will be forever grateful for her support and the many hours she has spent on this project with me.

Thank you to all those who could shed light on the life of migrants in the 1950s and 60s, especially Roswitha Pisch, Lisa Bootham, Stefanie Michel, Manfred Schueler, Domenic Martino and Agota Watt. Your stories were fascinating.

Thank you to all those who contacted me after reading *The Girl from Munich*, with your own stories, insights and kind words. It inspired me to work harder to bring you the best possible story in *Suitcase of Dreams*. Connecting with my readers always brings a smile to my face, especially when I'm writing, which can be a solitary business. It reminds me that this book is for you.

Thanks to my family and friends who have been so encouraging and supportive, especially Jane Kurta, my dear friend and first reader, Christine and Terry Blanchard, my gorgeous in-laws, and my fabulous husband Chris Blanchard for his practical support and advice, and expertise on all things related to carpentry and building.

Finally, I have to thank my number one cheer squad – my wonderful family. They wish me a good day of writing as they head off each day, they're the first ones I tell whenever I have exciting news or that I've reached the next deadline or milestone, they're the first to celebrate with me or listen when I have writers' block. They put up with me when I've disappeared into my story for hours at a time and are the first to tell me 'Good job' when I've achieved what I've set out to do. My heart swells with gratitude and love to see their pride in me. If nothing else I'm proud that I've shown my children that it's important to follow your dreams and with hard work, determination and perseverance, anything can happen! I wouldn't be here without the understanding and love of my husband and children. They make it all worthwhile.

Tania Blanchard

About the author

Tania Blanchard was inspired to write by the fascinating stories her German grandmother told her as a child. Coming from a family with a rich cultural heritage, stories have always been in her blood. Tania was discovered at one of bestselling author Fiona McIntosh's masterclasses. Her first novel, *The Girl from Munich*, published by Simon & Schuster Australia, was a runaway bestseller. She is working on her third novel, *Letters from Berlin*, which will be published in 2020. Tania lives in Sydney with her husband and three children.

To find out more, sign up to Tania's newsletter at www.taniablanchard.com.au or follow her at Facebook.com/TaniaBlanchardAuthor

If you enjoyed *Suitcase of Dreams* and *The Girl from Munich*, you'll love Tania Blanchard's new novel, *Letters from Berlin*, coming to a bookstore near you in 2020.

Read on for the prologue and first chapter, and be swept up in another gripping tale of love and loss in wartime Germany.

Prologue

Sydney, June 2019

The yellow envelope sat on Ingrid's lap like a lead weight.

'There's something I want to tell you.' The words left her mouth before she could recall them, and her daughter paused momentarily before she replaced the guitar on its stand. Natalie was classically trained, but even her soothing strains couldn't ease Ingrid's taut nerves. She felt nauseous and light-headed as the words hung between them for a second. But at least she'd said them.

'Is everything all right?'

Natalie joined her on the couch and the flash of concern across her daughter's face caused a wave of uncertainty to roll over her. Natalie was heavily pregnant with her first child. Maybe now wasn't the time to break the news, but the package felt like a bomb ready to explode and she could scarcely breathe.

'I've received some news from Germany. From Berlin to be exact.' Natalie's dark eyes darted to the thick envelope on her lap. Ingrid's heart was pounding now, but she had to continue. 'It's regarding the deceased estate of my mother . . . my biological mother. She died two years ago.'

'What?' The stunned expression on Natalie's face was hard to bear. 'Your *biological* mother . . . ? I don't understand.'

'I was adopted by Oma and Opa as a baby. I didn't know until I was about twelve.' Ingrid quickly reached out to hold Natalie's hand. 'They didn't tell me much, except that they couldn't have children and were overjoyed when they got me. That's when they decided to leave Germany for a better life, and we migrated to Australia in the early fifties when I was small. As you know, they didn't talk about the war and their life in Germany, not even to me.'

Natalie gripped her hand tight and stared at her, glassy-eyed. 'Did she . . . did Oma ever tell you anything about your birth mother?'

'She helped me look for her when I was twenty-one, but we found nothing. East German adoption laws – remember Germany was two different countries after the war – didn't allow access to the files or provide information about natural parents. And by the time the Berlin Wall came down I was married, and I had you. It didn't seem to matter anymore. I had my family. So I gave up the search.'

'Why didn't you tell me?' Natalie let go of her hand and sagged against the lounge, her face white and pasty.

'I'm sorry, but there was nothing to tell. It seemed kinder to everyone to just let it go. You had your grandparents, and they loved you so much.'

'But this changes everything.' Tears spilled from Natalie's eyes and she dashed them away with the back of her hand.

Ingrid felt her chest squeeze like a vice. She remembered when her mother had told her – the bewilderment, confusion, betrayal – and the questions that came after. She had a whole other family somewhere in Germany that she knew nothing about and she hadn't known where she belonged anymore. In that single moment her sense of identity had shattered and it took years for her to put the pieces back together. Now she understood how her mother had felt telling her the truth. How she wished she didn't have to put her own daughter through the same turbulent emotions, but maybe the parcel would offer some answers and together they could make sense of where they had come from. Who they were.

Ingrid leaned forward, reaching for her daughter's hand again. 'I know it's a shock, but now there's something to tell you, I don't want to keep it from you. Especially with the baby coming.' Natalie squeezed her hand and gave her a wobbly smile, making Ingrid sigh with relief. 'Do you want to know about your grandmother? The package is full of letters from her, maybe twenty or thirty.'

Ingrid wasn't at all sure, herself. She had no idea what they contained – and she knew there would be no going back after reading them. She watched Natalie's face, a faraway expression overcoming the dark features she'd inherited from some unknown ancestor. She had to do it for Natalie and her grandchild, if not for herself.

'Before today, I thought I knew who I was,' Natalie said softly, 'but now I don't know how I feel. I can only imagine what it might be like to give up a child, but she must have wanted you to know about her, writing all those letters.' She rubbed a protective hand over her swollen belly. 'It will never change how I love or remember Oma and Opa, but I think we owe it to her. I want to know our family story before the time comes to tell my own little one.'

Ingrid blinked away her own tears. 'I was hoping you'd say that.' With shaky hands she pulled out the papers inside the envelope.

Natalie touched her arm gently. 'We can take it slowly, one letter at a time.'

'Yes.' The first step was the hardest. 'And we'll do it together.' Natalie leaned across and kissed her cheek and Ingrid swallowed hard. 'All right, the solicitor has suggested we read this last letter first before reading the others in chronological order.' Picking up the single sheet, she inspected the delicate, spidery script, still written in fountain pen. This was her mother's handwriting. 'I'll translate as I go.'

'12th May, 2018,' she read.

To my dearest daughter,

My name is Susanna Christina Louise Göttmann. I am your birth mother. If you're reading this, then my years of searching are over. I've been looking for you for many years without success and now at ninety-three years of age, with time growing so short for me, I've appointed others to help find you.

You were three months old when I last saw you. All I knew is that you were adopted by a good family. I prayed that they'd love you as much as I did and that you'd have a good life. I tried to find you, but under the Soviet occupation and later, when we became East Germany, no rights were granted to parents who had given their children up for adoption, no matter the circumstance. Hope returned after the reunification of Germany but the new laws were just as restrictive. There was no way to trace you. But I never stopped hoping that, one day, I would find you.

I'm writing this letter in the hope that this is the first step of you getting to know me. I'd love nothing more than to look at you and hold you in my arms one last time before I die, but if it's not possible, I want you to know that I've never stopped loving you and thinking about you every day of my life. All I can do is tell you my story and hope you learn a little about my life, and about your father, too. You were born out of such love . . .

Ingrid put the letter down with trembling hands and glanced up at Natalie, who was staring at her, wide-eyed.

'She kept searching for you all those years and never found you.'

Ingrid nodded, feeling dazed, imagining what her birth mother had gone through. She had always wondered whether she'd been unwanted and abandoned, rather than given up for a chance at a better life. That had left her feeling that perhaps she was never been good enough, despite the love her adoptive parents had lavished on her.

Natalie hugged her tight. 'She loved you and she wanted you. You were born of love. That must feel good to finally know.'

'It does,' she whispered. Relief coursed through her, making her shudder, and more tears sprang to her eyes. But now there was something else – excitement tingled in her blood. Despite what effect the letters would have on them both, Ingrid wanted to know more. They had to keep reading. She wiped her eyes and turned the page over.

From the age of seven I grew up on a large estate outside Berlin, belonging to my godparents Georg and Elya Hecker. 'Gut Birkenhof' was about 300 acres and named for the ancient birch trees rooted into the hillside near the manor house that many locals believed had guarded the estate for hundreds of years. It was beautiful, straight out of a fairy tale, nestled between the forest and the Dahme river, and a magical child-hood home. After my parents Walter Gottfried and Anna Christina and my ten-year-old brother Friedrich were killed in an automobile accident in 1932 I went to live with Onkel Georg and Tante Elya there. Elya and my mother had been best friends since school, and she and Onkel Georg treated me like the daughter they'd never had. Their son Leo, who was the same age as Friedrich, took me under his wing and was kind to me, tolerating the annoying little girl who wouldn't leave him alone. He taught me about the farm, how to milk a cow, look after the horses; practical skills that kept me busy and distracted me from my grief and made me feel part of the family.

Like my parents, Onkel Georg was from ancient landed nobility, a 'Junker', and a very successful timber merchant, but the estate also had a substantial dairy operation, providing milk and cheese for Berlin, and produced crops like wheat and barley too. It was the largest and most productive estate in the area and the main source of work for locals. Onkel Georg insisted that Leo contribute to the family – no son of his would be a pampered heir – carrying in fresh milk from the cows, wood for the fire and helping him run the property so he could learn the business. There were servants in the manor house too and Tante Elya had a cook to help her in the kitchen.

Those were carefree days. Then I learnt about Hitler in school and how the Jews were considered unclean, corrupt and enemies of our great nation. The Nuremberg Race Laws of 1935 decreed that those with four Jewish grandparents were considered full Jews and no longer eligible for German citizenship, and those with two Jewish grandparents were 'Mischlinge', mixed race of the First Degree. It came as a great shock to me – my beloved Tante Elya was Jewish, originally from Russia, and this meant Leo was of mixed blood. One day, Onkel Georg brought Leo home from school after a terrible racial attack and our innocent childhood days were over.

By the time the pogroms of Kristallnacht erupted three years later and outright war was waged on Jewish citizens, I realised my beloved homeland was no longer safe for anyone who did not conform to Nazi views and policies. The mood in Germany was dangerous, and dark times were ahead. Trouble was brewing for our family, of that much I was sure . . .

1

January 1943
Tante Elya and I were finally alone in the parlour.

'We have to write that guest list if we're going to have your party in April,' she said, pouring a second cup of tea from the teapot, kept hot on top of the samovar. It was a beautiful vase-shaped silver urn, intricately decorated with brilliantly coloured enamel paint, like a delicate jewelled ornament. It had been her mother's and her grandmother's before her, and reminded Tante Elya of her childhood in Russia. Drinking tea in the afternoon was a daily ritual for her, carrying on the tradition from her family. It was something I enjoyed with her when I was home, finding a few moments of peace and tranquillity in an otherwise busy day and time for unhurried or private conversation between us.

'I don't want a big party,' I said, feeling mortified and excited at the same time.

Tante Elya had insisted on celebrating my eighteenth birthday in style despite the news filtering back about the terrible losses in Stalingrad on the Eastern Front and talk that the war was not going well for Germany. It was now grinding into its fourth year and all hope of a quick war had been lost. Even the relentless Nazi propaganda machine couldn't paper over the reality of Germans living daily with stiff rationing, continuous bombings, the loss of their menfolk and the bone-deep fear that the war would never end. It didn't feel right to be lavish but at the same time I was excited to be spending this special time with Tante Elya, planning my first grown-up party.

'Don't be silly, *myshka*. We have to make the most of what we have and enjoy the company of those we love because none of us know what tomorrow will bring.' Water flowed into the china cup from the tap on the bottom of the samovar, diluting the dark brew, and Tante Elya placed a sugar lump on my teaspoon before handing me the delicate cup and saucer. I knew she was indulging me. With Onkel Georg's contacts, we could still get luxuries like tea and sugar, but Tante Elya ensured we used them sparingly.

'Besides, you're the only girl I have and I want to spoil you a little.' She reached across the table and grasped my hand, her skin still warm from the teacup. 'Your mother would've done the same for you had she been here.'

My mother. The last memory I had of her was lying in a field of wildflowers – red poppies, and blue cornflowers the colour of her eyes – vibrant against her long golden hair, laughing at my father chasing after my brother and me as we played hide and seek. Then I was beside her and my father was tickling my cheek with soft stalks of grass before my brother called out a challenge to find him. We'd spent a week in East Prussia, at our property in Marienwerder, which my father had leased a few years earlier when we moved to Berlin for him to focus on his expanding law practice. I was lulled to sleep by the sound of the car as we travelled back to Berlin that night only to wake to screeching tyres, a loud bang and a feeling of weightlessness before impact and the terrible crash. There was nothing after that until I woke up in hospital to learn that my family was dead, taken from me in those few moments after hitting a lone deer on the dark road.

At the age of seven, I inherited everything, a more than tidy sum of money and the property that had been in my mother's family for generations. My mother's parents were gone too, and her brothers during the Great War. I was all that was left, but for a long time after, I'd wished that they'd taken me with them.

'Come, she wouldn't want you to be sad,' whispered Tante Elya, her dark expressive eyes misty. I knew she missed my mother terribly too – they'd been as close as sisters since Elya had arrived in Berlin as a young girl, having just lost her mother herself. She kissed my forehead and smoothed the long blonde hair from my face, her hands soft against my skin. 'Your parents would be so proud of you.'

All I could do was nod, quickly gazing out the large window that overlooked the garden, now blanketed in white after the heavy falls of snow the day before. The pale rays of afternoon sunshine sparkled on the icy branches of the trees, making me smile. It reminded me that even in the darkest moments, there was joy and hope to find. The death of my parents and brother had brought me my new family, and I loved them fiercely.

Tante Elya slipped a few sheets of writing paper across the table to me with a fountain pen on top. 'Think about who you want on your list while I jot down a few ideas for the menu. Then we can go through them together.'

I stared at the blank page while I sipped my tea through the sugar cube. My best friend Marika was the top of my list, of course, but I thought long and hard about which of my school and university friends I wanted to invite. I was in my first semester, studying history, languages and literature at the Friedrich Wilhelm University in Berlin, and had only been there a few months, but I had made friends quickly, bonding with students who lived on campus with me during the week. It was much like boarding school, with those who lived outside Berlin like me, but there were others who came from all over Germany too. Although I enjoyed the excitement and bustle of the city, I was glad to be home for a few days. Despite the persistent bombing raids over Berlin since early in the war, the city had sustained little damage and the rich cultural life of the capital was unchanged. Berliners were resilient and refused to let the war disrupt their daily lives and the dynamic city they lived in.

But I had seen another side to the war. For six months before starting university, I'd served with the Red Cross at the Beelitz Sanitorium just outside of Berlin, nursing horrifically injured soldiers from the front line. And the signs banning Jews from cafes, restaurants, parks, from fully enjoying the city and all it had to offer, so common that they had become invisible to most, were constant reminders to me that the Third Reich was also at war with its own people. I had begun to hate being in the city at the heart of it all, the seat of the Nazi government, and was always pleased to get home. I missed the river, the forests, the open spaces and tranquillity of life on the land, the welcoming smiles of the staff, the warm embraces from Tante Elya, Onkel Georg's updates about the farm, and Leo's dinner-time questions about my week in the city. The way life had always been before the Nazis had taken our homeland by the throat.

A knock at the door broke my reverie. 'Frau Hecker, there's a letter for you.'

'Thank you, Frieda. Bring it here and I'll read it now while I finish my tea.' The maid walked smartly across the timber floor, her steps becoming muffled on the Persian rug under the table. Tante Elya frowned as she took the letter and dismissed Frieda, who I realised had her coat across her arm, ready to go home to the village for the evening. It was a strange time to receive a letter.

'Do you want me to leave you in peace?' I asked, noticing Tante Elya's frown deepening as she turned the letter over in her hands.

'No, of course not,' she said as if coming out of a daze. 'You can write down some more names for the guest list while I read this. Then we can get back to planning your big day.' She smiled brilliantly but I could see the worry lurking in her eyes.

I set to work as she asked, but my heart wasn't really in it. My gaze darted across to her as she began to read the letter, her steaming cup of tea forgotten on the table. Suddenly the blood drained from her face and she put her hand involuntarily to her mouth, as if to prevent a gasp escaping her lips.

'Tante Elya, are you all right?' I put the lid on the fountain pen and placed it down next to the sheet of writing paper.

Her eyes were wide with fear as she glanced across to me. 'Susanna, can you tell Frieda to find Onkel Georg and ask him to come to the parlour?'

'Frieda's gone home, I think,' I said, already pushing my chair back to stand. 'I'll go and find him . . . That's if you're fine on your own.' Something terrible had happened, that much I knew.

She waved a delicate hand dismissively. 'I'll manage, but go quickly. I have to speak with him urgently.' I paused for a moment, hugging her impulsively, her small frame trembling, before I rushed out the door to find my uncle. Whatever was in that letter had shaken her to the core.

Although she was petite, Tante Elya commanded authority wherever she went. She had an inner strength, a core of steel that I suspected she developed when her family had fled Russia after the 1905 pogroms in Kiev when she was about the age I had been when I came to live with her. She had told Leo and me stories of being separated from her mother and brothers as they tried to flee after their house was attacked, then looted and vandalised, chased down the alleyways of the city by Cossacks on horse-back and the sounds of screams in her ears. She was finally reunited with her father who had watched horrified and helpless as a mob destroyed his office before racing away to warn his family of the impending danger. Only later did she learn that her mother had been crushed while trying to escape the rioting crowd while her brothers were swept away to safety by the sea of terrified people. Mercifully they didn't witness her fall, trampled to death by a soldier's horse in the mayhem.

Witnessing the carnage and slaughter of friends and family she had known and loved and the desperate dash to leave Kiev while too stunned and shocked to properly mourn her mother had left an indelible mark on her. Her father moved them west to Berlin, a progressive city where they could live in safety and he could set up his legal practice once again. He was determined to embrace German ways and secure a future for his children among well-heeled, educated, Christian German society where their Jewish heritage could pose no danger to them, and my mother was the one who took Tante Elya under her wing when she was the new girl at the expensive school her father sent her to. My mother was fascinated by Elya's Russian background and her Jewish ancestry and was fiercely protective of her, teaching her to modulate her halting, strangely accented German so that she spoke like a Berliner and introducing her to the world of the German aristocracy, making her a part of her own family. This was how she'd met Onkel Georg, whose family were old friends of my mother's family.

Tante Elya always told us that Gut Birkenhof had felt like home to her – here, she felt like she could be herself, a strange mixture of Russian, Jew and German. It was a place where she could raise her own family in safety and contentment, surrounded by the close-knit community. She was always the first one to help those in need and stand up for people who had been treated unfairly. The loss of her own mother had made her compassionate and kind and when my mother died, she understood what I was going through and made every effort to ensure I was not suffering alone. But whatever was in the letter had disturbed this strong, indomitable woman and for the first time I was truly afraid.

Onkel Georg was in his study. He didn't utter a word when I told him what had happened, only pressed his lips tightly together, pushed his chair back from the large walnut desk and walked quickly to the parlour where he closed the door firmly behind him.

I knew better than to ask questions. Although we outwardly appeared a normal German family, we lived in constant uncertainty, at the whim of changing Nazi sympathies and policy. Onkel Georg had managed to keep Tante Elya's name off the register of the Reich Association of Jews, but we were never sure if his efforts to keep Tante Elya safe would be enough. He had close connections to powerful Nazis due to his family's noble lineage and mutually profitable business dealings, securing large contracts years earlier with the Reichspost, Germany's postal system, and the Reichsbahn, the national railways, for timber, milk and agricultural produce. More importantly, Onkel Georg had trusted contacts in the Ministry of the Interior, which held all registrations and the 1939 census cards on Jewish heritage, and they had kept Tante Elya's details buried there. But we were well aware that the Reich Main Security Office, the RSHA, which oversaw the deportations of Jews from Germany with the might of the Gestapo behind it, could retrieve personal information at any time. There was always the concern that the Reich would invalidate marriages between German citizens and Jews. Most of the Jews remaining in Berlin after the pogroms surrounding Kristallnacht had been deported to ghettos in the East over the last year and a half, including one of Tante Elya's brothers and his family. The very few who remained were employed in factories and so-called Aryan businesses because of their level of skill and expertise, or like Tante Elya and Leo, were protected by marriage.

I pressed my ear to the door. I had to know what was happening.

'This letter just came,' I heard Tante Elya say. 'It's finally happened.' Her voice broke. 'I've been registered.' There was silence for a heartbeat or two.

'It must be Kalternbrunner, the new chief of the RSHA. He's SS, supported by Himmler, and it's no secret he's a fanatical anti-Sem-ite. If he got hold of those census documents . . . After everything we've done to ensure your safety.' I could hear the grim horror in Onkel Georg's voice.

'There's only so much your contacts can do. Even those highly placed Nazi officials can't help us anymore.' Tante Elya's voice shook.

Onkel Georg had cultivated relationships within the upper ranks of the government and Wehrmacht, the German armed forces. I'd seen him give visiting officials gifts, and Leo had told me he also sent them to their homes and offices: baskets of luxury items from across Europe, bottles of cognac, or even fresh meat, cheese and vegetables from our farm. He'd even taken to leasing out land and holiday or weekend cottages along the water to those wanting a more genteel lifestyle. All to remain a friend and asset to those who wielded power. As Leo had reminded me, keep your friends close but your enemies closer.

I had no illusions about what Onkel Georg was doing. My childhood innocence had been ripped away long before, when

I realised the effect Nazi racial laws had on my family and other Jewish families we knew. He'd been doing it for years, doubling his efforts after Kristallnacht. The consequences of providing false information in the census had been more severe than declaring Elya was Jewish, but social connections and the power that came with the upper class meant everything to the Nazis and so far he'd been able to keep Tante Elya and Leo safe. Gut Birkenhof was the source of the good local economy, employing over half the village at one time or another. And the longer the war went on, the more valuable raw materials and food products became and the government couldn't afford to lose a reliable supply. All this had kept Tante Elya protected and kept her off the official register, even though her heritage was known to some of Onkel Georg's Nazi associates. It had affected all of us, keeping me safe too – we'd heard stories of Aryan children being taken away from foster, adoptive or even step-parents who were found to be Jewish. It had protected Onkel Georg to some extent from the harassment metred out to Aryans married to Jews by Nazis and officials as well as local people. But I could only imagine what his efforts had cost him both financially and personally – he was not a political man and hated the Nazis as much as Leo and I did.

'I had a deal with them.' I heard Onkel Georg slam the table in frustration and anger.

'I know, and it's kept us safe this long. But it was bound to happen eventually. My worry is for you and Leopold, the effect it will have on you all. You'll be reviled as a traitor to Germany, and as my son, Leopold, will formally be recognised as a . . . *mischling*.' I heard the catch in her voice. It was a terrible word, calling those of mixed Jewish and German heritage, mongrels, half-breeds – just like animals.

'But you're both still legally protected. The register will reflect that you're in a lawful mixed marriage. Nothing will change.' Onkel Georg could be stubborn at the best of times, but what if he was wrong?

'Listen to me, Georg. Everything's changed. My identity card will be stamped with a 'J' and I can't go out now without wearing the Star of David. Everyone will know what I am . . .' Her voice was shaky. 'And what that now makes you and Leopold.'

'Not in the village. Everyone knows and loves us. We're family.'

'People already talk about why I have certain privileges, why I haven't been deported. There are those who think you should have already divorced me. When it becomes public knowledge about my status, there'll be no mercy from them.'

'But they've known you for over twenty years. You've always been the heart of this community. You're well loved.' Onkel Georg's outrage told me volumes. He knew what Tante Elya was saying was true.

'It doesn't matter. The resentment's already there. Some of them are restless with the presence of Nazis flocking to our door and spending extravagant weekends and holidays on the river. It makes them nervous. It's the only reason people have been polite up until now. With the Gestapo snooping around or breathing down their necks, now I'll have no freedom. If I put a foot wrong, they'll make sure I get what they think I deserve.' Tante Elya's voice cracked. It was no wonder. Memories of the persecution her family faced and their flight from Russia must have returned to her in full force. I knew she still had nightmares about Kristallnacht, where her brother's law practice in Berlin had been set alight and his son sent to Dachau in its wake.

'They'll come near you over my dead body.' The anguish and aggression in Onkel Georg's voice made my heart clench in fear. I swayed for a moment, clutching at the door frame, then swallowed and brought myself back under control. I had to hear the rest.

'Shh, don't say things like that.'

There was silence for a few moments.

'We have to get out while there's still a chance,' said Onkel Georg.

'What chance? Nobody wanted us four years ago when the quotas were tightened everywhere. Now emigration's forbidden to Jews, we'll never get a visa.'

'I'll try again. There must be a way. I'll go to the American Embassy and speak to your brother and uncles in New York.

I'll visit all the consulates if I have to. Even the black market. Somebody will take us.' My body shook at the desperation in his voice.

I remembered when they'd tried to sell the estate and make plans for us to all go to America. I had been devastated to leave our homeland but more terrified by the attacks on the Jewish people. I would have gone to the ends of the earth with my family if that had meant they were safe. But we couldn't leave. Reich officials had denied our request to emigrate, ironically because of the government contracts that protected our family. Onkel Georg was determined to escape somehow, even leaving the estate behind, but after Kristallnacht, the mass exodus out of Germany meant the quotas of countries like the United States were filled years in advance and some countries had closed their doors altogether. Tante Elya's youngest brother and his family had managed to emigrate but we missed out. There was nowhere for us to go.

Since then, despite Tante Elya's name being kept off the official register of Jews, Leo's life was made more restrictive. Proof of pedigree, including birth and marriage certificates of parents and grandparents, were required for university applications and Leo was denied entry into agricultural college, even though he was eligible. Acceptance was at the discretion of the university rectors and many did not want *mischlinge* at their institution. All he had ever wanted was to study agriculture, manage the estate and follow in his father's footsteps. Even Onkel Georg's enquiries to his Nazi contacts came to nothing. He was told what he already knew then: the frequent beaurocratic power struggles between various government ministries and departments as well as Nazi personalities made all dealings with the Reich uncertain. The decision could not be changed.

Like all the young men his age, Leo couldn't wait to serve his country and fulfil his duty as a patriotic German. But when he became of age for national service and conscription into the Wehrmacht, the law had just been revised to exclude half-Jews from the military and he was unable to join. With the call up of every friend and neighbour and reports of injury on the front lines to those we knew, the shame he carried only grew.

Leo felt useless I knew, but he'd encouraged me to serve with the Red Cross at Beelitz when I spoke to him about completing my Reich Labour Service, a duty all young citizens before joining the workforce were obliged to complete to assist in the war effort. And by proving I was a patriotic German, perhaps the authorities would continue to view our family with some approval. I couldn't stand by and do nothing, and perhaps it would even help our family. To help our young men injured while fighting for our country was an honour and I did it as much for Leo as for myself – he would have made such a fine soldier. But I was certainly not doing it for the Nazis, because I couldn't reconcile the Germany I was aiding with the Third Reich's brutal treatment of innocent Jews and their indoctrination of the German people.

Now everything seemed more precarious and the danger was so close to home. I clung to the hope of emigration that Onkel Georg had raised again. If we could just leave the fear and danger behind . . .

I didn't need to hear any more. I stumbled down the corridor, desperate for fresh air, thoughts jumbling in my mind. I suddenly felt so helpless and insignificant but I couldn't bear the thought of those I loved being persecuted. It was a future filled with unspeakable horror that chilled me to the bone.

Leo was in the stables. I met him coming out, silhouetted against the puddle of yellow light from the open door, which cast a cheery glow into dull and fading afternoon.

'I'll talk to you tomorrow,' I heard him say to a stable hand, his voice muffled by the heaviness in the air. It had begun snowing again, the sky low and leaden, as though threatening to oppress and suffocate us.

'Leo,' I called out, the sound falling flat, cocooned by the drifts of powdery white.

'What are you doing out here, Susie? It's too cold. Come on, let's go inside.' He reached my side and threaded his arm through mine. 'Aren't you supposed to be organising your birthday party with Mutti?' I leaned against him as much for warmth as for support. In my haste I'd forgotten my coat and gloves and my hands were nearly numb with cold.

'We were,' I murmured. 'But then . . .' I began to shiver, with cold and fear.

'Tell me inside.' He propelled me forward, along the path back to the house, now blanketed under fresh falls of snow, and refused to listen to a word until he had me rugged up in a blanket at the kitchen table, the rare indulgence of a hot chocolate in my hands.

The staff had retired for the evening and it was Frau Kraus's night off. She was the head of the household staff and cook and had been with Onkel Georg and Tante Elya for decades, but rather than live on the estate she'd insisted on remaining in her own home in the village. She'd left dinner gently simmering on the stove and the blast of warmth and smells of meaty broth and onions made me feel safe and secure, driving away the demons of the night.

I glanced at Leo sitting across from me, waiting for me to tell him what was wrong. He was only three years older than me but it still came as a shock to realise how he'd changed in the last few years. The last vestiges of childhood had left him and he was a man now, although his dark wavy hair still fell into his eyes as it had always done. I hadn't seen much of him since my final years at boarding school, then completing my National Service require-ments. He was straight-backed, tall and athletic like his father, and strong from his daily work on the estate; felling trees, chopping wood, baling hay, fixing machinery or carting milk. We'd lost some workers over the last year to old age, infirmity and the Wehrmacht, and as well as learning the business and management of the estate from his father, Leo was determined to fill the gaps and make himself as useful as possible. I knew that his guilt and frustration at not being eligible for National Service or the Wehrmacht drove him almost into the ground. I remembered well the visit from his two cousins on their way to the Eastern Front and how envious he'd been of them defending their country. They couldn't believe that he had been excluded from service because of his mother's Jewish heritage. The news that one of them had died at Stalingrad only a few months earlier had crushed him, made all the worse that he had died on Russian soil, fighting the Russians, his mother's countrymen. He'd said nothing to anyone but me, only worked harder than ever.

'So are you going to tell me what's bothering you? I have all night,' he said, folding his arms and leaning back in his chair.

I took a deep breath and told him everything I knew.

'I'm scared, Leo,' I whispered when I had finished. 'If something was to happen to your mother or you . . . ' I put the warm cup on the table, unable to finish.

'Don't worry, Susie. Vati will do everything to keep Mutti safe and I'm in no danger. It's only registration, and the law still protects her while she's married to Vati. I'm sure it's all just a formality and life will go on the same as it always has done.' He squeezed my hand across the table.

Relief coursed through me. Leo was always right. Onkel Georg would see to their protection as he always had and Leo would make sure his father's plans were carried out to the letter. 'I should get dinner. It's the last thing your mother will feel like doing right now.' I stood from the table and turned towards the stove. Leo's chair scraped across the floor as I ladled soup into a waiting tureen.

'They'll need us both tonight,' he said. 'Here, let me take the soup up, it's heavy. And I'll help you set the table.'

I nodded, feeling tears well in my eyes. 'We've always been a good team,' I whispered.

'It will be all right.' Leo put his arms around me and kissed the top of my head. He smelled of wood chips and the clean sweat of hard work and I hugged him fiercely, as though it would keep him safe forever. I wondered if he could still read my thoughts as he had when we were younger.

'You go up then,' I said, drawing myself away, heat flushing my cheeks. 'I'll be there in a minute.' Leo nodded and I thrust the tureen into his hands.

'Don't be long,' he said softly, holding my gaze with his dark eyes.

I stared after him for a moment and realised I was shaking. I couldn't escape the reality of our situation. There was no doubt that with Tante Elya's registration, the danger to us was greater than ever. The future was unpredictable and uncertain, but a future without Leo was unthinkable.

Leo meant everything to me. He was the love of my life.